35 CONTEMPORARY STORIES FROM THE SOVIET UNION'S FINEST WRITERS

MIKHAIL ZOSHCHENKO
One of the cleverest, most loved Soviet authors, Zoshchenko so incensed the authorities with the hilarious short fable titled "Adventures of a Monkey" that it became the State's excuse for a crackdown on post–Second World War literature.

KONSTANTIN PAUSTOVSKY
A clear and easy style disguised Paustovsky's deep philosophical concerns, and here in "Moscow Summer," his masterwork, he creates a tale of an architect who questions man's function in society and society's judgment of his function.

SEMYON BABAYEVSKY
Readers may compare "Grackles," a 1950s story of a man who marries the wrong woman, with some of the best contemporary Soviet films—ironic, critical, yet lushly romantic.

ISAAC BABEL
His verbal power and human insight is at its peak in "The King," a tale of a Jewish gangster at his sister's wedding, a hilarious, brilliantly written story that is vintage Babel . . . and so sharply satiric that it cuts to the bone.

ALSO AVAILABLE FROM LAUREL:
Great Russian Short Stories

D1205629

c.1

GREAT SOVIET
SHORT STORIES

Edited, with an Introduction, by
F. D. REEVE

A LAUREL BOOK
Published by
Dell Publishing
a division of
Bantam Doubleday Dell Publishing Group, Inc.
666 Fifth Avenue
New York, New York 10103

ISBN: 0-440-33166-8

Printed in the United States of America
Published simultaneously in Canada

New Laurel Edition

September 1990

10 9 8 7 6 5

RAD

CONTENTS

Contents

INTRODUCTION

Consciousness of our own vitality is one yardstick we press against our literature, not wishing to turn it into gossip, as Dr. Gogarty did, but insisting that reality be the final measure both of it and of us. The more we are aware of the energy moving in us, the more we require our literature to present an understanding of it; the more nearly real our literature is, the more nearly we understand ourselves.

What is real is not meretricious, though what is meretricious may be real. We do not live in Wonderland; our sentences are not tautologies; and a failure of consciousness is more foul than a failure of nerve though less easily noticed. When failure of nerve becomes a habit of consciousness, we are lost in that middle-class, *gut bürgerlich* culture of which the great bulk of our prose fiction has been the expression these three hundred years.

In America and Western Europe, the development of urban civilization and its institutions has compelled novelists to work either introspectively or ironically, to write from inside themselves or to advance mock-heroes—men who stand apart from the usual failures of nerve and failures of consciousness. In Russia, the political substance of life has, until recently, been so close to almost everyone—so *real*—so obvious, and so impelling that no intelligent man could avoid defining himself against it. Indeed, the novelist could take a position so clearly that he ran the double danger of literal punishment and unsuccessful allegory. Zamyatin's *We*, an allegory of life in the super-state, has never been published in Russia; he himself has been discredited. His work antedates Huxley's *Brave New World* by eight or ten years and, more importantly, is not so much a satire on a probable, future social development as an allegory of an existing political situation. His story "The Cave" (1922) is a picture, neither introspective nor mockingly heroic, of his understanding of the principles of a real government. The introduction of the New Economic Policy—a sort of holiday for shopkeeping and small enterprise—only temporarily delayed firm institutionalization of these principles. Once they were institutionalized, the figures and lines of literature changed. Olesha's novel *Envy* (1927), like his story "The Cherry Pit" (1929), presents the mock-heroic, or ironic, figure who, to move at all, must move first against himself, must by device and deviation rub his way clear of the unconscious, weak-kneed agents of happiness. I think it no accident that over two-thirds of the stories in this anthology were written and published in the first third of the period covered. Restrictions of censorship do not explain this.

Censorship exists in every country, and it will always exist in some sense, between the laws of libel and the dispensation of patronage. The censorship in Russia has been severe for a long time; in the last forty years, with ups and downs, it has been shockingly oppressive. There is probably nothing more vulgar about it, however, than the self-righteous indignation with which it is regarded by those not subject to it. All the opposition cannot bring back to life one man it has killed; all our substitution of *indignation* for study of contemporary Russian literature exposes only our own failure of nerve.

> Until the teacher wants to know all the facts, and to
> sort out the roots from the branches, the branches from
> the twigs, and to grasp the MAIN STRUCTURE of his
> subject, and the relative weights and importances of its
> parts, he is just a lump of the dead clay in the system.

This is from Ezra Pound's *Polite Essays* (1937). I mean to cite Pound *against* censorship, not for it. I mean that the only *real* opposition to censorship is immediate, as politics is immediate, as rebellion and revolution are immediate. I mean, also, in an unhappy and deep admiration, that that immediate political oppression in Russia is, in part at least, occasion for some of the literature we most venerate. *Doctor Zhivago* is not a violent book, but it is a profoundly anti-government book, a book that celebrates life and the life of literature against all modern institutions.

The present anthology is a collection of short prose fiction written in Russian in Soviet Russia. All the most notable authors are included, properly, and there are a number whose work is unknown or forgotten outside of their country. All of the stories have previously been published in the Soviet Union. Most of them could be published there now, though, to be sure, some of those that have been—"The Cherry Pit," "The Letter"—have been published as if they were historic documents (the world has changed that much!) and some—"Adventures of a Monkey"—have provoked stupid attacks, have served as excuses for overt political intervention in all intellectual affairs (the reinstatement of strict controls in 1946, after the Second World War).

The stories have been chosen on a dual standard: is it good? does it help indicate the shape of the development of Soviet Russian fiction after 1917, which the editor feels is an obligation of this anthology? The standard was not applied equally or evenly to all the material. Pasternak's "The Childhood of Luvers" (1918) is more excellent than indicative; Nikitin's "The Forest" (1922) is more indicative than excellent. Furthermore, the "development" of short prose fiction, besides applying to the "development" of other kinds of literature, includes various attitudes, tones, styles, subjects, techniques, figures, vocabularies, and points of historical relevance. The selection of stories was an effort to suggest all that; also, we include a story of obvious "social protest" and sympathy for the "underdog"—"The Hobgoblins" (1917)— by the man who has come to be regarded everywhere as sort of the George Washington of Soviet literature, Gorky, as well as "Grackles" (1957) by a prominent but internationally unknown writer who first published in 1940, has been very successful in the Soviet Union, and whose work is good.

There are stories of the Civil War, of famine, of bureaucratic stupidity, of cultural pretensions, of violence and unusual cruelty, of the "dailiest day" in people's lives. There are satires and parodies and an historical joke. There are stories of the tranquillity of nature, of the change brought about by the Revolution, of the inhuman suffering of the Second World War. There are stories of everyday Soviet life, with details, and of the desperation of everyday life, in the Soviet Union as elsewhere. I find the intimate poetry of "The Childhood of Luvers" deeply moving. Fedin's "The Orchard" (1920) presents, simply, the war between the old and the new. Ivanov's "The Child" (1921) refers to the naked violence of the Civil War. Leonov's "The Wooden Queen" (1923) seems one of the most successful and meaningful fantasies in any language. Babel's work is brilliant. Zoshchenko's satires on the new, official world are poignant, as are Ilf and Petrov's. Kaverin, like Olesha, vivisects penetratingly and, in a sense, surrealistically, that entelechy called the modern individual. Paustovsky, a sage, old writer of natural elegance, discusses ("Moscow Summer" [1930]) the disparity between a man's function in society and society's judgment of his function. I do not remember having read a story of greater horror than Valentin Katayev's " 'Our Father Who Art in Heaven' " (1946). Zhdanov's "The Trip Home" (1957) reminds us of the continuing skill of the good Soviet writers and of that change in value which these stories, in a body, announce.

The stories in this anthology are offered as the "facts." They are not all the facts, of course, but, perhaps, the "MAIN STRUCTURE" comes through them. After about 1930, after Stalin's success (1929) and after the organization of the central Writers' Union (1934), the Soviet world changed. So did its literature. Once industrialization was a fact, once political opposition was, by fiat, reduced to absurdity, the writers turned to the individual's isolation in a social context manipulated by a social machine over which he had no control. In short, *real* political opposition vanished. Censorship squashed the more valiant opponents; but the machine itself squashed the others. If industrialization is a fact, what then *can* the individual do? In those moments of respite allowed him—conspicuously, 1940-45, 1956-57—he must be most concerned with himself, his wife, his loves, his loneliness. The overtly political terms are then of little interest or matter. It is in this sense that the whole literary-political situation at present has an odd twist: our magazines are far more reluctant to take the work of Howard Fast or Semyon Babayevsky than Russian magazines are to take the work of Boris Pasternak (which they did) or J. D. Salinger (who has been translated into Russian with success).

This is the final irony: the conditions under which our writers work are those the writers in the Soviet Union would like to have, as, in its way, the "crowd" wants any kind of Western jazz. The absence of these conditions, however, forces the Soviet writer to respond to his environment in one of two ways: either to conform to it, for which he is rewarded and his readers are bored stiff; or to oppose it, however subtly, for which he is, if unlucky, persecuted, or at least quizzed (as Dudintsev was), and his readers are grateful. His opposition is *real,* as all good literature has always been and always will be. He is not a revolutionary; by no means. He is, indeed, an anti-revolutionary, standing as a symbol of peace more than Geneva itself, asserting those values of dignity and freedom by which we believe we genuinely live. The best modern Russian writers, with compassion and zeal, upbraid us for our failure of nerve by giving us the bright images and understanding of real consciousness.

F. D. REEVE

SEMYON BABAYEVSKY

GRACKLES

It was just growing light behind the Yegorlyk River as Yasha Konnik drove up to the cottage where I had spent the night and knocked on the shutter. While I was washing up and preparing for the journey, Yasha stayed right by my side. Smiling and confidentially addressing me as "thou," he related with friendly informality how the day before he had put his "decrepit old Cadet" over a pit and spent an hour and a half going over its "belly."

"You know, I listened and poked around like a regular doctor," he added, laughing. "That Cadet of mine's so temperamental that you have to tinker around with each nut and bolt or you won't move an inch."

I learned also that the driver's seat had been swept clean and a worn mat thrown over it; and that Yasha had not wanted to wake his wife, so he himself had heated the water, steamed his hands and shaved.

"Ever see a cheek gleam like that?"

It was already light. The village of Grushovka began to awaken and light its stoves. We drove along the still quiet street. Some cows were reluctantly emerging from a court-yard; somewhere a calf bellowed rendingly. I asked Yasha whether he would bring his accordion.

"You know as well as I do: it's against the rules," answered Yasha with a sigh.

"Couldn't we break the rules and take it?"

"Break them?" Yasha slowed up. "No sooner said than done."

He turned off onto a side street and drove up to a cottage covered by a weather-blackened thatched roof.

"My home," he explained. "I'll act quickly and quietly so as not to wake Galina. It'll be better that way. . . ."

On tiptoe he approached the threshold and cautiously pushed the door ajar.

Presently he came out, holding a worn black case in his hands.

At that moment the window flew open and a sleepy, good-looking woman peered out. Her shoulders were naked, and a loose braid adorned with a linen flower hung on her breast.

"Ah, my pet!" Her eyes flashed and she smiled not at Yasha but at me, as if seeking my support. "What kind of a husband did God send me—he doesn't take a step without his accordion!" Playfully forcing a laugh, she turned to me: "You had better tell that spouse of mine, Yakov Nesterovich, to leave his accordion behind and take the Victrola and a box of records instead. Then you might really enjoy yourselves."

I said that we would have a good enough time with the accordion. Without saying a word, Yasha hastily hid it in the luggage compartment, seated himself at the wheel, and we set off.

"Yakov Nesterovich," I broke the silence when we had driven out of the village, "instead of being bent over a steering wheel, you should be riding a horse, eh? Your last name's not that of a chauffeur."

"Just call me Yasha, like everyone else. . . . About my name, you're right—it's a horseman's name, everyone says so. A small mistake occurred at my birth. My father was a great horseman and also raised horses; my grandfather rode around with the Cossacks through the Black Lands. But it so happened I was born a misfit. I not only can't ride, I never even sat in a saddle. From my earliest years I was interested in motors. While I was still a youngster here in Grushovka, I got a job working for a mill as a mechanic's apprentice. Later on I was able to get a motor of my own, and then a steering wheel. In the war I drove for the Auto Brigade, as I'm doing now. And that's why I sit behind the wheel."

As soon as we were on the top of a hill, Yasha put his foot all the way down on the gas pedal and said jestingly to the Cadet, "Come on, buck up!" and the Cadet, trembling and jerking, shot down onto the expanse of the steppes. Wherever you looked, stubble and more stubble. The trail of an outmoded combine stretched before us—gray rainbeaten mounds of straw, low-lying bumps resembling rivets. The combine was moving through a brown field of sunflowers. Submissively the sunflowers bowed down to it as their dry top-heavy stalks came under its wing. Even the maize had yellowed. From it many-colored ears of corn poked out, reddish and blond at the tips. Flashing their black wings, a large flock of grackles rose up, flew past us, and then settled by the roadside on the mown sunflowers.

"They're grazing, damn them!" muttered Yasha, leaning over the steering wheel and stepping on the gas. "Doesn't that black devil of a bird get on your nerves?"

"Why should it? A bird's a bird."

"That's not how I look at it," objected Yasha. "The fact is, all birds are different. Listen, it's more than I can do to look at grackles calmly!" Yasha snorted and furrowed his brow menacingly. "If those birds walked instead of flew, I'd run them down in a minute!"

"What harm did grackles ever do you?" I began to get interested.

Yasha only sighed deeply. The road passed near a deep ravine. Below, along its winding bottom, the bushes were aflame with color and the whole landscape was dotted with huts belonging to some large farm. Then we again turned off onto the steppe, and Yasha, looking over at the dusty strip of road we had just traveled, said:

"What harm did grackles do me? I began to hate them because of a woman. You know, this event in my life might be very instructive for many men. . . . It's been a year now since I married Galya—the one who laughed at us from the window and advised us to take the victrola. I'm alive, but as for the kind of life I lead . . . ."

Yasha unexpectedly fell into deep silence. Soon we were entering Surkul. The long village scattered its mud-walled huts along the sloping ravine. Between the huts four ponds gleamed hotly, like four mirrors sunk in the ground.

We approached the administrative center of the *kolkhoz*, with its two leafy acacias at the entrance. I went to see the chairman and began discussing some business matters with him. Yasha drove the truck into the shade, under a tree. While I was talking with the chairman, I looked out the window and saw Yasha open the door of the truck, sit down and take up his accordion. The bellows quivered, but the full sound did not come forth; instead there was a tuneful whisper, not loud enough to disturb the peace of Surkul. Little children gathered around, and an old woman, staff in hand and dressed in a black blouse and skirt, like a monk, also stopped to listen. Crossing herself, she gazed with enchantment at the accordion, evidently remembering the good times of her girlhood. But Yasha kept his tufted head bent over the bellows and paid no attention to the children or the old woman; he just went on softly playing a sad tune— one which I didn't recognize.

Toward the middle of the day, when we were halfway to the village of Sukhoya Buivolo, the sky suddenly ruffled up and low blue-black storm clouds began scudding over us, moving west. Then there was such a heavy downpour that the road immediately became slippery. On the first hill we came to, our Cadet skidded and slid off sideways onto the wet stubble by the side of the road. From all indications we were going to be stuck for a long time. What could we do? We were sick at heart. Around us the deserted steppe was already deluged with water. The rain pelted incessantly against the canvas roof which covered us, the blurred windshield swam with tears. Yasha threw some sacking over his head, inspected the wheels and kicked them spitefully, as if they were responsible for our predicament. He didn't sit at the wheel, but got into the rear seat, lit a cigarette and took up his accordion.

"It's a real cloudburst, storm clouds all around," he said, putting his accordion on his knees. "If we had chains, we might give it a try, but without chains . . ."

He put his fingers to the keys. The bass rumbled and moaned, piercing chords rushed forth and tumbled about, shattering the monotonous song of the rain. Yasha played the waltz "The Waves of Amur" passionately, obliviously. Around us the steppe was becoming so soaked with rain that even the grackles, their wet feathers gleaming black, bristled and shivered on top of the dampened hayricks.

Suddenly the accordion stopped playing.

"Look!" said Yasha. "There are those damn birds again, right in front of our eyes. Didn't drop behind us an inch."

"But what have you got against grackles?"

"Well . . . I told you it was because of a woman. The story of my marriage is about as unpleasant as the weather. But we can't do much else now, so if you don't mind listening, I'll tell you about it." Yasha laid his hands on the bellows of the accordion and sighed. "I'll begin way back, from the war years, so you'll have some background . . . I don't want you to think I'm patting myself on the back, so I'll just say: I fought, as I was supposed to. I thought they'd send me to fight the Japs, but our outfit didn't get to go over there, so last fall they brought us home in triumph, with a lot of fanfare. I came back to my home town, Grushovka. I crossed the threshold of our cottage, embraced my old mother . . . Father didn't come back from the front . . . Well, anyhow, I embraced my old mother, and then we celebrated my safe return. We really did it up big. The fifth or sixth day—I don't exactly remember which—I took one to sober up on, put my accordion in its case and went to the petroleum plant. They needed a chauffeur there for a one-and-a-half tonner. Comrade Boriskin was delighted to see me, and we embraced like soldiers at the front, since he had just been demobilized too and had his major's epaulets stripped off only ten days before. An order was made out, I sat down in my truck and began to fall into the civilian rut. I fell into it naturally, without any trouble. A month went by, two. I was working along and getting adjusted. . . . Then my mother said: 'Yasha dear, you've done enough playing around and enough fighting, too. It's time you settled down with a wife and gave your old mother the joy of having some grandchildren.' It so happened that when the war came along I still hadn't been able to find a wife. Then the war—battles, campaigns, Warsaw, Berlin, and by the time I returned to Grushovka I was at an age when I ought to get married. I would come home at night, get bored, pick up the accordion and play a little—but I couldn't get into the swing of it, so pretty soon I'd put it down again. 'Well, Yakov,' I thought, 'your time has come.' I shared my thoughts with Ivan Kovalchuk. Do you know him? He was also in the front lines. Drives now for the Executive Committee. He's a reliable sort, infallible in his judgments about life. . . . So we talked. 'Get married,' he advised me, 'and don't delay. That'll cure your lethargy. But it's a serious matter. Make sure you pick a cultured woman, one who has a broad outlook on life and also knows something about the ideas of the Party. And she has to know how to get along with a man in matters of the heart too. We soldiers learned the score pretty quickly at the front, and the conditions of present-day life demand that women be on a par with their husbands in every way.'

"I thought things over very seriously. Who should I choose to travel through life with me? 'There's a real problem,' I think to myself. 'Where could I find a woman of culture and broad outlook in Grushovka?' And then, in response to the call of my heart, there appeared before my eyes not a girl, but a miracle in the shape of a girl. I admit she wasn't a girl in the literal sense of the word, but she was so youthful and good-looking she just charmed you out of your senses. You saw her in the window. True, she was sleepy then, and you know what that can do to a woman's looks. But she was still beautiful, in the way married life affects a beautiful woman. . . . You're probably wondering how she got to Grushovka. She came from Armavir to visit her uncle who's a bookkeeper at the petroleum plant, and I happened to be the one who drove her from the station. I seated her in proper style, took one look and before I knew what had happened I was being drawn to her as powerfully as when the steppe winds push you from behind in late fall, around the time when winter storms hit in Stavropol. 'There's no resisting that,' I thought. 'She's a magnet, not a woman!' This Galochka (her passport reads Galina Mefodevna Starodubova) is, without exaggeration, a real picture. She wears her hair high, her face is very white and lightly powdered and she keeps rolling her eyes in a way that is fatal to men. She always has a novel or a poem in her hands, and she speaks without any stumbling or hesitation, like a book—you never get tired of listening to her! She quotes the whole of Simonov from memory. . . . A very cultured woman! She wears a fur jacket, a tight skirt, rubber boots and a little fur hat on her head. To make a long story short, as one man to another, she's a real doll, and I fell in love with this doll head over heels and then some. . . . She intoxicated me."

"Did she intoxicate you or just captivate you?" I interposed.

"You could have taken your pick at the time," grudgingly admitted Yasha. "Whenever I happened to come out of this state of intoxication or captivation for a moment, I would think soberly: 'Maybe this is all wrong? Damned if I know where it will lead me!' So I thought I ought to turn to Kovalchuk and get some of his infallible advice. I introduced him to Galya. They talked very seriously about literature and politics, and even brought in atomic energy. Then Kovalchuk came up to me and whispered in my ear: 'There's a woman for you, Yakov! Take her, it's fate!'—'Well,' I think to myself, 'fate only knocks once, especially in such an attractive form. . . .' To make a long story short, as one man to another, my youth petered out like a garden hit by an autumn frost. I became a married man, and that, dear Comrade, is where my suffering and humiliation began in earnest. . . ."

Yasha struck a chord, ran his fingers lightly over the keys and listened attentively. Then he shook his head, lit a cigarette and looked for a long while at the rain-soaked stubble on the steppe and at the black specks of the grackles in the distance.

"What happened then?" I inquired sympathetically.

"It was awful," answered Yasha, drawing on his cigarette. "The whole thing started with a trifle. When we were finally alone together after all the commotion of the wedding celebration, Galochka came up to me and said in a very sensible tone of voice: 'Yasha, put your accordion away, the fun is over and we have to talk about our life now. Tomorrow we will buy two beds. In the department store I saw some twin beds complete with springs and nickel-plated headboards.' I timidly suggested: 'Why two beds, when we would be quite comfortable in one?' What I was telling her is the absolute truth. After all, are husbands and wives who sleep together in the same bed cramped? I also added: 'In Grushovka all the married couples sleep together.' She replied in the same sensible tone of voice: 'That's what Grushovka does, and this is what we do. I've lived in Armavir, and we will start our life on the new principles.'—'Well,' I think to myself, 'if it's to be on new principles, it's to be on new principles.' I had saved some money during my celibate life at the front. 'Nothing to be done,' I think to myself, 'but dip as often as necessary into my savings, as Mayakovsky used to advise.' To make a long story short, twin beds with gleaming headboards made their appearance in our home. No sooner was this accomplished than I heard Galya say: 'Yasha, we need a boudoir.' What an obnoxious word! 'True,' she says, 'your cottage is low-roofed, and it's impossible to be really comfortable in it, but let's put a trellis here and a divan and wardrobe there.' My heart beat faster. I dipped into my savings again. And then it was that the dancing bug bit my Galochka. 'Throw your accordion to the devil,' she says, 'and open yourself up to foreign culture. You fought in foreign countries, but you didn't learn to dance foreign style. In society foreign dancing is the criterion of culture.' I didn't say a word: if it's a criterion, it's a criterion. But it would be too bad to give up the accordion. So I think to myself: 'I'll do everything, even learn to dance, but I won't give up my accordion.' Galochka did what she said she would. She went to Stavropol, bought a Victrola and a boxful of records. She bought the records at the open market, not in a store, and they were somewhat dated and noisy beyond belief. Bang, crash, screech—it was miserable! From that time on jazz blues and jazz bands thundered in our cottage. As you see, I'm young and healthy and could still put up with that music, but my poor old mother almost had a fit. She ran away to a neighbor's house and hasn't come home since. 'Yasha, you move like a lumbering bear, so I'll start you off with the *pas de quatre*,' said Galochka, putting on a record and taking me by the hand. 'We will learn the first step, which in the *pas de quatre* is very simple. Here it is important to learn to make a sighing movement, as if you were about to swoon. We will learn it quickly and then pass on to the tango—also a slow dance, with a twofold movement. Then we will be ready to try the foxtrot.'

"That, dear Comrade, is how the foxtrot entered my life, god damn it! By day you drive a truck two hundred miles, come home tired, your whole body aching. You want to rest up, lie down for a while, but Galochka keeps at you with her tender glances—and then the foxtrots begin— All over Grushovka the rumor went around that a driver at the petroleum plant had lost his senses, driven his own mother out of the house and himself stayed glued to the Victrola all night. That was all rot, of course. I was still very much in possession of my senses; but I admit, I did begin to notice that my inner tension was increasing. In time things reached the point where because of the rumor everybody in Grushovka began giving me a wide berth—even acquaintances stopped greeting me. Whenever I appeared, the superstitious old women of the town would cross themselves and mutter exorcisms. I had friends—they gave me up too. Even Ivan Kovalchuk avoided me—that really hurt! He was the one who advised me to go into it in the first place, but when it came to grief he said: 'You, Yakov, are living an abnormal life.' And sure enough, I began to notice in myself a certain abnormal state of mind. I was well-fed and in pretty good physical health; it was just that my nerves were all shot. I was a trembling wreck. Everything shimmied and wobbled before my eyes as if I had anemia. I would sit at the wheel with my eyes on the road, and such black spots would appear before my eyes that the truck would seem to be lurching from side to side and not keeping to the road as it was supposed to. 'All right,' I thought, 'I've had it! Any more dancing and I'm a goner.' I asked Comrade Boriskin to transfer me to this Cadet. Then I went to a doctor. He examined me thoroughly, tapped me with a tiny hammer and waved his hands before my eyes. 'Your nerves are shattered,' he said, 'like the nuts and bolts of an old machine. You have to tighten up the nuts and repair the brakes; and in order to do that, domestic harmony and a generally normal life are essential.' He also advised me to have children. 'What kind of family life can you have without children?' he said. And then I opened up and told him everything, even about the foxtrots. And the doctor, who was obviously an intelligent man, said: 'Give your little ballet dancer a couple of children and she'll forget about her fox-trots.' "

"A good piece of advice. And did she have any?"

"Wait a minute. Well, I came home with this piece of advice and started a conversation with Galochka. Without beating around the bush I said: 'If you gave me the pleasure of having a little son or daughter, it would be a real blessing! . . . and it's the doctor's advice too.' She only laughed, raised her painted eyebrows and turned on the Victrola. My whole body jerked as if ants were running over it or as if it had received an electric shock. 'I have more things to do in life than that,' she said. 'Any little fool can bear children and mess around with diapers; and as for going around with your breasts full, that really takes the cake. . . .' And she said a lot more too. Finally I couldn't control myself any longer. Something in me snapped like a string, and I exploded with such rage that I don't even remember grabbing the Victrola and smashing it to pieces against my knee. The spring flew out the window and ended up tinkling somewhere in the street. Then I took the records and smashed them up too, one after the other, and I was about to take a swing at my wife when she started screaming. . . . I recovered myself and ran out of the cottage. It was after this fracas that our family drama really began, and when it will end I have no idea. If you only knew what pain I feel in my heart. I play the accordion to forget my misery, but after a while the pain grabs me again, like pincers. I'm still young, but my life is ruined. . . . What should I do, Comrade, tell me, give me some advice?"

"Perhaps you should take it to the People's Court?" I timidly advised him.

"I did that."

"And what happened?"

"They won't divorce us. . . . The court says there are no legal grounds. Twice the judge gave us a lecture about marriage and the family. I told him there was no family, and that the only thing we did together was play the Victrola and dance. And that's no family—it's sheer misery. Then the judge said: 'Tell me, Citizen Konnik, has your wife been unfaithful to you?'—'No,' I say, 'not that I know of.'—'And have you been unfaithful to her?'—'What do you mean?' I say. 'The idea never even occurred to me!'—'Then what grounds are there for divorce?' he says. 'You should become reconciled and preserve your love.' I tell him, in front of the whole court, that there's no love between us, and that the marriage is a farce from beginning to end. But the judge says: 'There is no evidence of marital infidelity. Seek a reconciliation with your wife and live a healthy normal life. The task of this court is not to divorce married couples, but to reconcile them in any way possible.' The judge was a young fellow—as curly-headed as a gypsy. And he took a fancy to my Galina. She made eyes at him and said with a brazen smile: 'The judge is right. I have no intention of granting the divorce and being left alone like a widow or an orphan, with no family and no roof over my head. And there's no law that can force me to give up married life.' She laughed again, and the whole courtroom laughed too. What a snake! She roped me into marriage—right to the death. And it's a living hell, with no letup in sight. . . . I can't take any more of it, and the law can't make me. I'm going to run away from home, anywhere my feet take me."

The heavy grinding roar of a motor drowned out the sound of the rain. A truck stopped beside us on the road, which was a network of little streams by now. A man wearing a raincoat and hood came toward us. It was the director of the Surkul MTS, a man named Gaivoronsky whom I knew slightly.

"You look as if you could use a hand!" he shouted. "What happened? Did your Cadet go off the road?"

He called for his driver to pull up closer. Our stalled Cadet was taken in tow. We turned back in the direction of Surkul and crawled along the drenched, swollen road. While Yasha sat gloomily at the wheel, I kept thinking about his story and still couldn't see what grackles had to do with it. However, I decided not to question him any further.

In Surkul Yasha put me on a passing truck, and I set out for Grushovka. I didn't see Yasha again for almost eight years. But in the spring of this year I found myself once more in the neighborhood of Grushovka and went to look for Yasha Konnik on the very first day. I didn't find him immediately. He no longer lived on the bank of the Yegorlyk, but on the outskirts of town, in a half-finished cottage. It stood there like a lonely child, behind a low clay wall. The doors and windows were missing, and you could see the white rafters, only half of which had been covered with tiles.

Yasha was just coming from the garden, which had been tilled and divided up in plots, and he was heading for the cottage. In his arms, with their hands clasped around his neck, were two little girls, one about two and the other about four years old. Behind him came a broad-faced, kerchiefed woman carrying a shovel and a rake on her shoulders. On seeing me Yasha's face lit up with joy. He lowered the older girl to the ground, handed the younger one over to the woman and, running up to me, shook my hand heartily. His appearance had changed visibly. He had grown an unattractive bristly, whitish mustache and looked much leaner and older. His uncommonly blue eyes had lost their luster, and little arrow-like wrinkles had crept up around them.

"Remember I said I'd run away?" said Yasha after we had entered the room, as yet unwhitewashed and furnished only with a table, a bed and two stools. "I left everything to that she-devil—took only what was on my back. And the accordion, of course—couldn't get along without that. Soon after I remarried. This is my wife Olenka, a Grushovka girl. And these are my daughters, Annushka and Zinusha . . . (Wipe your nose, you're not a baby any more.) At first we had a rough time of it, living from hand to mouth. We kept dreaming about owning our own cottage. But things finally got so bad I even had to sell the accordion. I felt bitter about it, but it had to be. I took out a loan, got myself in debt and patched together this hole. We're getting used to it. It's hard, but we'll manage until things straighten out for us."

"And how about the other one— What's she . . . ?"

"Just goes on dancing," Yasha interrupted. "Not alone, of course—she has her 'partners.' But that doesn't bother me, Comrade. She could walk on her head for all I care. The worst of it is that I haven't been able to get a divorce in all this time. It took only a fraction of a second to get hitched, but it's been eight years now and I still can't get unhitched again. I'm fed up with going from court to court, making complaints to public prosecutors and hiring lawyers. Oh!—that foxtrotting she-devil hitched me all right—with real chains! In court she makes a big scene about loving me and not being able to live without me, and says she won't grant me a divorce. What a rotten bitch! Because of her carrying-on the court always gives me the same answer: 'Your wife loves you, there are no grounds for breaking up the family.' You might as well put your head in a noose! And the fact that I have a family, as you can see—a real family of my own—that means nothing to the judges. Look at these girls! Now tell me: who do they look like? Their mother? No sir, they look like me—feature for feature! But by law these two beautiful children are not mine, they're not even registered in my name. I'm their blood father, but the whole thing is a farce—that's what's so hard to take. And that's the reason Olenka and I never even bothered to sign the registry and get papers—we just live as we are and put our faith in our love for each other. But it's all right, some day there'll be an end to this sorry mess. I'll get the cottage in shape and finish putting the roof on so the rain doesn't come in too bad. Then I'll take a leave of absence and go to see Voroshilov in Moscow. He'll put things right for me, you can bet on that."

"And meanwhile we'll suffer whatever comes," chimed in Olenka, blushing. "We've already suffered plenty. There's got to be some justice for us someday."

"There will be, there most certainly will be," I sympathized and turned to Yasha: "Remember, Yasha, you said you hated grackles? Why is that? I didn't want to ask you at the time. . . ."

"Grackles? Oh sure, I remember." Yasha became pensive, shook his head and began biting the end of his mustache. "After my conversation with Kovalchuk, when my fate was still undecided, I was on my way home thinking: 'Should I get engaged to Galya or wait a little, get my bearings and think things over?' I guess I had certain doubts and misgivings even then. But at that moment a flock of grackles rose over Grushovka. They circled around in the clear autumn sky— flew beautifully, the devils. And what a racket they made with their cries. I looked up at that noisy whirling flock of grackles, and such a lyrical feeling filled my heart that I couldn't think

sensibly any more, and in the morning I went to register for a
marriage license. . . . Of course I understand in my mind
that grackles are not to blame for my mistake in life, because
grackles are just grackles, and I am what I am. But in my
heart I can't understand it to this day. You know, even now,
whenever I see a flock of grackles, the whole of my ruined life
rises up before me, and I get so choked up with rage, words
can't describe it."

Translated by Richard Ravenal

ISAAC BABEL

THE KING

The wedding was over. The Rabbi sank down in an armchair, sat awhile, and then went out to look at the tables which lined the whole length of the courtyard. There were so many of them that they poked out through the gates into Hospital Street. The velvet-decked tables wound through the yard like a serpent, and on the upturned belly of that serpent were many-colored patches of velvet, and they sang in a choir of deep rich voices—those patches of red and orange velvet.

The living quarters had been converted into kitchens. Through the smoke-blackened doors bellied plump flares of flame, reeling drunkenly, and their smoky shafts lit up the broiling faces of old women with trembly chins and slobbery bosoms. Sweat, pink as blood, pink as the froth of a mad dog, trickled down those generous mounds of pungent human meat. Three cooks, not counting the scullery maids, were preparing the wedding supper, and over all the cooks reigned tiny hunchbacked Reisl, no less hoary and venerable in her eighty years than the scroll of the Torah itself.

Before supper a young stranger elbowed his way into the yard and asked for Benny Krik. And he took Benny Krik aside.

"Listen, King," said the young man, "I want to say a few words to you. Aunt Hannah from Kostetskaya Street sent me."

"All right," answered Benny Krik, nicknamed the King, "Shoot!"

"A new police chief took over yesterday, is what Aunt Hannah told me to tell you."

"I knew that the day before yesterday," answered Benny Krik. "What else?"

"The chief called all his men together and made them a speech."

"A new broom always sweeps clean," answered Benny Krik. "He wants to make a raid. What else?"

"But when the raid will be, do you know that, King?"

"It'll be tomorrow."

"King, it'll be today."

"Who told you that, Sonny?"

"Aunt Hannah told me that. Do you know Aunt Hannah?"

"I know Aunt Hannah. What else?"

"So the chief calls all his men together and makes them a speech. We have to rub out Benny Krik, he says, because where there's an emperor there can't be a king. And now's the time to do it, he says, because they're marrying off Krik's sister today and the whole gang'll be there for the wedding."

"What else?"

"So the cops begin to get jittery and say: if we make a raid today and spoil his celebration Benny'll get mad and a lot of blood'll be spilled. But the chief only says: 'I have my pride to consider.'"

"O.K., take off," replied the King.

"What do I tell Aunt Hannah about the raid?"

"Tell her Benny knows about the raid."

And he took off, that young man. Three of Benny's boys followed him and said they would be back in half an hour. And they were back in half an hour. And that's the story.

The guests did not seat themselves at table according to age. Foolish old age is no less pitiful than faint-hearted youth. Nor according to wealth. The lining of a heavy purse is sewn with tears.

At the head of the table sat the groom and his bride. This was their day. Next to them sat Sender Eichbaum, the King's father-in-law. That was his right. You ought to know the story behind Sender Eichbaum, since it is no ordinary story.

How did Benny Krik, bandit and king of bandits, get to be the son-in-law of Sender Eichbaum? How did he get to be the son-in-law of a man who owned sixty milk cows minus one? Well, it happened during a raid. Not more than a year ago Benny wrote Eichbaum a letter.

"M'sieur Eichbaum," he wrote, "tomorrow morning be so kind as to put twenty thousand rubles under the gateway to number 17 Sofievskaya Street. If you refuse, something so unheard of will happen to you that Odessa will never stop talking about it.

Respectfully,
Benny the King"

Three letters, each more threatening than the last, remained unanswered. Then Benny took action. They came by night—the nine men with long poles in their hands. The poles were wrapped with tar-coated tow. Nine flaming stars were lit in Eichbaum's cattle yard. Benny smashed the locks on the barn doors and began leading the cows out one by one. Another bandit was waiting to receive them, knife in hand. He felled each cow with a stunning blow and plunged his knife into its bovine heart. On the blood-soaked ground the torches bloomed like fiery roses, and in the air the shots boomed out like thunder. The shots were meant to scare off the milkmaids who had come running toward the cow shed. And the other bandits also began shooting in the air, because if you don't shoot in the air you might end up killing somebody. But when the sixth cow had mooed its death-moo and fallen at the feet of the King, Eichbaum came dashing into the yard in his drawers and demanded:

"What do you think you're doing, Benny?"

"No money for me, no cows for you, M'sieur Eichbaum. Simple arithmetic."

"Come in the house a minute, Benny."

And in the house they came to an agreement. The slaughtered cows were divided equally between them, and Benny promised Eichbaum protection in the future, sealed with a written guarantee. But the real wonder occurred later. During the raid, on that dread night when slaughtered cows were moaning and calves were slipping in their mothers' blood, when the wild flares danced like whirling blackamoors and screaming milkmaids shrank in horror from the grinning muzzles of the trusty .38s—that was the night when into the yard, clad in a low-cut chemise, dashed old man Eichbaum's daughter—Tsilya. And the King's victory turned into his defeat.

Two days later Benny surprised Eichbaum by returning the money he had taken from him, and shortly after that paid him an evening call. He was dressed in an orange suit, and beneath one cuff gleamed a diamond bracelet. He entered the room, greeted Eichbaum politely, and asked for his daughter's hand in marriage. The old man had a slight stroke, but came out of it. He still had twenty years or so left in him.

"Listen, Eichbaum," the King said to him, "when you die, I will bury you in the First Jewish Cemetery, right by the gates. I will erect for you, Eichbaum, a monument made out of pink marble. I will make you an elder of the Brodsky Synagogue. I will give up my specialty and become your business partner. You will have two hundred cows, Eichbaum. I will kill all the dairymen except you. No thief will ever set foot on the street where you live. I will build you a summer place way out past the end of the streetcar line. . . . And remember, Eichbaum, you were no Rabbi in your youth, either. Will-forgers don't like to be reminded of the fact, do they, Eichbaum? . . . And your son-in-law will be the King, not some young snot, but the King, Eichbaum. . . ."

And he got his way, that Benny Krik, because he was passionate, and passion rules the universe. The newlyweds spent three months in fertile Bessarabia, three months full of grapes, rich food and the sweat of love's embraces. Then Benny returned to Odessa to marry off his forty-year-old sister Deborah, who was suffering from goiter. And now, having told the story of Sender Eichbaum, we can return to the wedding of Deborah Krik, sister of the King.

For the wedding supper they served turkey, roast chicken, goose, stuffed fish and fish soup whose lemon lakes reflected glimmers of mother-of-pearl. Over the heads of the dead

geese swayed flowers, like lavish plumages. But does the
foamy surf of the Odessa Sea cast roast chicken ashore?

All our choicest and most noble contraband, those delica-
cies for which each distant land is most renowned, wrought
on that blue and starry night their own sweet mischief and
delicious charm. Exotic wines warmed the stomach, gently
wobbled the legs, giddied the brain and called forth sono-
rous belches like blasts of a war trumpet. The black cook
from the *Plutarch,* which had put in three days before from
Port Said, managed to get past customs with fat-bellied bottles of Jamaica rum, oily Madeira, cigars from Pierpont Mor-
gan's plantation and oranges from the outskirts of Jerusalem.
That is what the foamy surf of the Odessa Sea cast ashore,
and that is what sometimes came the way of the Odessa
beggars at Jewish weddings. But Jamaica rum was all that
came their way at Deborah Krik's wedding, and so, when they
had guzzled their fill like unclean swine, the Jewish beggars
began to beat deafeningly with their crutches. Eichbaum
stood with his waistcoat unbuttoned, surveying the tumultu-
ous gathering with one eye screwed up and hiccupping amia-
bly. The orchestra played a fanfare. It was like a divisional
review. The fanfare carried everything before it. The gangsters sat huddled close together and were at first extremely ill
at ease in the presence of strangers, but later on they began
to open up a little. Lenny the Rooski broke a bottle of vodka
over his girl-friend's head and Manny the Gunner shot into
the air. But enthusiasm reached its height when, according to
ancient custom, the guests began to present the newlyweds
with gifts. The shamuses from the synagogue leaped up on
the tables and, accompanied by a riotous blare of fanfare,
sang out the amount of each gift of rubles or silver spoons.
Then the friends of the King showed that the blue blood and
Moldavian chivalry of yore were not yet extinct. With ineffa-
bly nonchalant movements of the hand they tossed onto the
silver trays gold coins, rings and strings of coral.

These aristocrats of the Moldavanka region were dressed
in tight-fitting waistcoats; their shoulders were framed by
russet jackets, and on their fleshy feet the sky-blue leather
bulged and cracked. Standing up to their full height and
sticking out their stomachs, the bandits clapped in time to

the music, shouted the traditional, "Kiss, Kiss," and threw
the bride flowers, while the forty-year-old Deborah, sister of
Benny Krik, sister of the King, disfigured by disease with her
swollen crop and eyes which popped from their sockets, sat
on a mountain of pillows beside the sickly youth, now mute
with misery, whom Eichbaum's money had purchased.

The bestowing of wedding gifts was almost at an end, the
shamuses had grown hoarse, and the double-bass was no
longer in tune with the violin. The yard was suddenly filled
with a faint odor of burning.

"Benny," said Papa Krik, an old drayman known as a
roughneck from way back, "Benny, you know what I think? I
think the soot's on fire in the chimney."

"Papa," replied the King to his drunken father, "just go on
drinking and eating and don't worry your head about such
nonsense."

And Papa Krik followed his son's advice. He ate and he
drank. But the smoke fumes were becoming more and more
pungent. Off in the distance a fringe of sky grew pink, and
then a tongue of flame, slender as a sword blade, shot upward. The guests perked up and began sniffing the air, the
womenfolk gave out frightened little squeaks and squeals.
The gangsters eyed one another meaningfully. Only Benny
noticed nothing.

"What's happening to my celebration?" he cried despair-
ingly. "Dear friends, keep eating and drinking, I beg you!"

But just then the same young man who had come earlier
appeared in the yard.

"King," he said, "I want to say a few words to you."

"Well, go on," replied the King. "You always have a few
words up your sleeve."

"King," the unknown young man giggled, "it's really too
funny for words: the police station's burning like a candle."

The shopkeepers were dumbfounded. The gangsters
grinned at each other. Sixty-year-old Manka, ancestress of
the suburban bandits, put two fingers in her mouth and
whistled so piercingly that her neighbors jumped with fright.

"Manya, you're not on the job now," Benny cautioned.
"More nonchalance please, Manya."

The young man who had brought this astounding piece of

information was still splitting his sides with laughter. He kept tittering like a schoolgirl.

"The forty of them come piling out of the station," he recounted, his jaws working hard, "and start off on the raid. They don't go more than fifty feet when the whole thing goes up in flames. Why don't you run over and take a look?"

But Benny refused to allow his guests to go over and watch the blaze. He himself set off with two of his comrades. The whole station was blazing merrily away. The policemen, wagging their buttocks, were running up and down the smoke-filled stairs and throwing trunks out the windows. In all the confusion the prisoners made their escape. The firemen were filled with zeal, but there did not seem to be any water in the nearby pump. The new chief of police—the broom that always sweeps clean—stood on the opposite sidewalk and nibbled the ends of his mustache, which had curled in toward his mouth. The new broom stood motionless. Benny passed right by the chief and gave him a military salute.

"Good health to you, your Excellency," he said sympathetically. "There's a rotten piece of luck for you, eh? It's a living nightmare!"

He turned his eyes toward the burning building, slowly shook his head, and clucked:

"Ts-ts-ts."

When Benny returned, the lanterns in the yard were flickering out and dawn was just appearing in the sky. The guests had departed and the musicians were dozing, their heads resting on the necks of their double-basses. Deborah alone was not thinking of sleep. With both hands she was urging her timorous husband on toward the door of their bridal chamber, keeping her bright devouring gaze fixed on him all the while—like a cat holding a mouse in her jaws and ever so gently testing it with her sharp teeth.

Translated by Richard Ravenal

A LETTER

Here is a letter home dictated to me by Kurdyukov, a fellow from our detachment. It deserves not to be forgotten. I took it down without correction or change and give it in its original form, word for word.

Dear Mama, Evdokiya Fyodorovna: In the first lines of this letter I hasten to inform you that, praise the Lord, I be alive and well, of which I wish to hear the same from you. And also I bow to you very deep, so my face goes all the way down to Mother Earth. . . . (*This is followed by a list of relatives and godparents of all kinds. Let us skip that and pass over to the second paragraph.*)

Dear Mama, Evdokiya Fyodorovna Kurdyukova: I hasten to write you that I am in Comrade Budyonny's Red Cavalry, and here too is godfather Nikon Vasilich, who is at the present time a Red Hero. They took me on in the Political Section, where we transport literature and newspapers to all parts of the front—the Moscow Central Executive Committee's *Izvestia*, the Moscow *Pravda*, and our own relentless paper *The Red Cavalryman*, which every front-line fighter wishes to read, and after that he hacks up the Polacks with heroic zeal, and I am living now with Nikon Vasilich in swell style.

Dear Mama, Evdokiya Fyodorovna: Send me whatever you can, to the limit of your powers. I request you to slaughter the little spotted boar and make me out a parcel to Comrade Budyonny's Political Section, to be received by Vasily Kurdyukov. Every night I go to sleep on an empty stomach and without any blankets, so it is mighty cold. Write me a letter about my Styopka to say whether he is alive or not, I request you—take good care of him and write me about him—does he still limp or has he stopped, and also about the scabs on his front legs, and whether he has been shod or not. I request you, dear Mama, Evdokiya Fyodorovna, do not fail to bathe his forelegs, using the soap I left behind the ikons, but if Papa has used up the soap, buy some in Krasnodar and God will never forsake you. I can write you also that the country here is very poor, the peasants and their horses hide in the forests from our Red eagles, there is little wheat and what you see of it is so fearful small it tickles us. The farmers sow rice and oats too. The hops grow on sticks here and come up very straight: they use them to make their own brew.

In the next lines of this letter I hasten to write you about Papa, how he did in brother Fyodor Timofeich Kurdyukov back about a year or so ago. When our Red brigade under Comrade Pavlichenko was advancing against the city of Rostov, treason broke out in our ranks. Papa was a company commander with Denikin at that time. Them that saw him said he wore medals on him like under the old régime. And on account of the treason we all got took prisoner, and brother Fyodor caught Papa's eye. And Papa began to cut Fedya up: "Swine, Red dog, son of a bitch," he calls him, and lots of other things; and he kept cutting him up till it got dark and brother Fyodor Timofeich gave out and died. I wrote you a letter then to tell you Fedya was buried without a cross, but Papa caught me with the letter: "You're of your mother's slutty stock," he says, "sons of that bitch. I knocked her up before and I'll do it again; maybe I'm all washed up, but before I go I'll stamp out my seed just to even up the score," and things like that. He made me suffer like Jesus Christ the Saviour. Only I managed to get away from him and made it back to Comrade Pavlichenko's side. And our brigade received orders to go to the city of Voronezh to fill out the ranks, and we got reinforcements there and also horses, packs, pistols and everything else we were supposed to have. About Voronezh, dear Mama, Evdokiya Fyodorovna, I can tell you that it is a swell town, a mite bigger than

Krasnodar, the people in it are very nice-looking, and you can swim in the river. They gave us two pounds of bread a day, a half pound of meat, and enough sugar for us to drink sweet tea breakfast and supper, and we forgot what it was like to be hungry, and for dinner I used to join brother Semyon Timofeich to eat pancakes and goose, and after that I would lie down for the night. At that time the whole regiment wanted Semyon Timofeich for commander because he was such a daredevil, and the order came through from Comrade Budyonny, so he received two horses, a decent uniform, a private cart for his stuff and the order of the Red Banner, and wherever we went I was always treated like his brother. Now if some neighbor begins to make trouble, Semyon Timofeich can give it to him good and proper. Then we began to chase General Denikin, killed them by the thousands, and drove them into the Black Sea, but Papa wasn't nowhere to be seen, and Semyon Timofeich kept on the lookout for him all the while because he missed brother Fedya bad. Only, dear Mama, Papa did just what you would expect, knowing his stubborn nature—he had the nerve to dye his beard from black to red and took up in the city of Maykop dressed in civilian clothes, so nobody living there knew he was the same one as used to be a constable under the old régime. But the truth will always come out; godfather Nikon Vasilich happened to see him in the cottage of one of the townspeople and wrote a letter to Semyon Timofeich. So we jumped on our horses and covered a hundred and fifty miles—me, brother Senka and some fellows from our village who wanted to be in on it.

And what did we see in the city of Maykop? We saw that the rear doesn't sympathize with the front at all, and the whole place was full of traitors and Yids, like under the old régime. And in the city of Maykop Semyon Timofeich made things good and hot for the Yids that locked Papa up in jail and wouldn't hand him over because Comrade Trotsky said not to slaughter prisoners, so they would try him themselves and see that he got what was coming to him. But Semyon Timofeich took matters in his own hands and proved he was a regiment commander and deserved all the orders of the Red Banner he got from Comrade Budyonny, and he threatened to kill anyone as made trouble and wouldn't deliver up Papa's person, and the fellows from our village backed him up with threats. And in the end Semyon Timofeich got hold of Papa and started whipping him around, and he lined up all the fighting men in the yard like in military style. Then Senka splashes water on Papa Timofey Rodionych's beard, and the red dye starts to drip down him. And Senka asks Timofey Rodionych:

"Am I treating you all right, Papa?"

"No," says Papa, "you're treating me bad."

Then Senka asks:

"And Fedya, were you treating him all right when you cut him up?"

"No," says Papa, "I was treating Fedya bad."

Then Senka asks:

"And did you think you'd ever be treated bad too, Papa?"

"No," says Papa, "I didn't think I'd ever be treated bad."

Then Senka turns round to us fellows and says to Papa: "And you know what I think? I think if your boys ever got their hands on me I'd be a goner too. And now, Papa, we're gonna finish you off."

Then Timofey Rodionych begins cussing Senka up and down and shamelessly insults his mother and the Mother of God too, and he starts punching Senka in the face, and Semyon Timofeich sends me out of the yard, and that's why, dear Mama, Evdokiya Fyodorovna, I can't write you about how they finished Papa off, because they sent me out of the yard.

After that we were quartered in the city of Novorossiisk. About that city it can be said that there is no dry land behind it, only water, the Black Sea; and we stayed there through to May. Then we left for the Polish front and we're here now knocking the daylight out of the Pans.

I remain your loving son, Vasily Timofeich Kurdy-

ukov. Mama, be sure to look after Styopka and God will
never forsake you.

Such is Kurdyukov's letter, not a single word of which has
been altered. When I had finished, he took the written sheet
and slipped it behind his breast pocket, against his bare
chest.

"Kurdyukov," I asked the boy, "was your father a bad
man?"

"My father was a dirty dog," he answered sullenly.

"And how about your mother?"

"Mother's decent enough. Here's our family in case you
want to see."

He held out a battered photograph to me. In front was
Timofey Kurdyukov sitting rigidly erect, a broad-shouldered
hulk of a man wearing a village constable's cap. He had high
cheekbones, a well-combed beard, and stupid lusterless eyes
that were fixed in a beady stare. Seated beside him in a little
bamboo armchair was a frail, loosely clad peasant woman
with bright, wasted features and a timid, worn look on her
face. And standing against the wall, against the provincial
photographer's wretched backdrop of flowers and doves,
towered two stalwarts—two monstrously huge, stolid, broad-
faced louts, goggle-eyed and stiff as ramrods: these were the
elder Kurdyukov brothers, Fyodor and Semyon.

Translated by Richard Ravenal

BORIS BEDNY

MOSQUITOES

I

Between them stood a table, a respectable office table, made for the purpose of writing bills and memoranda, making drafts and estimates, drawing diagrams and doing lots of other useful things. In Voskoboynikov's opinion the table was certainly not intended for lovers' quarrels, but nevertheless at this very table just such a quarrel was going on.

An incomprehensibly strange Anna hurried to get in as many insults as possible so that it would be harder for Voskoboynikov to break through the thorns and barbs and end the quarrel. That he would manage to break through somehow, Voskoboynikov didn't doubt for a moment, and he only waited patiently for Anna to run out of breath; to try to make peace immediately was a waste of time.

A typewriter was sputtering and clattering maliciously behind the thin partition to the next room. A July rainstorm was howling loudly outside the window.

"Your behavior for the past few days has been simply abominable!" Anna declared. "Yesterday I finally realized that I've been mistaken about you before. It's better for us to break up. It's a good thing we've come to this conclusion in time, before we had managed to do something really stupid!"

"Speak for yourself," Voskoboynikov said sullenly, "I've never had such . . . mean ideas."

Anna gave a sarcastic laugh. The typewriter clicking came

to a stop behind the partition and an oppressive silence fell over Voskoboynikov. Only the soft even rain falling on the window and the annoying drone of a mosquito above their heads broke the silence. The mosquito circled above them persistently, trying to decide which one to sting. Voskoboynikov waved it away and asked, "Did you decide all this just because I didn't go with you to the theater yesterday? But believe me—I really couldn't have gone. When the director goes away I have to run my head off. Why even today I only managed to break away after some urgent business at the Trust."

Anna looked at him disdainfully and leaned against the table. She had an expression on her face of a person listening to a subordinate making excuses for doing bad work. This overbearing expression infuriated Voskoboynikov and he said angrily:

"You Trust workers haven't the slightest idea what we go through when the timber-rafting is in full swing."

"I'm not talking about the theater," Anna answered wearily. "I'm simply convinced that we're . . . too incompatible . . . I mean this very seriously!" Catching the disbelieving look on Voskoboynikov's face, Anna's voice grew higher:

"Everything's finished, is that clear? Finished, finished . . ."

"Listen," Voskoboynikov began threateningly, but just at that moment the door squeaked lightly and a strange young man carrying a briefcase came into the room.

While he took some papers out of the case and handed them to Anna, Voskoboynikov managed to look him over thoroughly. The young man had a faultless part in his hair and thin, expressive eyebrows. He also cast a sidelong glance at Voskoboynikov and turned away immediately, disapproving of everything about him: his baggy oilskin raincoat, his two-day beard and all the worries and experiences of a district engineer as well. Obviously the young man had guessed that he and Anna were quarreling—or at any rate his well-defined eyebrows seemed to Voskoboynikov to be poised in the position of a person who has guessed that he has walked in on a quarrel.

"But they haven't shown the balance of the fuel oil again!"

Anna said, leafing through the papers, and she slammed the table with her hand so hard that the copper cover of the inkstand tinkled.

Voskoboynikov was amazed that Anna could think of some kind of fuel oil at such a time. In a flash the young man lost all his luster, and even his impeccable part was a little crooked, or so it seemed to Voskoboynikov. "She has them all at her mercy," he thought approvingly.

The young man muttered something unintelligible about a delay in the accounting department while Voskoboynikov looked steadily at Anna with the intense, relentless eyes of a man in love. He noticed the little wrinkles at the corners of her mouth and a little slanted crease above her left eyebrow. Anna's eyes were dry and caustic, as if she hadn't slept the night before. But just the way she was now—tired, unhappy —she was dearer to Voskoboynikov than the carefree, schoolgirl Anna that he knew only from his favorite photograph. And my God how he needed her!

Voskoboynikov was certain that if Anna had any idea of how much he needed her she would make peace with him immediately. For a moment he imagined how he'd embrace her when this absurd quarrel was resolved and his lips grew dry, his hands felt light and impatient, almost ready that very moment to embrace and caress Anna. Her lips were moving, uttering cold businesslike words but Voskoboynikov thought only of how not very long ago he had kissed these calm lips; if only they had their own memory apart from Anna's, then surely they would be remembering that kiss at this very minute. But everything seemed to show that neither Anna herself nor her lips remembered anything about it now. This was appalling and incomprehensible. Voskoboynikov almost said it aloud: appalling and incomprehensible.

His behavior abominable? Then she didn't understand a thing! Simply, he loved her and resented the fact that they managed to be together so rarely, that she never made the slightest effort to get together with him more often. She hadn't once gone out of her way to visit him at his settlement during the whole long northern winter. . . .

The young man with the briefcase left, closing the door carefully behind him. Anna's eyes met Voskoboynikov's and quickly turned away. She wasn't feeling too well either now, that was clear. Suddenly she struck him as a lost little girl. He felt an impulse to help her to understand, to lead her to the right path. But he didn't know how to do it; some sort of wall seemed to stand between them.

"We have to find another place to talk," Voskoboynikov said appeasingly. "Too many disturbances here."

"What's the use of going from bad to worse?" Anna asked with the same unapproachable hostility as before, and Voskoboynikov realized that her incomprehensible bitterness toward him was very serious indeed and that his chances were bad. "Everything's finished, do you understand? Finished!"

"Is that so?" Exasperated, Voskoboynikov got up from the table.

How lightly she erased everything that had been between them.

Anna also got up and sighed, relieved . . . it seemed to Voskoboynikov that the conversation was nearing an end. He suddenly wanted to hit her. He removed the cover from the inkstand and twisted it around to give his hands something to do.

"Now I see that you never loved me," he said bitterly.

"That's simply not fair," Anna said quietly, "but think anything you want."

She turned toward the window and began to fix her hair with a particular movement of her hand, circular and cozy somehow, that Voskoboynikov had noticed and loved long before, and suddenly he forgave her everything.

"Anya," he whispered to her and stretched out his hand.

"Don't try any tricks," Anna said harshly, moving away from him, and Voskoboynikov suddenly felt as if he had received a blow.

"But tell me how my behavior has been so abominable," he said tonelessly, stalling for time.

Anna sighed impatiently.

"At this point, you know, that's an academic question."

An academic question! That did it for Voskoboynikov. He turned around abruptly and marched to the door. At the door he stopped for a moment, said, "Oh well, so long," and walked out.

II

The rain had just stopped and the last drops were still falling away from the gutters. The same truck that had been there when he had entered was still standing in front of the building. The driver was studiously chewing on a purple radish and finishing off a slice of sausage which he had just begun when Voskoboynikov entered the Trust. For the driver, that sausage contained the whole conversation with Anna. Voskoboynikov grinned and buttoned his raincoat.

Relieved of its watery burden, the sky was beginning to fill with little lively white clouds. They moved in the direction of Voskoboynikov's settlement, as if they were showing him the way home. The sun emerged in a narrow blue clearing, spreading out its wide, hot rays. The glass of the clean windows flashed blindingly and the wet rooftops glistened smoothly. A bright rainbow made a high-vaulted bridge across the river.

Voskoboynikov walked mechanically along the slippery sidewalk. The ordinary workaday world of a small northern city went its way about him. At a construction site axes were chopping away. Trucks loaded with boxes, bales and long planks that jutted out from the back, rolled along slowly, splashing through the puddles. Soft-drink vendors wearing their old-fashioned tulle headdresses sat like bored princesses in their blue plywood booths. People hurried about their business, jostling and passing Voskoboynikov. Noisy barefoot children played in the rivers and oceans created by the downpour.

At first the general indifference to his fate upset Voskoboynikov, but gradually he began to feel calmer and better, almost as if he had dissolved his bitterness in the crowd. "Not such a bad idea to have so many people in the world," he decided, "and everyone has his own place in the world, his own troubles and joys. . . ."

"Mister, get my kite!" a round, tow-headed little boy of about six asked Voskoboynikov, tugging urgently at the flap of his raincoat. "Please, mister!"

The boy shuffled his discolored bare feet with impatience.

The rag-tail of his homely, notebook paper kite was caught in a branch of a larch tree.

Voskoboynikov obediently climbed up on a low latticed fence and holding on to a branch thickly covered with light-green needles that resemble caterpillars, he freed the tail of the kite. The little boy gave a joyful shout and scampered away without thanking Voskoboynikov, splashing pigeon-toed through the puddles. The clumsy damp kite, listing backward, floated low in the air behind him.

Voskoboynikov watched the progress of the kite for a long time. If he and Anna had met before the war and had married right away, he thought (for some reason Voskoboynikov was certain that people got married more quickly and simply before the war than now), they might already have had a little boy like that one. "Let's blame the war for everything. It's big enough to take care of everything," he said to himself and walked ahead.

Passing by a grocery shop Voskoboynikov noticed an enormous dummy bottle displayed in the store window. He remembered that the universally conventional procedure for all unhappy lovers was to drown their sorrows in wine. Not wanting to differ in any way from his fellow sufferers, Voskoboynikov entered the store. He selected a bottle of cognac, but after emptying all his pockets he realized that he didn't have enough money.

"There goes my universally conventional procedure!" Voskoboynikov smiled at his failure and bought a bottle of light wine. "I'll drink it with Stepanovna," he decided, dropping the bottle into his deep raincoat pocket.

Voskoboynikov searched out his speed boat at the landing. Petya, the helmsman, was stretched out on a seat in the back, reading a pamphlet on the origin of the species.

"Have you found out yet who people are descended from?" Voskoboynikov asked amicably.

"It's beginning to make a little more sense," Petya answered, starting up the motor, "it turns out that apes aren't our predecessors after all, but that they're a parallel line springing from a common ancestor. Something like cousins."

Voskoboynikov heartily congratulated Petya and asked

him to let him out on the opposite shore. He decided to get off the boat and go the rest of the way by foot: he wanted to be alone a while longer, to try to figure out once and for all what had happened between him and Anna.

"Why should you want to crawl about in the bushes?" Petya protested in that querulous, patronizing tone peculiar to chauffeurs and helmsmen asserting their authority. "Or do you want to check if the wood on the beach has dried out?"

"I want to check how much has dried, how much is drying . . . everything. . . ." Voskoboynikov said.

"Well, that's a different story," Petya allowed generously and brought the boat smartly up to the bank.

Petya dashed away, waving good-by with his cap, and Voskoboynikov made his way through the high wet grass. The oilskin raincoat was quickly soaked through and knocked against his knees with a tinny sound. A large, hungry mosquito landed on his hand. Voskoboynikov watched patiently while the mosquito drank its fill of blood and then took off, sated and tipsy. The farther he got from the city the more mosquitoes there were. A buzzing cloud of them accompanied Voskoboynikov, stinging him mercilessly, but he didn't chase them away, finding some sort of strange, agonizing satisfaction in their sharp bites, as if he were getting even with himself for his failure with Anna.

Voskoboynikov stopped at the bend of the river and stood for a long time, watching a whirlpool. The dark, oily water churned and foamed noiselessly. He kicked a lump of earth into the pool with the tip of his shoe. A short splash and the water closed over the lump. Not a single ring appeared on the water. Only a step separated Voskoboynikov from the whirlpool. He thought speculatively, somewhat offhandedly, that if he took a step now in his coat and shoes, he'd never get out; he'd be sucked in immediately and pulled down to the bottom. At his funeral the pompous controller Ivushkin would deliver a speech with oratorical pretensions. . . . Maybe then Anna would feel sorry. . . .

Voskoboynikov grinned at his absurd thoughts and still gazed steadily into the water. A heavy golden-reddish log was going around in the whirlpool. The factory stamp was clearly visible on the end of the log. It was soon joined by two dark spruce pulpwood logs, and then several thin pieces of pit-prop. More and more pieces of wood came floating down from around the bend of the river. Obviously the main floating barrier of the Byeloborsk station was open. Voskoboynikov swore quietly. Tomorrow the telephone calls would start pouring into the office, the Trust, to the Party headquarters: "Raft-making operations at a standstill due to a lack of wood; please take measures."

"I'll take measures!" Voskoboynikov said out loud and walked quickly to the camp.

He broke off a walnut branch from a nearby clump and thrashed it fiercely about his face and neck, waving away the mosquitoes.

Next to the sawmill that marked the beginning of the settlement, several couples were dancing between the mounds of sawdust. The accordion player was perched on top of a high pile of scrap, playing with his eyes closed, completely oblivious. There weren't enough boys and the helmsman Petya, having managed to dock his tub, was dancing with all the girls one after another, blushing, sweaty and happy.

"Where are your boy friends, girls?" Voskoboynikov asked.

"They all ran away. We're so beautiful they couldn't stand it!" a pert supervisor of the log-sorters answered. "Come with us, Andrey Petrovich, and we'll dance or we'll sing you something about love."

"Not me!" Voskoboynikov waved her away. "I'd only spoil your fun!" And he added almost gaily, "I'm finished with love!"

III

The evening hush had already settled on the office building, broken only by the light clicking of the abacuses in the book-keeping department. In the controller's office bald, sun-burned Ivushkin was carefully ruling wide sheets of paper. The ruler was too short and Ivushkin had to place it on the paper three times to get a line, but the lines turned out straight; the controller prided himself on his accuracy.

"What's with Sizhma?" Voskoboynikov asked.

"Previous communications have broken off." Ivushkin waved his hand hopelessly.

At the end of the early spring timber-rafting in the upper reaches of the river, all the binding wire was left at the Sizhma area. A week before, the director of the timber-rafting administration, Potapov, had gone to Sizhma to hurry the local workers in getting together the wire and sending it down to the lower stations where the timber-rafting was in full swing and the supply of wire was rapidly dwindling. To hope that the Trust would help them was useless: a long-awaited barge with equipment was grounded somewhere near the mouth of the river. They could only be saved by the Sizhma wire. And, to top it all off, yesterday's storm had broken the telephone connections with Sizhma. Now Voskoboynikov couldn't find out how Potapov was progressing with the wire-gathering.

"Ring Sizhma every half hour," Voskoboynikov ordered the telephone operator, and began to look through the telephone messages from the other sections.

He wanted to roll up his sleeves and get to work immediately so as not to think about Anna. But as if to spite him there was nothing to do right now: the binding and raft-making operations were going smoothly, the tugboats were working well. Everyone was requesting more wire, but Voskoboynikov had nowhere to get it.

"I can't make it myself!" he said angrily and telephoned the Byeloborsk station.

Voskoboynikov railed at least five minutes at the Byeloborsk head for letting the wood escape before he realized suddenly that he was venting on him all his fury for his quarrel with Anna as well as for the shortage of wire. Abashed, he hung up the phone.

"Well, you've certainly learned how to abuse the workers," Ivushkin said mockingly, remarking the first time since he had come to work for the bureau that Voskoboynikov was ashamed of himself for scolding the lumber workers.

"You're a good teacher. . . ." Voskoboynikov said, searching his pockets for a cigarette.

He felt a heavy object in his pocket, and realized only after a moment that it was the bottle of wine.

"Where's Stepanovna?" he asked severely.

"The secretary went to town," answered the telephone operator. "There's a new comedy playing at the movies."

"The hell with her!" Voskoboynikov grumbled and went off to his room in the building next to the administration office.

He spent a long time trying to uncork the bottle with a penknife. The cork broke and he couldn't pry it out. Finally he got angry and pushed the cork into the bottle. Then he cleared all the books off the table, reversed the tablecloth, sliced some sausages and opened a can of his favorite vegetable preserves. After a critical look at the table he went to the cupboard and got a bunch of onions—a gift from Stepanovna who swore that the fulfillment of the Plan depended primarily on the amount of vitamins consumed by the heads of the bureau, and therefore stuffed the engineer with vegetables from her kitchen garden. But he didn't feel like drinking alone. "I'll invite Ivushkin," he decided unexpectedly, surprising himself, as he didn't particularly like the garrulous controller.

Ivushkin didn't have to be coaxed long, only wanting to know the occasion for drinking on a work day.

"An event not included in the Plan," Voskoboynikov answered vaguely and the controller laughed as if he understood what was behind it all.

They drank a glass of wine. It turned out to be weak and sour.

"Like kvass," Ivushkin announced.

"Have something to eat," Voskoboynikov said guiltily, "here's some sausage and some preserves. I'm sorry it doesn't quite go with the wine."

The controller lifted the bottle and read the label, squinting nearsightedly. He asked, as if he were giving an examination:

"Andrey Petrovich, what do you know about Tsinandali?" Ivushkin was fond of educational conversations.

"I think that's some mountain or other in the Caucasus," Voskoboynikov answered uncertainly.

Ivushkin was delighted and declared didactically, rubbing his bald head and displaying his superior knowledge:

"Tsinandali is a village in the higher Telavsky district of the Tiflis province, and the center of the Kahetian wine industry."

Remembering that the controller liked to read odd volumes of the Brockhaus-Efron Encyclopedia in his spare time, Voskoboynikov didn't argue with him and poured another glass of the Kahetian product. Neglecting the vitamin-filled onions, Ivushkin pulled the plate with the sausages nearer to him and asked very seriously:

"What do you think, will England hold out in Singapore or not?"

"To tell you the truth," Voskoboynikov admitted candidly, "I haven't given the matter much thought. Haven't had time, somehow . . . you know how it is . . . maybe we can leave that problem to the diplomats and limit ourselves to timber-rafting?"

The controller was in principle opposed to any limitations and began to prove that every sensible person who followed all the periodicals carefully and who didn't lack the ability to make independent judgments (he especially underlined independent judgments) could understand anything, even the most delicate questions of international politics. It was clear that Ivushkin was a man of firm convictions and so, to pacify the controller, Voskoboynikov quickly admitted that he personally was unable to make independent judgments in matters of international politics.

"That's quite a different matter!" Ivushkin took pleasure in humbling the engineer, "but I can tell you authoritatively: England won't leave Singapore voluntarily!"

Ivushkin began to prove conclusively why England would not leave Singapore voluntarily. Voskoboynikov kept nodding his head, agreeing with everything, trying not to provoke an argument with the militant controller, but thinking all the while: What could Anna be doing now? Sleeping? Reading? Doing some kind of housework, or maybe sitting at the movies, watching the new comedy with Stepanovna? Was she thinking of him? He thought about Anna kindly, just as he had yesterday or a week ago, before there had been any

quarrel, and catching himself at this he suddenly was angry
that he had already forgiven her everything.

"Thinking of me! Not a chance!" He said the last words
out loud: "Not a chance!"

Ivushkin thought he was talking to him.

"You're quite mistaken," the controller said coldly. "Why
right next to Singapore is Malaya, and to talk as you do
means that you really don't understand anything about the
colonial question."

Offended, Ivushkin pulled the dish with the conserves toward him and quietly polished off Voskoboynikov's beloved
vegetable marrows. As he was leaving, the controller said:

"Anyhow, my friend, you shouldn't have bought that
kvass. It's both expensive and bad. Nothing like hard liquor.
That's much healthier for you—it polishes the toxins. . . ."

Voskoboynikov was terrified that his guest would now begin to enlighten him on the matter of toxins, but Ivushkin
only scolded the engineer for being impractical and wished
him good night. To be someone's guest and then curse him
out was just like Ivushkin.

IV

After the controller's departure, his solitary bachelor quarters seemed even emptier and uglier to Voskoboynikov. He
remembered how last winter he had dreamed of seeing Anna
in this room. And she hadn't come once the whole winter.
Not once!

He took out one photograph of Anna that he always carried with him in a not too successful effort to brighten their
frequent separations when he was off on business trips.

It was her old school photograph. A young, angular Anna
was standing alone in a sunlit forest glade. The wind was
twisting her thin white dress to the side. A cluster of ox-eyed
daisies standing tiptoed, were staring out of the grass. Her
dress was short in the prewar fashion and her hair, too, was
worn short in a style girls don't wear any more these days.

Her girlhood had passed without him. . . . It was not the
first time that Voskoboynikov regretted that he hadn't known
Anna at that time. He would have written her letters from the

foxholes and front hospitals, and she would have marked the progress of his battery on her map. But it wasn't only a matter of letters. Simply, their love hadn't undergone any ordeals; there had been no long waiting, no romance, really.

Everything about their love was too commonplace. They had met early last spring at the lumber conference. Voskoboynikov had criticized the work of the Trust and without knowing Anna had made fun of her for an overfondness for telephone messages. At the break Anna had come to him to explain, and that evening after the meeting they had bumped into each other in the cloak room. It turned out that Anna's coat and Voskoboynikov's had hung next to each other all day.

"A good omen," said the cloak-room attendant, embarrassing Anna. Voskoboynikov secretly gave the former a large tip.

They had talked and talked the whole evening, walking about the town, taking the quietest, most remote streets. Voskoboynikov accompanied Anna to the porch of her house. There she wished him good-bye, jokingly cautioned him not to fall through the ice on the way home and invited him to call on her when he came to the Trust. He took her up on the invitation and began to call on her. But they met rarely. Three dozen meetings in the fifteen months of their acquaintance, and hundreds of telephone conversations— that was really all that was left for him to remember now.

Most of the time they met at the Trust, conversing briefly in muted voices at the same table where they had quarreled today. Whenever Voskoboynikov managed to find some free time they went to the movies or the theater. Remembering his student days, the political battles, the brigades, the congratulatory glass of kissel for the successful students, Voskoboynikov named these infrequent evenings "culture parties." Anna, who had entered college just before the war and hadn't lived through all these things, couldn't understand how anyone could use such a tasteless name for such simple and ordinary things as going to the movies or to the theater.

They knew for the last half year that they loved each other, but still they hadn't managed to get married. One thing or another stood in their way. In the beginning, Anna had

wanted Voskoboynikov to change jobs and come work at the
Trust, but he refused, disliking any administrative work. He
finally persuaded Anna with his plan that they both live in
town but keep their old jobs. Then they waited for the apartment Anna had been promised in a new building under construction. Whenever they took a walk they made a special
detour to feast their eyes on the building and they always
called it "our house" in their conversations. The construction went along briskly and the house was finished even
before the scheduled date. And it turned out a beautiful
house! Voskoboynikov and Anna were especially delighted
by the façade with its round stucco balconies that looked like
swallows' nests. The time was drawing near for the housewarming, and Anna, who wanted Voskoboynikov to think her
an economic housekeeper, was especially pleased that they
would thus be able to kill two birds with one stone: to cele-
brate the housewarming and the wedding at the same time.
But suddenly, for some reason, the higher authorities assigned Anna's apartment to another Trust employee, and
now whenever they went for a walk, they carefully avoided
that section where the beautiful house with the birds' nests
balconies was standing.

Voskoboynikov didn't want to move into Anna's apartment; Anna lived with her mother and older sister, and the
sister didn't like the engineer. . . . Damn it, how many ridiculous trifles keep a person from living his life the way he
wants! Apartments, job locations, unpleasant relatives . . .
Judging by all our accomplishments, Voskoboynikov mused,
people in the future will consider us giants, but how many
adversities hobbled the feet of those giants—trifles, mainly,
yet still capable of causing pain. But Voskoboynikov was
convinced that the pain would not last long—temporary suffering, that was all. He and Anna couldn't break up forever
on account of such an absurd business! He thought too much
of himself and of her for that. If such a mosquito-bite, such a
petty trifle, can ruin a person's life, then one simply might as
well give up, lie down and die! . . .

But why after all did Anna get so angry with him? Is it
possible that the world came to an end because he didn't take
her to the theater last night? From the very beginning of the

timber-rafting season they had met only a few times at the Trust and never with any privacy. Anna had been very happy when she found out that he had bought tickets for yesterday's play; but yesterday the steamship line had suddenly refused to accept a raft for transit, Voskoboynikov had to represent his bureau before the Disputes Committee, and half an hour before the play was to begin he called Anna and told her that the "culture party" would have to be called off. She was silent for a long time and Voskoboynikov even began to wonder if she had heard him.

"But, Andrey, I'm already dressed," she finally blurted out, "all dressed up for the theater. . . ."

At that time this purely feminine argument had struck him as ludicrous, and he had thought condescendingly that a woman, even such a clever and independent woman as Anna, was still always a woman. Voskoboynikov told her cheerfully that he'd try to find time soon for a new, more fortunate "culture party" and hung up; the steamship line representative was hurrying him to come down to the raft. Now, however, Anna's argument didn't seem ludicrous at all, and Voskoboynikov reproached himself belatedly for his rudeness and callousness. He hadn't of course been able to go to the theater, but he could have consoled Anna somehow instead of insulting her with his insensitive cheerfulness.

And this morning he had behaved even more stupidly: to give up and leave so readily. He should have persisted and argued and in any case he should never have left Anna until he had convinced her that it was impossible, simply impossible for them to break up. He needed to talk to Anna immediately. He cleared off a corner of the table and started to write her a letter, thankful that someone had invented reading and writing.

Voskoboynikov wrote that he couldn't possibly believe that everything between them was finished: that simply couldn't be so. Even though it was all his fault, still they couldn't break up forever on account of a misunderstanding. He begged her to answer him by letter when she had forgiven him, or better yet to come to him herself. Then just her coming would answer all his questions and they could make up their quarrel without any needless talk or mutual re-

proaches. Afraid that Anna might be delayed because she
didn't know where he lived, Voskoboynikov described mi-
nutely how to find his house and he even drew a little map.
Then suddenly he couldn't remember whether his door was
the fourth or the fifth in the corridor, even though he had
lived in this house for over a year. He darted out of his room,
scared some young couple in the darkened corridor, and
ascertained that his door was the fourth. Then he stood on
the porch for a short time before returning to his room, so
that the young couple wouldn't think that the chief engineer
of the timber-rafting bureau runs out into the corridor at
night to count doors. While he was writing out the envelope
he began to think how stupid and naïve this letter would
seem to Anna if she didn't want to make up. He remembered
how they had stood facing each other and Anna had said that
all his questions were academic. Without rereading it, Voskoboynikov hastily put a stamp on the letter and threw it into
the mailbox outside the office building. And as soon as the
letter had slipped with a quiet rustle into the insatiable slot of
the mailbox, Voskoboynikov felt relieved, as if he had just
concluded a very important and complicated matter.

To his surprise he slept better than he had expected. Twice
during the night he was awakened by the telephone operator.
First the manager of the Trust was calling to inquire about
the delivery of the finished rafts to the steamship line, promising at the same time that the bureau would receive sometime the next evening a ton of wire returned by local users of
wood. The second call brought bad news: a propeller had
broken on a tugboat of one of the local stations. Voskoboynikov ordered a boat to be sent from the Byeloborsk
station and went back to sleep.

Toward morning Ivushkin appeared to him in a dream,
dressed in short knee-breeches and a cork helmet, shaking
his finger at Voskoboynikov and pontificating:

"Until you master the colonial question, you won't see
Anna and you'll never get a telephone connection with
Sizhma!"

V

The thin, hysterical whining of a saw from the lumber mill awakened Voskoboynikov. He lay motionless for a minute, not yet remembering his quarrel with Anna, enjoying the simple, healthy pleasures of waking up. He went over leisurely what was necessary for him to do that day, and just as he was deciding to check the various stations to see if the last remnants of wire had been used up, the thought of yesterday's break-up with Anna flashed into his still sleepy brain. His memory obligingly reminded him also of last night's all-forgiving letter, and Voskoboynikov made a wry face, annoyed at having been so weak-willed. Why it was as clear as day that if Anna could put an end to everything because of such an absurdity, that meant that she didn't love him.

After he had cleared his head with some cold water from the sink, Voskoboynikov consoled himself with the fact that all was not lost yet: the ill-fated, sentimental letter was lying in the mailbox, and he could still ask the letter carrier Ksenia to let him have it back.

Five telephone messages had accumulated during the night, all about one and the same thing: the stations needed wire.

"What's with Sizhma?" Voskoboynikov inquired.

"Not a sound," the telephone operator answered guiltily.

Voskoboynikov was soon caught up in the usual commotion of a working day. He redistributed the remainder of the wire to the stations, asked the backwater station to hurry up with the boats under repair, signed some bank checks and orders to the Trust, argued on the telephone with the steamship line who unreasonably demanded a reduction in the capacity of the rafts.

Absorbed in his work, it seemed to him that he was just the same as ever today, but Stepanovna, sharp as usual, noticed something peculiar about the engineer. Voskoboynikov caught her questioning glance a few times. And when they were alone in the office, Stepanovna said quietly:

"Why are you so gloomy today, Andrey Petrovich? Has something happened?"

"No, everything's O.K." Voskoboynikov answered what seemed the truth to him, but Stepanovna, looking hurt, shook her head doubtfully and began to rustle some papers.

"She didn't believe me—that means it shows." More than anything else at this point, Voskoboynikov was afraid of warm human pity.

Voskoboynikov talked with workers, foremen, the construction engineer.

The wife of the foreman Ilin came in to complain that the directress of the nursery school had canceled the children's trip to camp. The name of the camp was similar to Anna's last name—only the vowels were reversed. And the dandyish construction engineer suddenly reminded him of the young man who had come into Anna's office while they had been quarreling. Anna was everywhere. Whatever he did, some aspect of it was invariably associated with Anna.

It would be very easy to hear Anna's voice—all he needed to do was to stretch out his hand to the telephone and ask for her number. Every day she would be so near and yet so inaccessibly far from him. And in a week or a month or a year he would hear that she was often seen in the company of some handsome young man or other, or maybe he himself would bump into them on the street, the town being so small. And then on just such an ordinary busy day as today he would hear that Anna had gotten married, and then surely he wouldn't be able to control himself and he'd call her up and wish her happiness in her married life. . . .

"A jolly picture!" Voskoboynikov got up from the table and stood for a while by the map, automatically looking for the town he was born in, and he sent for the directress of the nursery school.

The directress was pleasant to look at—tall and pretty and rosy. But talking with her turned out to be much less pleasant.

"Why haven't you sent the children to camp yet?" Voskoboynikov asked sternly.

"There was no transportation and I'm not a boat, if you please!"

Voskoboynikov gave a look at Stepanovna to see if she agreed with his opinion of such outrageous behavior. Stepanovna confirmed with a glance that she too didn't approve of the beautiful directress.

"That's no reason," Voskoboynikov said. "This morning some boats went down for refueling and they might have taken the children to camp, but you never even made the effort to inquire at the controller's office."

"I know your boats and your controllers," answered the directress scornfully, "you never get anywhere with them!"

The directress rudely turned away from the engineer, as if she really had wanted to say: "Why should I bother with you, Anna's rejected lover." But she said, "I suppose Mrs. Ilin tattled to you. Well, just tell me what they'll find in this camp?"

Voskoboynikov didn't allow himself to be provoked to anger.

"Have you forgotten what it was like when you were little? The memories of camp last all year long for children. They get a rest there, gain a little weight. Why it's a marvelous place, with a pine forest and lots of sunshine and fish in the streams. . . ."

"You've been a grown-up longer than I. I'm younger than you . . ." the directress objected validly, "and the pine trees have nothing to do with it. It's all a matter of the food. At our nursery school they drink tea with milk but in camp they get cocoa. Just give me some cocoa and you'll see what happens! That's what you have to understand."

Voskoboynikov wanted to appeal again to Stepanovna to sympathize with him silently at the directress' absurd reasoning, but he remembered in time that the secretary herself was crazy about vitamins and he refrained.

The whole trouble, Voskoboynikov decided, thinking about the nursery-school directress, was that she had become aware too soon of her own beauty. That led her to develop an unpleasant overconfidence, made her superficial and kept her from succeeding now with such important people as, for instance, himself. But judging by the imperturbable expression of the directress, one could assume with certainty that she didn't even realize what she was missing and of course hadn't the slightest regret about having lost

the respect of such an important person as the head engineer
of the timber-rafting bureau.

"Send the children to camp today," Voskoboynikov said
out loud, and he ordered the controller to take one boat off
towing duty.

Ivushkin stared at the engineer, unable to understand what
was going on. Voskoboynikov himself was always furious
when any boat was used for some purpose not directly connected with the timber-rafting, and now he had dreamt up
this children's charity. Voskoboynikov firmly withstood
Ivushkin's withering glances and asked him to mark down on
the order for the boat to pick up the promised ton of wire at
the Trust warehouse on the return trip. The controller only
shook his head, wondering if it were possible, strictly speaking, to call the trip of the boat from the camp to the warehouse a return trip.

The letter carrier Ksenia came into the office. She took the
out-going mail from Stepanovna and inquired with her usual
patter:

"Andrey Petrovich, are there any orders for the Trust?"

After ten minutes in the company of the unpleasant nursery-school directress, Voskoboynikov looked with pleasure
at Ksenia's simple, sun- and windburned, frostbitten face. A
bundle of letters was sticking out of her open mailbag and
Voskoboynikov thought he recognized the blue envelope of
last night's all-forgiving letter.

"Hurry up with those orders!" Ksenia said brazenly.

Voskoboynikov had observed long ago that she always
began to be rude when she felt guilty about something or
other. But now he was in no mood to hunt for Ksenia's
imaginary transgression.

"There are no orders for the Trust, but there is one little
thing . . ." Voskoboynikov said easily, trying to cover his
embarrassment.

Ubiquitous Stepanovna tore herself away from her work
and listened eagerly. If he took the letter back now the secretary would surely understand everything, he thought, and
out of the goodness of her heart she would offer him her tart,
old-womanish pity.

"Do you sell postcards at the post office? Buy me a dozen."

He handed her the money for the postcards. Ksenia carefully put away the money in a little child's oilskin purse with a gay red button. The button clicked loudly and maliciously, as if it were laughing at his indecision. Voskoboynikov followed the departing letter carrier with his eyes. Her shoes were worn and one shoulder, pulled down by the bag, was lower than the other. . . . If only he hadn't written all that about his room number or if only he hadn't drawn the map! . . . It was still possible to overtake Ksenia in the corridor and get the letter from her, but Voskoboynikov suddenly felt sick to death of all his attempts to save his self-respect.

"Let Anna laugh at his letter if she finds it funny. Whatever will be, will be. . . ."

All day long the office was attacked by hosts of mosquitoes and clouds of small gnats. They stung faces and hands, crept into ears and eyes and mouths. It was a windless day and the neighboring swamp sent forth millions upon millions of insects. Several times during the day Glasha, the cleaning-woman, carried with great ceremony, a brazier with burning coals and pine cones through all the rooms. A thick cloud of milky-white smoke trailed after the brazier and all the workers stopped their work and watched Glasha with amusement as she walked through slowly and solemnly, fully aware of the responsibility of the work she was doing.

The aromatic, resinous smoke unexpectedly reminded Voskoboynikov of the half-forgotten scent of incense; his mother had been religious and had taken him to church often in his childhood. He thought how unfortunate it was that his memory would retain this ancient smell, this early rubbish, to the end of his days, while it would forget many more recent and more important things. This subconscious contraband was like dirt tracked in from the outside: he'd always carry with him, even to Communism itself, these old and unnecessary memories.

The relief-bringing smoke quickly dispersed and the mosquitoes attacked the office with renewed vigor. Voskoboynikov's hands were swollen from bites and his face and neck burned as if he had been scalded. Stepanovna suffered bravely for a long time but finally she couldn't stand it any longer: she put on gloves and covered her head with mosquito netting. The horn-rimmed glasses of the secretary glimmered mysteriously through the black gauze netting and modest Stepanovna began to resemble a wise Martian. Only the controller Ivushkin had his triumph: for some reason the mosquitoes didn't bite him.

"They sense a relative!" Stepanovna whispered.

VI

At noon the best diesel launch in the whole outfit, the Number 9, went out of order. That meant that the Byeloborsk station was left without any towing power and within two or three hours they would have to stop work on the rafts.

Reporting the breakdown of the "Nine," Ivushkin looked venomously at Voskoboynikov, as if he really wanted to say: "Look what's happened, while we're transporting children to camp with tugboats!" Voskoboynikov countered with another glance that he couldn't have foreseen the breakdown of the launch that morning, but Ivushkin, wiping his bald head, seemed to answer, "But that's what you're head engineer for, to foresee everything. The State isn't paying you good money for your beautiful eyes!"

It was clear that Ivushkin wouldn't forget this matter and would make sure to place all the blame on the head engineer at the next production meeting when the station heads complained about the controller's service. "Oh, you nincompoop!" Voskoboynikov thought good-naturedly and asked him to telephone the repair station.

"I just called them," Ivushkin informed him. "Not one of the launches will be out of repairs before this evening."

"Comrade Ivushkin," Voskoboynikov said quietly, "please call the repair station."

Voskoboynikov asked the controller of the repair station how many launches the neighboring raft works had under repair. Situated farther downstream the neighboring raft works appropriated for itself the wood lost by the upstream raft-makers and almost always won the prizes at competitions. The neighbors were not on good terms with each other: they were forever fighting about wood, floating barriers, riggings. Voskoboynikov felt for a long time how abnormal such relations were, but somehow there was never time to undertake a radical change in customs that had developed over the past ten years.

The repair station controller answered that the neighboring raft works had only one launch under repair.

"Only one out of all!" Voskoboynikov exclaimed with delight and asked Ivushkin to connect him with the manager of the Trust.

Ivushkin, intrigued, quickly reversed the lines on the switchboard and inclined a fleshy, curious ear toward the engineer. Voskoboynikov explained to the manager their desperate situation in respect to towing power and asked that one launch from the lower works be temporarily assigned to them, leaning heavily on the argument that all their raft-making operations were in full swing while their neighbors were at a standstill because of a lack of wood.

"Nothing doing," said the manager, "learn to use your own tows correctly."

Ivushkin couldn't hear what the manager said, but his expression grew condescending and disapproving, as if he were ashamed of the engineer for turning to the manager with such unimportant requests.

It was lunch time and the office was packed with raftsmen. Adroit in the water, they moved with constraint in the crowded room, not knowing what to do with their own hands. Voskoboynikov indicated with a nod for them to take seats on the sofa and very gently asked Ivushkin to telephone the lower raft works.

"A useless waste of time!" Ivushkin said patronizingly, getting a line on the switchboard. "You won't live to see the day they'd help you out. Why should they cut their own throats?"

Many of the raftsmen nodded their heads in agreement.

The head engineer of the lower establishment, Cheremukhin, came to the phone. Voskoboynikov hardly knew him; they had happened to meet only a few times at the Trust or the Regional Committee of the Party.

When he discovered who was calling, Cheremukhin unexpectedly was delighted.

"Andrey Petrovich, why I think this is the first time we've

ever spoken together on the phone. That's a bad thing—
we're neighbors and don't know each other. When the timber-rafting is over you must come for a visit. I'll treat you to
some marinated mushrooms. My mother-in-law is the greatest specialist in these parts for marinating mushrooms. . . ."

Voskoboynikov decided that the time was ripe and without
procrastinating further asked him to send them up a launch
before evening for their work.

"We'll pay you back well when the occasion arises. . . ."

The raftsmen on the sofa looked amazed, Ivushkin got up
from the table: in the whole history of the raft works such a
thing had never before happened!

"You've sold me!" Cheremukhin laughed. "You're either a
very crafty fellow or . . . very simple."

"I try to be crafty," Voskoboynikov answered modestly.
"Well, what about that launch?"

"I know the director will call me names, but so what . . .
I'll give you the launch. Two conditions: don't use the boat
later than nine p.m. and as soon as the river rises I'll expect
you for those delicious mushrooms!"

"No later than nine . . . and I'll come without fail. . . ."
Voskoboynikov said calmly, as if he were used to getting help
from the other raft works every day, and he asked Ivushkin to
notify the Byeloborsk station that they'd have a launch within
the hour.

The raftsmen on the sofa exchanged puzzled looks,
Ivushkin was blinking with embarrassment and Stepanovna
the Martian giggled a little underneath the mosquito netting,
proud of her favorite's success.

A warm wave of happiness he hadn't felt for a long time
swept over Voskoboynikov. Damn it, he loved this work—the
bustle, the sleepless nights, the unexpected obstacles at every step that characterized the lumber industry—no longer a
seasonal one as in the past, but still not a completely assimilated industrial branch that was planned to the last detail
with no surprises or malicious jokes of Mother Nature. . . .
In his position as technical director of the enterprise, Voskoboynikov tried to plan the work, to avoid stoppages and
accidents, but he felt a certain pleasure especially at those

times when despite his plans unforeseen obstacles came up, and he managed to overcome them, to bend them to his will, overcoming blind chance and the forces of nature.

This was what made life worth living. He felt a consuming joy in being alive and somehow he thought of Anna in quite a new way. He had never considered this before, but it turned out that life was quite possible without Anna, and such a life had its joys too. It was not in her power to close off all roads to him, to throw him off balance completely. Other things held Voskoboynikov firmly anchored to life. For instance, meeting a new, spiritually rich person. This was greater than he had imagined, greater than living for love alone. And if his fight with Anna weren't resolved—he would go on living and doing his not very great, but in the long run not too insignificant, work.

VII

In the afternoon Voskoboynikov made a tour by boat of the nearest raft-making stations. The helmsman Petya, knowing the head engineer's weakness, let the motor run full speed. The boat ran swiftly along the water, nose high in the air, drenched by a glittering, silvery spray, scattering floating logs, barriers and rowboats in its wake.

The river was engaged in a strenuous working life. Low tugboats pulled long caravans of barges with flour, bricks and farm machines upstream. The wire shortage had not slowed down the raft-making operations yet. Logs floating down from the logging camps at the upper reaches of the river were being sorted on the water and joined firmly with wire into bundles so that they wouldn't separate when formed into rafts and would last the whole long trip down to Archangel. Small hard-working tugboats were towing these bundles downstream to the raft-making stations.

The steep banks were picturesque, but Voskoboynikov had no time now to think of beauty. He remarked to himself that as he watched the bundles being towed he didn't even notice the wood, but saw only the binding wire and it struck him that he was now like a sick person who doesn't feel the healthy parts of his body but concentrates all his thoughts on the one sick part.

At each station Voskoboynikov made a round of the sorting and raft-making operations, checking the quality of the sorting and the strength of the wire bindings. He just wanted to catch somebody using too much wire, but the binders at each station were as careful as if they were binding the bundles of wood with gold rather than steel wire. Voskoboynikov even inspected the rigging warehouses in his search for binding materials, but they were all deserted and quite empty.

It was now as clear as day that without the Sizhma wire they would never last out until the arrival of the barge. The devil picked just this time to break the telephone connection!

Voskoboynikov begged the pardon of the head of the Byeloborsk station for picking on him unfairly the day before.

The Byeloborsk head had worked at timber-rafting for thirty years and had seen many things in his time. His was the burden of worrying about an early freezing up of the river, a late thaw, the wood drifting into the bushes or getting stuck in the shoals, the unfulfillment of the towing Plan, the over-expenditure of materials, the negligence of the seasonal workers and many other great or little, real or imaginary troubles and misdemeanors. The various authorities bawled him out, dressed him down, told him off, spit in his face, threatened to throw him in prison and cursed him out time and time again. All this was done by mouth or by letter in the fatherly twenties. Then, with the introduction of technical means of communication to the lumber camps, it was by telephone, and, later, even on the radio—graphically demonstrating their flexibility and their ability to make use of the latest technical developments.

It became a habit with him to hear all sorts of abuse, almost as if this were included in the unwritten range of duties outlined by his position: first a brigadier, then a foreman and now the head of a station. Many years of careful performance of this duty had hardened him to the very worst curses. Habit, like a coat of armor, protected his feelings against any scolding. And as the years went by and he climbed higher on the official ladder, he himself reached perfection in this not too difficult art, and on occasion he too knew how to "cuss out," tell off, or dress down his subordinates. In a word, the Byeloborsk head was an old salt, hardened to various scrapes, and not so very easy to amaze.

At first he simply didn't understand when Voskoboynikov begged his pardon, and thought that the educated "little engineer" was only preparing to "eat him out" especially hard. But when Voskoboynikov repeated his pardons once again, the old veteran suddenly understood him—not with his intellect but from a memory of a certain dream that had haunted him in his youth, a dream that lay dormant for many years at the very bottom of his soul, about the possibility of other, more pleasant relations between people bound together by common labor. All his previous experiences left him completely unprepared for these new relations. Without his usual coat of armor he suddenly felt unprotected and bare and he was as dumfounded as a schoolboy. His face reddened as he blushed comically and somehow clumsily, as if he were just beginning some hard and unfamiliar work.

"Well, really . . . really," he muttered with embarrassment, "all sorts of things happen in the world. . . ."

"Exactly! Things happen. . . ." Voskoboynikov agreed readily, finding it pleasant—a very human fault—to feel himself self-critical and magnanimous, and wanted other people —above all, Anna—to behave toward him just as tactfully and fairly as he did toward them.

It suddenly occurred to him that Anna had just received his nocturnal letter, at this very minute. She was opening the envelope, unfolding the paper, now she was reading it. Maybe everything now would turn out all right with them. . . .

"All sorts of things happen," Voskoboynikov said quickly, "but it's not necessary for them to be," looking the old lumberman straight in the eye but seeing only Anna before him and trying to lead her to the only right decision.

The head of the station brought out a handkerchief the size of a good tablecloth and began to wipe his face, perspiring from his extraordinary experience. Then he looked away to the side, unable to stand Voskoboynikov's unseeing gaze, and stewed angrily.

VIII

Voskoboynikov went home quite late that evening. As before, only the dry clicks of the abacuses could be heard in the deserted office; the bookkeeping department was struggling with its quarterly accounts. Catching sight of him, the telephone operator hoarsely began to call Sizhma, without any hopes of an answer.

On his desk there was a careful pile of postcards weighted down by a little mountain of change. Voskoboynikov fingered a bright new coin and smiled to think of his agitation that morning.

Some practice students from the technical school came in, a boy and a girl. The letter carrier Ksenia slipped into the office after them, sitting down on the edge of the sofa. Voskoboynikov looked at her questioningly.

"It's forbidden to be in the office now!" she said defiantly and he knew that his former assumption about the letter carrier's guilt had been correct.

"Sit down," Voskoboynikov allowed, guessing that Ksenia wanted to speak alone with him.

The students brought him a sheet of time-keeping data. The girl quailed before the head engineer of the Timber Rafting Bureau and was astonished by the speed of his computations on the slide rule and by the fact that he knew the simple formulas by heart as he corrected the mistakes. The boy stood at attention, looking Voskoboynikov searchingly in the eye, silently demanding that he lay out for them all his wisdom and hold back nothing. The girl looked a little like Anna in her schoolgirl photograph and the boy reminded Voskoboynikov of himself: he was also the mistrustful type. And to complete the resemblance the boy seemed to be in love with his schoolmate and scowled jealously every time she especially admired the head engineer's mathematical talents.

"Don't be afraid, you little idiot, I won't take away your treasure!" Voskoboynikov thought fondly.

Ksenia carefully closed the door after the students had left and said rudely:

"Andrey Petrovich, write a note to the locksmith to come

open the lock . . . he won't come unless *you* order him . . . he says he's busy. . . ."

"What lock?"

"To the mailbox! I lost the key somewhere or other. I thought maybe I had dropped it at the post office yesterday, but no, they didn't find it. . . . Why is it, Andrey Petrovich, that if you lose something useless you always find it, but lose something important . . . that's the last you'll ever see of it. Once I knew a case . . ."

"So," Voskoboynikov said, getting up from the desk, "that means that you haven't collected the letters since yesterday morning and all the letters deposited in two days and a night are still lying there?"

Ksenia stuck out her chin belligerently, ready to fight and defend herself.

"Who mails letters at night?" she said to begin with, trying to make her crime smaller. "People sleep at night!"

Voskoboynikov wrote a note to the locksmith. Ksenia immediately subsided when she was certain he wasn't going to scold her, and begged him shyly at the door not to tell anyone about her negligence.

"People sleep at night," Voskoboynikov repeated mechanically, remaining alone in the office and going up to the window. The mailbox hung outside the office next to the window and Voskoboynikov could see clearly a green corner of it. It suddenly struck him very funny that the letter had lain right next to him the whole long day, some three yards from his desk. Voskoboynikov measured the distance with his eye and decided that he was mistaken: the mailbox couldn't be more than two and a half yards from his desk.

He went home to his room. He found unexpectedly that he felt like doing some housework. He set the teapot on the electric plate, washed the floor and cleaned the cupboard and table. Then he battled with the mosquitoes. He made a small bonfire on the stove out of candles, papers and pine branches torn from a besom broom.

Voskoboynikov smoked out the room until it became impossible to breathe. Then he let the excess smoke through the transom, took off his shirt, and sat down to have tea informally, in his undershirt. His eyes were tearing from the smoke but, in recompense, not one single mosquito droned in his ear. Voskoboynikov gulped down the unsweetened tea with a lump of sugar melting on his tongue and proudly surveyed his room, cleaned by his own hands; he thought resignedly: "Well, we'll just live alone! . . . What can we do if women don't realize how good we are!"

The door burst open without a knock.

"Sizhma is on the line!" the telephone operator blurted out.

Choking on his tea, Voskoboynikov rushed to the office, pulling on his coat on the way.

The thick, calm voice of Potapov hummed in the receiver.

"You must be tired out without me. I know, my friend . . . I sympathize. . . . The wire is on the way already, you can expect it tomorrow around noon. I'll be coming myself by plane in two or three more days. . . . Suffer just a bit more, my friend, break your weak, intellectual bones. . . . And I've thought up a new little thing to build, my friend. . . ."

The director loved technical novelties; he was known up and down the river as a passionate admirer of dams, and Voskoboynikov pricked up his ears.

"To build what? Speak more clearly. . . . Another dam?"

Potapov laughed joyfully and a little guiltily.

"Why can't we dry out the wood every year by means of lowering the river rapidly? I'll talk you into it . . . you'll work the project out!"

"Well, we'll see about that!" Voskoboynikov said implacably. "I'm not about to indulge your fancies: my job is engineering and construction."

"Tut tut tut," the director teased Voskoboynikov, "an engineer, and you're afraid to build!"

"How much wire did you get? Will there be four tons?"

"Guess again . . . more!"

"Six?"

"They're sending seven tons!"

"Well, that's splendid," Voskoboynikov said happily. "Now we'll have more than enough to hold us until the barge arrives. We'll even be able to give some to the lower raft works."

"Is this something new?" Potapov asked, amazed. "No charity! Let them find their own wire!"

"No, we're going to help," Voskoboynikov said firmly. "I'll explain to you when you come."

He put down the receiver and thought about the director condescendingly: "Now he's dreamt up some sort of new dam . . . and he probably isn't taking into account the flood tides. . . . He's up to building anything!"

Attracted by the noise in the office gloomy Ivushkin appeared.

"Now we're living!" Voskoboynikov welcomed him with a joyous tone, as if he wanted to convert the controller with his own personal delight. He couldn't stand to see gloomy faces around him when he himself was happy.

Ivushkin said nothing and only looked enviously at the engineer. The controller envied him his youth and energy, his established position in the world and, finally, he envied the fact that a few tons of wire could make the engineer so happy. There didn't exist any wire in the world that could have cheered up Ivushkin. He sensed the engineer's superiority over him with the sharp resentment of one who is a failure. He had nothing that could compare with Voskoboynikov.

Ivushkin was a rolling stone. Once he had studied at college but he never finished. He had been married, but had divorced and lost his family. In search for better jobs he had traveled all over the country: he had worked in the south and in the far north, he had changed professions dozens of times and now in his old age had gotten stuck here, quite by chance, and had become a lumber worker. Even his one consolation—his diversified knowledge gleaned from encyclopedias—seemed scrappy, obsolete and unnecessary now to Ivushkin.

Voskoboynikov lightheartedly threw open the door to his room and froze on the doorstep as if he had stumbled. On a chair in the middle of the room sat Anna, looking a little angry and embarrassed as proud people do when they have to admit they were wrong. She was wearing his favorite cherry-colored dress, and all the things in the room—the table, the cupboard, even the sink—looked somehow different now, as if they realized that the lady of the house had arrived. All the things had clearly deserted to Anna's side and had acquired a new, unexpected meaning, as if they had been made exclusively to surround Anna, to set off her cherry-colored dress, to conceal her dirt-stained shoes. She had walked!

He stood at the door for a long time without moving, without dropping his eyes from her, still not really believing and afraid that she might suddenly vanish if he moved his eyes or took a step.

"Close the door," Anna said quietly, "you'll let in the mosquitoes."

Translated by Marie Winn

MIKHAIL BULGAKOV

THE ADVENTURES OF CHICHIKOV

A Poem in Ten Items with a Prologue and an Epilogue

"Hold him, hold him, you fool!" Chichikov shouted to Selifan.

"I'll use my broadsword on you!" shouted a courier with mustaches a yard long, galloping toward them. *"Don't you see this is a government carriage, the devil flay your soul?"*

PROLOGUE

A strange dream. It was as if, in the kingdom of the shades, over the entrance to which an inextinguishable lamp flickers beside the inscription "Dead Souls,"* a satanic joker had opened the doors. The kingdom of the dead began to stir, and an endless line filed out of it.

Manilov in his fur coat, mounted on huge bears, Nozdryov in someone else's carriage, Derzhimorda on a fire truck, Selifan, Petrushka, Fetinya. . . .

And last of all *he* appeared, Pavel Ivanovich Chichikov, in his celebrated chaise.

And the whole band moved into Soviet Rus, and then amazing events occurred there. And what they were the following items will show.

* The title of a famous novel by N. V. Gogol. This story is a mock-extension of it, with references also to other work by Gogol.

I

Having changed from his chaise to a car in Moscow and
dashing in it through the Moscow gullies, Chichikov was
cursing Gogol roundly:

"May blisters as big as haystacks run under both his eyes,
the son of the devil! He has dirtied and fouled my reputation
so that I can't show my face anywhere. For if anyone finds out
I'm Chichikov, in the flesh, they'll throw me the hell out in
two shakes! And I'll be lucky if they only throw me out,
otherwise they'll stick me in Lubyanka prison, God forbid.
And it's all Gogol's fault, may he and all his relatives . . ."

And meditating in this manner he drove through the gateway of that same hotel from which he had departed a hundred years before.

Everything there was exactly the same: the cockroaches
peeped out of the cracks, and there seemed to be even more
of them, but there were some slight changes. For example,
instead of the sign "Hotel," there hung a placard inscribed
"Dormitory No. so-and-so," and of course the dirt and filth
were such as Gogol could not have even conceived.

"A room!"

"Show yer order."

But the brilliant Pavel Ivanovich did not hesitate even for
an instant.

"The manager!"

Lo! the manager, an old acquaintance, baldheaded Uncle
Pimen, who had once kept the "Akulka" but has now opened
a café on Tverskoy Boulevard in Russian style with German
trimmings: orgeats, balsams, and, of course, prostitutes. The
guest and the manager exchanged kisses, whispered together, and the matter was arranged in an instant without any
order. Pavel Ivanovich had a bite of whatever God had provided and dashed off to arrange for work.

II

He appeared everywhere and captivated everyone by his
bows a little to one side and the colossal erudition which had
always distinguished him.

"Fill out the form."

Pavel Ivanovich was given an application form a yard long, which contained a hundred questions of the trickiest sort, such as "Where from?" and "Where have you been?" and "Why?"

Pavel Ivanovich had not been seated even for five minutes before he had filled out the form completely. Only his hand trembled as he submitted it.

"Well," he thought, "they'll read right away what sort of treasure I am, and . . ."

And absolutely nothing happened.

First, no one read the questionnaire. Secondly, it came into the hands of the young lady registry clerk, who dealt with it in the usual fashion: she treated it as an outgoing document instead of an incoming one, and then she immediately shoved it away some place, so that the questionnaire vanished into thin air.

Chichikov grinned and started work.

III

After that everything was even easier. First of all, Chichikov took a look around and saw that positions on every side were filled by his own men. He dashed into an office where rations were supposed to be issued, and he heard:

"I know you, you misers, you'd skin a cat alive and give it to me for a ration! But you give me a side of mutton and kasha. Because I won't put that frog you're serving into my mouth, even if you coat it with sugar, and I won't take your rotten herring, either!"

Chichikov looked and saw Sobakevich.

As soon as Sobakevich had come in, he had first gone up to claim his ration. And he actually got it! He ate it up and asked for seconds. They gave him some. Too little! Then they dished up a second meal for him. He'd had an ordinary ration, so they gave him a shockworker's ration. Too little! They gave him some sort of reserved ration. He gulped it down and asked for more. And he made a terrible row about it. He cursed them all for "Judases," said that scoundrel sits on scoundrel and prosecutes scoundrel, and that there was only one decent man, the clerk, and that he too was a pig, to tell the truth!

They gave him an academic ration.

As soon as Chichikov saw how Sobakevich acquired rations, he immediately made arrangements for himself as well. But of course he did better even than Sobakevich. He obtained a ration for himself, for his nonexistent wife and child, for Selifan, for Petrushka, for the uncle he had told Betrishchev about, for his old mother, who was not in this world. And academic rations for all. So that his groceries had to be delivered by truck.

And having solved the food problem in this way, he moved onto other government offices to get jobs.

Once dashing along Kuznetsky Street in his car, he met Nozdryov, who immediately informed him that he had already sold his watch and chain. And in fact he was wearing neither watch nor chain. But Nozdryov did not despair. He told how lucky he had been in a lottery, where he had won half a pound of vegetable oil, a lamp chimney, and soles for a child's shoes, but how he had had no luck later on, and how he had thrown in his six hundred million rubles, damn it all. He told how he had proposed to the Ministry of Foreign Trade to export a shipment of genuine Caucasian daggers, and it had. He would have earned billions by it, except for the rascally English, who had noticed that the daggers were marked "Made by Savely Sibiryakov," and had rejected the whole lot as defective. He dragged Chichikov to his room and poured out some wonderful cognac, supposedly obtained in France, but which tasted, however, like straight illegal vodka. Finally, he lied so much that he began to assert that he had been given eight hundred *arshins* of textiles, a light blue automobile trimmed with gold, and an order for living space in a building with columns.

But when his brother-in-law Mizhuyev expressed doubt about this, he cursed him out, not as a Sofron, though, but simply as scum.

In short, Chichikov was so sick of him he did not know how to get away from him fast enough.

But Nozdryov's stories gave him the idea of taking up foreign trade himself.

IV

And so he did. Again he filled out a form, and he began to get busy, and he put himself forth in all his glory. He brought sheep in double sheepskins across the frontier, and under the skins there was Brabant lace; he smuggled in diamonds in wheels, shafts, ears, and in all kinds of places.

And in a very short time he had five hundred oranges in capital.

But there was no stopping him, and he submitted an application to the proper quarter, expressing his desire to take a lease on a certain enterprise, and he painted in extraordinary colors the profits that the government would derive from it.

At the government office the mouths just fell open; the profit was indeed colossal. They asked to be shown where the enterprise was. Certainly. It is on Tverskoy Boulevard, right opposite Strastnoy Monastery, across the street, and it is called the "Pampas on Tver-Boul." An inquiry was sent to the proper quarter to find out if there was anything of the kind there. The answer was that there was, and that all Moscow knew of it. Fine.

"Submit a technical estimate."

Chichikov had the estimate already at hand.

The lease was given to him.

Then Chichikov, losing no time, dashed to the proper quarter:

"An advance, please."

"Submit an authorization in three copies with the necessary signatures and seals."

In less than two hours he submitted the authorization, too. In completely proper form. As many seals as there are stars in the sky. And the signatures were all there.

"Manager: Never-Mind-the-Trough; Secreta Pitcher-Snout; Chairman of the Tariff-Estimate Commission: Elizabet Vorobey."

"Right. You'll get the order."

The cashier only grunted when he glanced at the sum on the order.

Chichikov signed for it and carted away the banknotes in three horsecabs.

And then he went to another office.

"Give me a loan with my merchandise as collateral."

"Show us your merchandise."

"By all means! Let me have your agent."

"Send the agent here!"

Hey! the agent is an acquaintance too—Emelyan the Loafer.

Chichikov picked him up and took him along. He brought him to the first cellar they came to and showed it to him. Emelyan saw an incalculable quantity of merchandise lying there.

"Hm, yes. And it's all yours?"

"All of it."

"Well," said Emelyan, "in that case I congratulate you. You're even more than a millionaire, you're a trillionaire."

And Nozdryov, who had tacked onto them at this point, poured more oil on the flames:

"See that car driving in the gate, with the shoes in it?" he asked. "Those are his shoes, too."

And then he grew excited, dragged Emelyan into the street and pointed out:

"See those stores? Those are all his stores. Everything on this side of the street is all his. And what's on the other side is his, too. See that streetcar? That's his. The street lamps? They're his. See? See?" he said as he turned him around in all directions.

Emelyan begged him: "I believe it! I see, only let me have some peace!"

They drove back to the office.

There they asked, "Well, how was it?"

Emelyan only waved his hand:

"It's indescribable," he said.

"Well, if it's indescribable, give him $n + 1$ billions."

v

Later Chichikov's career assumed dizzying proportions. The mind cannot grasp what he was doing. He founded a trust to make iron from sawdust, and he obtained another loan. He became a shareholder in an immense co-operative and fed all

Moscow on sausage made from animals that had dropped dead. When the landowner Mme. Korobochka heard that "everything was settled" now in Moscow, she wanted to acquire some property, so he formed a company with Zamukhryshkin and Uteshitelny and sold her the Manège, the building opposite Moscow University. He contracted to electrify the city, a job that would not get anywhere for three years, and, making contact with the former mayor, he erected some sort of a fence and put up landmarks so that it would look like planning, and as for the money issued for electrification, he wrote that it had been stolen from him by Captain Kopeykin's bandits. In short, he worked miracles.

Soon the rumor ran through Moscow that Chichikov was a trillionaire. Enterprises began rushing to get him as an expert. Chichikov had already rented a five-room apartment for five billion, and Chichikov was already dining and supping at the "Empire."

VI

But suddenly the crash came.

Chichikov was ruined, as Gogol had correctly predicted, by Nozdryov, and finished off by Mme. Korobochka. Without the least idea of doing him a bad turn, but simply because he was under the influence of liquor, Nozdryov babbled casually about sawdust and about how Chichikov had leased a nonexistent enterprise, and concluded it all with the statement that Chichikov was a swindler and deserved to be shot.

The public began to think about it, and winged rumor flew like a spark.

And at this point stupid Mme. Korobochka shoved her way into a government office to inquire when she could open a bakery in the Manège. In vain they assured her that the Manège was a government building and that it could not be bought nor could anything be opened in it; the dumb woman understood none of it.

The rumors about Chichikov kept getting worse. People began to be puzzled about what sort of bird this Chichikov was and where he had come from. Gossip started, each item more malicious and monstrous than the first. Uneasiness descended upon them. Telephones jangled, conferences started. The Commission on Construction met with the Commission on Observation, the Commission on Observation with the Section on Living Quarters, the Section on Living Quarters with the People's Commissariat of Health, the People's Commissariat of Health with the Main Administration of Handicraft Industries, the Main Administration of Handicraft Industries with the People's Commissariat of Education, the People's Commissariat of Education with the Proletcult, etc.

They rushed to Nozdryov. That was, of course, stupid. Everyone knew that Nozdryov was a liar and that not a single word of his could be believed. But Nozdryov was summoned, and he answered every question.

He declared that Chichikov had indeed leased a nonexistent enterprise, and that he, Nozdryov, saw no reason why he shouldn't have, since everyone was doing it. To the question whether Chichikov was a White Guard spy, he answered that he was a spy, and that recently he had been due to be executed but had not been, for some reason. To the question whether Chichikov was a forger of false bank-notes, he answered that he was a forger, and even told a story about Chichikov's extraordinary skill, how when Chichikov had heard that the government was going to issue new notes he had rented an apartment in Marina Grove and from there had issued counterfeit notes for eighteen billion rubles, two days before the real ones were issued, at that, and when they suddenly raided the apartment and sealed it up, Chichikov changed all the notes for genuine ones in a single night, so that later even the devil himself could not have told which were genuine and which were counterfeit. To the question whether it was true that Chichikov had changed his billions for diamonds in order to escape abroad, Nozdryov answered that it was true, and that he himself had undertaken to help him and co-operate with him in this matter, and if it were not for him nothing would have come of it.

After Nozdryov's stories everyone was plunged into complete despair. They saw that there was no way of finding out what Chichikov was. And there's no way of knowing how it all would have ended if it had not been for one man out of the whole crowd. True, he had never had a copy of Gogol in his hands, any more than the others, but he had a small dose of common sense.

He exclaimed:

"Do you know who Chichikov is?"

And when everyone eagerly asked in chorus:

"Who?"

He pronounced in a voice of doom:

"A swindler!"

VII

Only then did the light dawn. They rushed to find his application form. It was not there. In the "in" box. Not there. In the file. Not there. Ask the registry clerk. "How would I know? Ivan Grigorich has it."

They asked Ivan Grigorich, "Where is it?"

"That's not my business. Ask the Secretary." Etc., etc.

Suddenly and unexpectedly it was found in a basket for unnecessary papers.

They started to read it and were stupefied with horror.

First name? Pavel. Middle name? Ivanovich. Last name? Chichikov. Social Status? Gogol character. Occupation before the Revolution? Purchase of dead souls. Draft status? Neither fish nor fowl nor good red herring. Party affiliation? Sympathizer (with whom—unknown). Were you ever arrested? A wavy line. Address? Turn into the courtyard, on the third floor on the right, ask the field officer's wife, Podtochina, in the information office, she'll know.

Signature? A blotch!

They read it and turned to stone.

They shouted at Instructor Bobchinsky, "Rush to Tverskoy Boulevard, to the enterprise he leased, and in the courtyard where his merchandise is, maybe you'll find out something."

Bobchinsky returned. His eyes were round.

"An extraordinary occurrence!"

"Well?"

"There's no enterprise there. That's the address of the

Pushkin Memorial. And the merchandise wasn't his, it belonged to the American Relief Administration."

They all began to howl: "Holy saints! What geese we've been! We gave him billions! Now it seems we'll have to try and catch him!"

And they started to try and catch him.

VIII

The finger pressed the button:

"Send the messenger."

The door opened and Petrushka appeared. He had long since left Chichikov and was now working as a messenger in a government office.

"Take this package immediately and be off immediately."

Petrushka said, "Yes, sir."

He immediately took the package, immediately set off, and immediately lost it.

They telephoned Selifan at the garage.

"Send the car. Quick."

"Right away!"

Selifan bestirred himself, covered the motor with a pair of heavy pants, put on his chauffeur's uniform, jumped into the seat, whistled, honked, and flew out.

What Russian does not love a swift ride?

Selifan did, and therefore at the very entry to Lubyanka he had to choose between a streetcar and a store window of ornamental glass. Selifan in a brief instant chose the latter, turned away from the streetcar, and screaming, "Help!" drove like a whirlwind into the store through the window.

At this point even Tentetnikov, who was in charge of all the Selifans and Petrushkas, lost his patience.

Fire them both!

They fired them. They applied to the Labor Bureau, which sent Plyushkin's Proshka to replace Petrushka and Gregory Ride-but-Never-Get-There to replace Selifan. And meanwhile events rushed onward!

"The authorization!"

"Here it is."

"Ask Never-Mind-the-Trough to come here."

It turned out that this could not be done. Never-Mind-the-Trough had been purged from the Party two months previously, and he himself had purged himself from Moscow immediately afterward, since there was absolutely nothing for him to do there.

"Pitcher-Snout?"

He had gone to the ends of the earth somewhere to be in charge of a province section.

Then they started to look for Elizabet Vorobey: He didn't exist! There was, it is true, a typist Elizabeth, but she was not Vorobey. There was an assistant to the deputy of the junior clerk of the Assistant Manager of the Subsection named Vorobey, but his first name was not Elizabet.

They caught hold of the typist.

"So you're the one!?"

"Nothing of the kind! Why me? Here the name Elizabet ends in a t, and does mine? On the contrary!"

And she burst into tears. They let her alone.

And while they were dealing with Vorobey, the lawyer Samosvistov secretly let Chichikov know that the hue and cry had begun, and all trace of Chichikov naturally disappeared.

And in vain they dashed by car to the address he had given; at the turn to the right there was of course no information office, there was only an abandoned and destroyed public dining hall. And the cleaning woman Fetinya came out to them and reported that there ain't no one here.

Next door, it is true, at the turn to the left, they found an information office, but there was no field officer's wife there, only a certain Sidorovna Podstega, and of course she was ignorant not only of Chichikov's address but even of her own.

IX

Then despair descended on all. The matter became so confused that even the devil himself could not have found anything to his taste in it. The nonexistent lease was mixed up with the sawdust, Brabant lace with electrification, Korobochka's purchase with diamonds. Nozdryov had stuck with the case, and both the sympathizer Emelyan the Loafer and the non-Party Antoshka the Thief were involved, and a Panama hat turned up with Sobakevich's ration cards in it. And the whole province set to writing!

Samosvistov worked without stopping and mixed into the stew some robberies of trunks and a case of falsified expense accounts for government trips. (This case alone led to the involvement of up to 50,000 people.) Etc., etc. In short, God knows what all started to happen. Those who had the billions stolen out from under their noses and those who were supposed to find them dashed here and there in horror, and only a single incontrovertible fact confronted them. "Once there were billions, and they've disappeared."

Finally some uncle Mityay rose and said,

"Well, lads, it's sure we'll have to appoint an investigating commission."

X

And at that point (what doesn't happen in dreams!) I emerged, like a *deus ex machina*, and said:

"Assign the case to me."

They were amazed.

"But you—could you—would you be able?"

"Don't worry," said I.

They wavered. Then they wrote in red ink:

"Assigned to him."

Then I started in. (I've never had such a good dream in my life.)

Thirty-five thousand motorcyclists rushed up to me from all sides.

"Do you need us for anything?"

"I don't need you," I said. "Don't interrupt your work. I'll manage it myself. Alone."

I took a deep breath and barked so that the window panes rattled:

"Send me Lyapkin-Tyapkin! Immediately! Get him on the phone!"

"It's impossible to get hold of him. The telephone's broken."

"Aha! Broken! The cords torn out? Well, don't let it dangle there doing nothing, string up the man who's reporting it to me!"

Lord! What happened then!

"Please, sir! . . . What are you . . . This, er . . . heh, heh! Right away! Hey, repairmen! Wires! Mend it immediately!"

In two shakes they mended it and gave it to me.

And I pushed on:

"Tyapkin? The scoundrel! Lyapkin? Arrest him, the rascal! Get me the lists! What? Not ready? Get 'em ready in five minutes, or you'll be on the death list! Who's that? Manilov's wife is the registry clerk? Throw her out! Ulinka Betrishcheva is the typist? Out with her! Sobakevich? Arrest him! Is the villain Murzofeykin working in your office? and Shuller Uteshitelny? Arrest them! And whoever appointed them, too! Grab him! And him! And this one! And that one! Out with Fetinya! Send the poet Tryapichkin, Selifan and Petrushka to the Accounting Section! Put Nozdryov in the cellar . . . this minute! This second! Who signed the authorization? Get him here, the rascal! Even if he's at the bottom of the ocean!"

Thunder rumbled through hell.

"He's a devil, this guy. Where'd they get him from?"

I went on: "Get me Chichikov!"

"Not . . . not . . . er . . . we can't find him. He's hiding."

"Oh, hiding? Wonderful! We'll put you in prison in his place."

"Plea . . ."

"Shut up!"

"In a minute . . . Just a . . . Wait just a second. They're hunting."

And in two instants they found him!

And it did Chichikov no good to grovel at my feet and tear his hair and tunic and to insist that he had a dependent mother.

"Your mother!" I thundered. "Your mother? Where are the billions? Where's the people's money? Thief! Cut him open, the scoundrel! He has diamonds in his stomach!"

They cut him open. There they were.

"Is that all?"

"Yes, sir."

"Put a rock around his neck and down an ice-hole with him!"

And peace and quiet descended.

I reported by phone:

"All clear."

I received the answer:

"Thank you. Ask for whatever you want."

Then up I jumped beside the telephone. And I almost poured out to the receiver all the items of expense which had been tormenting me for a long time.

"Trousers . . . a pound of sugar . . . a twenty-five-watt bulb . . ."

But suddenly I remembered that a decent man of letters should be unselfish, so I lost heart and blurted into the phone:

"Nothing but a bound edition of Gogol's works, like the one I recently sold in the second-hand market."

And . . . lo! on my desk was Gogol with gold lettering.

I was so glad to see Nikolai Vasilevich, who had consoled me more than once on bleak, sleepless nights, that I bellowed:

"Hurray!"

And. . . .

EPILOGUE

. . . of course I woke up. And there was nothing: no Chichikov, no Nozdryov, and, most important, no Gogol. . . .

"Ah well," I thought to myself, and started to get dressed, and life again paraded before me in its ordinary way.

Translated by Lydia W. Kesich

Nikolai Chukovsky

The Tramp

I

In 1916 Misha became twelve years old. Misha was curly-haired, broad-shouldered, and thick-legged. Only his dark, rotten teeth spoiled his appearance. He lived with his father and mother in a southern town. His father owned six fish stores in various parts of the town.

Every evening Misha went to the main street and met some friends there. They would set off to stroll along the avenue in a noisy gang. When they spotted some mild-looking passer-by, they would begin to argue hotly among themselves. When the passer-by was very near, Misha would suddenly turn to him and say, "Listen!"

The passer-by would stop, whereupon Misha would turn his back on him and continue his argument. The passer-by, thinking that they had forgotten about him, would prepare to walk on. But Misha again stopped him: "Wait!"

The passer-by waited while Misha argued about how many watermelons the hold of the *Andromeda* held or how many steps there were between Cathedral Street and Greek Street. Then, as though he had suddenly remembered him, he said, "Go on. I don't need you."

And the passer-by walked off listening to the laughter behind his back as it sailed through the branches and into the warm, darkened sky.

Sometimes it happened that Misha got into a scuffle with a friend and when some peace-loving fool began to pull them

apart and quiet them down, they, forgetting their fight,
would begin to tweak his cheeks good-naturedly.

He was a joker, this Misha.

At that time Misha had cost his father a great deal of
money. The war with Germany and Austro-Hungary was in
progress, and his father had purchased his release from military service. But in spite of all these expenditures, Misha's
position was becoming continually less sure from day to day.
He was being seen too much by the whole town. The governor himself, they said, was displeased that Misha was still not
at the front. And Misha's father felt that it was necessary
somehow to arrange things differently for his son.

After some efforts he arranged for Misha to be taken as a
clerk in the provisions department of a prisoner of war camp.
The camp was located in Central Asia. Misha, in a greatcoat
and fur cap, left for there in the fall.

The war prisoners were building a railroad. Before the
winter snow came, when the frozen steppe sounded under
foot, they were separated into groups of six men each and
assigned to lugging rails. A guard was stationed with each
group of six. The six took a rail and carried it to the embankment. The guard walked along holding a rifle. Black-mus-
tached Croats and Bosnians walked behind, in the same order, in single file. They had still not been issued mittens, and
the skin was torn from their hands—their fingers were frozen
to the iron. From a distance these human chains on the
frozen steppe seemed like musical notes on gray paper. They
worked until darkness, and then they lay down on the hard
ground, stretching their legs toward the smoky, dried grass
and manure bonfires.

When Misha arrived, he soon made himself at home and
fitted himself into the situation. He didn't sit with the clerks
for long. They appointed him a receiver and began to send
him to Askhabad for goods. He became famous in the camp
administration as a gay blade and storyteller. He frequently
told the story about the passenger who continually asked
what the next station was called.

"Papaville," they told him. "And the next?"—
"Mamaville"—"And after that?"—"The villes of all the relatives!"

Misha was very much in demand. He was invited first to one house then to another. He enjoyed the complete confidence of the authorities. They began to give him the most delicate assignments, such as to carry off provisions designated for the war prisoners to Askhabad and there sell them to black-marketeers. At first Misha was shocked, then he became accustomed to it. He had to do business with a huge number of people, and because of this Misha was earning more than his father made from all his six fish stores. And with each month Misha became more and more successful, more and more jolly.

In the spring of 1917, when the steppe became green and sultry, when the meetings began to be held and the news about the deposition of the tsar reached Central Asia, Misha began to buy sterling pounds. Together with the speeches of Kerensky, the news came to the camp that an inspection party was coming from Tashkent. It was decided to sacrifice someone, to ascribe to one the sins of all in order to save the rest. The choice fell on Misha. He was young, inexperienced and a stranger to everyone there.

They grew still more cordial toward Misha. In short, they gave him the opportunity to steal as much as he liked. And so he took provisions to Askhabad in whole transport units, while the camp bookkeeper, meanwhile, ascribed all the former losses and forgeries to him.

But Misha was shrewd, and when the steppe turned from green to parched yellow, he crammed all his sterling pounds into his boots and, providing himself with an official assignment, set out in a cart to the neighboring village.

From there it was twelve versts across the steppe to Persia. At sunset Misha left his horse in the village and set out to the south. It was a rolling steppe, and he attempted to remain in the low spots between the hills. The crimson sky glowed, and a hot dry fog rolled over the ground in a violet haze.

It had become almost completely dark, and the sunset had become a narrow band, when Misha suddenly noticed a man sitting on the slope of a hillock. The man got up. He stood on the slope directly above Misha and seemed to Misha to be huge. He asked something from above in a low voice and an incomprehensible language. Two or three words were similar to Russian and Misha suddenly guessed that this was a Croat who had run away from the camp. Recently everything had gone to pieces in the camp, and prisoners frequently ran away.

Misha gave no reply, and the Croat bent over right up to his face and peered into it. Misha stood immobile, feeling the breathing of the Croat on his cheeks. Suddenly the Croat cried out, and Misha understood that he had recognized him.

The Croat began to speak rapidly, and it was all the more frightening because there were occasional comprehensible words in this unintelligible speech. Then he punched Misha in the face.

Misha spit out all his dark teeth, lost consciousness and sank into the stiff grass. When he came to, the sun had already set. Large, low stars hung over the steppe. Without strength and afraid to stir, Misha lay on his back and looked at the stars. Hours passed, the constellations slowly passing overhead. All was quiet about. And suddenly from afar, three rifle shots sounded in the stillness—one after the other.

Misha listened attentively, but again quiet, unmoving, stone-like, set in.

When the night became grayish, Misha got up and started walking forward slowly. A narrow band of dawn appeared in the east, the peaks of the hillocks were reddish. Making his way, bent over, across a flat, open field, Misha stumbled in the grass. When he glanced at his feet, Misha saw that the toe of his boot had caught on a man's leg. He recognized him—it was the Croat.

During the night border guards had killed the Croat. In his tattered clothes the dead Croat was similar to a rag doll. His unmoving, protruding eyes with their lower eyelids drawn back stared upward.

Misha stood and looked at the Croat. Then he struck him in the face with his heel. And he ran forward not looking. He ran until he reached the shore of a small river. This stream, he knew, was the border.

It was already completely light. There was not a soul about. He took off his boots, and, carrying them on his shoulders in order not to wet the sterling pounds, he started to ford the stream. The water was warm and yellowish. Sharp, brittle reeds broke with a dry cracking.

On the Persian side he crawled into the bushes near the water and lay down. He washed his swollen face and drank for a long time. His gums were bleeding. A gray lizard looked at him from a gray stone. The sun was rising over the hills.

II

Having purchased a gray suit and a soft hat in the Persian town of Asterabad, he arrived in Teheran by mail carriage. There he rented a room with an Armenian family who spoke Russian. He invented a new surname for himself and at first was very careful because he didn't know whether or not the Russian authorities would try to haul him back from Teheran. But reports of more and more new occurrences were coming from Russia, and little by little Misha began to realize that the Russian authorities weren't concerned about him.

His toothless mouth was ghastly, and in the fall he went to a dentist to get himself gold teeth. It turned out that the dentist was a Russian émigré and was even a native of that same town where Misha had been born. Misha told him about how he and his friends had clowned with passers-by on the avenue, and the dentist laughed heartily—he had spent his youth on that same street. He told Misha that before he could put in new dentures, it would be necessary to remove the roots of the teeth remaining in his gums. This was very painful, but Misha agreed. Every five days he went to the dentist, who would tear out several of his roots. By the new year, 1918, two rows of golden teeth shone in his mouth.

Under the Persian sun these teeth glistened so brightly that everyone who spoke with Misha involuntarily squinted. Misha was satisfied in spite of the fact that the dentist had taken almost a quarter of his capital from him.

Having received his teeth, Misha began cautiously to attend to his affairs, searching for ways to employ his capital. There were a good many Russian tradesmen in Teheran, and he gradually succeeded in becoming acquainted with them. They liked him because he was a joker and because they guessed that he had money. And little by little he began to take part in several affairs and joint enterprises.

But his work in the war prisoners' camp had spoiled him. Slow, intricate business dealings with an infinitesimal profit were not for him. He was not suited for that sort of thing: he wanted a real killing.

Such a killing, however, did not turn up.

He lived in Teheran for a whole year, buying and selling all sorts of paltry nonsense, but there was no profit, and his money dwindled. He quit Teheran and traveled around Persia selling insurance. But the Persians had no fear of fire in their mud houses, and no one bought policies. His money was diminishing. He was cheered only by rumors of civil war in Russia—so that all traces of his theft be destroyed.

Destitute Persia tormented him. He left there and went at first to Baghdad where English forces were then stationed and, after several months, to Syria, which was occupied at that time by France. In Alexandretta he posed as the representative of the Wrangel government and began to sell various Russian papers. This was a magnificent idea, and Misha took heart. But, unfortunately, the real representatives of the Wrangel government appeared in Syria and exposed him. Misha left Syria and moved to Palestine.

Wearing a white suit and a pith helmet, he rented the best room of the hotel in Jaffa—with mirrors, a bath and a view of the Mediterranean Sea. He represented himself as a rich man precisely because his affairs were in poor shape. He felt that, if he did not succeed in completing some extraordinary deal, he would be lost. And so he hurriedly and eagerly sized up the situation.

That was the time when England was setting up the Jewish state under its protection. Daily new steamships deposited more and more crowds of refugees from Rumania, Hungary, Lithuania and Poland in Jaffa. They transported them to different regions of the plains and gave them little plots of wild, stony land. Misha happened to see how, gathered into little bands on the plains, they carried away stones, and he remembered the Croatians who in the same way and on the same sort of plain had carted rails. This similarity excited him, and he directed all his attention to the new settlers.

He began to observe the activity of one American charitable organization which distributed clothing among the immigrants. This clothing was donated by New York Jews. In the chests of worn and cleaned cast-offs, excellent things turned up: practically new dresses, silk underwear, sweaters, men's suits, overcoats and even furs. All this was transported to the Palestinian settlements and distributed completely free.

A hungry immigrant who received as a gift a coat of heavy material or a woolly sweater and did not know what to do with these things under the desert sun would set out to sell them. He would also sell the underwear because he had nothing to buy food with. But all his neighbors, too, were selling coats, sweaters and underwear. There were no buyers. No one would give even small change for clothing.

Having calculated the remnants of his wealth, Misha rented an old and dirty little Ford and in the course of a month visited all the villages between Jaffa and Jerusalem, between Bethlehem and Nazareth, and between the Dead Sea and the coastal valleys where the Philistines once lived. He bought skirts, dresses, coats, jackets, trousers, furs. When the Ford became completely full, he drove all that he had purchased to Jaffa, stored it away there, and again set out after booty. Many of the Jews spoke Russian. This helped him because they looked on him as one of their own. He told the men a very funny story about how a rabbi took a bath. He knew how to get along with women even better than with men.

He loaded chests of good clothing on the next steamship bound for Constantinople. He knew for certain that the prices for clothing in Constantinople were very high. There was a war going on in Turkey. Turkey had entered the war in 1914 and now it was already 1921 and Turkey was still at war. After the surrender of Germany in 1918, the Turks still had to fight the Greeks, their sultan, and the English for a long time. In Constantinople there were no goods, and the prices for clothing continually went up and up.

He sat happily on the deck under a canopy, ate pineapples, which he cut into golden chunks, and looked at the warm, blue sea. There were French ladies on the steamship—dark-browed, slender, wearing rose-colored dresses. By feeding the seagulls a roll, he managed to attract their attention. The red-beaked gulls, in disarray, hovered around him for the bread. Misha tossed pieces of it upward, and the gulls swallowed them in flight. Misha knew only a few French phrases which he had learned in Syria, but the ladies understood him perfectly.

In Constantinople he unloaded his naphtha-saturated goods.

Constantinople was at that time full of White Russian soldiers who had fled the Crimea, recently occupied by the Reds. He met fellow countrymen everywhere—in restaurants, hotels, on the streets. The appearance of their downcast faces afforded him satisfaction: he felt his superiority over them, the scoundrels and ne'er-do-wells. He met and talked with them and even treated several to beer. He told them about Papaville and the rabbi's bath and vaguely hinted at his wealth.

He really was quite rich as they offered him large sums for his goods. But he was in no hurry to sell. He looked about and kept his ears open.

He met one Armenian merchant who had just arrived from Tiflis. The Menshevik Georgian government which was at war with Soviet Russia was in Tiflis. This merchant dealt in everything and knew the prices for any goods anywhere. It was he who told Misha that good clothing was worth at least twice as much in Tiflis as in Constantinople.

Misha's plans changed at once. Bales of rags turned into bales of gold. He broke off his negotiations with the Constantinople purchasers, packed his goods on a steamship, and set sail across the Black Sea for Batum.

Batum was overcrowded and restive. People were sleeping under palm trees on their suitcases. Crowds stormed the steamship on which Misha arrived—everyone wanted to go to Constantinople. Merchants, landowners and officials were converging there, on the shores of Batum, from all over the Caucasus. The Reds were approaching Tiflis.

"You madman!" they told Misha in the café when they found out that he was going to Tiflis.

But the thought that such a remarkable undertaking, almost brought to its conclusion, could suddenly collapse seemed to Misha incredible. He was not afraid of the Bolsheviks. In Persia everyone feared the Kurds; in Arabia, the Bedouins—but he well knew that one could sell anything one wished to both the Kurds and the Bedouins. He loaded his riches into two freight cars and sent them to Tiflis.

He rode in an empty train. In the opposite direction, the trains were overflowing—people were sitting on bumpers, roofs, engines. When he arrived in Tiflis, Red flags were already hanging here and there, and workers were walking the streets singing songs.

He spent the night in a hotel filled with people who had not succeeded in fleeing. Everyone attempted to be as quiet as possible, and they even walked along the corridors on tiptoe. Outside there was shooting.

In the morning he strolled over to the railroad station to look at the wagons containing his goods. Red Army units walked along the empty streets. A commissar, a huge Caucasian in a black, shaggy fur cap, was in charge of the station. He didn't know anything about Misha's two boxcars and didn't want to know anything about them. Misha himself went to search and for a long time rushed along the sidings. People with rifles were standing by the warehouses and the trains. They chased Misha away, but he returned.

Finally a watchman, with whom he had started up a conversation, told him that the freight train, which had arrived yesterday from Batum, had not been unloaded and had left before daybreak for Baku.

Misha cursed the Constantinople Armenian who advised him to go to Tiflis and got aboard a heated freight car which in three days brought him to Baku through a region only recently cleared of Whites.

His cars weren't in Baku. But he had their numbers written down in his notebook, and, from the numbers, he found out from the stationmaster that they had been sent to Rostov. He spent four nights in front of the ticket window in Baku and succeeded in getting a ticket to Rostov. In Rostov he found out that his wagons had gone to Voronezh.

It was the month of March, and Misha was seeing snow for the first time in many years. There was not much snow in Rostov, but in Voronezh it had only just begun to thaw.

Misha arrived in Voronezh before his wagons. He remained in Voronezh a week, waiting. Finally, they arrived—he himself saw them on the rusty supply sidings. He wandered around them, grieving. Their tightly closed doors were sealed up.

Misha took out his travel papers, issued in Batum under the Whites. But the railroad men, when they had seen the seals, advised him not to show these papers to anyone. Misha understood that his Palestine goods were no longer his. He was beside himself. Now he no longer believed that the Bolsheviks were similar to the Kurds and Bedouins. All day he walked about the streets of Voronezh stifling the anger and the terror that he felt.

During the night his freight cars left. He again dashed in pursuit. He did not know what he would do when he caught them, but it was not within his power to leave them. He rode after them to Kazan. They were not in Kazan, and he raced farther to Sarapul, to Krasnoufimsk, Sverdlovsk. Spring turned to winter, and everything became colder. There was more and more snow all around. He rode trains without end through mountain valleys, through dark, rising forests.

He finally caught up with his cars in Chelyabinsk. They were standing on a rail siding. Dirty snow was melting around them.

Misha ran along a low embankment. Having run up to the cars, he glanced inside. It was dark and empty in there. Only a few flakes of naphthaline glittered on the floor.

III

He arrived in his own home town, but he didn't find his father there. He found nothing in town old or familiar. Stores were boarded up, and those which were doing business belonged to the co-operatives. Not one of his friends or relatives remained. By chance he met an old man who had previously worked in his father's fish store, and this old man told him that Misha's mother had died, and his father had been in prison several times as a bourgeois hostage, and that a half year ago he had moved to Petrograd, not wanting to

live any more in his home town, where he was too conspicu-
ous.

Misha sold his leather suitcase in the market place, sent his
father a telegram and left for Petrograd. His father met
Misha at the station but Misha recognized him only when he
rushed to embrace his son. What had become of his father!
He had been so imposing and stately, stout and mustached,
and had worn a frock-coat made from material thick as armor, and walked with his head thrown back. But now nothing
remained of his former lordly air; he seemed quite small and
mouse-like—he had a gray peasant's blouse hanging over his
sloping shoulders, his mustacheless face was full of flabby
spots and empty hollows, there was a wide, moist bald spot,
gray fluff behind his ears, and he had the swollen veins of the
aged on his temples. Of his former self only a barely perceptible fish smell remained.

His father was overjoyed to see Misha, although it seems
he was a little disconcerted to note that Misha did not even
have a suitcase. They traveled across town by foot. The
bright May sun illumined the broad streets. When they entered the front door and began to climb the stairs, it seemed
to Misha that his father was a little shy.

His father's apartment, however, was not bad. The furniture, which was ragged and dirty but expensive, crowded the
rooms. The abundance of locked trunks, cupboards and
chests led Misha to think that there was something or other
in these trunks, cupboards and chests. In front of him, there
was suddenly a rustling, stirring sound, and a stout, middle-
aged woman in a flowered robe came toward him. She was
fair-skinned and black-eyed. "Oho!" thought Misha.

This was his father's new wife. It turned out that his father
had managed to marry again after the death of Misha's
mother. He remained, uncertain, on the threshold of the
room and waited to see how Misha would meet his stepmother. But the meeting went off very well. The stepmother
embraced Misha around the neck with her large hands, drew
close to his face and kissed him. She had a drawn-out south
Russian accent, and, without stopping, she told him how glad
they were to have him and how lonely his father had been for
his son.

"But where are your suitcases?" she asked. . . .

They put Misha in the very back room. A dirty window looked out on the court. By the wall, between two cupboards, stood a shabby leather sofa, and Misha at once lay down on it.

Day after day, night after night he lay on this sofa and got up only when it was time to eat. When he had eaten, he would again lie down. He never went out on the street. Days passed, nights passed, summer came, oppressive hot air blew into the small window from the court, while he just lay and looked at the dirty plaster curls on the ceiling.

Sometimes his father came to see him, sat down on the edge of the sofa and talked about business. The New Economic Policy had begun, private enterprise was allowed and his father had hopes. He had already opened a fishstall in the market place . . . an insignificant, penny-ante affair. But in the meantime he succeeded in establishing several of his old business connections with fish-dealers in the north—connections which none of the other fish-sellers there had. If he had capital now, in such a large city as Petrograd, he could develop a first-class business. His father sighed. Unfortunately, he had not managed to save anything. Now if it had happened that Misha had brought something or other from abroad . . . but since he had not brought anything, there was no sense in talking about it. In such a situation it would be a good idea if Misha got a Soviet job. Really, why not get one? It wasn't a question of salary—they would give him almost none—but they would regard the family differently. . . .

"Tell me, Papa, how do you sit down on the bench in the train?"

His father thought a bit.

"With my ass," he answered simply.

"But I had a real seat!"

No, Misha was not idiot enough to take a job. He would have nothing to do with that here. What kind of sense is there in doing something in a country where the government itself conducts business, where land and factories are not bought and sold? Misha felt as though he were a prisoner. He lay on his sofa and thought about escaping.

Sometimes, when his father was not at home, his stepmother came to see him, well-rounded in her robe and with slippers on her bare feet. Smiling, she sat down on the edge of the sofa by his feet and tried to start a conversation. She very much wanted to know what he had done abroad, and she questioned him closely. But he was morose and uncommunicative. Then she began to talk about herself. She told how she had lived in the town where Misha was born, and how she had a friend there who had gone abroad with the Whites. She was prepared to go after him, but she was one day late, and the train had already gone. So she married Misha's papa who was old, but good. Once, while he was listening, Misha got up from the sofa, embraced her and kissed her. She cried out, tore free and ran away. He didn't run after her. He again lay down on the sofa.

He lay and listened to what she was doing on the other side of the wall in the bedroom. At first she sat quietly, then she began to walk about, her heels clicking loudly. Perhaps she wanted to attract his attention. But he lay there and was quiet. In ten minutes she quietly went up to the door of his room. She was standing behind the door. He listened to her breathing, but he didn't move from his place. "Let her stand there," he thought.

His father, returning from the market, would come to see him as usual but he no longer talked to him any more about getting a job. He would glance at him, sigh and always act as though he expected something from him. Several times, as though by chance, he spoke of several rich fish-sellers in the north who were occupied with a new business: transporting people to Norway on their boats. He had known these fish-sellers for about twenty years, and they knew him. What did they want? Only the word of a dependable man, yes, and money. . . .

At these words Misha's insides always turned over, but he gave the appearance that he was totally indifferent. He was in no hurry. He would still lie on the sofa and wait. With time his father would become more generous.

The stepmother stopped visiting his room, but she often stood behind his door. She no longer spoke with him as freely as in the beginning and became terribly frightened when he looked at her. He sometimes amused himself by staring at her face for a long time at dinner in his father's presence without saying anything, smiling or blinking. She became disconcerted under his glances, sighed, and sweat came out of every pore on her face.

Summer passed, and his father's business was continually expanding and expanding. Soon Misha understood from his talk that he had not just one stall in one market place but several stalls in various market places. He had already surveyed a location where he could open a fish store. In this store there would be a large aquarium with live fish. Although he still walked about in the gray peasant's blouse and sighed that he had nothing left, his eyes looked full of confidence, and more and more often Misha recognized in him his old habits and ways.

"Mishenka," asked his father, sitting close to him on the sofa, "would you like me to give you a letter of recommendation?"

"Are you driving me out, Papa?" asked Misha.

His father smiled, looked into his eyes and said nothing.

Misha refused to take the letter if his father would not give him money. But his father still thought that Misha had some money. He gave him only a thousand old Nikolai notes, swearing that they would accept it for transport. Misha did not take anything and lay on the sofa as before. Then his father began to add to the sum. He added gradually from one day to the next. He stopped at five thousand Nikolais.

"I don't need paper abroad," said Misha, "give me something more substantial."

But he finally understood that his father would not give anything better. July ended, August was beginning. If he did not leave before autumn, he would have to wait until the next year. Misha took the letter and the five thousand.

His father became cheerful. Misha also grew cheerful. They both were very happy. Misha went to the railroad station to find out when the train left for Murmansk. When he returned, he told his father and stepmother that the train to Murmansk went twice a week, on Tuesdays and Saturdays. It was Wednesday. There remained three days till Saturday.

On the following day, when his father was not at home, Misha heard the splash of water behind the wall in the bedroom. He got off the sofa, walked down the hall and knocked on the bedroom door. His stepmother with disheveled hair and wearing her flowered dressing gown stood in the middle of the room and held a white glazed wash basin in her hands. Upon seeing Misha, she dropped the wash basin, and water spilled all over the floor. Misha silently walked right up to his stepmother, kicking away broken pieces with his feet. He grabbed her and kissed her. She offered no resistance.

In ten minutes, sitting beside her on the edge of the bed, he proposed that she go with him. He showed her the letter written by his father and addressed to a certain Fyodor Akimovich Lapshin at the outpost of Ust-Shan. He told her that he had purposely lied in his description of the trains, and that the Murmansk train really did not leave on Saturday at all but tomorrow, on Friday, at two-forty in the afternoon, just when his father would not be home. She was frightened, despondent and depressed . . . but she agreed to everything.

He told her that they would have to have a little something abroad at first, or else they would be lost, and asked if his father didn't have money. But it turned out that she had no idea what his father did and did not have. It seemed that his father kept his dealings hidden from her and kept nothing at home. At first Misha did not believe her, then he became angry. When she saw that he was angry, she became terribly frightened. She rummaged in the bureau and drew out from under a pile of linen, two little earrings wrapped in paper. These earrings were her personal property. He held them up to the window and looked them over. His face lit up. Diamonds, obviously real. Yes, this was as good as cash. He directed her to sew the earrings into the lining of his trousers. She did.

In the evening his father was even more happy than yesterday. He continually slapped Misha on the back, was concerned that Misha not catch cold on the way and constantly expressed regrets that he had nothing to give him. Misha was also extraordinarily gay and burst out laughing and winked. The happy people were sitting at the table, the father beside the stepmother, and Misha opposite them. His father had obtained a small bottle of spirits. Misha downed a glass and told about how a husband and wife went to sleep but their blanket was short. The husband drew the blanket up to his chin, and his legs stuck out. The husband looks and sees that not four, but six are protruding.

"Hey," said the husband poking his wife, "why do you and I have six legs?"

"Fool," says the wife, "where do you see six? There are four. Count again."

The husband counted legs once more—again it came out six.

"Ah, you don't know how to count," cries the wife. "Get out of the bed and count like you should."

The husband got out and began to count.

"You're right," he said, "there are four legs."

His stepmother sighed, and her eyelashes became wet. His father and Misha laughed heartily. Laughing, Misha loudly slapped his palms on his knees, and the yellow reflection of his teeth flitted across their faces.

On the next day, Friday, his father left home early. Misha heard the door close after him but for a long time lay in his room on the sofa. On the other side of the wall in the bedroom, his stepmother was fussing about. She was crying. He continued to lie there until eleven-thirty, and then he dressed and went to her.

Fearfully, she wiped her swollen eyes. Open suitcases stood on the floor, but she evidently did not know what to pack in them. He opened her dresser, looked over her underwear and her dresses and gave her advice. Folding and packing things gradually diverted her, and she took heart. He walked about the room and whistled, while she showed him first one thing and then another, asking whether she should take it or not. If he saw that the piece pleased her, he advised her to take it. Both suitcases were full, and still new packages and bundles crowded the floor. She asked him what time it was about three times, but he always told her not to hurry. He said that when the time came he would go for a cab.

She began to get dressed at ten to two. It was two when he went out for the cab, leaving her in the apartment alone with the things. Not hurrying, he went down the stairs and walked to the corner. In his pocket lay the letter. Five thousand

Nikolais were hanging on his chest in a little linen sack. The two earrings were sewn into his trousers.

Twenty-five minutes remained before the departure of the train. Misha hailed a cab and, without stopping for his stepmother, drove to the station.

IV

Misha slowly walked along the shore of the bay. The waves almost touched his feet. The huts of the outpost Ust-Shan skirted the bay in a semicircle. In the bay, the bare black masts of the fishing boats swayed. Behind the masts a cawing flock of gulls circled like a wheel spinning forever. Behind the huts loomed the bare stone crags of the hills. The large sun was hanging quite low; one could look at it without squinting. Long, blackish-red shadows extended from the rocks.

In his lifetime Misha had been on the steppes of Central Asia, in Persia and in Arabia. He had seen the Mediterranean Sea and had seen the islands of the Greek archipelago and the Bosphorus. Now he was walking along the shore of the Arctic Ocean. But both in the past and now, he was indifferent to what he saw around him. Wherever fate might bring him, he remained just the same. His surroundings changed, but Misha was immutable, like a piece of small change going from pocket to pocket.

Reaching the limits of the settlement, he glanced around and found a hut standing apart from the others on the slope of the mountain. Then he turned around to see whether anyone was following him. But it was desolate all around, and he slowly made his way up the slope.

A lanky adolescent of about seventeen greeted him on the porch.

"Who do you want?" he asked Misha in an unfriendly way, blocking his path.

"Does Fyodor Akimovich Lapshin live here?"

"What do you want him for?"

"I have a letter," said Misha, "from Petrograd."

"From Petrograd," repeated the youngster slowly, as though it were the first time he had ever heard this word.

Then—to Misha's good fortune—a gruff and deep voice rasped from behind the door: "Let him in, Kondraty."

Kondraty moved to the side, and Misha opened the door which was covered with shaggy felt.

The stuffiness engulfed Misha. The windows of the room were heavily covered and did not let in light. In the first moment, Misha could make out only the half-open door of an iron stove where loose slabs of peat were burning, immersed in flame as though in water, and the little lights of many lamps in the corner before the icons.

The icons covered the whole right corner from floor to ceiling. In front of each glimmered a small lamp, and one large lamp—a communal one, the size of a soldier's mess-tin —hung in front of the whole icon display. The icons depicted heads cut off by swords, emaciated faces (from the temples of which crawled black serpents), hellish bonfires surrounded by the swinish and horse-like devils' faces.

"Could he really be hiding money behind the icons?" thought Misha. "No, he's not so simple. He hides his money in the ground."

When Misha's eyes became accustomed to the darkness, he made out a middle-aged peasant, who was sitting on a bench. The man was broad-shouldered, thickset and had shaggy eyebrows. His beard was gray on the outside, but its black core, shaped like an egg, clearly shone through the gray hair. His firm dark eyes, without any gleam, were fixed upon Misha.

"Fyodor Akimych?" asked Misha.

The peasant silently surveyed Misha's face. Then he spoke out:

"You might at least have taken off your hat before the icons."

"It's going to be difficult with him," thought Misha, hurriedly pulling his cap from his head. He felt that he was afraid of this peasant.

"I have brought you a letter."

Misha took out the letter and extended it to Lapshin. When he had taken the letter, Lapshin got up and went over to the lamps. He read for a long time, noiselessly moving his lips. Misha waited. He wanted to have a smoke. He fished out a cigarette and leaned toward an icon lamp to light up, but he didn't dare. "Who knows what sort of customs they may have?" He gingerly took the cigarette out of his lips and hid it in his pocket.

When he had read it through, Lapshin carefully folded the sheets and held them to a lamp. The flame crawled along the paper and finally reached his brown fingers with their large, cracked nails. Then Lapshin threw the light black flakes on the floor.

"Kondraty!" he cried.

Kondraty entered, carrying an earthen pot in front of him. He placed the pot on the table and set out two bowls and two pewter spoons.

"Sit down," said Lapshin to Misha, and Misha obediently sat down.

Lapshin poured soup into each bowl. Misha took his spoon and began to eat. Lapshin sat directly opposite him and also ate. Kondraty did not sit down.

The heat was unbearable. The soup stank of fish oil. But Misha swallowed it, having decided to submit to everything. When the soup was eaten Kondraty carried away the pot and brought boiled fish on a plate. Lapshin licked over the bones with his thick lips. Misha carefully spat out the little fish bones onto the bottom of his coat.

"My papa writes you . . ." Misha tried to begin, feeling that somehow his voice was too high and not his own, and stopped short.

Lapshin didn't say anything.

After he had waited, Misha began again:

"You see, I'm not without money, Fyodor Akimych, and I fully understand . . ."

Lapshin acted as though he weren't listening. He sucked bones, drew them out of his mouth with his fingers and deposited them along the edges of the plate.

"I can even give tsarist money."

Misha sighed and the sweat flowed along his cheeks and down his collar.

"Even fifteen hundred . . ."

"Five thousand," said Lapshin.

Misha wanted to laugh and say, "You're joking," but he

said nothing, and his laugh did not come. Lapshin continued to eat silently, looking at his plate. "Just don't give him anything until he's transported you," thought Misha.

"Hand it over," said Lapshin, standing up from behind the table.

Misha drew his amulet out from under his blouse, ripped it open, and gave Lapshin all his money. Lapshin, with one movement of his fingers, spread out the bills like cards, pushed them together again, and thrust them into his pocket.

Then he opened the door to a little room, put Misha in there, and left him there alone. The room was tiny, with one little window so small and low that one could look through it only by bending over. Misha bent over and looked but saw nothing except rocks. Without undressing, he lay down on the bed.

"Well, it doesn't matter," he consoled himself. "Tomorrow I'll be there."

He lay there that way for many hours without hearing anything but the crash of waves breaking on the shore. No one came to see him. He tried not to sleep . . . he was convinced that he would not go to sleep, but he fell asleep before he knew it. A light knock at the window awakened him.

Misha got off the bed and went up to the window. He saw Lapshin's face very near. The edges of his black beard were gray and seemed to shine. Lapshin waved his hand.

Misha went out onto the porch. He gasped—so furiously was the wind blowing. A brownish cloud swept along the ground concealing the huts and the rocks. The wind chased, swirled and whirled the cloud around. Misha at once became soaked to the shirt. It was almost dark, although, through the flying mist, Misha at times saw the sun hanging over the horizon.

Lapshin appeared out of the haze. A double-barreled gun was hanging across his shoulders.

He shouted something to Misha, but the wind carried his words away and Misha didn't hear anything. Lapshin led him right next to the water along the pebbles. The wind blew from the shore and pushed them in the water. Sometimes the mist broke for an instant, and Misha saw now the long crest of a wave, now the corner of a house.

Misha ran, trying not to lose Lapshin in the haze. They passed the entire outpost and went farther. In half an hour, panting from the wind, they reached the promontory.

Kondraty was sitting in a boat, bailing water out of it with a tin can. Misha crawled into the boat and sat on a cross-plank. Lapshin moved the boat off the sandbar and jumped into it.

The shore soon disappeared. There was nothing around except waves and the swirling darkness. The boat was rocked headlong by the wind. Kondraty and Lapshin rowed.

Misha's entire soul had been shaken out on the waves, when suddenly quite near he saw the tall black hull of a fishing motorboat. Kondraty caught hold of a rope and crawled up along it, and Lapshin, in spite of his weight, followed after him with ease. Misha also grabbed for the rope, but his feet slipped, and he was totally incapable of ascending. Then Lapshin tied a rope to himself and pulled Misha onto the deck as though he were a sack.

Almost immediately, they raised the sail and hauled in the anchor chain. The boat set out to sea through the haze. In twenty minutes they started up the motor.

In the cabin, near the small iron stove it was warm, but one became more nauseated in the warmth. Misha grabbed the copper handrails and crawled out on the deck. There he sat down near the mast. The wind pierced through him. Waves washed the deck and licked his boots. But he no longer protected himself—he had long ago become wet through.

Behind Misha's back, Lapshin stood at the wheel. He didn't glance at Misha, he was looking at the sea. But his proximity oppressed Misha who shivered and attempted to take up less space.

Having turned to stone on deck and not having the strength to bear the cold, Misha again went down into the stuffiness of the cabin. He lay down on a berth attached to the side of the ship. Next to him, behind thin boards, the water was splashing. When Misha turned on his left side, the diamond earrings sewn into his left pants' leg dug into his leg. Exhausted by the rocking and the close air, he tossed from side to side and listened to how Kondraty, leaving the motor for a minute, tossed some firewood into the stove and heated the tea-kettle. The hours passed.

Finally, from the effusion of light around the hatch, Misha understood that it had cleared up outside. He jumped up and went above.

The fog vanished, the sun, hanging overhead, shone, and the shadow of the mast, wavering, lay on the water. The atmosphere was clean and clear.

The boat was heading straight for shore, which was now not far.

This was the shore which Misha had to reach. It was the entrance to that world in which those laws of life so dear to him held sway.

Misha glanced at the ridge of the hills, trying to make out homes and people. But there were neither homes nor people, only the fiery-brown hillsides, crevices, boulders. Here and there along the slopes there was dark-green creeping vegetation.

The boat stopped in a wide bay without heaving the anchor or even cutting the motor. The shore shielded it from the wind, and it at once became warmer. With his hands, Lapshin drew the dinghy right up to the side by the rope and jumped into it. The gun barrels on his shoulders reflected the pale blue of the sky.

"Jump!" he shouted to Misha.

Misha jumped, sat down and grabbed the sides of the boat with his hands—the boat was pitching heavily. Lapshin silently rowed to shore.

When he had jumped out on the crunching pebbles, Misha at once ran from the sea. He wanted to leave Lapshin as soon as possible. But Lapshin suddenly said, "I will show you the way." And Misha did not dare contradict him.

They made their way up along the side of the hill. The sun softly warmed their shoulders. Misha walked ahead, Lapshin behind. Wild berry bushes reached to their waists, and at each step large watery berries could be heard falling to the ground.

"I can't go any farther," said Lapshin suddenly. "Go alone." And he halted.

Misha went on up without saying good-by. He had gone

about fifty steps, when suddenly he felt that Lapshin was still standing there and not going away. He turned around.

Lapshin, having pressed the butt of the double-barreled gun to his shoulder, was carefully aiming at him.

Misha ran upward.

At that moment he heard a shot.

Lapshin had missed.

The twigs of the bushes bent under Misha's legs. He waited for the second shot as he ran desperately. If only he could reach the crest of the hill and hide behind it.

For one moment he saw from the top of the hill, approximately two versts away, a wooden barrack with an unknown flag on its roof.

The second shot rang out, and Misha fell on his back, just short of the crest. He fell head down, with his legs and his mouth opened. Lapshin thrust his arm through the sling of the gun and unhurriedly walked toward him.

He unfastened all the buttons on Misha and ransacked the pockets, one after another, of his coat, jacket and trousers. The pockets were empty, and he tore off Misha's blouse searching for something on his body. But there was nothing on his body either.

Lapshin stubbornly turned the corpse over and felt it from all sides. They both were slowly sliding down the side of the hill. The sun gleamed on Misha's teeth. Lapshin carefully examined Misha, but the earrings, sewn into his left trouser leg, did not come under his touch.

Giving up hope, Lapshin, with great force, struck Misha in his opened mouth with the heel of his boot. The gold teeth fell out. Lapshin got down on his knee, thrust his fingers into Misha's throat and drew out the two golden dentures. With the flap of Misha's jacket, he carefully wiped the spit and blood off them and put them in his pocket.

Translated by Andrew Field

ALEXANDER FADEYEV

ABOUT LOVE

(Old Pim is telling a story in the forecastle of a three-masted schooner sailing from Southampton to Honolulu.)

"Even as a child I had an insatiable curiosity about life and about people. I was particularly interested in the girls, but as soon as I was old enough to fall in love with one of them I began to think: what about this pretty little lass walking by me on the street, and how about the one with whom I loaded wood today? And I couldn't help being attracted to them too. But my first love didn't let me show an interest in other girls because she loved me alone, and since I couldn't love her alone, I resented her demand as an encroachment on my freedom. . . . The girls that followed were pretty much the same in this respect—only in some cases they were even more possessive." *(Pause.)* "I'm a good materialist, you know, but I've got something of the adventurer in me too. I would be in love with a girl, but I'd also feel like going fishing or skiing or off to Sydney with the lads, and since these were things she couldn't do with me, she would ask me to stay home. At that moment my life seemed to shrink into a narrow circle, I would begin to feel depressed, my love for her would vanish, and in the end I'd throw her over along with the rest. But I continued to love life, and so far life had dealt kindly with me. There I was, twenty-three and not a care in the world, and the girls loved me because the one who loves less is always the stronger." *(Pause—Old Pim blows a puff of smoke and continues.)*

"One day I met a girl from Boston by the name of Valery. I liked her a lot and let her know it, but I also told her what kind of a chap I was. Then I went off to Sydney with a clear conscience, carrying her picture in my pocket. Everything was progressing quite normally until something very extraordinary happened: I began to miss her! We corresponded, she came to see me, I went to see her. Her love was very uneven. Sometimes she was completely indifferent to me, at other times she told me how much she loved me. For the most part that happened when we were excited by physical proximity. She would ask: 'Do you believe me?' I believed her, because I knew that she was sincere with me, but a strange dread gripped my heart. I knew that physical attraction sometimes caused two people to swear their love for each other and for the moment believe they were really in love: only later would they discover that their love had been a mirage. Great love, obviously, has other roots than this. My own intelligence and experience inclined me to put more faith in what she said when she was somewhat farther away from me. And what she said then was that she was indifferent to me. Besides, she used to stare shamelessly at every dark-eyed man she saw. In short, she loved me in the same way I had once loved other girls. Life plays strange tricks! You'd think I had found a perfect solution. I could go on being the same old carefree Pim—ski or go off to Sydney with the lads and have my passing affairs with other girls (without neglecting my little Valery, of course); and Valery was also free to do whatever she pleased. Then, when it finally came time to part, there would be no regrets and we would come away with friendly feelings for each other and pleasant memories of our love. But no! I loved my little Valery from Boston in the same way the other girls had once loved me. I continued to go off to Sydney and to ski as before, but now I did it out of habit rather than desire. In other words, I no longer cared to go fishing without my little Valery from Boston, I no longer felt like going off to Sydney without my little Valery from Boston, and I was no longer interested in the girls I saw on the street, because I was interested only in my little Valery from Boston.

"In my love for her I reached unprecedented heights, and I was terrified at the thought of falling from them—afraid that I would plunge to my destruction. The inconstancy of Valery's love began to torture me. You know, I'm a very down-to-earth and uncomplicated fellow; I demand that even the greatest love should be strong, simple and wholesome. But with her this was impossible. From the very depths of my nature I, carefree twenty-three-year-old Pim, revolted against 'psychologizing,' and I was torn by a desperate conflict between my love for unpredictable Valery and the pull of my old habits. My thoughts began whirling in a vicious circle, and I was shattered by my 'fall from the heights.' I began to feel depressed, became gaunt and joyless. I tortured myself unmercifully. One day I broke down and wrote her about my state: there was no one else to whom I could unburden myself. Once I had written her I became calmer and began to do some serious thinking about my situation." *(Old Pim lit his pipe; from somewhere came the heavy tinkle of an anchor chain.)*

"To begin with, I realized that I would never be able to leave Valery first, since in love the stronger is the one who loves less, whereas I was the one who loved more. But I also knew that torturing myself further would only lead to insanity. I began to feel ashamed of myself. 'Pim,' I said, 'it's easy for you to enjoy yourself—fish, ski and go off to Sydney —when you're not all involved with the girl you love. That's simple enough. The real trick would be to remain the same old good-natured, carefree life-loving Pim even if you happen to "fall from the heights"—even if your little Valery from Boston leaves you!' And while I was thinking these thoughts life again began to bubble in my veins, I felt my muscles grow taut and my eyes regained their brightness. I thought: 'I shall be the same old carefree Pim; I shall give thanks to life and to my little Valery from Boston; I shall give thanks for the chance to love her and for her letters which I used to kiss like a little boy, and for the sufferings which my love for her brought me: for it was all part of life, and life is beautiful, and life always conquers death!' By this time it was already night. From the river came the wailing of sirens; a gust of spring blew in through the window; beyond the river, shrouded in a mist dark as night, stretched the fabled expanse of the steppes. I decided to write her again. Let her know that carefree twenty-three-year-old Pim had survived. I wrote: 'I cannot forget you, my little Valery from Boston, and I love you—thank you for that. But I will not cry my heart out any longer. I will go off to Sydney; I will fish and I will ski; I will be as patient and as wise as an old wolf of the steppes. If you leave me I will kiss your letters and remember you everywhere I go, and I will love every word you spoke or wrote and treasure all my memories of you. And one of two things will happen. Either you will leave me and I will "fall from the heights" without plunging to my destruction, for I am still carefree twenty-three-year-old Pim! (It will be hard and the pain will last a long time; but I will recover and go to Sydney and from Sydney to Singapore, for the world is a big place!) Or your love for me will be strengthened, and then you will wish to go with me to Sydney and wish to go fishing and skiing with me, and I will gladly do many of the things you wish to do: but you will still be Valery from Boston and I will still be carefree adventurous Pim, since the world's a big place and it's a worthless love that limits the freedom of the loved one, for love is joy and "man was created for happiness as were the birds for flight." ' " *(Pim paused; it had grown dark, and we became aware of all those beautiful little nocturnal happenings which it would be idle to try to describe. The captain stumbled against the threshold as he came out of his cabin, spat and swore.)*

"But how did it turn out?" timidly inquired a young blue-eyed cabin boy who had barely entered the world but already had his own little Valery from Boston.

"It doesn't really matter how it turned out," said Old Pim after a short pause. "And anyhow I'm not going to tell you. But if you ever happen to meet her, maybe she'll tell you about it herself. . . ."

Translated by Richard Ravenal

KONSTANTIN FEDIN

THE ORCHARD

The floods always came with the blossoming of the orchard.

The orchard began at the knoll and seemed to roll down the slope to the bank, where there stretched a palisade, and white willows had been planted in a row, as straight as if they had been cut across in bangs. Through the tangle of their twigs glowed the brocade robe of the water, and over the treetops lay a gleaming stream, of the river perhaps, or perhaps of the sky or the air—of something incorporeal and blinding.

Up the river another orchard began; beyond it, a third, a fourth.

Across the river spread a small glade cut by a shallow ravine, where field maple waved on the landslides in gay sprouts.

This was the whole little world. Behind it lay unused land, with bald spots of wormwood and feather grass, and little bushes of dead immortelle, cornflowers and bindweed grew along the wattle fences of the orchards.

A mantle of whitish dust covered the whole wasteland, and, twisting somewhat carelessly, two or three deep-rutted roads ran in different directions.

That year the river came right up to the palisade itself, and the white willows stood exhausted from the excess of dampness, glossy with oily young greenery. The wattle fence had bloomed in places, the naked, peeled stubs curling with fragrant sprouts. The muddy yellow waters of the flood mewed like a kitten and rubbed against the slope of the knoll.

The knoll was covered by a spotted shawl of white and pink blossoms. A border of cherry trees, bright as the sun, framed the orchard with a thick fringe, concealing the fence.

The clusters of pale pink blossoms closed over every branch, every twig, and swallowed all the trees in their downy embrace. It was as if everything had congealed in immobility, as if it had submitted to the mystery of spring.

The orchard was in bloom. . . .

Previously, at this time of year, the old mistress used to come from the city and settle in her country house. Belted by a broad veranda, the house stood almost at the top of the knoll, and from the wooden tower which jutted up from the roof of the building, one could see the river and the vacant land behind the orchard, and the monastery crosses on the edge of the town.

The mistress had long since lost the use of her legs, and she was wheeled in a chair. In the mornings she would ride out onto the veranda and would spend the whole day there, looking all around her with calm, observant eyes.

Her son, the owner of the orchard, a taciturn, quiet man, visited his mother very rarely, but when he came he would take the gardener Silanty with him and would set off to wander through the orchard, stopping by the strawberry beds or at some marvelous apple tree, about which the gardener had an inspiring story to tell, or at the hothouse, where Silanty was growing hyacinths and roses.

The friendship of the master and the gardener had grown close long ago, when the master had first undertaken to cultivate an orchard and had hired the hale, hard-working, tireless peasant Silanty and had built him a strong, roomy frame cottage at some distance from the main house.

They respected each other, it seemed, for their reticence and their inability to do anything over again. For both of them, whatever was said was as good as done. And they both worked hard, purposefully and sensibly.

When the young orchard took root, neither master nor man wasted time talking about it. They only walked from sapling to sapling, squinting at the snowy whiteness of the blossoms which dotted the thin branches and surreptitiously glancing over at each other.

"It ought to do well?" the master asked, affirmatively.

"Why not?" the hired man agreed cautiously.

They were both young and strong then and each put his whole life into this orchard.

The orchard took root readily and began to grow quickly, spreading its mighty shoulders wider and wider with every spring. The roots of the apple trees, the pear trees and the cherry trees intertwined into a solid ball, and the gardener's life was sucked into them by the living tentacles, and it grew with them into the earth.

He lived like a bear. In winter he hibernated for a long time. Snowdrifts piled up along the fence and the orchard was secure from people, cattle and snowstorms. Silanty's wife put fuel in the stove from morning till night, and he just sat or lay on the stove and waited for spring.

Slowly, ponderously he would move from the stove to the table, like a granite boulder, passive, unhewn, mute, cold.

But when the fragrant spring arrived, the granite would suddenly acquire warmth, and, thawed out, gradually begin to be poured into the mold which would quit him with the last ray of the autumn sun.

The bear awoke with the orchard. . . .

That spring Silanty felt alarmed. In the fall the master had ordered the house closed up tightly, had sold off the last of the winter apples which had just been picked from the trees, and had gone away without saying where or for how long.

From his wife and neighbors the gardener had learned that all the landowners and merchants had run away, and that a rebellion had swept through the cities and countryside, but he did not like to talk about it, and he ordered his wife not to talk.

When the roads had been driven smooth, some men had appeared in the orchard who tore down the signboard with the master's name from the gate and ordered Silanty to come to town.

"I've been wondering about it for a long time, about the master's sign hanging there while the orchard is Soviet," said Silanty, smiling into his beard and picking up the sign.

"We'll paint it over," one of the townfolk said.

"You need another, what good's this? It's just a rotten plank, not a signboard."

Silanty did not go to town. He thought that he would get out of it somehow, it would blow over. But he did not get out of it.

The blossoms began to fall, the ovaries glistened in shaggy black plumelets, the leaves started to grow, catching up, as if behind, choking on the juices which so far had nourished the pale pink cover of blossoms.

The hoeing had to be done, but there was no one to do it. Before, around this time, they used to get a whole horde of women and girls from the neighboring villages.

Between the rows of apple trees, if you bent down to the ground, you used to be able to see the bare white calves of the working girls trampling the ground around the short trunks of the trees, the glittering hoes rising and falling, the red hems of the pinned-up skirts keeping time to them. The earth echoed under the frequent blows, and the voices of the women would hop from branch to branch and plunge into a thicket of cherry trees like peals of bells.

"Hi there, Mashutka! Come pick bast pieces!"

Now everything was quiet, mute.

Every day the sun climbed higher and higher. By the porch of Silanty's cottage the earth cracked, the nights set in, breathless and humid, and the orchard lay waiting for a watering.

One man could not handle the situation, no one showed up from town, and Silanty wandered about from morning to evening, his hands at his sides, gloomy and angry. He cursed his woman obscenely, as he had never done before in his life, and, when he finally made up his mind to go to town, he even beat her.

He decided that on the way he would visit his close friend who had worked for a long time as a guard in a brick shed and was a smart, crafty sort of peasant who could see to the bottom of things.

As they sat at the lindenwood table, white from the scrubbing brush and knife, Silanty's friend drank apple tea from a painted saucer, and while the unpolished spigot of the samovar splashed boiling water into a potbellied teapot, he spoke cunningly and with little grimaces:

"There's masters for you, let me tell you! Their own mother would weep. They don't know a thing. Just stop in at their *soviet*, you'll find out for yourself."

From the window they could see the wide gates, standing open. Behind them loomed gray buildings, like a factory or warehouse, just as dull and long as the brick sheds.

"Just take our business here," the guard went on. "There's nothing so hard about bricks. But nothing gets done with them in this business, either. Things get stolen day and night, but there are no thieves! It's gone so far that there's not a single brick left in the whole factory. Nothing to throw at a dog!"

Silanty returned from the city only toward evening, as it was growing dark. After silently eating his supper, he stretched out in the middle of the room. He liked to sleep on the floor in summer; it smelt of oily tar, and the coolness from the damp cellar was wafted through the cracks.

But before day began to break he woke his wife, ran into the shed for a shovel and a hoe, picked a heap of oakum out of the squat bales, fixed a new tar brush, filled the tar bucket, and, rolling up his sleeves, told his wife:

"Pray to the sunrise. The Lord is merciful, maybe we'll manage."

He crossed himself with a sweeping motion, touched the ground with his finger, gathered up shovel, hoe and oakum into his arms, ordered his wife to bring the bucket of tar, and went down the slope toward the river, firmly planting his legs wide apart, which were bent at the knees in the country fashion.

A huge clumsy watering engine sprawled on the bank there, all in poles and logs like elbows propping up the absurd machine; it was inoffensive and silent, despite the monstrous gear wheels and shafts, sleepy after its hibernation, incongruous among the peaceful greenery of the dressy white willows.

Silanty examined the chutes which branched off down the sides of the trough at the top of the watering engine, glanced into the well, then sat down on the ground with a grunt, pulled off his boots, and unwound his leg wrappings. Then he got up, unbuttoned his pants, which were as capacious as a Volga longshoreman's, and they slid down like an accordion and lay in a large eight around his feet.

His wife silently watched Silanty's hairy, sinewy legs, cutting through the tangled blackberry bushes and trampling and bending the lush unmown grass to the ground.

It was quiet. The raspberry tint of the morning was creeping up from beyond the river, reflected on the still, mirrorlike surface of the water. Like exhausted arms, the branches of the willows hung limp and, when a bird awoke in their depths, trembled with fright.

Silanty carefully climbed down into the well, which was full of chips, twigs, and all sorts of refuse that the flood had brought. He steadied himself with one foot on the framework and one on the ladder and began to throw out the refuse.

Then he shouted up, loudly and shortly:

"Watering engine!"

The gardener's wife lay with all her weight on the working beam to which they used to harness a horse, and the orchard, the expanse of the river, and the whole sky resounded with squeaks, screeches, and groans. The buckets squelched, catching one after the other, the teeth of the gear wheels crunched, the clumsy slow shafts screeched, and the peaceful machine reluctantly began to grumble, as if irritated at being aroused from its motionlessness.

The world of birds hidden in the thickets seemed to have been waiting for this signal, and in answer to the groans of the watering engine, a general clamor enveloped the whole orchard, was scattered through the bushes, and mounted upward in unrestrained joy to the sky, stopping there as if bewitched by the monstrous red sphere which had risen on the horizon.

Silanty climbed out of the well soaking wet, his shirt clinging to his body, bent with weariness, but cheerful and satisfied.

"The scoops are intact, thank God."

He climbed up, covered the trough with tar, climbed onto the end of the horizontal shaft and checked the gear wheels, then he got dressed, sent his wife home, and began to tar the chutes and to clean the gutters which were overgrown with grass.

The hope suddenly arose in him that everything would work out, that he would only have to get busy and do some work, and he shoveled and dug, chopped with his ax, and calked the chutes as diligently as if he wanted to make up for all the weary weeks of inactivity.

A chattering robin perched over the gardener's head hastened to tell him about something important, and Silanty called out good-naturedly, wiping his sweaty neck with his sleeve:

"You chirping away, birdie? Look what a busy thing you are! Well, go on, keep chirping!"

He had to get a horse to start watering. The watering engine turned out to be in order, he and his wife could weed out the ditches, only there was no one to do the hoeing. But if they'd give him a horse they'd let him have some workers, too.

Like a black storm cloud a flock of starlings flew over and covered an apple tree, fussing and making a racket in the branches. Silanty whistled piercingly, flourished his hoe and dashed after the fleeing birds, shouting and cursing, until the last starling had flown over the fence into the next orchard.

At dinner he told his wife:

"I'll have to get busy, there's no other way, if we're going to get things done. You know, to tell the truth, there was plenty to do when the masters were here, too. Only it all worked out smoother. But nowadays, in times like these . . ."

The next day he went to town. There they assured him they'd send a horse and men.

But days went by, the sun baked down, the greenery turned black and dried up, but no one came, as if they had forgotten that the orchard stretched on the knoll was waiting for watering.

Silanty started rushing here and there. He ran over to the brick factory, to some gardeners he knew in the next village, but there were no horses anywhere and no one was going to work.

Once, on the way back from town, the gardener went down

to the river, examined the silent engine, wandered along the bank, picked some little green apples from a parched tree and brought them to his wife.

"Do you see these sour apples? I picked them off the anise tree."

He threw the hard wrinkled apples on the table and added:

"The tree's become just like a wild one."

Then he sat down on the bench and stayed there till evening, not moving, looking out the window, from which he could see the motionless orchard bathed in sunlight.

When darkness fell he sighed and said to himself:

"Let it die. There's no one to bury it for. . . ."

The whistles of the birds and the rustling of the orchard were joined by the piercing voices of children. To the house where the old lady had once lived there came schoolchildren from town, a dozen quick-eyed, bright little boys under the supervision of a teacher, a pathetic young woman, all skin and bones.

On the veranda, once quiet and mute, the loud-voiced crowd of newcomers invented games, scattered over the knoll like peas, hiding up in the trees, behind the panes of the hothouse, in the cellar of the main house and in the garret, in all the little corners and cracks of the infirmary, in the withered raspberry beds. There was no hiding place or thicket where the cry of young voices did not resound, and it was as if there were hundreds and thousands of them instead of a dozen.

Soon a crowd of little children appeared at Silanty's cottage, and the teacher declared in businesslike tones:

"Set aside two plots for us for planting."

"What are you going to plant?" asked the gardener.

"Beans, radishes, all sorts of vegetables."

"What a time for it now!"

They had nailed a rag to the gate, decorating it with fancy lettering:

"Children's Colony."

From the tower from which the city and the whole district could be seen, hung a red banner, fluttering in the breeze and flapping perkily day and night.

In the evening the harsh, jerky words of some songs were wafted from the balcony, floating over the treetops, and Silanty heard in them something that was so alien to the orchard, so insolent and evil, that he pressed his hands against his head and rocked from side to side, like a dog which cannot stand the sound of bells ringing.

Scowling and wordless, he opened his mouth when his wife began to pour out her soul in her grief and loneliness to the cook who was employed by the colony and told about the royal apple which the infirmary used to be filled with.

"And now look," she squealed, growing sad, "the worm has eaten it all down to the ovaries."

"Now," Silanty blurted out discontentedly, "now it seems like everything's been dismantled by hand."

"So the masters have gone, and it seems like they've taken everything with them."

"And now we have these brats, these madcap kids," the cook went on, and all three of them poured out their indignation in a single stream of sighs, reproaches and regrets until it was time for bed.

Three boys, barefoot and in ragged shirts, climbed onto the long bough of an old apple tree, hung from it upside down and rocked as if it were a trapeze; then they rode it like a horse and crawled right out to the end. The bough rocked smoothly, springingly supporting the unaccustomed burden, then creaked, cracked, and slowly bent its branches down to the ground.

The acrobats gave a warlike cry, broke into infectious laughter which gaily echoed through the orchard, then suddenly, breaking off their cries, dashed headlong between the trees up toward the main house.

Silanty rushed after them. Bent over so as not to hit the branches with his head, leaping over the ditches and with his hands keeping from running into the apple trees in his flight, he ran like a young beast chasing its prey, skillfully skirting the barriers and holding his breath so as not to betray his nearness to his victim by a single sound, and calculating every movement, feeling how every bound fired up the anger in him.

Fear drove the children. The danger redoubled their skill,

and they dashed on without looking back, exchanging warning shouts, rushing indiscriminately into patches of nettles and gooseberries, breaking off branches and twigs in their way, stumbling, falling, instantly jumping up again and rushing on like mad.

When Silanty sprang onto the veranda of the main house right behind them, the boys darted indoors, and before the panting gardener, covered with sweat, stood the outraged teacher.

She scowled and declared in amazement:

"How can you frighten children like that? You must be mad."

These words seemed to Silanty so out of place, and the thin little girl of a teacher seemed so pathetic and strange, that all his anger was packed into one quiet threat:

"I'll smoke you out of here like rats."

That day the whole colony went to town for some reason, and the main house stood quiet and empty, as it had been before.

At dinnertime, Silanty walked out the gate.

Before, at this time of year, the drays would drive out of the orchard, one after the other, overflowing with early-ripening fruit and crammed with baskets of berries. Now the ruts of the road were overgrown with creeping grass, and the familiar creaking of the carts could not be heard anywhere.

"It seems like they've taken everything with them," thought Silanty, and began lazily watching two peasants in the distance, approaching from the direction of the brick sheds.

When they came up to him, they asked whose orchard it was.

"Why do you want to know?"

"They've sent us to hoe."

"Why so early?" grinned Silanty. "Nowadays everything's Soviet. . . ."

Then he questioned them in detail and when he was sure that the men had been sent to him, he declared:

"This isn't the place! I've never heard of that orchard."

"Where'll we go now?"

"Dunno, wherever you were sent. But everything's all right here, we just finished the second watering. Impossible."

He gave a brief laugh after the departing workmen, then returned to the cottage and sent his wife to town, inventing an urgent household errand.

When the hubbub of the birds had fallen silent, and the evening quiet had descended upon the earth, Silanty climbed into the hayloft, gathered a pile of straw from the corners, and dragged it up to the main house.

Then, as he was putting the kindling under the house, he came upon the signboard with the master's name, taken down from the gate the previous spring and hidden in the hayloft. He held it for a moment in his hand, turned it over, then pushed it deeper into the straw and went for a new armful.

As he was returning to the main house, he picked up a dry fallen branch, placed it under the other side of the house, and struck a match. The dry straw caught fire readily and the branch crackled gaily.

Having set fire to the main house, Silanty quietly drew back, sat down on the ground, and began to watch the bright smoke circling in rings around the wooden pillars which supported the roof of the veranda and the balconies. Like black lace, the carved decorations fluttered, and the rosy flame climbed through the countless chinks.

Thick as soot, the smoke screwed upward right into the sky, then suddenly, as if it had summoned up its strength, the mighty red bonfire cast off its smoky cap.

The house burned like a candle.

Silanty sat motionless, hugging his knees in his sinewy worker's arms, gazing into the fire.

He sat there until a frantic woman's scream burst upon his ear.

"Silushka! God help you! What have you done? How'll we answer when our folk come back?"

Then he tore his gaze away from the flames, looked severely at his wife, and said, more to himself than to her:

"What a fool you are, woman! Will they ever be coming back?"

And she immediately fell silent, and like her husband she stared with motionless eyes into the flame.

Over their aged faces quivered the rosy reflection of the dying fire.

Translated by Lydia W. Kesich

Olga Forsh

The Dolls of Paris

That day Paris was adorned with bright yellow, black-lettered posters. From afar the posters looked like sunflowers full of ripe seeds. Come closer—and you see announcements about a "gala" affair. Seven orchestras, celebrities: dark-skinned Josephine, Sacha Guitry, Charlestons, and the President. They listed the attractions, exclaimed the inevitable *"Épatant!"*

The "gala" affair was for the benefit of war victims with facial wounds. These unfortunates had nicknamed themselves *"gueules cassées,"* a name that cannot be translated into any language. Thus, in the tradition of old French bravura, they chose to laugh in order not to cry.

The photo placard of the main "characters," displayed along with the poster, had a movieland headline, "Masks of Horror."

One glance at the placard made it clear that such human wrecks must be kept out of sight, must be kept somewhere out of town the way lepers, madmen and others who disturb our complacent life are kept.

"Such wounds used to have but one issue, death!"

"Now they are the triumph of medicine. Doctors find it especially flattering to save the lives of such people."

"They certainly haven't done them any favors! According to the Code Napoléon, they are not even considered invalids. But since they were never expected to live, naturally no category was created for them. To be an invalid officially, one must be legless, armless, paralyzed . . ."

"But no, m'sieur, I beg your pardon . . . Mine is more horrible than yours. Here he is, the worst of all! Everyone will agree, if they make a comparison. He's had both his jaws removed, that's why his face looks like soft dough tied up in a thin kerchief. And look here, his nose, cheeks, and mouth—it all runs together into a mass. And notice that this horror is the result of forty operations."

"It's rumored that their wives have left these unfortunate men."

"And you yourself, madame, be honest, what would you have done in their place?"

"Oh, I can't imagine. . . ."

"Still, although expensive, we'll take the tickets. The price is steep, but it'll be worth it. Black Josephine alone . . ."

"The hell with it, Paris will dance a six-months' bellyful for these *'gueules cassées.'* "

"Don't you think that such a means of helping one's neighbor has a certain charm?"

Lobov wanted to shout that the means were outrageously vulgar, that it betokened an intrinsic savagery which is more frightening than an extrinsic savagery because it is more hopeless. But he said none of that. Making his way out of the crowd, he merely began to walk faster than usual along the boulevards. And for some reason Lobov began to seek a Russian equivalent for *"gueules cassées."* "Bashed-in kisser, bashed-in mug." In Russian, however, it smacked of bar-room brawling and had none of the biting irony of the original French.

Lobov now recalled that he had first heard that expression in Moscow from the old woman Barbier, the ex-governess who had attached herself for good to a certain well-known family.

The old woman liked to boast of the culture of her native land where the eternal flame burns in honor of the Unknown Soldier, and where her son, Colonel Jean-Marie, is treated so very generously by the State that, in addition to being fully maintained, he even gets his favorite tobacco, as a gift.

This very Colonel Jean-Marie, seriously wounded in the

face, was one of the *"gueules cassées."* And Lobov recalled the most important thing—that he had promised the old woman Barbier that he would look for her granddaughter Louise Barbier, the colonel's daughter, in Paris.

Louise's silence was killing the grandmother. "Perhaps she's already married and, being frail, is afraid to have children. Or she has suddenly become rich and is living on the Riviera. Well, in that case she's justly ashamed to write. All the women in our family have conducted themselves properly!"

The old woman Barbier was unable to hazard any further guesses. For Louise's future children, she gave Lobov an old medallion depicting her as a child with a round face and large eyes. He had this very medallion in his wallet. Lobov took it out and looked at it.

"This girl has blue eyes," he decided, and suddenly made up his mind not to postpone the matter, but to go at once to Louise's last place of employment to find her address.

The doll factory where Barbier's granddaughter might still be employed was located in the nearby district. The concierge led Lobov to the top floor of a very old building. There the sign "Femmosa" shone red on blue. The concierge proudly added, " 'Femmosa' is the name of the composition of the 'natural female body,' discovered by the owner of the factory. Dolls for both hemispheres are made in this building."

Lobov went up the stairs, passed the sign on the right reading "Waiting Room," hastened to the end of the corridor, entered a huge room, and was awestruck. There before him was a mortuary of Lilliputians.

On large, longitudinal tables there lay mountains of tiny female bodies of genuine human color. Thousands of eyes, blue ones, black ones, with brilliantly shining pupils, hypnotized with their monotonously fixed look. The eyes of the separate heads of the large dolls drying on the shelves looked down strangely and uneasily.

Through the open doors came an angry snorting, like camels spitting at each other. It was the boss's "secret," the famous "Femmosa" formula for the "natural female body" squelching in a huge kettle.

A girl-mannequin, tall, her eyebrows thinly drawn in the latest beauty-parlor fashion, nibbling at her "Vampire Red" lips, painted pupils on the dolls, evenly, quickly, without stopping, like a machine. As she finished each one, she handed it over to her neighbor who with two strokes of a brush brought out its high color. A third pair of hands fashioned the lips—first a heart, then Cupid's arrow.

Further on, the bodies of the female Lilliputians were taken out of their clay molds, washed and placed on Turkish toweling for drying.

Were it not for the terribly cloying odor of the "natural female body" and the champing of the mash in the kettle, one would have thought that silent madmen were engaging here in eternal play.

"Did Louise Barbier work here?" Lobov ventured and drew closer. "Her grandmother in Moscow asked me to look her up."

The fingers of the girl painting the pupils trembled slightly and spilled some black paint on the doll's orb, causing it to grow dull and suddenly to look like a sad, living eye. The girl said without looking up, "I'm Louise Barbier. Please go to the waiting room. I'll be done in a moment and I'll join you."

An apprentice showed Lobov to the waiting room where he, as a chance visitor, ought to have stayed in the first place, and said, "Here, m'sieur, is our customer's room. If you like, m'sieur, you may look over the display of our line."

With a most obliging gesture, the apprentice pointed out the shelves around the room and left. Smart lines all ready for sale were perched on the shelves. Marquesses were embracing marquises on little, gold, Louis XV sofas; Negro maidens were kicking out their black legs from beneath purple velvet; nude dolls à la Nana, in gloves and slippers, smiled wantonly from under their lampshade-hats on which was written in large letters, "Gifts for bachelors."

Here were samples of orders from the two Americas, Sydney, and England. Under the label "province" were dolls of smiling womenfolk with baskets and a crying black and white Pierrot.

Here were good-luck dolls for taxis, living rooms, alcoves, and sports. Souvenir dolls, orders from the big Ritz and

Crillon restaurants, to be handed out as mementos to guests who paid thousands of francs for their supper.

From behind all that tulle and spangles, frightful *"poupées bolcheviques,"* in bright red Circassian costumes, carrying huge axes and bayonets, glowed flaming red. Their scarlet Caucasian caps, made out of artificial sheep's fur, bore the inscription *"chapeau russe—Astrakhan."* For some strange reason, these Bolshevik dolls had been ordered by the city of Grenoble.

Lobov was so engrossed that he did not notice Louise enter. Tears filled her eyes and her "Vampire Red" lips twitched as she said, "If my grandmother has been having a difficult time, I'd rather not hear about it. I'm in no position to help her with anything."

Lobov hastened to describe in glowing terms the old woman Barbier's retired life with good friends. Louise then beamed with joy. Her mannequin face suddenly became so similar to the childish face on the medallion that Lobov inadvertently told her so, as he handed her the gift from her grandmother. And it seemed to both of them that they had known each other for a long time.

Louise shed a few tears over the medallion, then showered Lobov with questions, interrupting herself every so often with childhood recollections. ". . . Grandmother Barbier and I used to sail a boat in the pond in the Luxembourg Gardens. How happy Grandmother was when Louise's boat took the lead! There, too, we used to play in a ring with the whole family. Father was then handsome and happy. Oh, these simple things are not easily forgotten. . . . Tell Grandmother that the chairs in the Gardens which were free then are now, since the war, eight sous a chair, as in church."

"And isn't there anything else you want me to tell your grandmother? You know she's been dreaming of a grandson," Lobov said, but caught himself short as Louise began to flare up.

"There are no children in Paris," she said spitefully.

"If you are free this evening," Lobov said respectfully, "let's dine together, and then you can show me Paris."

"The Place de l'Opéra is a good place to dine, and I don't mind taking a walk after work."

Louise's face again became mannequin-like, her eyebrows pencil-thin.

They left in silence, crossing the long boulevard toward the renowned historic cathedral. The doors were wide open. Nuns dressed in dark blue, their beads tinkling softly like light chains, were swallowed up by the black depth as soon as they entered. Rows of candles burned far in the back, and beyond them an ancient Gothic stained-glass window glittered like precious stones. The organ played beautifully; the sound rushed in chords to the dome as if along a staircase, fell and, barely audible, rose again in the black abyss. Suddenly the sound became stronger and grew into a passionate, tremendous wail.

Lobov wanted to go in, but Louise shook her head firmly, walked on and said, "I can't set a foot in there any more. All through the war I used to run there morning and night until Father returned. My prayers were certainly answered, that's for sure!"

She stopped abruptly and turned her brightly illuminated, stony face toward Lobov. He was once again amazed by her eyebrows which were not penciled, not shaved, but somehow incomprehensibly gathered into a thin line, hair by hair.

"Do you know what my father calls himself? A football! His whole face is bandaged forever, forever! Oh, are you perplexed by my eyebrows? No, they are not shaved, but plucked. The beauty parlor charges fifteen francs per appointment. And a complete 'facial and hair-do' costs thirty francs. And that's every week! The competition, you know, is too great! Smart Parisian women are preferred to provincial girls when it comes to getting a job. But let's walk faster. I can't wait to get to les Batignolles. After our idiotic work, when you've been wrung out like a dishrag, you need fun and noise, like a pick-me-up. Here's a bar, let's have a drink!"

The evening lights brought a new world into being on the square. Taxis with shining covered roofs, still fearful of the rain that had just come down and was threatening to start again, moved in a solid stream. Their polished red roofs reflected the blue lights of the stores and the blinking eye of the Metro. The policemen raised their white sticks and the taxis stopped dead, turning the square into a stagnant sea, playing in an overflow of gasoline. The policeman lowered his stick and the taxis growled and moved on.

Place Vendôme was somewhat more peaceful. The lights of the magnificent Hotel Ritz made the gray asphalt in front of the Colonne Vendôme shine like water. In response to it, dancing like dew under the sun, diamonds shimmered in the plate-glass show-windows.

Gardens of artificial flowers blossomed forth in its center, subduing the live flowers through their greater vividness and size.

A little Napoléon, wearing a garland and cloak, fused with the darkness so that his famous column did not rise upward, but, on the contrary, fell headlong downward and pierced the granite.

"It's been a long time, however, since I've been here," Louise said. "Last time I dropped in to see our senior designer Claude. She struck it lucky! Like me, she used to paint pupils on dolls when, like in a fairy tale, an American appeared with a big order. He saw Claude and offered her a 'situation.' Now in New York, she has her own car and her Negro servant. Isn't it true that everything in life depends on luck? My father says about the cripples from Les Invalides that 'there you've got lucky men; they've chopped off their legs, but not their noses.' And you want me to write Grandmother about my father? What am I to tell her? Perhaps that the faceless are eating out their hearts in envy at the legless, or that soon there'll be no place for them where they can lay their heads because private means have become exhausted and the State does not list them in any category? And I've heard people cracking jokes: 'They used to make less of a fuss over these victims—formerly they died—but on these, you see, they operate.' Father has had fifty major operations and more and more lie ahead. . . ."

Lobov wanted to tell Louise about the "gala" affair for the benefit of the *"gueules cassées,"* since she had obviously not yet managed to see the posters. But he lacked the courage. And how was he to tell her unless he sounded like that voice in the crowd. "Paris will dance a six-months' bellyful for your father!"

On the contrary, Lobov began to make a faint-hearted

effort to prevent Louise from seeing, as long as she was with him, the bright-yellow poster which, like a sunflower full of ripe seeds, was beaded with cramped black letters. And Louise, excited by childhood recollections and her father's fate, looked neither left nor right, but walked on her high heels toward the Place de l'Opéra in order to get from there as soon as possible to the amusements in les Batignolles.

But they could not get through to the square. Traffic was at a standstill. People were crowded together not only on the sidewalks and on the stairs of the Opéra, but shoulder to shoulder throughout the square. Benumbed, their heads lifted upward, they awaited the news of the arrival of the American flyer.

Above the roofs, fiery letters coupled to one another like cars on an endless train, now spelled out special news, now advertisements, against the black, starless sky.

"What's that? It can't be! Oh, how foul!"

Louise grabbed Lobov by the sleeve and, stretching hard on her toes and turning pale in anger and pain, she repeated word for word the text of the very same "gala" affair which Lobov had a short while before read in the crowd.

From behind the large hotel, on the turret of a neighboring house high above all the others in the city, a train of lights announced: *"Au profit des gueules cassées!"* At the flashing of the events, the crowd, like the one in the morning, applauded dark-skinned Josephine, Sacha Guitry and the President. At the end it was announced exactly where one could get "the main characters" of "the masks of horror" for two francs.

Someone in the crowd said, "The main characters of the masks of horror must be a really cheerful booklet. Let's go get it."

Louise shouted to Lobov, "I want this really cheerful booklet too."

Lobov wished Paris would go to hell, and like a guilty man followed Louise. The store was crowded. The booklet was being snatched up eagerly.

Beneath the clear photographs of the nonhuman faces was inscribed a quatrain which the salesmen, before wrapping the booklet in paper, read aloud with pseudo-classic animation.

"What are all the sufferings and our bashed-in mugs to us, as long as they hastened our victory even a little . . . ?"

"And this one here is called 'my father.' " Louise pointed to a photograph depicting a uniform with decorations. Above the uniform protruded something not unlike a head of cheese, entirely swathed in crisscross bandages. Looking closely Lobov saw not a mouth, but a slit for the reception of food, and buried in the bandages a lurking eye. This eye alone glistened with intelligence, anger and grief. The eye betrayed a living person.

"A good example of the *'gueules cassées,'* " the salesman praised him obligingly. Louise turned sharply and ran toward the exit. Lobov had a hard time catching up with her.

"Why are you following me?" She turned furiously. "Do you really expect me to show you around the bars? Get yourself a night-guide. . . ."

Lobov hailed a taxi.

"I'll take you home."

They drove in silence. They got out. Embarrassedly, Lobov asked for permission to call again. . . .

"There's no point in your calling," Louise said very calmly, "and it would make it more difficult for you to lie to my grandmother. And you must lie. But don't tell the old woman that her handsome and clever son of whom she had been so proud is now a football which they kick around with their feet."

Louise's voice grew stronger, became hard and cruel. Lobov recalled the organ and how its sounds, hardly having been born, suddenly grew into a threatening, stupendous wail.

Lobov was overcome with confusion. He cast a glance at Louise's face and saw that it looked dreadful. It was the face of a doll inspired with great human wrath.

"Isn't it trampling on, isn't it kicking people with one's feet, I ask you," Louise repeated again, "to dance for the benefit of such utter misery at some foul 'gala' affair? You're all played out, you men. Yes, you're played out! Cowards, gas-bags . . . no, it's not for you to create a better life. And women have only just begun to understand . . . but give us time! time! We won't be chattering, we'll act! Good-by. There's no need for you to come again.''

Louise slammed the door and Lobov left for home.

A warm, soft rain was falling. Bending with the wind, the flame of the Unknown Soldier danced in slender tongues under the Arch. And to the rhythm of its dance, an absurd verse by Captain Lebyadkin jeeringly raced through his head:

> *Backward girl or George Sand-ette,*
> *Doesn't matter, now exult:*
> *You're a nurse with dowry now—*
> *Spit on it all and be on top!*

Translated by Ira Goetz

MAXIM GORKY

HOBGOBLINS

I

One humid summer night, in a remote roadway on the edge of town, I saw a strange sight. A woman who had waded into the middle of a huge puddle was stamping her feet and splashing dirty water around, as children do. As she splashed she sang through her nose a dirty song, where the name "Tommy" rhymed with the word "roomy."

A mighty thunderstorm had passed over the city that afternoon, and a heavy rain had drenched the muddy, clayey soil of the roadway; the puddle was deep, and the woman's legs had sunk into it almost to the knees. Her voice indicated that she was drunk. If she were to fall down while dancing around, she might easily choke on the watery mud. I pulled the top of my boots higher, waded into the puddle, and, taking the dancer by the arms, dragged her onto dry land. At first, apparently, she was frightened and followed me silently and submissively, but then she tore her right hand free with a powerful jerk of her whole body, struck me in the chest, and screamed, "Help!" And she stubbornly waded back into the puddle, dragging me after her.

"To hell with you!" she muttered. "I won't go. I'll get on without you, so you get on without me. Help!"

A night watchman appeared out of the dark, stopped five steps from us, and asked crossly, "Who's making the racket?"

I told him that I was afraid the woman would drown in the

mud and I wanted to pull her out. The watchman examined the drunken woman, spat loudly, and ordered, "Get out, Mashka!"

"Don't want to."

"Get out, I tell you!"

"Won't."

"I'll give it to you, you slut," the watchman threatened without anger, and he turned to me, good-natured and talkative. "She's a local woman, an oakum picker, Mashka Froliha. Got any cigarettes?"

We lit up. The woman strode boldly around in the puddle, shouting, "Bosses! I'm my own boss! I'll take a swim if I want to."

"I'll give you a swim!" warned the watchman, a powerful, bearded old man. "That's the way she is every night, see, making trouble. And she has a son at home without any legs."

"Does she live far from here?"

"She ought to be killed," the watchman said, without answering me.

"She should be taken home," I suggested.

The watchman snorted in his beard, looked into my face by the light of his cigarette, and walked away, stamping his boots hard in the sticky soil.

"Take her! Only look at her mug first."

The woman sat down in the dirt and shoveled it up with her hands, singing wildly through her nose, "So o-o-over the o-o-ocean . . ."

A big star out of the black emptiness above us was reflected in the dirty, greasy water not far from here. When the puddle was covered with ripples, the reflection disappeared. I waded back in, took the singer under the arms, stood her up and pushed her with my knees out to the fence. She leaned against it, waving her hands and challenging me, "Well, beat me, beat me! Never mind, beat me! Oh, you brute, oh, you tyrant, well, beat me!"

When I had leaned her up against the fence, I asked her where she lived. She raised her drunken head, looking at me with her dark spots of eyes, and I noticed that the bridge of her nose had fallen in and the remnant of it stuck up like a button; her upper lip, stretched upward by her deformity, revealed her tiny teeth, and her swollen little face was smiling repulsively.

"All right, let's go," she said.

We went along, knocking against the fence. The wet hem of her skirt whipped against my legs.

"Let's go, dearie," she said in a grumbling tone, apparently becoming soberer. "I'll take care of you. I'll give you a little comfort."

She brought me into the yard of a big two-story house; carefully, like a blind woman, she made her way between carts, barrels, boxes, and scattered piles of logs, then stopped before a sort of hole in the foundation and invited me to "climb in."

Clinging to the sticky wall, with my arm around the woman's waist, hardly able to support her body, which kept slipping away from me, I went down the slippery steps, groped for the thick pad of felt and the hook on the door, opened it, and stood on the threshold of a black hole, hesitant to step further.

"Is that you, Mom?" asked a quiet voice in the darkness.

"Me, me."

The smell of warm rot and of something resinous hit me heavily. A match flared, and the little flame lit up a pale childish face for a second and then went out.

"Who else would come in to you? It's me," the woman went on, leaning up against me.

Again a match flared, a glass rang, and a thin ridiculous hand lit a small tin lamp.

"My little comfort," said the woman, and swaying she fell over into the corner, where a wide bed lay ready, only slightly raised above the brick floor.

Caring for the flame in the lamp, the child turned down the wick when it flared up and began to smoke. His little face was serious and sharp-nosed, with lips swollen like a girl's, a face drawn with a fine brush and strikingly out of place in this damp dark hole. When he had finished with the light, he looked at me with eyes that seemed somehow shaggy and asked:

"Is she drunk?"

His mother, lying across the bed, sobbed and snorted.

"She must be undressed," I said.

"Undress her, then," answered the boy, lowering his eyes.

And when I began to pull the wet skirts from the woman, he asked quietly in a businesslike way:

"Should I put out the light?"

"Why!"

He fell silent. As I pulled his mother around like a sack of flour, I took a look at him; he was sitting on the floor, under the window, in a box made of wide boards with the words

W I T H   C A R E

N. R. Co.

printed in black on it. The sill of the square window was level with the boy's shoulder. Along the wall stretched several narrow little shelves, and on them lay piles of cigarette and match boxes. Alongside the box in which the boy was sitting there was another box, covered with yellow and apparently serving as a table. Putting his funny and pitiful hands behind his neck, the boy gazed up at the dark panes of the window.

When I had undressed the woman, I threw her wet dress onto the stove and washed my hands at an earthen washstand in the corner. As I dried them on my handkerchief, I said to the child, "Well, good-by!"

He glanced over at me, and asked with a slight lisp:

"Should I put the light out now?"

"Just as you want."

"And you're leaving, you're not lying down?"

He stretched out his hand, pointing to his mother.

"With her."

"Why should I?" I asked stupidly, in amazement.

"You should know," he said with terrible simplicity, and stretching, he added, "they all do."

I glanced around in embarrassment. To my right was the top of an ugly stove, there were dirty dishes on the hearth, in the corner behind the box were bits of tarred rope, a pile of oakum that had been picked out, logs of wood, chips, and a yoke. The yellow body stretched and snored at my feet.

"May I sit a bit with you?" I asked the boy.

He looked at me distrustfully and answered, "She won't wake up until morning."

"But I don't need her."

I squatted down next to his box and told him how I had met his mother, trying to make a joke of it. "There she was, sitting in the mud, raking it with her hands as if they were oars, and singing."

He nodded his head, smiling palely and scratching his narrow little chest.

"She's drunk, that's why. Even when she's sober she likes to be mischievous. She's like a child all the same."

Now I examined his eyes; they really were shaggy. The lashes were extraordinarily long, and lovely little curly hairs were growing thick on the eyelids. Bluish shadows lay under his eyes, emphasizing the paleness of his bloodless skin, and his high forehead, with a wrinkle over the bridge of his nose, was covered by a tousled mop of curly reddish hair. The expression in his eyes, so attentive and calm, was indescribable; I could hardly bear his strange, inhuman gaze.

"What's wrong with your legs?"

He moved around, and from the rags freed a withered leg, like a little poker, raised it with his hand, and put it on the edge of the box.

"That's the kind of legs I have. Both of them have been like that since I was born. They don't walk, they're not good for much."

"And what's in those boxes?"

"That's a menagerie," he answered. He picked up his leg in his hand as if it were a stick and put it back in the rags at the bottom of the box, then with a friendly open smile he suggested:

"Do you want me to show you? Well, then, sit down. You have never seen anything like this ever before."

Skillfully using his thin, disproportionately long arms, he rose up on his trunk and began to take the boxes from the shelves, offering me one after the other.

"Look, but don't open it, or they'll escape! Put it to your ear, listen. What's that?"

"Someone's moving around there."

"Aha! That's the little spider sitting in there, the bum. His name is Drummer. He's smart!"

His magnificent eyes came alive with tenderness, and a smile played over his bluish face. Working quickly with his skillful hands, he took the boxes from the shelves, put them to his ear, then to mine, and told me excitedly, "And here's Anisim, a cockroach, he boasts as bad as a soldier. This is a fly, Mrs. Government Official, the worst bitch you ever saw. She buzzes about all day, cursing everyone, she even pulled Mummy's hair. Not the fly, the government official's wife, who lives with windows looking out on the street, the fly only is like her. And this is a black cockroach, a big one, the Boss; he's all right, only a drunkard and a shame. He drinks too much and crawls around the yard naked and hairy like a black dog. Here's a beetle, Uncle Nikodim, I caught him in the yard; he's a pilgrim, one of the swindlers; he pretends to be collecting money for the church. Mummy calls him Cheapskate; he's one of her lovers too. She's got as many lovers as you want, like a fly, even if she doesn't have a nose."

"She doesn't beat you?"

"Her? What an idea! She couldn't live without me. She's good, but she's a drunkard, well, they're all drunkards on our street. She's beautiful, and gay too. A terrible drunkard, the whore. 'Stop swallowing that vodka, you fool, and you'll be rich,' I tell her, but she just laughs. She's a woman, so she's stupid. But she's good, when she wakes up you'll see."

He smiled so enchantingly that I wanted to roar and shout to the whole city my unbearable, burning pity for him. His lovely head rocked on his thin neck like some exotic flower, and his eyes burned more brightly in excitement, attracting me with irresistible force.

As I listened to his childish but terrible chatter, I had forgotten for a moment where I was sitting, and suddenly I saw again the prison window, small and spattered with mud from the outside, the black maw of the stove, the pile of oakum in the corner, and at the door, on the pile of rags, the body, yellow as butter, of the woman who was his mother.

"Is it a good menagerie?" the boy asked proudly.

"Very."

"I don't have any butterflies, butterflies or moths."

"What's your name?"

"Lenka."

"Same as mine."

"Yeah? And what sort are you?"

"Just so-so. No special sort."

"No, you're lying. Everybody's something, I know that. You're nice."

"Perhaps."

"I can see that! You're a scare-cat too."

"Why a scare-cat?"

"Oh, I know." He smiled slyly and even winked at me.

"But why do you say I'm a scare-cat?"

"Because you're sitting with me; that means you're scared to go out at night."

"But it's getting light."

"Well, then you'll go."

"I'll come to see you again." He did not believe me, covered his sweet shaggy eyes with his lashes, and after a short silence he asked:

"Why?"

"To sit a while with you. You're very interesting. May I?"

"Go ahead. Everyone comes to see us."

He sighed, and said:

"You'll fool me."

"No, really I'll come."

"Come then. You'll come to see me, not Mom, to hell with her. You make friends with me, all right?"

"All right."

"Fine. It doesn't matter that you're grown up. How old are you?"

"Twenty-one."

"And I'm twelve. I don't have any friends, only Katya, the water carrier's daughter, but the water carrier beats her for coming to see me. Are you a thief?"

"No, why should I be a thief?"

"You have a terrible looking face, thin and with the kind of nose that thieves have. Two thieves come here, one, Sashka, is a fool and mean, but the other, Vanechka, is as kind as a dog. Do you have any little boxes?"

"I'll get some."

"Get some! I won't tell Mom you're coming."

"Why not?"

"I just won't. She's always glad when men come a second time. You see, she loves men, the bitch, it's just a shame. She's a funny little girl, my Mom. She got along for fifteen years and then had me, and she doesn't know herself how it happened. When will you come?"

"Tomorrow evening."

"In the evening she'll be drinking already. And what do you do, if you don't steal?"

"I sell Bavarian kvass."

"You do? Bring a bottle, huh?"

"Of course I will! But now I must be on my way."

"Go ahead. You'll come?"

"For sure."

He stretched both long arms out to me, and I also pressed and shook those thin cold little bones with both mine, and without looking back at him I climbed outside, like a drunk.

It was getting light; over a damp pile of sagging buildings Venus flickered as it faded. From a dirty hole under the wall of the house, the square panes of the basement window stared at me, cloudy and dirty, like a drunken woman's eyes. In a cart at the entrance a red-faced peasant was sleeping, his huge bare legs wide apart, his thick, stiff beard, white teeth glimmering in it, jutted toward the sky. The peasant seemed to be laughing venomously and murderously, with his eyes closed. An old dog with a bald spot on her back, probably scalded by boiling water, came up to me; she sniffed my foot and whined quietly and hungrily, filling my heart with unnecessary pity for her.

In the streets and the puddles left after the night, the morning sky was reflected, blue and rose. The reflections gave the dirty puddles a repulsive, excessive, offensive beauty.

II

The next day I asked the kids on my street to catch beetles and butterflies. I bought some pretty little boxes at the drug-

store and set off for Lenka's, taking along two bottles of
kvass, cookies, candy and rolls.

Lenka received my presents with great surprise, opening
his sweet eyes very wide. By daylight they were even more
magnificent.

"Oo-oo-oo!" he exclaimed in a low, unchildlike voice,
"how much you brought! Are you rich or something! How
can you be rich, you're dressed bad, and you're not a thief,
you say. Look at those boxes! Ooo, I don't even want to
touch them, my hands aren't clean. Who's that there? Hey, a
beetle! How brassy he is, even green, oh, gosh! Will they run
out and fly away? Hey—"

Suddenly he shouted gaily:

"Mum, climb down and wash my hands, just look what he
brought! This is the same one who came last night and
dragged you in like a cop, he's brought everything! His
name's Lenka too."

"Say thank you to him," I heard a soft, strange voice say
behind me.

The boy nodded his head many times.

"Thank you, thank you!"

A thick cloud of rather hairy dust hung in the basement,
and through it I discerned with difficulty the disheveled head
and disfigured face of the woman, and the glitter of her teeth,
her involuntary, ineradicable smile.

"Hello!"

"Hello," the woman responded; her nasal voice sounded
soft but cheerful, almost gay. She looked at me, squinting,
and seemed to be mocking me.

Lenka, forgetting me, chewed on a cookie and murmured
as he carefully opened the boxes. His lashes threw a shadow
onto his cheeks, emphasizing the blueness under his eyes.
The sun peeked through the dirty window panes, dull as the
face of an old man, and a soft light fell on the boy's reddish
hair. Lenka's shirt was unbuttoned across his chest, and I saw
his heart beating behind his thin little bones, raising the skin
and the barely perceptible nipple.

His mother climbed down from the stove, wet a towel at
the washstand, went up to Lenka and took his left hand.

"He's escaped! Wait, he's escaped!" he exclaimed, and

twisted his whole body completely around in the box, throwing out the stinking rags under him and exposing his blue motionless legs. The woman laughed, digging through the rags, and she shouted too, "Catch him!"

She caught the beetle and put it on the palm of her hand, looking it over with quick eyes of cornflower blue. She said to me, as if we were old friends:

"There are lots like this."

"Don't crush it," her son warned sternly. "Once when she was drunk she sat on my menagerie and crushed so many of them!"

"You forget about that, my little comfort."

"I was burying and burying them."

"But I caught them for you myself afterward."

"You caught them! Those were scholars, the ones you crushed, you idiot! I bury those who die under the stove, I climb out and bury them, that's my cemetery. You know, I had a spider, Minka, just like one of Mum's lovers, one who used to come, he's in prison now, rather fat and merry."

"Oh, you, my darling little comfort," the woman said, smoothing her son's curls with a dark little hand with blunt fingers. Then nudging me with her elbow, she asked, her eyes smiling:

"Isn't my son handsome? How about his eyes, huh?"

"Take one of my eyes, but give me back my legs," Lenka offered, grinning and examining the beetle. "What a . . . an iron one! So fat! Mom, he's like the monk, the one you wove a ladder for, remember?"

"Why on earth!" And with a laugh she started to tell me about it.

"Well, you see, this great monk stopped by here one day, a huge one, and he asked me, 'Could you make me, Madam Oakum Picker, a ladder out of rope?' Well, all my life I'd never heard tell of such a ladder. 'No,' I said, 'I don't know how.' 'Well, I'll teach you then,' he says. He opened his cassock, and he had a thin rope wrapped all around his belly, a long rope, and a strong one! He taught me. I wove and wove, and I kept thinking, 'What's he need this for? Maybe he's going to rob a church?' "

She laughed and hugged her son around the shoulders, still caressing him.

"Oh, those jokers! He came at the time set, and I said to him, 'Now you tell me, if you need this for burglaries, I won't give it to you!' He laughed slyly. 'No,' he says, 'that's to climb over the wall. We have a big wall, a high one, but we're sinners, and the sin lives outside the wall. Understand?' Well, I understood; it was for him to get to the women at night. He and I laughed and laughed."

"You're a great one for laughing," said the boy, as if he were the older, "but you'd do better to start the samovar."

"We haven't any sugar."

"Go buy some."

"But there's no money."

"Oh, you drinker, you! Take some from him."

He turned to me. "Do you have some money?"

I gave the woman some money and she jumped up quickly, took down from the stove a little samovar, smudged and dented, and disappeared behind the door, singing through her nose.

"Mom!" her son shouted after her, "wash the window, I can't see anything. She's quite a woman, I tell you!" he went on, accurately distributing the boxes of insects on the cardboard shelves, which were suspended from pieces of twine attached to nails hammered into the slots between the bricks in the damp wall. "What a worker! When she begins to pick out oakum she raises such a dust you can hardly breathe! I yell, 'Mom! carry me outdoors, I'll stifle in here!' And she answers, 'Just bear it awhile,' she says, 'I'll be bored without you.' She really loves me, that's all. She picks and sings, she knows a thousand songs!"

Excitedly, his wonderful eyes sparkling, raising his thick brows, he began to sing in a hoarse alto, "There's Orina lying on the feather bed . . ."

After listening for a bit, I said:

"That's a very filthy song."

"They all are," Lenka explained readily, and suddenly he started. "Hey, the music's come! Quick, lift me up!"

I raised his light bones, wrapped in a sack of thin gray skin, and he eagerly stuck his head through the open window and froze still, while his withered legs swung helplessly, knocking against the wall. In the yard a hurdy-gurdy was whining irritatingly, tossing out the remnants of some melody; a child was shouting joyfully in a deep voice, and a dog was howling in accompaniment. Lenka listened to the music and quietly whimpered through his teeth, humming the tune.

The dust had settled down in the basement, and it had become lighter. Over his mother's bed hung a cheap clock; the pendulum, about as big as a penny, limped over the gray wall. The dishes were left unwashed on the hearth and a thick layer of dust lay over everything, especially on the spider webs hanging like dirty rags in the corners. Lenka's abode recalled a trash heap, and the excessive monstrosities of poverty, pitilessly offensive, thrust themselves upon the observer at every step in this hole. The samovar began to hum gloomily; the hurdy-gurdy, as if scared by it, suddenly fell silent, and a hoarse voice yelled, "Get out!"

"Take me down," said Lenka with a sigh. "They chased him out."

I sat him in his box, and he made a face and rubbed his chest with his hands, coughing carefully.

"I've got a pain in my chest, it's not good for me to breathe real air much. Listen, have you ever seen devils?"

"No."

"Me neither. I keep looking under the stove at night to see if they'll come. They don't show themselves. But devils live in cemeteries, don't they?"

"What do you want with them?"

"It's interesting. Mightn't there be one devil who's kind? Katka the water carrier's daughter saw a little devil in the cellar, and she was scared. But I'm not afraid of horrors."

Wrapping his legs in the rags, he went on cheerfully, "I love them, even. I love bad dreams too. Once I dreamed about a tree growing upside down; the leaves were all over the earth and the roots stretched up to the sky. I even sweated all over and woke up from fear. And Mom dreamed that she was lying naked and a dog was eating up her stomach, he'd take a bite and spit it out, take a bite and spit it out. Or that our house suddenly shook and started to ride down the street, going along and slamming the doors and windows, and the cat of the government official's wife was running after it."

His pointed shoulders shuddered, and he took a candy, unfolding the colored paper and smoothing it out carefully, and then he put it on the window sill.

"I'll make things out of these papers, nice things. Then I'll give them to Katka. She likes nice things too, bits of glass, or china, pieces of paper, everything. But listen, if you keep feeding a cockroach, will he grow as big as a horse?"

He obviously believed this. I answered, "If you feed him well, he'll keep growing."

"Sure!" he exclaimed joyously. "But Mom just laughs at me, the dumbbell."

And he added a dirty word, insulting to women.

"She's dumb! You could feed a cat up quite fast till he's as big as a horse, couldn't you?"

"Why not? Sure!"

"Oh, but I don't have the food. Wouldn't it be wonderful!"

He was even trembling with excitement, pressing his hand tightly against his chest.

"Flies would be flying around as big as dogs! And you could use cockroaches to cart bricks; if he's as big as a horse he'd be as strong! Right?"

"The trouble is they have feelers."

"The feelers wouldn't be any trouble, they'd be like reins, the feelers. Or say a spider crawls around, a huge one, as big as—who? A spider even as big as a kitten would be scary! I don't have legs, but if I did! I'd work and feed all the animals in my menagerie, I'd sell them and buy Mom a house in the open field. Have you been in the open fields?"

"Of course I have!"

"Tell me what it's like, huh?"

I began to tell him about fields and meadows, and he listened attentively, not interrupting me, his lashes lowered over his eyes, and his little mouth opened slowly, as if he had dozed off. When I saw this I began to speak more softly, but his mother appeared with the boiling samovar in her hands, a paper bag stuck under her arm, a bottle of vodka in her bosom.

"Here I am!"

"Grand!" sighed the boy, opening his eyes wide. "There's nothing, just grass and flowers. Mom, you should find a wagon and take me out into the open fields. Or else I'll die and never see them. You're a bitch, Mom, really!" he ended, hurt and sad.

His mother gently reprimanded him, "Don't swear, you shouldn't. You're still little."

" 'Don't swear!' That's all right for you, you can go where you want, just like a dog. You're lucky. Listen," he turned back to me, "is it God who made the open fields?"

"Probably."

"But why?"

"For people to go walking in."

"The open fields!" the boy said, smiling thoughtfully and sighing. "I'd take my menagerie there and let them all out. 'Go for a walk, you house pets!' But listen, where do they make God, in almshouses?"*

His mother shrieked and literally rocked with laughter; she tipped over onto the bed, kicking her feet and hooting:

"Oh, you . . . Oh, my Lord! My little comfort! Yes, what was it, that those cheap icon painters make God . . . Oh, I'm laughing so hard, you funny little thing . . ."

Lenka watched her, smiling, and swore gently but dirtily.

"She's giggling like a little girl! She loves to laugh."

And he repeated the curse again.

"Let her laugh," I said. "It doesn't hurt you."

"No, it doesn't," Lenka agreed. "I'm angry with her only when she doesn't wash the window. I ask her and ask her, 'Wash the window, I don't see the light of day,' but she keeps forgetting."

The woman washed the tea dishes as she laughed, winked at me with her light blue eyes, and kept saying:

"Isn't my little comfort wonderful? If it weren't for him I'd have drowned myself long ago, that's the truth. I'd have hanged myself."

As she said it, she was smiling.

* The Russian for almshouse is *bogadel'nia*, derived from the old expression "For God's sake." The boy interpreted it as "a place which makes God."

And Lenka suddenly asked me, "Are you a fool?"

"I don't know. Why do you ask?"

"Mom says you are."

"And why did I say it?" exclaimed the woman, not in the least embarrassed. "You brought a drunken woman in from the street and put her to bed, then you went away, so there you are! I didn't mean anything bad by it. And now you're telling on me, oh, you . . ."

She talked like a child, and her words reminded me of a half-grown girl. Her eyes were also childishly clear, and the noseless face, with the raised lip and the exposed teeth, seemed all the uglier. Like a nightmarish joke, but a funny one.

"Well, let's have tea," she invited us, ceremoniously.

The samovar was on the box beside Lenka, and the mischievous little jet of steam, stealing out from under the battered lid, touched his shoulder. He put out his hand under it, and when the palm was moistened by the steam he wiped it off on his hair, meditatively narrowing his eyes.

"When I grow up," he was saying, "Mom will make me a little cart, and I'll ride through the streets as a beggar. When I get something, I'll roll out into the open field."

"Oh-oh," sighed his mother, then laughed quietly. "He thinks the open field's heaven, poor dear! But there are only camps there, and rascally soldiers, and drunken peasants."

"That's a lie!" Lenka interrupted her, frowning. "Ask him what it's like, he's seen it."

"And haven't I?"

"You're drunk!"

They started to argue, just like children, as heatedly and illogically. Meanwhile a warm evening had already arrived outside and a thick dove-colored cloud stood motionless in the reddening sky. It was getting dark in the basement.

The boy finished his mug of tea, broke into a sweat, and with a glance at me and his mother he said, "I've eaten and drunk all I can, and gosh, I even feel like going to sleep."

"Go to sleep, then," his mother advised.

"But he'll leave! Will you go away?"

"Don't be afraid, I won't let him go," the woman said, nudging me with her knee.

"Don't go," begged Lenka; he shut his eyes, and stretching luxuriously he lay down in his box. Then he suddenly raised his head and said reproachfully to his mother, "You should marry him, get married like the other women, instead of hanging about for nothing with all sorts, they only beat you. But he's kind."

"Go to sleep now," said the woman softly, bending over her saucer of tea.

"He's rich."

The woman sat silently for a minute, sipping tea from the saucer with her awkward lips, and then she said to me, as if I were an old friend, "Well, that's the way we live, quietly, him and me, and no one else. They call me a good-for-nothing out in the yard. Well, so what? There's no one for me to be ashamed before. Then too, see how my looks are ruined? Anyone can see right off what I'm good for. Yes, sir. My little boy has dozed off, my little comfort. Do I have a good kid?"

"Yes, wonderful!"

"I can't get enough of admiring him. Isn't he smart?"

"A genius."

"That's right! His father was a gentleman, an old man. One of those—what are they called? They have offices—oh, Lord! They write papers?"

"Notaries?"

"That's it, that's what he was! A nice old man, kind. He loved me, I was a maid in his house."

She covered her son's naked legs with a rag, straightened the dark pillow under his head, and started to speak again, casually. "Suddenly he died. It was at night, I had just left his room, and he fell to the floor with such a crash, and his life went with it. Do you sell kvass?"

"Yes."

"For yourself?"

"For the boss."

She moved closer to me and said, "Don't look down on me, young man. I'm not contagious now, ask anyone you like down the street, they all know."

"I don't look down on you."

Putting on my knee a small hand with the skin peeled off the fingers and the nails broken, she went on tenderly, "I'm

very thankful to you for Lenka, you gave him a holiday today.
It was a good thing you did."

"I must go," I said.

"Where?" she asked in amazement.

"I've got work to do."

"Stay!"

"I can't."

She looked at her son, then through the window at the sky,
and said softly, "But stay anyway. I'll cover my mug with a
kerchief. I want to thank you for my son. I'll cover it up, all
right?"

She was speaking in a way that was irresistibly human, so
tenderly, with such feeling. And her eyes, her childish eyes in
her deformed face, smiled, not with the smile of a beggar, but
with that of a rich man, who has means to express his gratitude.

"Mom!" the boy shouted suddenly, shuddering and raising himself up, "they're creeping up! Mom, come here!"

"He's had a dream," she said, bending over her son.

I went outside and stopped in thought. Through the open
window of the basement, a gay song, sung through the nose,
poured out into the yard. The mother was singing a lullaby to
her son, carefully enunciating the strange words:

> The hobgoblins are coming,
> They bring sorrows with them,
> They are bringing sorrows,
> They'll tear our heart to pieces!
> Oh, woe is me, oh, woe!
> Where'll we hide, oh, where?

I quickly left the yard, clenching my teeth so as not to burst
into tears.

Translated by Lydia W. Kesich

VASILY GROSSMAN

THE SAFETY INSPECTOR

I

Whenever his wife became angry and would begin to talk loud and fast, the sound of her voice seemed to Korolkov like the buzzing of a drill run by a muscular and persistent dentist.

Korolkov had his own theories on how to get along with his wife, theories taken from his engineering experience. As a safety inspector in the anthracite mines, he had devoted more than a few years to studying explosions in underground workings. His job had made him a skeptic. The methods of locating black-damp—sudden dangerous accumulations of methane gas in domes and even well-ventilated passages—are complicated and involved. In his work, Korolkov came across much that was beyond scientific prediction.

And when his wife would begin to grumble and be cross while he was quietly reading his after-dinner newspaper, Korolkov would not express but only think to himself;

"Put the whole Joint Commission Under the Chairmanship of Academician Skachinsky in my place—and what would they do? Not a single thing."

His friends often advised him to leave his work as safety inspector.

"There's no sense to it at all; it's no good," they said, "it's the lousiest job in the mines. If the safety inspector tries to do his job, the operators get mad: 'He stopped work in the drift'; 'He made the men stop sorting and switched them to timbering'; 'He closed off a gaseous coal-face.' They get mad, the operators, and then they do him dirt. And if the safety inspector stops trying to do his job, it's worse: he's got to answer for men's lives with his own skin. Whatever happens, he's the first to answer for it. In a mine, anything can happen: rockfalls, cave-ins, defective cables, fires, explosions, cars running wild, ropes parting, men falling, defective timbers. . . ."

"How many times have they had you on trial, Apollon Markovich?" his friends asked.

"Didn't count them," said Korolkov, "I don't keep statistics on my personal life."

The short, thin and stooped engineer, with a ridiculous tie around his stringy neck and its prominent Adam's apple, took an angry and stubborn view of his world, and had no intention of leaving his work as safety inspector.

And as Korolkov could not imagine himself without his difficult job, neither could he imagine life without his wife.

It was she, his long-jawed and forbidding spouse, who once went down into a gallery wrecked by an explosion to bring up her husband, burned half to death, to the surface. For twenty years, she had been moving with Korolkov around the mines of the Don Basin. She had lived with him for two years in a sod hut in far-off Karaganda. She had suffered the maddening heat of the Kazakhstan Desert, the fierce frosts of the Tyrgan, and the viciousness of the Ural bedbugs in the dormitory at the Cheliabinsk mine.

True, her personality was a little stolid. Korolkov figured that hers was a woman's personality—unexplainable and unpredictable. A mine, especially a mine with gas, also had a woman's personality.

An order from the People's Committee for Heavy Industry found Korolkov in the Don Basin, in one of the mines of the Budenny Mining Directorate.

The mine superintendent called Korolkov in and, snickering and rustling his papers, he said, "I've got a little tidbit for you here, Apollon Markovich, from Moscow."

Korolkov yawned and said quietly, "I've seen lots of different kinds, and in my time I've swallowed a couple of tons of them."

"Then choke on this one," said the superintendent.

Korolkov was surprised at the superintendent's malicious tone.

"Well, what's wrong?" he asked angrily. "Is it because I shut down Number Four? What did they scribble up there now? A warning? Hauling me on the carpet? Well?"—and he reached out for the papers.

The superintendent said with difficulty, "In the first place, you still owe us two buckets of rectified alcohol, I swear you do. But take a look at this: a transfer to the Central Safety Inspection Agency, with an expression of personal gratitude, three-thousand-ruble prize, and to top it off, a guarantee of living quarters in Moscow." Glancing up at Korolkov's frowning face, he had to laugh: how could you connect this miracle with the gloomy safety inspector sitting before him?

Korolkov decided that somebody was pulling his leg, and then he thought that there must have been some mistake in Moscow—but when he had convinced himself that the order was real, he was upset. Going down into the mine, he kept spitting and shaking his head disapprovingly.

It was a long time before he left the mine. He was especially critical that day; he reported the straw boss in charge of the drift and fined the leading foreman, a man respected by everybody. In the evening, he went home and told his wife the news.

"God knows what they're thinking," he said, looking at her. "Those brains up in Moscow have decided to pick me out for a reward: three thousand in prize money, and they're transferring me to Moscow as senior inspector. 'A little tidbit,' the superintendent called it."

He looked at his wife and kept wondering how she would take such a turn of events. Polina Pavlovna acted in a most unexpected way: she met the news without a word.

At dinner, she kept studying her husband with her eyes, as though she had just discovered in him a terrible and dangerous vice.

Korolkov, aiming at a pickled tomato with his fork, glanced

up at her and asked, "Why do you keep staring at me like a dodo?"

Polina Pavlovna said in a tight voice, "Apollon . . ." and for the first time in their life together, she began to cry.

Korolkov was at a loss, and, without trying to comfort his wife, he went off to a general meeting at the mine surveyor's.

That night, he asked her, "What made you start crying, Polia?"

She explained, and when he heard what she was saying, Korolkov shook with laughter. "So I'm supposed to go chasing after the young Moscow girls? Have you lost your mind, or what? Take a good look at this mug of mine. Leave you! Who would want an old wreck like me? Besides, it's only with you that I can perform as a man."

"What will you do with me in Moscow then?" asked Polina Pavlovna, trying to convince herself. "I'm old and ugly and touchy, and dumb to boot. Do you think I remember what they taught us in school? Professors' wives will be coming to see you there. What can I say to them? You'll be ashamed to death of me. . . ."

Korolkov looked at her, puzzled, and finally he, too, began to wonder. He went to the mirror to see if he might still have a chance.

He filled his chest with air and puffed out his cheeks, trying to make himself better-looking, but Korolkov didn't like his looks in this puffed-up state either and shrugging, he released the air from his chest. Then he went to bed, but he couldn't sleep.

That night, Engineer Korolkov recalled his youth, the first years of his married life. He had worked in the "Ivan" mine, some twenty versts away. Polina Pavlovna then flaunted a light blue sarafan, and she had plaited her hair into braids. True, even then she had a horseface, a trifle longish. A friend of Korolkov's, the carefree head miner Vanka Kuzhelev, a blunt and rough man, tried to talk him out of getting married: "What are you doing, man? We have forty horses in our stable at the mine, each as good as the next; quiet, good horses. What do you need that skittish one for?"

Kuzhelev died in 1912, during a fire in the central shaft. How much coal had been dug since then! How many people had come, grown old and died, and others come to take their places! And much had happened in the mines during these years: electricity, air hammers, new mining methods, God knows what all.

So they were transferring him to the central office. Who could have done him this good turn? He just couldn't understand it. It seems that there wasn't a man in the mining industry with whom Korolkov had not exchanged curses. And strangest of all was that someone in Moscow was keeping an eye on him: where and when he had worked, what he had done; it was all spelled out in the order. "In 1930, prevented disaster at Mine 17-17 bis." Have they nothing better to do at the central office? It's no joke to dig up such nonsense in those huge archives. Sit around in Moscow? Like hell he would. Polina Pavlovna could take care of the apartment; he would drive out to the Moscow Basin; they've got brown coal there; he'd have to see it once before he died. They say that in the Moscow Basin, the soil itself is bloated with gas, and that the coal is impregnated with carbonic acid, as in the Mexican mines. One look at Moscow Basin coal, and there's no reason to go to Mexico. He still didn't fall asleep for a long time, but kept thinking about how strange a woman's mind is. Just look at all she thought up. It's really hard to believe. He remembered his youth again, and Polina's light blue sarafan. And the thought of the sarafan brought on a feeling of sadness, a feeling unfamiliar to Korolkov. He could see it now, that light blue sarafan with its little white flowers. When he was just a kid, he had planned to organize a journey to the center of the earth.

Korolkov sighed and suddenly regretted that there had been no children. He would have said now, "See, young man, how much people think of your father. They're calling him to Moscow."

All sorts of surprising nonsense crept into his head and kept him from sleeping.

II

Everybody was surprised at Korolkov's good luck and congratulated him. Fadeyev, the head of the mine rescue station and an old friend of Korolkov's (they once had been through the disaster at the Gorlov mine together), drew Korolkov into his office. Winking slyly and chuckling, he started to ask about it all.

"You're a smooth one," said Fadeyev, "it's really amazing how things worked out for you. Tell me though, who helped you fix it up, and make up that list and send it off to Moscow? I'll have to try it too, by God. Who did you send it to? To Andrey Fridrikhovich?"

"What's the matter with you, Nikolai Tikhonovich?" said Korolkov. "I only found out about it yesterday myself; I didn't send anything off to Moscow."

But Fadeyev wouldn't listen; he was carried away.

"Come on, you tightwad," he said, shaking his head. "Are you asking me to believe that they made it up themselves? 'Apollon Markovich Korolkov in 1927 exemplarily put a number of mines on gas-safe conditions, and in 1932, he transferred his experience in the Don Basin to the huge mines of the Kuznets Basin Coal Directorate.' Sneaky bastard, you didn't forget a thing. Did it take you two weeks to write it up?"

Korolkov pressed his hands to his chest and said, "Nikolai Tikhonovich, by God I didn't do a thing. I myself even forgot what I did there; it was little enough, anyway. And yesterday I read the order and remembered: that's right, that's how it was. The thought never entered my head that I was transferring my experience to Siberia. You know me better than that, don't you?"

Here, Fadeyev became serious and said, "O.K., friend, I can see you're going to be a bastard about it. If you don't want to be honest with an old friend, to hell with you."

Suddenly, Korolkov's blood boiled, and he asked, "So you think I'm a sneaky bastard then?"—and without waiting for an answer, he left, slamming the door so hard that the cap of the safety lamp hanging on the wall clanked.

Korolkov had to go to a small mine, Number 5-S. A mud-spattered buggy was waiting for him in front of the mine office. The old driver, a retired coal cutter, one of the few who recovered after the terrible explosion of 1908, threw back the leather apron of the buggy and said, "Let's get going, Apollon Markovich. I brought your mine clothes from the bathhouse."

"I have to get my lamp," said Korolkov, "I don't like the lamps in 5-S; they leak."

"I brought your lamp," answered the driver. "I wrapped it up in some rags."

The way to the mine was over a dirt road, and the wheels of the buggy sank into the mud. All around lay the heavy, wet earth, covered with the half-rotted bits of last year's growth, but here and there on the hillocks green patches of young grass could already be seen. White clouds floated in the sky, clouds not sullied by coal dust; the sun shone bright and strong. A warm wind was blowing from over Makeyevka way. It was born not in Makeyevka, but on the shores of the Azov Sea, and its moist breath gladdened the hearts of the riders. Even the despondent old horse, it seemed, felt something, and he flared his nostrils.

The buggy was bouncing heavily on the bumps, but Korolkov didn't notice it. By now, he was really upset. What the hell is going on, anyway? It wasn't just some joke, everything that happened yesterday! Somebody had an eye on him; somebody was interested in his work and in his life. Korolkov looked around on both sides: it seemed to him that even now this mysterious Muscovite was walking along in the fields and watching him. "So, you're going to Number 5-S, Apollon Markovich?"

They reached the mine. Korolkov wandered over toward the pile-driver, swinging his lamp. The mud under his feet sighed and soughed, caught at his shoes and tried to pull them off.

The round-shouldered mining inspector had walked thousands of times like this across muddy mine yards, swinging his lamp. And never once in all those long years did it occur to him that he might one day live in Moscow, walk on sidewalks of asphalt in light, polished shoes, or stroll down a boulevard in the evening—stop in at some little pavilion and listen to the music, and have a glass of tea with lemon. All his life, Korolkov had lived around the remotest and roughest mines. Whenever he had gone to Makeyevka, he looked at the town park and paved streets and would shake his head. "Yes, this is really the life."

He rode the screeching cage down into the mine and walked along the main drift. Reaching the first incline, he stopped and listened carefully. The train of coal cars rumbled, and testing its whistle, shrieked piercingly. Carpenters passed by with saws, and down the incline came a timber man looking at the overhead timbers and swinging his ax.

Korolkov sighed heavily and walked along the passage. He inspected a few faces, checked the ventilation doors and examined the timbers in a new passage. Then, grunting and sighing, he crawled into a conduit. The gas foremen particularly disapproved of Korolkov's nasty habit of inspecting conduits. Crawling along conduits was the last thing anyone considered necessary. The ventilation office called Korolkov all kinds of names for his stupid interest in these negligible ducts, through which not only a man but even a current of air could squeeze only with great difficulty.

The conduits were in bad shape, and crawling on his belly along the narrow passage partly blocked by fallen rock, Korolkov scraped his right hand so badly that it bled. Whenever he penetrated to some such remote place, he liked to talk out loud to himself. But now, it seemed to him that he was not alone. His observer, following him with the soft footfalls of a miner, advised, "You'd better rest, Apollon Markovich; it is extremely harmful at your age to crawl into places where there are gas accumulations."

Korolkov had had enough, and muttered angrily, "What's the big idea? You're always poking your nose into everything!"

When he reached the surface, Korolkov went to the office.

The head engineer at Number 5-S, Kosmatov, was an old friend of Korolkov's. At one time, they had both been caught in a rockfall at the Rutchenkovka mine, and they lay for six hours, growing stiff, under a cross-strut supporting the face. They had said good-by to the surface and tried to comfort each other.

Kosmatov met Korolkov with a laugh. He already knew everything, and of course, nothing could have been funnier than what had happened.

A broken-down old coal-miner, a safety inspector, five times hauled into court, who fell from one misfortune into another, who was fired twice and who had made scores of enemies and set as many against himself, who had grubbed in all the God-forsaken mines in the country—suddenly he receives the gratitude of Moscow, and his biography is written out with complete details. Looking at Korolkov, Kosmatov shook his head in amazement and shrugged helplessly. Korolkov, however, was not inclined to discuss the changes in his life.

"You know, Stepan Trofimovich," he said, "I was in your eastern section, and the conduits are caving in, and the ventilation's not worth a damn—if you don't watch out, I'll shut down the whole section. Your mine comes under the second category."

"Come off it," smiled Kosmatov, "would you get me on a regulation?"

"I know the regulation," said Korolkov. "They had me up three times for that regulation. But still I'm going to make out a report on it. I'll give you ten days to take care of it."

"So that's the way it is," said Kosmatov, looking intently at Korolkov's black fingers as he wrote. He added, "Give me a couple of weeks, anyway; I have to speed up production—it's the end of the month—for the record."

Korolkov handed him the paper.

"You're pushing me, you no-good," Kosmatov said angrily. But then he shrugged and suddenly was in a good mood again. "O.K., to hell with you; you're only doing your job. How about it: have they sent a sketch of your apartment yet, and with hot water probably?"

He started to laugh again, slapping his thigh.

On his way back, Korolkov was irritated. Why did all his friends act so stupidly? He began to feel a kind of triumphant mood take hold of him more and more strongly, a mood he had never felt before. Thoughts came into his mind about his life, about people long gone, and about his good and hard job.

"Yes, Nikifor, what do you make of it? They remembered me of all people, me, a broken-down old engineer."

"Who else, if not you?" answered Nikifor. "They know

everything in Moscow." And he added, "Yes, they know all right up there. I remember how two hundred and seventy men were lost in the mine, and the Tsar sent a telegram; he grieved over it."

"What's the Tsar got to do with it?" said Korolkov, thinking. "The Tsars are nothing to us, Nikifor. Here I am, moving to Moscow—I'll submit a project to the Kremlin, to raise monuments to all the engineers and head miners who were lost in the mines. I ought to write a book, too, about how they lived, what levels they worked on. And a simple inscription on the stone. Coal cutter—let's say for instance—Gerasimov, worked on levels with a fifty-degree drop. He cut 100,000 tons of coal. There, that tells everything. Such men they were —Nikolai Nikolayevich Chernytsyn—and who remembers him now?"

"Ye-e-es," agreed Nikifor seriously, "somebody ought to write that book."

At home, a surprise was waiting for Korolkov.

Polina Pavlovna was dressed up fit for a birthday party. She had put on a light blue dress, new to Korolkov; her face was powdered and her lips unusually red.

"What's all this?" asked Korolkov. "Been eating raspberries in March?"

All at once, he didn't feel like teasing her any more.

His wife looked at him with bright, cold eyes and said, "I'm not going to any Moscow."

"What? What?" said Korolkov, turning.

"What's the matter, are you deaf?" she said, and repeated word by word, "I'm not going to any Moscow. I know what will happen."

"Hmph," thought Korolkov, "some 'tidbit.' She went off to Karaganda, but doesn't want to go to Moscow."

Korolkov knew that nothing increases the destructive power of an underground explosion as much as the very least, insignificant opposition. A shock wave moves more or less peacefully along empty drifts of some major section, but it has only to meet an obstacle—some sort of light ventilation door—and the pressure of the explosion increases unbelievably; cars are flattened like pancakes, and iron rails, ripped from the ties, are twisted into odd shapes.

Polina Pavlovna, in the light blue dress which somehow recalled that earlier sarafan, looked at him, waiting.

And perhaps for the first time in his life, departing from his basic theories, Inspector Korolkov did not allow the shock wave to dissipate itself along an empty drift.

"Now, Polia, what are you talking about?" he said, smiling from a feeling of strength and right. "Just imagine: out of the goodness of his heart, Ordzhonikidze invites me to come, politely, and in good faith, and all at once I refuse! Why, he'd be hurt for the rest of his life."

Translated by Sam Driver

ILF AND PETROV
(ILYA ILF AND EVGENY KATAYEV)

ON A GRAND SCALE

Behind a huge writing table, its sides carved with snipes and bunches of grapes, sat Semyon Semyonovich, director of the plant. In front of him stood the superintendent in yellow-patch cavalry breeches. Superintendents for some reason or other like to drape their official bodies in semi-military dress, as if their task consisted in constant fancy-equitation and crop lashing rather than in placid counting and recounting of electric bulbs and in fastening brass stock numbers to closets and chairs.

"So then, Comrade Koshachy," Semyon Semyonovich said with vehemence, "get us some smoked salmon, or, better yet, fillet of salmon and, well, some ham, sausage, cheese, and some of the more expensive canned stuff."

"Sprats?"

"That's just like you, Comrade Koshachy. Sprats! Why not stuffed squash or hog beans? The Rubber Trust served canned burbot liver at its last banquet and you come up with sprats! I say crabs, not sprats. Write: twenty baskets of crabs."

The superintendent was going to object and even opened his mouth, but said nothing and started to write.

"Crabs," repeated Semyon Semyonovich. "And five kilos of fresh caviar."

"Isn't that a lot? Last time we got three kilos and it was quite enough."

"You think it was enough and I don't think it was enough. I observed."

"Forty rubles per kilo," said the superintendent somberly. "Well, what of it?"

"Nothing, except that the caviar alone will cost us two hundred rubles."

"I've long wanted to tell you, Comrade Koshachy, that you lack perspective. A banquet's got to be a banquet. An appetizer, a hot dish, even two hot dishes, ice cream, fruit."

"Why this grand scale?" muttered Koshachy. "Of course, I don't deny it, we fulfilled our monthly plan. Fine. We can serve tea, beer, red caviar sandwiches. What's wrong with that? And, besides, we gave a banquet last week in honor of our business manager's fiftieth birthday."

"Nevertheless, I don't understand you, Comrade Koshachy. Forgive me, but you are a sort of morbidly stingy person. What have we, a grocery? What are we, petty tradesmen?"

The superintendent lowered his eyes, defeated by the arguments.

"And, finally," continued Semyon Semyonovich, "buy a decent set of tableware, for God knows what you have been serving on. Different-sized plates and wine glasses. Last time they drank wine in cups. Do you know what this means?"

"I know."

"If you know, then go to the commissary and get everything we need. Things can't go on like that."

"The commissary is very expensive, Semyon Semyonovich. And we have a limited budget."

"I am better acquainted with the budget than you are. We are not thieves or embezzlers and are not going to shoplift the fillet of salmon. But why should we pretend to be poorer than we are? Our enterprises are not incurring any losses. And if we offer a friendly supper, so let it be a real supper. We ought to hire a jazz band, invite entertainers, and not that Tambov choir, whatever its name is. . . ."

"Lyrists Ensemble," said the superintendent hoarsely.

"Yes, yes, we don't want those balalaika strummers any more. Invite a good singer, have him sing us something. 'Sleep, my joy, sleep, the house is dark and deep.'"

"But such an entertainer," said Koshachy in a tearful voice, "will strip us to the bone."

"Why, good grief, you're a strange man! *You* he'll strip to the bone? For our million-ruble budget this is of no importance."

"We'll have to hire a taxi for the entertainer," whispered the superintendent dolefully.

Semyon Semyonovich looked intently at the superintendent and said heatedly:

"Forgive me, Comrade Koshachy, but you are really a tightwad. A regular miser. Such a type, forgive me, is even found depicted in literature. You're a Plyushkin! A Harpagon! Yes, yes, and please don't contradict. You have the nasty habit of contradicting all the time. You're a Plyushkin, and that is all there is to it. Even my deputy complained about your absurd, provincial niggardliness. You still did not get around to buying decent furniture for his office."

"He has good furniture," said Koshachy sullenly. "He's got everything he needs for his work: six Swedish chairs, one writing table, another table—a small one—a pitcher, a bronze ash tray ornamented with a dog, a beautiful, new oilskin sofa."

"Oilskin!" groaned Semyon Semyonovich. "Get him leather furniture tomorrow. Do you hear? Run over to the commissary."

"Leather, Semyon Semyonovich, costs fifteen thousand."

"Money again! It's simply disgusting to hear. What are we, beggars? One must live on a grand scale, Comrade Koshachy, one must have a socialist perspective. Got that?"

The superintendent pocketed the tape measure he had been twisting in his hands and, his leather-patch breeches rustling, walked out of the office.

In the evening at tea Semyon Semyonovich listened with a bored expression to his wife jotting down something on a slip of paper and saying joyfully:

"It'll be fine and inexpensive. Four bottles of wine, a liter of vodka, two boxes of anchovies, three hundred grams of fillet of salmon, and ham. Then I'll make a green salad with fresh cucumbers and prepare a kilo of sausages."

"Nonsense!"

"Did you say something?"

"I said, 'Nonsense.' "

"Is anything wrong?" asked his wife worriedly.

"Yes, there is," answered Semyon Semyonovich dryly. "For example, every cucumber costs one ruble fifteen kopecks, that's what's the matter."

"But the whole salad requires only two small cucumbers."

"Yes, yes, small cucumbers, fillet of salmon, anchovies. Do you realize how much all that will add up to?"

"I don't understand you, Semyon. My name day, we'll have visitors, it's been two years since we entertained, though we ourselves have been constantly calling on everyone. It's really embarrassing."

"Why is it embarrassing?"

"It's embarrassing because it's rude."

"Well, all right," said Semyon Semyonovich dully. "Let's see your list. And so, we strike out all that. There remains . . . in fact, nothing remains. Now then, Katya, here's what you get. Get a bottle of vodka, and a hundred and fifty grams of herring. That's all."

"No, Semyon, we can't do that."

"We certainly can. Everyone will tell you that herring is the classic appetizer. I even read something about that in literature."

"Semyon, this will be a disgrace."

"All right, all right, in that case add a box of sprats. But mind you don't get Leningrad sprats. Ask for the Tula brand. It's true they're cheaper, but they're much more nourishing."

"You'd think we're paupers!" cried his wife.

"We must build our life on the basis of the strictest economy and rational utilization of every kopeck," replied Semyon Semyonovich gravely.

"You make a thousand rubles a month. Why should we pretend to be poorer than we are?"

"Katya, I'm neither a thief nor an embezzler and am not obliged to feed a band of greedy acquaintances on my hard-earned money."

"For shame!"

"I'm paying no attention to your outburst. I have a budget and have no right to overstep its limits. Do you understand? I have no right!"

"But who can such a miser take after?" said his wife, addressing the wall.

"Rail at me, rail," said Semyon Semyonovich, "but I warn you that I'll continue to exercise firm financial discipline, no matter what you say."

"I'll say it and keep on saying it!" shouted his wife. "Kolya has been running around a month now with holes in his shoes."

"Why bring Kolya into this?"

"Because, because he's our son."

"All right, all right, don't shout. We'll buy the little rascal a pair of shoes. In due time. Now, what else do you need? Out with it, quickly. You want a piano, a harp?"

"Never mind the harp, but we need a stool for the kitchen."

"A stool!" squealed Semyon Semyonovich. "Why a stool? But of course! Let's buy leather furniture for the kitchen right away! It's only fifteen thousand. No, my dear Katya, I'll bring order into our home."

And he went on and on explaining to his wife that it was high time to put an end to the senseless spending, feasting and similar free squandering and dissipation of the socialist kopeck.

He slept well.

Translated by Ira Goetz

VSEVOLOD IVANOV

THE CHILD

I

Mongolia—a wild and joyless beast! The rock is a beast, the water a beast; even the butterfly, even it tries to sting.

What kind of heart the Mongolian has, no one knows. People say he goes about in animal skins, looks like a Chinaman, and took to living far from the Russians across the desert, Nor-Koi. And, another thing they say, he'll go off beyond China and India to deep-blue, unknowable lands on seven shores. . . .

Those Kirghiz from around the Irtysh River, who had fled from the Russian war to Mongolia, flourished here near the Russians. Everyone knows that their heart is like mica, worthless, transparent through and through. They came here without hurrying and brought with them their herds, their children and even their sick.

But the Russians had been driven here unmercifully—they were strong and healthy peasants. They had left their excess weakness behind on the rocks and mountains: some died, some were killed. Families and tools and cattle were abandoned to the Whites. The peasants were as evil-tempered as wolves in spring. In ravines, in tents, they lay and thought about the steppe, about the Irtysh. . . .

There were some fifty of them with Sergei Selivanov at their head, and the detachment was known as "Comrade Selivanov's partisan detachment of the Red Guard."

They were bored and lonesome.

While the Whites were driving them across the mountains, there was terror in their hearts from the rock, immense and dark, but when they came to the steppe, it was dull and sad. Because the steppe was like the Irtysh steppe: sand, stiff grasses, a firmly forged sky. Everything was strange, not your own, unplowed, wild.

And, moreover, it was hard without women.

At night they told obscene soldiers' stories about women, and when it became unbearable, they saddled the horses and went out after Kirghiz girls on the steppe.

And the Kirghiz girls, seeing the Russians, fell submissively on their backs.

It was bad, repulsive to take them—motionless with tightly closed eyes, as if they were sinning with cattle.

The Kirghiz—they feared the Russians—moved far off into the steppe. Seeing a Russian, they would threaten with rifles and bows, whoop, but not shoot. Maybe, they didn't know how to.

II

The detachment's paymaster Afanasy Petrovich Trubachov was a regular cry baby, and, like a baby's, his face was small, beardless and ruddy. Only his legs were long and powerful like a camel's.

But when he mounted a horse, he became stern. His face grew distant, and he sat there gray, angry and terrible.

On Whitsunday three men were sent on detail—Selivanov, paymaster Afanasy Petrovich, and secretary Drevesinin—to look for good forage grass on the steppe.

The sands steamed under the sun.

A wind blew from above, from the sky, the sultry heat rose from the earth to the quivering sky. The bodies of the men and animals were hard and heavy as rocks. Melancholy.

And Selivanov said hoarsely:

"What kind of meadows are over there?"

They all knew. He was speaking about the Irtysh. But the sparsely bearded faces were silent, as if the hair had been seared by the sun like the grasses on the steppe. Their eyes, slitted like a fishhook wound, burned red. Heat.

Only Afanasy Petrovich responded plaintively:

"Is there really drought there, too, boys?"

The small voice was tearful, but the face did not cry, and only the tired and panting horse under him had aching tears in its big, long eyes.

Thus one after another the partisans went off into the steppe along paths beaten by wild goats. . . .

. . . The sands glowed dully. A suffocating, sand-smelling wind stuck to one's shoulders and head. Sweat burns in the body, but cannot force its way out through the dry skin. . . .

Toward evening, as they rode up out of a hollow, Selivanov said, pointing toward the west:

"Here come some travelers on the move."

To be sure, right on the horizon the sands were tossing a red-hued dust.

"Kirghiz, probably."

They started arguing about it: Drevesinin said that the Kirghiz lived far off and did not come near Selivanov's ravines. Afanasy Petrovich said it was Kirghiz for certain, it was Kirghiz dust, thick.

But when the sand had rolled the dust up close, everyone decided:

"Strangers . . ."

The horses sensed it from their masters' voices—something alien was being carried on the wind. They pricked up their ears and fell to the ground long before the command. Gray and yellow horse carcasses lay in the gully helpless and absurd with legs thin as poles. Was it from shame that they had closed their big frightened eyes and breathed fitfully?

Selivanov and paymaster Afanasy Petrovich lay on the edge of the gully. The paymaster cried, sniffling. So as not to feel frightened, Selivanov always kept him nearby, and from that childish crying his heavy peasant's heart was almost gladdened and strengthened.

The path unfurled dust. The wheels clattered intermittently. Like dust the long black manes curled and wreathed in the collars.

Selivanov said confidently:

"Russians . . . Officers."

And he called Drevesinin out of the gully.

Two persons in peaked caps with red bands sat in a new
little wicker cart. Their faces were imperceptible in the dust,
as if the red bands were floating in a yellow cloud. A rifle—
the muzzle sticks out when the hand with the whip emerges
from the dust.

Drevesinin reflected a minute and said:

"Officers . . . on business, probably. An expedition . . .
That's clear."

He winked mischievously:

"We'll show them, Selivanov, old boy."

The cart carried the people along, bore them along sturdily. The horses. They were having a fine time of it, and
behind, like a fox with its tail, the cart covered up the tracks
with Mongolian dust.

Afanasy Petrovich drawled tearfully:

"Don't, boys. . . . Better take them prisoners. . . . Let's
wait about killing them."

"You aren't afraid . . . are ya? . . ."

Selivanov became irritated and, as one unbuttons a button,
threw back his rifle bolt noiselessly.

"This is no place for tears, paymaster."

What enraged them most of all—the officers appeared on
the steppe alone, without an escort, as if there were a host of
them, as if they were death to the peasants. There, for example, an officer was standing up straight, gazing around the
steppe, but he could not see much: dust. The evening wind
blew red on the scorched grasses, on two rocks near the
ravine, like horses' carcasses. . . . Which rocks? Carcasses?

In the red dust the cart, wheels, people and their thoughts
. . . whirling along.

They fired. . . . Whooped. Fired again.

Simultaneously knocking against one another, the caps fell
into the cart.

The reins went slack, as if snapped. . . .

The horses darted . . . nearly bolted. But suddenly their
withers foamed milk-white. . . . Shuddering along the powerful knots of their muscles, they lowered their heads and
stopped.

Afanasy Petrovich spoke:

"They're dead. . . ."

The peasants came up and took a look.

The red bands were dead. They sat shoulder to shoulder, their heads thrown back, but one of the dead was a woman. Her hair fell undone in the dust—half yellow, half black, and the soldier's tunic was raised high by a woman's breasts.

"Strange," said Drevesinin. "It's her own fault . . . shouldn't put a cap on. Who wants to kill a woman? Society needs women."

Afanasy Petrovich spat:

"You bourgeois beast . . . You don't have any feeling, you bastard. . . ."

"Hold on," Selivanov interrupted them. "We're not thieves—we have to make a list of the people's property. Give me some paper."

Under the front compartment in a small Chinese wicker basket, among the rest of the "people's property," lay a little white-eyed, white-haired child. A corner of a brown blanket was clutched in his tiny hand. Unweaned, small, he whimpered slightly.

Tenderly Afanasy Petrovich said:

"You see now . . . probably he's telling in his own way how . . ."

Once again they felt sorry for the woman and did not take her clothes off, but the man they buried naked in the sand.

III

Afanasy Petrovich rode back in the captured cart, holding the child in his arms and, rocking him, crooned very softly:

> *Nightingale, nightingale-pipit . . .*
> *Little canary . . .*
> *Who sings so plaintively . . .*

He remembered the little village of Lebyazhy—his home, the stables with the cattle, his family, the little children—and wept softly.

The baby cried, too.

The loose, crumbling, scorched sands raced along and cried softly. The partisans raced along on the low, firm-

fleshed Mongolian horses. They were scorched-faced and
scorched-hearted partisans.

Sun-stifled wormwood drifted along the path, like sand,
fine and imperceptible.

And the sands were like wormwood—fine and bitter.

You paths, goats' paths! You sands, bitter sands! Mongolia
—the wild and joyless beast!

They examined the officer's belongings. Books, a suitcase
filled with tobacco, shiny steel instruments—among them,
on three long legs, a square brass box with compartments.

The partisans came near and examined, touched and
weighed them in their hands.

They smelled of sheep fat. They ate a lot from nothing else
to do, and their clothes became all greasy. High cheekboned
ones with soft thin lips, from the Don Cossack villages;
swarthy ones with long black hair, from the lime pits. And all
of them had legs curved like shaft bows and throaty steppe
voices.

Afanasy Petrovich picked up a brass-headed tripod and
said:

"A telescope," and screwed up his eyes. "A good telescope. It must have cost a pretty bit. They looked at the
moon with it, boys, and discovered gold fields there. . . .
You don't have to pan it, it's like flour, the purest gold. Chuck
it in the bag. . . ."

One of the young city boys guffawed:

"Listen to those tales, for God's sake. . . ."

Afanasy Petrovich lost his temper:

"So I'm lying, huh, you stupid bastard? You better watch
it. . . ."

"Who're you telling to watch it?"

Afanasy grabbed his revolver.

"All right, cut it out," said Selivanov.

They divided up the tobacco, but the instruments were
handed over to Afanasy Petrovich—as paymaster he might,
when the opportunity arose, be able to barter them for something with the Kirghiz.

He laid the instruments in front of the child.

"Here, play. . . ."

The child did not see: he whimpered. Afanasy tried everything, he even broke out in a sweat. Still the child whimpered and would not play.

The cooks brought dinner. There rose a heavy smell of butter, porridge and cabbage soup. Broad Semipalatinsk spoons were fished out of boot tops. Around the camp the grass was trampled down. Up above on the cliffs a sentry shouted:

"How much longer for me? I want some grub . . . Send . . . send the relief!"

They finished eating and remembered—they had to feed the baby. The child was whimpering incessantly.

Afanasy Petrovich chewed up some bread. He shoved the soggy lump into the moist opened little mouth and smacked his lips:

"Try—try it . . . little one . . . eat it up, little goblin . . . 's good."

But he closed his tiny mouth and turned his head away—he would not take it. He cried through his nose, thinly, shrilly.

The peasants came over; they stood around him. Over the heads they peered at the child. They were silent.

It was hot. Cheek bones and lips shone from mutton. Shirts were unbuttoned, feet bare, yellow, like the Mongolian soil.

Someone suggested:

"He wants some cabbage soup. . . . Let's try some cabbage soup for him. . . ."

Some soup was cooled. Afanasy Petrovich dipped a finger into the soup and put it into the baby's mouth. The good greasy cabbage soup ran down his little lips onto his little pink shirt and onto the blanket.

He would not take it. He whimpered.

"A pup's smarter—it'll eat from your finger. . . ."

"What do you mean a dog, this's a human being. . . ."

"What next! . . ."

There was no cow's milk in the detachment. They thought of giving it some mare's milk, they had plenty of mares. It was no good—kumiss gets you drunk. He might fall sick.

They broke up into groups among the carts and talked the matter over. They were worried. And Afanasy Petrovich rushed around among the carts, a tattered Caucasian coat

over his shoulders, his eyes small, also tattered. His small
voice was thin, troubled, childish, as if the child itself were
running around, complaining.

"What's going to happen? But he's got to eat, doesn't he?
Do something, why don't you, you bastards. . . ."

They stood there broad, powerful-bodied, with a helpless
look.

"It's woman's work. . . ."

"Of course it is. . . ."

"From a woman he'd have eaten a ram. . . ."

"Well, now, that's right."

Selivanov called a meeting and declared:

"You can't let a little Christian lad die like a beast. The
father, let's say, was a bourgeois, but what about the child?
It's innocent."

The peasants agreed:

"It's not the child's fault. It's innocent."

Drevesinin guffawed:

"Grow, kiddy. He'll grow up with us and fly to the moon
. . . to the gold fields."

The peasants did not laugh. Afanasy Petrovich raised his
fist and shouted:

"What a bastard you are. The only scoffer in the detachment."

He shuffled around a bit, swung his arms and suddenly
cried out shrilly:

"A cow . . . He needs a cow! . . ."

They responded unanimously:

"Without a cow—it's death. . . ."

"We got to have a cow. . . ."

"Without a cow he'll conk out."

Resolutely Afanasy Petrovich said:

"Boys, I'll go get some cows. . . ."

Drevesinin interrupted him insolently:

"To the Irtysh, to Lebyazhy? . . ."

"No point in my going to the Irtysh, you prize ass. I'll go to
the Kirghiz."

"To swap for the telescope? Go, benefactor."

Afanasy Petrovich lunged at him; he bawled angrily:

"You carrion dog! You want to get it in the puss?"

But seeing that their swearing got out of hand, the chairman of the meeting, Selivanov, cut them short:

"That's enough. . . ."

And they voted as follows: Drevesinin, Afanasy Petrovich, and three others were to go to the Kirghiz villages on the steppe and drive back a cow. If possible two or five, since the cooks were running out of meat.

They hung their rifles on the saddles and put on fox-lined Kirghiz jackets so as to look like Kirghiz from a distance.

"Good luck."

They wrapped the child up in a blanket and laid him in the shade under a cart. A young lad sat by him and every now and then for his and the baby's amusement fired off his revolver into a wormwood bush.

IV

Oh, you Mongolian sands, you joyless sands! Oh, you rock— you sad blue rock, you deep-earthed hands, you evil hands!

The Russians cross the sands. Night.

The sands smell of heat, wormwood.

In the village dogs bay at a wolf, at the darkness.

In the dark wolves howl at hunger, at death.

The Kirghiz fled from death.

"Will we drive the herds away from death?"

A green, suffocating darkness shivers over the sands, the sands barely retain it—now it breaks off and flutters toward the west.

The village smells of burning dung and straw, of sour milk. Gaunt, hungry Kirghiz children sit by yellow campfires. Beside the children lie bare-ribbed, sharp-faced dogs. The *yurts** rise like hayricks. Beyond the *yurts* is a lake, rushes.

Suddenly from the rushes hollow shots rang out into the yellow campfires:

"O-o-a-at! . . ."

At once the Kirghiz sprang out of the felt *yurts.* They shouted fearfully:

* A tent made of skin.

"Ui-boi . . . Ui-boi, the Red Russians are coming. . . . Ui-boi . . ."

They leaped on their horses. The horses were kept saddled day and night. The *yurts* thumped. The steppe thumped. The rushes shrieked like a wild duck:

"Ai-ai, Red Russian—White Russian, ai-ai . . ."

One graybeard fell head first off his horse into a kettle, a cauldron, and tipped it over. Scalded, he howled in a deep full voice. And nearby a shaggy dog, his tail between his legs, timidly poked his hungry mug into the hot milk.

The mares whinnied softly. As if frightened by wolves the sheep thrashed about in the sheepfold. The cows panted as if short of breath.

And the submissive Kirghiz women, seeing the Russians, submissively lay back upon the felt rugs. . . .

Drevesinin guffawed lasciviously:

"Are we stallions, or something? . . . We don't always want to. . . ."

He hastily strained some milk into a small flat Austrian flask, and, cracking his whip, herded the cows with their calves toward the *yurts.* The untethered calves, swiftly nudging the soft udder with their heads, joyfully seized the teats in their large soft lips.

"Well, how do you like that, they're hungry, the little bullocks. . . ."

And Drevesinin fired his revolver at the calves.

Afanasy Petrovich was still riding around the village and was about to go off after Drevesinin, when suddenly he remembered:

"Gotta have a feeder. The idiots, they forgot a nipple! . . ."

He rushed from *yurt* to *yurt* looking for a nipple. The fires in the *yurts* had been put out. Afanasy Petrovich seized a firebrand and, scattering sparks, coughing from the smoke, searched for a nipple. The torch was sputtering in one hand, and in the other he held a revolver. The nipple was nowhere to be found.

The submissive Kirghiz women, covered with coats, lay out on felt rugs. The babies were squalling.

Afanasy Petrovich lost his temper and in one *yurt* shouted at a young Kirghiz woman:

"A nipple, you dumb bitch, give me a tit!"

The woman began to weep and quickly started undoing her silk coat and then pulling off her shift.

"Don't hurt me. . . . Ai . . . Ai . . . Take me. . . ."

And beside her on the felt rug wailed a baby swaddled in rags. The woman was already spreading her legs.

"Ai . . . Ai . . . take me. . . ."

But just then Afanasy Petrovich seized her breast, squeezed it and whistled joyfully:

"Hey . . . Now there's a tit. Eh! What a sturdy one!"

"Don't hurt me. . . . Don't . . ."

"All right, don't quack. Come on! What a sturdy one!"

And he dragged her by the hand after him.

The torch fell—it went dark in the *yurt.*

In the dark he sat the woman on the saddle and, every once in a while feeling her breasts, raced back to the Selivanov ravines, back to the detachment.

"I found her, boys, eh," he said happily and he had tears in his eyes. "I'll find her, brother, if I have to dig her up from under the ground."

v

But at the camp it turned out—Afanasy Petrovich had not noticed in the dark—that the woman had brought her own baby with her.

"Let her keep it," the peasants said, "there'll be enough milk for both of them. We have cows, and she's a sturdy one."

The Kirghiz woman was silent and stern and nursed the babies out of everyone's sight. They lay beside her on a felt rug in the tent—one white, the other yellow—and wailed as one.

Only a week later, Afanasy Petrovich lodged a complaint at the general meeting:

"She's cheating us, Comrades: that Kirghiz woman's a hussy, she nurses unfairly—she gives the whole breast to her own, but ours gets what's left over. I spied on her, men. You just take a look. . . ."

The peasants went over and looked: they were babies like all babies; one white, the other yellow, like a ripe melon. But it looked as if the Russian were thinner than the Kirghiz.

Afanasy Petrovich spread his arms:

"I gave him a name, Vaska . . . and you see what happens. . . . What a trick."

Drevesinin said without so much as a grin:

"But you're a sickly one, Vaska, you're half dead. . . ."

They found a pole and measured it on a shaft so that one side would not overbalance the other.

The babies were suspended from the ends to see which one was heavier. Swaddled in rags and suspended on hair ropes, the babies whined. They smelled of that delicate baby's smell. The woman stood by a cart and, not understanding anything, cried.

The peasants were silent. They were watching.

"Let 'em go," said Selivanov. "Let go of the scales."

Afanasy Petrovich took his hands off the pole and immediately the Russian child went up.

"See, the little yellow-mouthed bastard," said Afanasy angrily, "he stuffed himself."

He picked up a dried-out ram's skull which had been lying around and put it on top of the Russian baby. The babies were then evenly balanced.

The peasants raised a cry and shouted:

"By a whole head, boys, she overfed hers, eh? . . ."

"It's hard to keep track of her. . . ."

"What a beast . . . See how she's fed him."

"Who was supposed to watch her? . . ."

"We have other things to do than look after babies!"

Some of the staid peasants supported this:

"How can you keep track!"

"After all, she's his mother. . . ."

Afanasy Petrovich stamped and shrieked:

"So you think a Russian should die because of some foreigner . . . Vaska die? My Vaska?"

They looked at Vaska—he lay there white and thin.

The peasants felt bad.

Selivanov said to Afanasy Petrovich:

"Then you take him . . . and . . . a . . . perhaps . . .

let him go . . . let him die . . . that Kirghiz brat. A lot of them were killed anyway. It's all one . . ."

The peasants glanced at Vaska and went off silently.

Afanasy Petrovich seized the Kirghiz baby and wrapped him in a ripped bag.

The mother wailed. Afanasy punched her lightly in the teeth and went out of the camp into the steppe. . . .

VI

A day or two later the peasants were standing on tiptoes beside the entrance to the tent and looking over each other's shoulders inside where the Kirghiz woman was nursing the white child on a felt rug.

She had a submissive face with narrow eyes, like oat seeds; she wore a violet silk coat and small morocco boots.

The child was pounding his little face into her breast and patting her coat with his tiny hands; his legs were kicking comically and clumsily, as if he were hopping.

The peasants looked on with a mighty laugh.

The tenderest of them all was Afanasy Petrovich. Sniffling, he said tearfully:

"See, he really likes it! . . ."

But beyond the canvas tent ran the ravines, cliffs, steppe, alien Mongolia—no one knew where.

No one knew where Mongolia ran—Mongolia, the wild and joyless beast.

Translated by Thompson Bradley

IVAN KATAYEV

THE WIFE

The water flowed along broadside, thick in appearance and
smooth. Lowering my fingers into it, I was prepared to feel
even a slight coolness, but it turned out to be tepid, almost
impalpable. With his oars, Strigunov chased little eddies
along the water; they flew by me, spinning, toward the stern,
and disappeared. Their edges, bottle-green, with a soft melting bend seemed to me the height of gracefulness and I
became engrossed in the beauty of the water's lines, compa-
rable only to the lines of the human body—and the contour
of the descending captive Volkhov*, powerful and sleek as
the contour of a Greek back, and the sea wave, smoothly
arching its neck to break, and, as hissing foam, run up the flat
shore. At this moment we were overtaken by a boat with two
pair of oars. From the boat a young girl with lively curls set
loose from under a pink band, squealed:

"Hey, boys, don't get your pants wet!"

Her friend, sitting at the front oars, calmly laughed; her
face, pale with powder, was passionless and fat like a melon.
She said in a deep bass, referring to Strigunov:

"He's got frog glasses on, but doesn't know how to row."

Sitting at the rudder, their young man, in bow tie and a cap
shoved down on his nose, stretched a thick accordion. He

* Volkhov—a river near Novgorod.

was unconcernedly looking in the direction of the women's beach.

Strigunov disconcertedly looked about, hurriedly thinking up something caustic, but while he collected himself, the girls pushed on, laughing and trying to splash us: their boat started moving away. The accordion continued confidently to play "Little Bricks." The girl in the pink scarf picked up the melody in a high voice and over the river, like a mist, stirred that sadness always heard in a receding song.

Strigunov at last said embarrassedly:

"Well, what impudent babes! . . ." was silent, and added, "I don't think I row badly; they had no call for comment."

The oars in his hands jumped in complete disorder.

I smiled.

"Just don't dig so deeply. Bring them back further."

When we were getting into the boat Strigunov bravely rolled up his sleeves, and now it made me sad to see his thin, indoor-bluish arms. All of him is like that, narrow shouldered, kindly-decent, lacking in that live gaiety which moves through the body in one's blood; he was thoroughly gay only when, in his opinion, it was necessary for the purpose at hand.

Strange are these casual Moscow meetings with people who have been completely shoved aside and hidden by the years. Who plans those scrutinous glances which recognize you with difficulty in streetcars, baths, in the corridors of the Local Committee and Central Committee, those ecstatic and strained "ah's!," those cordial or cautious handshakes?

I met Strigunov in the regional committee building at an agitation-propaganda meeting which was never held. On a little balcony leading out into the garden sat some five people fruitlessly waiting. From above they contemplated a bitter struggle of a game of *gorodki** on the square next to a plaster Marx. One of them commented with a familiar, indignant stutter:

"The devil took someone to call a meeting on Saturday! People go swimming, go to the country. And as far as I can recall there's even a special pamphlet about Saturdays."

---

* A game played by striking a structure of chocks with a stick.

I looked around. His enormously round glasses in a black frame were in the way, but behind them were Strigunov's squinting eyes, the color of a November sky.

When the people who were waiting angrily scraped their chairs and left, cursing, we went off to go boating. And here is the dusty gold and blue Moscow River slipping under us and the smiling greenery of the Golitsin Hospital garden, the mossy sandstone of its embankment with two white columned rotundas, refracted at the edges and reflected with perfection in the sleeping water.

In the empty, burned-out July evening one perceives a certain repressed anticipation in this southwest corner of Moscow, separated by the Krymsky Bridge. Here one senses all the languid youth of a city born anew, striving to preserve and irretrievably squandering its energy.

The right bank—the ornate squalor of an exhibit with the faded blue of the Turkestan pavilion, faded like youth, like the memory of Asiatic wanderings. Then—an untouched farmstead remoteness of juicy orchards; the Golitsin, Neskuchny, Manon country homes, behind them, behind the Andreyev Home for the Aged—the genial bend of Vorobyovka.

The left bank—boring embankments, sluices, shacks covered with spittle, and the hesitant, rocking run of Number 24 along new tracks, laid on dogs' bones, necks of bottles, and building rubble, all the way out to the endless spaces of the ancient Pyshyn truck gardens—the great cabbage plantations. There is the undivided kingdom of huge, glum pigs, which wander, touching the earth with their nipples, around the rusty sheet metal shacks.

Dusty chronic July boredom rules over both banks, over this entire outskirt world. And fatigue, fatigue is in the dead air pierced by a hot sunset ray, in the orchards which lower their branches to the water, in the river which has already stilled and doesn't breathe.

But the silent gigs fly on the water, the upward stroke of ten oars like the sweet sigh of attention. The wooden amphitheaters of the bathhouses swarm with people, are mottled with striped bathing suits, glisten with bare shoulders. A ceaseless hubbub is all around—the thunder of wagons and streetcars on the bridge, the distant echoing of the railway station, the accordion and the flowing boating songs; and in the free, lightly flying sky sparkles a hydroplane like a silver dove in the Sunday heights.

"Here a city will be laid down"—a new city which will trample the desert of truck gardens and dumps, which will chain the rotten shores in granite; it will step over the river to the Vorobyovsky Hills. It is already being pulled here, beckoned by suntanned, golden-locked youth, rushing on light oars *à la brasse* and with a sharp shoulder cutting the waves, noisily splashing in a water-polo game.

We were approaching a railroad bridge. The blood-red flattened sun went behind the roof of a beer brewery; the exciting and fresh smell of beer wafted in the air; a cool shadow fell on the water. In this shade, damp and greenish, Strigunov's face, consumed by eyeglasses, seemed to me inhumanly skimpy, almost disappearing. I looked at his dry, sucked-in cheeks, at his light thin hair receding far back before the gulfs of his forehead. He rode intently, rocking back and forth, and was pleased with this occupation since it is recommended by the press and is especially valuable for those persons occupied in intense mental labor. He informed me of this when I proposed to take his place at the oars.

"A good thing, brother, this athletics. Up to now I somehow never had the time. Too much work, you know—academic, Party and lecturing, but, beginning this fall, I've already made a plan for myself to take up winter sports and the like. It's absolutely necessary."

I already knew from what he had told me that he was finishing the Science Research Institute to which he transferred from Sverdlovka*, that he already lectured somewhere at a workers' school and in night schools, and had even published a special article in the Institute monthly dedicated mainly to the reprimanding of heterodoxies. He already was, according to all evidence, an ideologist and an academician in embryo, popular in his circle, making jokes in his own way at meetings, in spite of his faint stuttering and

* Sverdlov Communist Institute.

constrained movements. He also happened to mention that his work was directly supervised by a prominent Party man.

I thought that Strigunov's life was probably rushed, but in its own way full and interesting. Then I remembered that he was married and asked:

"Well, and how is your wife? Varya, isn't it? Yes, Varya."

Strigunov put down his oars, looked aside and took off his glasses. Then he started wiping them with a handkerchief.

"Varya? All right, as usual." Keeping silent, he put on his glasses and added, "She lives near Moscow, in Zvenigorod, you know. Works in a library there, comes into town occasionally; she has the child, too."

"You have a child of your own already?"

"Well, sure—it'll be four years soon. A rather gifted little chap, name is Liebknecht."

"Why Liebknecht?"

"Well, just like that."

Strigunov shrugged as if from a sudden wind, buttoned his collar and resolutely took up the oars again.

I, however, recalled the story of his marriage, almost extinguished in my memory. And as soon as I thought of it, that distant year stood before me, as if it were yesterday, a troubled yet happy year, like all that is past.

I remembered Strigunov lying on the table in the printing office *Poarm*, which he was in charge of. He is lying on thick stacks of newspapers, covered with a coat, looking at the ceiling and dreamily scratching himself. Under his head is a fur cap. This is how I used to find him when I dropped in before midnight to pick up a fresh edition of the newspaper, printed with reddish ink on reddish wrapping paper. On the table a smoky lamp is winking—the commune supplied electric current in limited quantities. Behind the dusty barred windows, a wet southern February, the city drowning in black slush. We rolled cigarettes and smoked, spoke of demobilization, which according to all information was at hand, and of the fact that it wouldn't be bad to have something to eat now. The political department at the time distributed half a pound of crumbly cornbread and two rusty herrings apiece.

"You don't have anything?"

"Nothing."

"Well, we'll fall asleep without it. Good night."

I would go out into the night, the dirt, the rotten yellow fog, wrapping my overcoat tight.

In the spring, the sharp-eyed typesetters began to tease Strigunov. He was seen strolling in the gardens with the political department's chorister, Varya, a yellow-haired, fat-legged contralto. She lived in the neighboring village, an out-of-towner; her two brothers, strong boys, recently partisans, worked in a copper shop. Before the coming of our army, Varya sang in the church choir, then she joined us. She came to love Strigunov for his misery. As is the custom, the white acacia bloomed like mad, the little town was choking in the sweet, heady mist. They wandered along the streets, in the melon fields on the outskirts of town, stopped at the village. Varya's mother, an old woman, fed her guest sour milk; in the fall she fed him watermelon and eggplant, thinking that, although he was a skinny chap, he was, nonetheless, a commissar. The scorching August nights spent on the yellow grass by the shore of a clayey, turbulent little river completely weakened Varya. She stroked Strigunov's hair, kissed his hands; but Strigunov was serious, had lice, and most of all wanted to eat. He could stroll, ate eggplants and cornmush with ramson with pleasure, but didn't know how to do anything else. He went off to sleep in his office, on the stacks.

We, the members of the political department, knew of this through the printing office guard, who was from the same village as Varya (she once quietly complained to him and he talked about it later, embellishing it to the laughter of all the typesetters); we were used to the idea that nothing would come of it and were very amazed when Strigunov, one day in the fall, announced that he had been married the day before. He himself told us later on how it happened.

At night someone knocked on the window, he unlocked the door, and Varya entered. She stood awhile rolling and unrolling a ball of string, rattled the knobs on the abacus, and said:

"Let's go."

Strigunov asked where.

"Let's go, you'll find out when you get there."

He got angry:

"You've lost your mind! I won't go anywhere, I'm sleepy.
The typesetters will be here soon."

He got back up on the table and started wrapping himself
up in his coat. Then Varya went up to him, firmly took him by
the arm, pulled him off the table and led him out, protesting,
to the square. She led him to Commandant Street, opened
the door of some house with a key, and led him into a room.
There already stood a clean open bed, on the wall hung a
calendar and portrait of Lunacharsky.

"Here's where we'll live," announced Varya, "please don't
act the fool."

Strigunov stayed.

All of us, his buddies, were violently indignant on account
of such a bourgeois action on Strigunov's part; we foretold
that he would now become a petty old woman, and that,
generally, it was all over for him as a Party man. We teased
him:

"Well, man, they wrapped you up right well. Didn't have a
chance, did you? Just you wait—your mother-in-law will
make you milk the goat, salt melons. . . . What do you think
—they'll feed you for nothing?"

Strigunov smiled absentmindedly. But in about two weeks
we were convinced that not only didn't he go sour or deterio-
rate, but somehow became especially youthful. Even earlier,
he was one of the real talkers in the unit, spoke long and
confusedly on every issue, stressing rather his proletarian
descent—he was a Voronezh bookbinder.

"And I think, as a laborer, simply, that the whole question
here is of Menshevik eructation. . . ."

Now he began to speak more boldly, without reservation
and even longer. When Antoshkin, the property man and
wardrobe master of the political department's troupe, out of
hunger appropriated a general's uniform and sold it at the
bazaar for food, Strigunov solemnly and sternly, stuttering
nevertheless, demanded at the meeting immediate expulsion
of Antoshkin from the Party and handing him over for trial.
On that day, he was in particularly good form and seemed to
be rejoicing. Antoshkin was expelled and tried. After this
Strigunov started requesting to go to the big meetings, and
he was sent. Then he organized a live newspaper out of his

typesetters, went with them on a truck to factories, acted as master of ceremonies and, they say, provoked applause. It seemed that he felt behind him a trustworthy wall of caring adoration, clean clothes, planned meals, and came to believe in his own predestination.

Soon he invited us for pancakes.

We appeared at the little room on Commandant Street, a greedy and suspicious mob. Strigunov met us by a large table set with indescribably lovely things, including sour cream and salted watermelons. Varya appeared with a mountain of pancakes, a bit frightened, arms bare, and her cheeks rosy from the heat. We greeted her with a gay and greedy roar. At the height of the feast, Strigunov walked over to the window, looked along the street and then pulled out a fifth of cherry brandy from under the table. Up until then we had been gulping the greasy pancakes, cheeks puffed out, in religious silence, and became noisy only after a few glasses of wine which was sweet and smelled of beet juice. Later, everything became gayer. The supply of brandy didn't diminish, from somewhere a mandolin appeared in Strigunov's hands, he began to play it, sweetly holding his head to one side—we didn't know that he was the possessor of such talents. We asked Varya to dance and she floated off in slow motion, glancing at us with dignity and a distant fire in her eyes. We shouted songs, argued, excitedly recalled the shifts, deaths, blizzards of last year and the year before.

Taking our leave, satiated and filled with unusual braveness and inspiration, we shook Varya's hands for a long time and vowed her our friendship and passionate sympathy.

During the next several months, many of us began to joke that we were on the Strigunovs' rations. One could visit them at any time, have dinner and supper, of course—one at a time, sort of in turn. The village at first frowned upon Varya, her mother begged her in tears: "Secretly, but get married," but the jolly brothers, the coppersmiths, shut her up and the old lady gave up. The generous flow from the village didn't diminish, and Varya looked at our hollow cheeks, straining in motion while chewing, with an unchanging, kind curiosity. Gradually we were filled with gratitude and acceptance with regards to this marriage which worked out so well for everyone. We also knew that in the evenings Strigunov and Varya read Plekhanov and Maxim Gorky aloud, that she herself never mentioned the church and had already handed in an application to the Party. No come-down! Furthermore, the majority of us were hardly past twenty, this was the first marriage in our life, before our eyes, after so many years of male loneliness and neglect. We joyfully followed this marriage, knowing, each one to himself, that soon it would be our turn, too. At that time the wave of real loves, marriages, and hurried childbirths which later powerfully spread all over a Russia which was coming to itself after wars, famines, and wanderings, was just beginning to mount. This wave brought together lives which were formerly separated.

Toward the end of the winter, Strigunov went to Moscow for type. I began to drop in at Commandant Street rather frequently—only because Varya herself begged me to. On the next day after parting with her husband, she stubbornly, teeth clamped, longed for him, and I, better than the others, knew Strigunov, and could talk the most about him. Putting away the hot, thick, brown string-bean soup which Varya had cooked specially for me, I was supposed to, without rushing, tell of mine and Strigunov's misadventures on the Don and in the black city of Lugansk; of what a good, honest, working, talented, brave, inventive, kind chap Strigunov was, and how we all valued him. This wasn't a lie, because in those years all the people about me were really fine and loved one another.

There appears before me that little room, neatly kept and adequately heated, where on the wall, besides Lunacharsky, there is now a host of photographs, postcards and for some reason even Guy de Maupassant, with extravagant mustaches. The coal lamp fades, due to the evil pranks of the commune, and once again slowly glows to light. Varya's large cheekbones keep appearing out of the half darkness, then darken again. I lazily talk about Strigunov, swirling my spoon, and when I become silent, Varya gets up to give me more soup, or to put a piece of lamb with thick white fat on my plate. "Just keep talking, dear, I'll feed you to the hilt," I could read in Varya's movements. Well, what could I do? I kept talking. Then, having eaten so much that there was no room for anything more, I began taking my leave. Varya looked at me pleadingly, holding me tightly by the hand. Nonetheless, I left. I didn't feel anything toward her, only a cozy happiness because this year, after all, I didn't perish; I'm well-fed and my life is going to be a full one, and she, Varya, is also happy because she loves Strigunov, because she knows how to make life stable and clear. That's all. My time simply hadn't come yet.

Strigunov returned from Moscow with an even greater sense of direction and rather triumphant. He'd heard the leaders, he now knew everything first hand and would of course explain everything to us. Varya and I met him at the station, she clung to him, he concernedly kept tearing away from her, anxious about the unloading of the type. Afterward, she led him home by the hand, proudly looking about and didn't pay attention to me any more. Only at the door of the house did she point me out to Strigunov:

"Well, thank him; without him I would have died from sorrow. He was the only one who didn't forget me—kept coming over to console me."

Strigunov briefly glanced at me and thanked me. I said:

"Oh, come on, it's nothing."

Soon after returning, Strigunov burst out at all meetings, elucidating greatly and in detail the frightening, unexpected NEP.

Later he was demobilized before me and went to the north, taking Varya with him. The years were different, rosy; large apples fell in the orchards, large babies were born. . . .

. . . The boat gave a big bump and stopped. I came to. Evidently we had got stuck on some shallows. Strigunov was already fussing at the prow, ineptly pushing off with an oar. Over us, like a huge shadow, stood Vorobyovka; the sharp slopes were curled with groves; above, the lights at the trolley stop lit up, transparent and green like grapes. Over the other sloping shore a wide glow had already spread; low in the distance Moscow rustled and sighed in the faint twilight and also winked her first lights.

With concerted effort we got out of the shallows, changed places, and I hurried the boat back, going with the current. We were again quickly going past familiar shores: tree after tree, house after house went by, the hulk of the bridge moved closer and hid the spire of the rest home, then the rest home sprang into view again, and after it, the entire dim length of the river.

Strigunov, sprawled out in the stern and evidently slightly stirred by the quiet, the plashing, the clear color of the water and sky, began to speak more warmly, more thoughtfully of his work, plans, and whom he had met. Then he unobtrusively slipped into reminiscence, I encouraged him, and the past—persistent, still alive, quickened, became more defined. That's the way it always is when two people, looking into one another's eyes, enter its mists. I reminded Strigunov of the printing office, of the pancakes, of the argumentative battles at the Party army conference.

He laughed, remembering, and then said, trying to speak with feeling:

"Yes, friend, the good years—you can't knock them with anything. However, what were we then?—milksops, boys. Much of the foolishness that we perpetrated in those days is still being answered for. In personal life as well as generally . . . You say, a gay time, enthusiasm and so forth," he continued, although I hadn't said anything about enthusiasm, "but precisely for this, so to say, impulsiveness, some people have to pay. Take me. My life is now more or less organized, all roads are open, but one or two things weigh me down, are in my way, hamper me. . . ."

"What weighs you down?" I asked with studied disbelief, comprehending that he had softened up and would now probably tell me everything. I put down the oars. The boat slowly went with the current, on its own. Over the left bank the red glow had become fiercer and thicker; there, above, a hack, a group of people, the trolley mast, were impeccably drawn with india ink—black on red; a fine brush had drawn all the spokes in the wheel and the cane in a citizen's hand. Strigunov looked at all this frowning.

"You see," he said, "you know the circumstances of my marriage. I couldn't do otherwise at the time. Although, actually, nothing bound me to it. Well, I just got sucked into it, consumed. . . . And the girl, it seemed, was all right. . . . I'm speaking of Varya," he explained. "That is exactly what weighs me down. That is, I haven't done anything with respect to this; the issue isn't resolved for me yet. I don't know if it will be resolved. The thing is, that we haven't separated finally, because she doesn't want to, and I'm also bearing with it. All of this drags on for us, because we haven't the strength to break it, although it has been clear for a long time that nothing can come of it. It didn't work out—period. It's a long story to tell, but the point is, that we have an unequal marriage, rather like a morganatic one, you know—they had them before.

"You laugh—what nonsense, the times, so to speak, are different—but those are the facts. How did it happen? Well, at first, you know yourself, I started making her over, developing her, or whatever. We read and discussed together. She's rather gifted and she assimilated quickly. And it was hard for her because—well why? The village, pots and pans, an orthodox mother; the regent in the cathedral choir—he was for her the top man—a philosopher! And what sort of a pedagogue was I then? Myself of proletarian descent, taught the value of a jug of milk. At first, together with her, we really did accomplish a thing or two. She was accepted into the Party, demobilization, Voronezh, Moscow—there she really got going. I went to Sverdlovka and she, we decided, would stay awhile with practical work, since we needed money—didn't have a dime between us. She went to work as a salesgirl—she wanted to sing, but it didn't work out—in Moscow they have enough singers without her. But nevertheless she worked in a unit and went to lectures and meetings in the Polytechnicum and the Colonnade Hall.

"In general she began to develop noticeably, figured everything out independently, conversed with everyone who dropped in to see me—we lived in a family dorm—made comments which were rather to the point. I'd look at her and say: My Varya is coming up! Excellent, very good. It's true, though, she didn't read very much—not enough time and not in the habit—used to it only with me. And I, of course, didn't have much time left for her—only at night. Sverdlovka, brother, spins you about, gets all of you, head and hands. Also, I had a great desire to study; too many meetings in those years, I gave of myself and more of myself, with no replenishments. However, Varya went about energetically

and was rather happy, although she missed me a bit. . . .
She really loved me. And how! I'd pulled her out of a hole;
she saw what is called the light, through me: new people, new
horizons—Moscow. . . . Well, everything was going along
—she worked, ran about. Planned to study the next year. And
then, suddenly, how do you do!—pregnancy, a baby. . . .
The delivery was a difficult one, broke her up quite a bit.

"Well, as for me—I came home after the club sessions,
took a look at the child, petted him, laughed a bit. But for her
there was really a lot of fuss. Then they increased the curriculum
for us at Sverdlovka. She didn't go back to work after the
allotted leave—she was allowed not to work. And so it went.
My work—the further I went, the more there was; studies got
more difficult, they gave me a Party assignment on a regional
scale. So, of course, I went to the theater with the boys, and
to debates—this is also enlightenment. As for Varya, she, of
course, couldn't leave the baby. When I did ask her to go out
and suggested she get a nurse—it can be done cheaply—she
herself didn't want to go. But still her mood at the time was
pretty good—a lot of work, no time to think; although we had
begun to quarrel now and then—can't avoid that: I was nervous
from the constant rush and so was she. Furthermore,
the honeymoon doesn't last for a lifetime. It got worse as
time went on. As a result, understandably, she got completely
behind. She went to meetings infrequently; well,
meetings only help in the beginning, then you've got to act
on your own. I, on the contrary, moved fast, was completely
reborn. New thoughts, new demands. Comrades would visit
me, we'd talk, but for Varya this was all Chinese; she'd remain
silent. But she wanted, unquestionably, to be interesting to
me and to show my friends that Strigunov's wife was no fool,
no bourgeois. She became sad, took up her books again,
tried to talk. But whatever she said never hit the mark. We'd
try to pretend that we didn't notice, but she herself did, and
blushed; and it wasn't very comfortable for me. Another year
went by and she somehow entered the *Rabfac*—they accepted
her only as a first-year student. But me!—I was far ahead;
there was no catching me. I had already finished Sverdlovka
(may I add, brilliantly), I was sent to the Science Research
Institute. Here all the people are finer, thoroughly educated,

and I wasn't doing so badly myself. As for Varya . . . How can I put it to you? . . . She began to irritate me more and more."

Strigunov became silent and rubbed the tip of his nose.

"Well, since I've begun, I must finish. And the end is short. The whole thing is, that if Varya didn't love me so much, if she didn't drag herself after me, then probably it would be easier for me. Because I can see how frightened she is, actually shaking, that I'll get fed up with her, that I don't need her. So—she's not attractive—but you can live with her, though she's become rather bossy, sort of hasty. She keeps looking into my eyes, asks me about everything, tries to give me good advice. And what sort of advice! I'm a frank person; sometimes I tell her that she's talking nonsense, and then she looks at me with terrible eyes. Cries at night, I say: 'Cut it out, Varya, tears won't help; you have to study, work on yourself.' She wouldn't say anything.

"As for the *Rabfac,* things were pretty tight for her there— maybe the child hindered her. She was left back the first year. Well, then a curious thing happened. Last summer she went away with the child to a resort. Took a load of books with her. I took a deep breath—a load off my back. I had become part of a close circle at the Institute. We went to the country, drank a bit together, although I don't like to. When Varya is around, all of this is out—she's jealous. Not that she makes scenes, but her looks are enough to make your heart wilt. Excuse the expression, her eyes are like a beaten dog's. Then letters started coming from her. Often in very thick packets. I'd take a look at them in my spare time and saw that she was crucifying herself in them for me. Showing herself off. Here was ideology for you, and quotations, and all sorts of landscapes. The sun goes down, the sun comes up, clouds, rivers. Not bad, by the way. It turns out she's observant and that her style is good. Even I felt drawn to nature's bosom. I wrote her about this, praised her. So she covered me with them— Leo Tolstoy or Lebedinsky, no less! Ten pages each, and all about the beautiful nature which surrounds their resort. What an amazing place, I thought, a blessing.

"Then she returns, tanned, happy, and the child looked better—it was a pleasure to look at him. Oho, I said, Lyonka

(we call him Lyonka for short), time for you to join the
Pioneers soon. And Varya is happy—I'd paid attention—and
immediately began to suck up to me. Well, all right, I'd also
missed her a bit—you can't live without a dame in our time of
plenty. The next morning she went to the market and I sat
down at the table, thinking. The books that Varya had
brought with her were stacked on the table. Mechanically I
leafed through them, glanced at the pages, and suddenly
something sticks me right in the heart. I'm looking at *A
Sportsmen's Notebook*—something is very familiar. I took
Varya's letters out of the drawer, started comparing, and
became horrified. Mother, mine! She copied, copied everything, all the descriptions, like a schoolgirl! From Turgenev,
from Chekhov . . . the places were marked with crosses in
the margins. She even took from Stepniak-Kravchinsky. Copied everything about the sunsets from 'A House on the
Volga.' . . . I almost choked. To me, her husband! Well, all
right, I thought. . . . She returned; I had weighed it in my
mind and decided that such doings are not to be forgiven—
it's ridiculous and stupid. I led her by the shoulders up to the
table, opened the books, got the letters and said: 'Well,
Varya, I've made some discoveries here while you were out.'
She understood everything, dashed to the books, slammed
them shut, held them down with her hands and looked at me,
pale as paper and her eyes were huge, as if death were before
her. I even became frightened. 'What for, Varya,' I said. 'This
is, of course, a trifle, although it is a bit ridiculous.' At this
point she rushed to me, pressed herself to me and burst into
tears, and how! I put her to bed, calmed her. She stopped
crying, just bit her lip and breathed heavily. I wanted to be
done with the matter and told her in the end, more or less
gently, that I was ready to forgive her this deception, because
most of all she was deceiving herself by this, and that this
method of attracting her husband was both naïve and pathetic and nothing more. And suddenly, can you imagine, at
these words she leaps up, grabs me by the hair and bites me
in the chest, in the shoulders and the devil knows where,
while screaming and thrashing. I tore myself from her, although she had already thrust herself away and had fallen to
the wall, trembling. She was waiting for me to beat her or

something. Her face was distorted, disgusting. A great rage, you understand, rose in me, also; just to give it to her once, so she'd crack. But I remembered myself in time—what am I, a Party member or not? Really! I turned and left, didn't even slam the door. That's the whole story."

Strigunov was silent.

"But it isn't actually. We made up, of course. I gave her a real tongue-lashing, pointing out the savageness of her behavior. She asked forgiveness, I forgave her. But naturally, everything got much worse after that. For a long time now, I can't stand the sight of her, can't bear her. She's awkward, big and healthy. She walks at a distance, her heels rattle, and I twitch all over. And she's become completely stupid, speaking entirely objectively. Maybe when she's not with me, she's all right, but when she is, out of fright and effort, she'll pull something that makes everyone exchange glances.

"So, she doesn't want to separate, she begs me, saying she'll improve; and I'm not throwing her out—where could she really go? Although she's still in the Party, she has no qualifications. I could keep the child with myself—he's a big boy by now. Well, so, in May she finally came to the conclusion that she is unhappy with me, and through the MC she left for Zvenigorod, leaving the *Rabfac,* I think. She works as a librarian at the club. She comes sometimes with her son, hangs around, looks at me ecstatically—she's pleased that I am a candidate for a doctorate—and makes me unhappy. I couldn't say that I'm having an affair with someone, no, I'm careful about such things now, and I don't have the time. But still, every day I see a countless number of intelligent, elegant and developed women who wouldn't keep Varya for a cook. Who knows—maybe I will fall in love some day, the devil likes to play around, and there you are—this thing is getting me down. A sad remnant, so to say, of war communism. . . . I'm fed up! . . . That's the bit, brother. . . ."

It was dark all around but still the air was saturated with the glowing of space. The sky above us became deep and greenish, foretelling a calm August. The quays spilled into the water like golden flames. Over Zamoskvorechye and Khamovniki floated the same condensed rumble, reflected by the water and the ring of the hilly shore. At the exhibit the carousel drum boomed, the wind orchestra sang out dreamy waltzes, flowing into the general hubbub, into a solitary song of a Saturday world and unending labor.

Here, right past the Krymsky Bridge, next to the former handicraft pavilion, two solitary many-storied houses once stood on the empty lot. In one of them I lived and met the week of October battles which was so horrible for me. In the pavilion there was, at the time, a military plant evacuated from Warsaw.

In back of the house where the exhibit is now housed, were gardens where I went skiing in winter; right there on the shore, during the week of battles, stood a Bolshevik three-bore gun, firing at the Kremlin. All the windows in the house burst. The first post-October months whirled me off like a leaf, and I got back here only in 1919. Passing along the Krymsky rampart, I glanced at my house and saw the sky through it: it was destroyed or had burned down—I don't know, except that everything had crumbled inside of it and the bare beams stuck out. In '23 both houses were torn down to make way for the exhibit. They are no more. I can only point at the air and say: Here, on the fourth floor, was our dining room. I can also close my eyes and recall that house as you recall the face of a person who has died.

Three currents of time had come together in me after Strigunov's story. They enveloped my heart in the hot steam of excitement, and for the first time I felt this city not as a collection of streets, people and institutions, but all of it together, how it lies on the fields, and through the years, with me and without me, surrounded by its parks and railroad stations in a network of routes, in the ring of its seventeen counties.

The western night wind flies over Zvenigorod and cools Varya's hot cheeks—I haven't seen them for six years; then the river Moscow, a misty white ribbon snakes below, in the fields, then the country settlements, gardens, stifling canals of streets, and now the wind is ruffling my hair while I silently press on the oars.

Translated by Natalie Bienstock

VALENTIN KATAYEV

"OUR FATHER WHO ART IN HEAVEN"

"I want to sleep. I'm cold."

"Lord! I want to sleep too. Get dressed. And that's enough nonsense. Enough. Put on your scarf. Put on your cap. Put on your boots. Where are your mittens? Stand still. Stop squirming."

When the little boy was dressed, she took him by the hand and they left the house. The boy was not yet fully awake. He was four years old. He shivered from the cold and stumbled along. It was just beginning to get light. There was a frosty blue fog outside. The mother tightened the scarf on the boy's neck, straightened his collar, and kissed his sleepy, mischievous face.

The dry wild grape vines, hanging from the broken-down wooden arcades, seemed sugary from the hoarfrost. It was twenty-five degrees below zero. Thick steam poured out of their mouths. The courtyard was littered with ice-covered garbage.

"Mama, where are we going?"

"I told you—for a walk."

"Then why did you take a suitcase?"

"Just because. Now be quiet. Don't chatter. Keep your mouth closed or you'll catch cold. You see how cold it is. Better look where you're going or you'll slip."

A doorman dressed in a sheepskin coat and a white apron with a nameplate on his chest stood at the gate. She walked past him without looking. He closed the door silently behind them and fastened it with a great iron hook. They set out along the street. There was no snow—everything was covered with ice and frost. And wherever there was neither ice nor frost there was smooth stone or earth as smooth and hard as stone. They walked under the bare, black acacia trees which were shaking resiliently in the cold.

The mother and son were dressed almost identically. They wore quite good coats made of artificial monkey-fur, soft leather boots and gaily colored wool mittens. The mother wore a checked kerchief on her head and the son wore a round monkey-fur cap with ear-flaps. The street was deserted. When they reached the crossing, the loudspeaker of the public address system gave such a loud crackle that the woman started. But she realized at once that the morning broadcast was beginning. As usual, it began with the crowing of a rooster. The exceedingly loud voice of the rooster shouted musically along the length of the street, heralding the beginning of a new day. The boy looked up at the loudspeaker.

"Mama, is that a rooster?"

"Yes, darling."

"Isn't he cold up there?"

"No, he's not cold up there. Now don't squirm. And watch where you're going."

Then the loudspeaker crackled again, and a gentle, childish voice repeated with angelic tones:

"Good morning! Good morning! Good morning!"

Then the same voice, slowly, with great feeling, recited the prayer:

"Our Father Who art in heaven, hallowed be Thy name, Thy kingdom come, Thy will be done . . ."

On the corner the woman turned away from the wind and almost ran up the alley, dragging the boy behind her, as if this too loud and too gentle voice were pursuing her. Soon the voice stopped. The prayer was finished. The wind blew from the sea across the icy passages of the streets. Ahead of them a bonfire was blazing, surrounded by a crimson fog, with a German guard warming himself beside it. The woman turned and crossed to the other side. The boy ran beside her, stamping his little leather boots. His cheeks were as red as cranberries. A frozen drop hung beneath his nose.

"Mama, are we taking a walk now?" the little boy asked.

"Yes, we are."

"I don't like to walk so fast."

"Be patient."

They walked through a courtyard and came out on another street. It was already light. The pink dawn shone brittlely through light and dark blue clouds of steam and hoarfrost. It was so cold that one's jaws shut and puckered just from its rosy color as from something sour. Several people appeared on the street. They walked in one direction. Almost all of them carried bundles. Some pushed their bundles before them on carts, or dragged along loaded sleds that scratched the bare pavement with their runners.

From all ends of the city, on this morning, people with heavy loads trudged slowly in one direction, like ants. These were Jews on their way to the ghetto. The ghetto was set up in the Peresip district, in that dull, depressed part of the city where scorched oil tanks stood at sea level, looking like traveling circus tents. The Fascists had surrounded a few dirty blocks with two rows of rusty barbed wire and left only one entrance, as in a mousetrap. The Jews made their way under the railroad bridges. They slipped on the icy sidewalks. There were old people among them who couldn't walk and some people sick with typhus. These were carried on stretchers. Some would fall down and remain lying there, leaning back against a lamp post or hugging an iron hitching post. Nobody was escorting them to the ghetto. They were going there by themselves, without any convoy. They knew that whoever stayed home would be shot. Therefore they were going by themselves. Anyone who gave shelter to a Jew would also be shot. For one hidden Jew everyone living in the apartment would be shot, without exception. From all parts of the city, along steep slopes, under railroad bridges, the Jews made their way to the ghetto, pushing their wheelbarrows before them, leading their bundled children by the hand. They walked one behind the other, like ants, passing houses and frost-covered trees. They walked past locked doors and gates, past smoky bonfires where German and

Rumanian soldiers warmed themselves. The soldiers paid no attention to the Jews and went on warming themselves, stamping their boots and rubbing their ears with their mittens.

It was horribly cold. It was unusually cold even for a northern city. But for Odessa it was simply monstrous. Such cold hits Odessa once in thirty years. A tiny circle of sun shone weakly through clouds of thick blue and green steam. Hardened sparrows lay on the highways, killed in mid-flight by the cold. The sea was frozen to the very horizon. It was white. The wind blew in from it.

The woman looked like a Russian. The boy also looked Russian. The boy's father was a Russian. But this meant nothing: the mother was a Jew. They were required to go to the ghetto. The boy's father was an officer in the Red Army. The woman had torn up her passport and had thrown it into the ice-covered toilet that morning. She had gone out of the house with her son, counting on walking about the city until everything calmed down. She thought she'd manage it somehow. It was insane to go to the ghetto. That meant certain death. And so she had begun to walk about the city with her son, trying to avoid the most crowded streets. At first, thinking that they were taking a walk, the boy was quiet. But soon he began to misbehave.

"Mama, why are we walking all the time?"

"We're taking a walk."

"We never walk so fast. I'm tired."

"Be patient, darling. I'm also tired. But you see I'm not misbehaving."

She noticed that she really was walking too fast, almost running, as if someone were chasing her. She made herself slow down. The boy looked up at her and hardly recognized her. He saw with horror her swollen, bitten lips, the lock of hair, gray with frost, hanging untidily out of her kerchief, and her fixed, harsh, glassy eyes. That kind of eyes he had seen before only on his toy animals. She was looking at her watch and didn't see him. Squeezing his little hand, she dragged the boy behind her. He grew frightened. He began to cry.

"I want to go home. I want to go peepee."

Hastily she led him behind a billboard covered with German notices. While she unbuttoned and then buttoned him, shielding him from the wind, the boy continued to cry and shake from the cold. When they began to walk again he cried that he was hungry. She took him to a milk-bar, but two Rumanian policemen in heavy fur coats and dogskin collars were eating there; because she had no documents and was afraid they'd be arrested and sent to the ghetto, she pretended she had walked into the wrong store by mistake. She excused herself and quickly slammed the door. The boy ran after her, understanding nothing and crying. The next milk-bar was empty. Relieved, they crossed the doorstep with a horseshoe nailed to it. There the woman bought a bottle of fermented milk and a thick roll for the boy. The bundled little boy, sitting on a tall chair, drank the fermented milk, which he loved, and chewed on the roll and she thought feverishly about what to do next. She could think of nothing. But there was an iron stove burning in the milk-bar and at least they could warm up. It seemed to the woman that the proprietress of the milk-bar was looking at her too carefully. She quickly began to pay the bill. The proprietress looked out of the window uneasily and invited the woman to sit by the stove a while longer. The stove was red-hot. It was almost cherry-colored, a little darker. Sparks flew about from it. The heat made the boy sleepy. He could hardly keep his eyes open. But the woman began to fidget. She thanked the proprietress and told her she was in a hurry. But still they sat there for nearly an hour. The sleepy, full little boy could hardly stand on his feet. She shook him by the shoulders, straightened his collar and pushed him lightly toward the door. He stumbled over the horseshoe. The woman took the boy's hand and again led him along the street. The street was lined with old plane trees. They walked by the dappled plane trees with their soft, frost-covered bark.

"I want to go to sleep," said the little boy, screwing up his face from the icy wind.

She pretended she didn't hear him. She knew that their situation was desperate. She had almost no friends in the city. She had come here two months before the war began and then found herself stranded. She was completely alone.

"My knees are frozen," the little boy whimpered.

She took him to one side and rubbed his knees. He quieted down. Suddenly she remembered that there was, after all, one family in the city whom she knew. They had met on the steamer *Georgia* on the way from Novorossiisk to Odessa and then several times afterward. This was the young Pavlovskys: he was an instructor at the University, and she had just finished the building trades' school. Her name was Vera. The women had taken a liking to each other and had managed to become friends while the steamer was going from Novorossiisk to Odessa. They had visited each other a few times afterward. The men too had become friends—once they had even gotten drunk together. Another time they had all gone together to a soccer game—Kharkov vs. Odessa. The Pavlovskys had rooted for Odessa; she and her husband had rooted for Kharkov. Odessa won. God, what went on then in that huge new stadium overlooking the sea! Screams, howls, columns of dust . . . They almost came to blows. But now it was only pleasant to think about. Pavlovsky was out of town, in the Red Army. But Vera was stranded too, hadn't managed to get evacuated. Recently she had seen Vera in the Alexandrovsky market, and they had even chatted for a while. But it wasn't safe to stop too long at the market place. The Germans started round-ups almost every day. The women spoke for hardly five minutes. They hadn't met since then. But probably Vera was in the city. Where else could she go? The Pavlovskys were Russians. She might try to sit it out at Vera's. In any case, she could leave the boy there. The Pavlovskys lived quite far away, on Pirogovskaya and the corner of Frantsuzky Boulevard. The woman turned around.

"Where are we going, Mama? Home?"

"No, darling, we're going visiting."

"Where?"

"Do you remember Aunt Vera Pavlovsky? We're going to visit Aunt Vera Pavlovsky."

"Good," said the boy, reassured. He loved to go visiting. He became more cheerful.

They walked across the Stroganovsky Bridge over the street leading to the harbor. The street was called Karantinny Hill. Below stood a group of rectangular sandstone houses. Some of them had been reduced to piles of rubble.

Some had been burned down. The round arches of another bridge could be made out at the bottom of the hill and beyond the arches the angular ruins of the harbor came into view. Farther still, above the burned-out, fallen rooftops lay the white sea, frozen to the horizon. On the horizon itself a band of unfrozen water shone deep blue. Several Rumanian troop-ships painted lead gray stood in the ice near the ruins of the famous Odessa lighthouse. Above the city on the mountain, far off to the left, the dome of the municipal theater shone like a sea shell through clouds of pink and delicate light-blue steam. The fencing of the Stroganovsky Bridge was made up of a long row of high, iron spikes. The spikes were a severe black. Below, people were climbing up Karantinny Hill with buckets. The water splashed out of the buckets and froze on the pavement, glistening like glass in the opaque light of the pink sun. All this was very beautiful. If worse came to worse, they could stay for a while at the Pavlovskys' and figure out what to do next.

They walked a very long time. The boy was tired but did not misbehave. He tramped on quickly in his little leather boots, just managing to keep up with his mother. He wanted to get to Aunt Vera's as fast as possible. He loved to go visiting. His mother wiped his whitened cheeks several times on the way. A bonfire was burning on the sidewalk next to the house where the Pavlovskys lived and some soldiers were warming themselves around it. The house was large, divided into several sections. The gate was locked with a chain. A round-up was going on. The documents of everyone going in and out were being checked. Pretending she was in a hurry, the woman walked past the gate. No one paid any attention to her. The boy began to misbehave again. Then she took him in her arms and began to run, stamping her feet on the dark-blue lava-stone sidewalk. The boy calmed down. Again she began to roam about the city. It seemed to her that she was appearing in the same places too often and that people were beginning to notice her. Then she had the idea of spending a few hours at the movies. The showing started early since to be on the street after eight was forbidden on pain of death.

She felt nauseated and dizzy in the close, smelly hall,

packed with soldiers and prostitutes driven in there, like
herself, by the cold. But at least it was warm and they could
sit down. She undid the scarf on the boy's neck and he fell
right asleep, clutching her arm with both hands. She sat
through two shows without leaving the hall, barely following
what was happening on the screen. It seemed to be a war
newsreel and then a comedy or something like that: she
couldn't catch the thread of it. Everything was muddled.
Sometimes the screen was filled with the head of a pretty girl
with blond ringlets snuggling her cheek against the flat chest
of a tall headless man, then they would sing a duet, then the
girl would get into a sleek sports car, then sometimes there
were black fountains of explosions, one, two, three, four in a
row—with a tinny roar as if someone were tearing roofing
iron into long strips—one, two, three, four strips in one
stroke while black hunks of earth came down like hail, striking the tin drum, and tanks crawled along the shell-scarred
earth with funeral crosses, grinding and plunging and shooting still longer tongues of flame and whirling streams of
white smoke.

A German soldier wearing embroidered felt boots and a
Russian fur cap with ear-flaps was leaning heavily against the
woman's shoulder and tickling the boy's cheek with a big,
dirty finger, trying to wake him up. He smelled strongly of
garlic and raw alcohol. He laughed good-naturedly all the
while, repeating idiotically, "Don't sleep, bube. Don't sleep,
bube."

"Bube" means "little boy" in German. The boy didn't
wake up, but only moved his head slightly and whimpered in
his sleep. Then the German dropped his heavy head on the
woman's shoulder, putting one arm around her, and began
to knead the little boy's face with the other hand. The woman
kept quiet, afraid of making the soldier angry. She was afraid
he'd ask to see her documents. The German smelled of
smoked fish. She was nauseated but made a terrific effort not
to flare up. She kept persuading herself to stay calm. After
all, the German wasn't doing anything especially awful. He
was simply a boor. An altogether decent Fritz. Bearable.
Moreover, the German soon fell asleep on her shoulder. She

sat without moving. The German was very heavy. But she was glad he was asleep.

The girl with the blond ringlets moved across the screen again, and long shafts of black and white rays moved through the whole theater with her. And with an iron roar the black fountains flew up, and tanks crawled on, and German battalions marched across the desert sands, and an enormous German flag was mounted on the top of the Eiffel Tower, and Hitler with a little sharp nose and a lady's chin barked out from the screen, sticking out his womanish rear end, rolling his eyes and opening and closing his mouth very quickly. He opened and closed his mouth so quickly that the sound came a little behind: arf, arf, arf, arf. . . .

Soldiers were pinching girls in the dark and the girls were squealing. The hall was terribly hot and stuffy and smelled of garlic, smoked fish, raw alcohol, aspirin and the Rumanian perfume "Chat-Noir." Still and all, it was better here than out in the cold. The woman had rested a bit. The boy had had enough sleep. But the last show was over and they had to go out again. She took the boy by the hand and they set out. The city was completely dark. Only the dense, frosty steam curled in among the darkened houses. It made one's eyelashes stick together. Smoking bonfires, almost smothered by the cold, were burning in the streets. Somewhere, from time to time, solitary shots rang out. Patrols walked up and down the streets. It was after eight. She picked up the sleepy child and began to run, almost out of her mind from the one thought that a patrol might stop them. She chose the most deserted alleys. Plane trees and acacias, covered with frost, lined the streets like ghosts. The city was empty and dark. From time to time a door would open in that blackness, and along with the bright band of light suddenly lighting up the frozen cars by the entrance, the passionate, piercing squeak of a violin rushed out for a moment. The woman ran safely to the Shevchenko Park of Culture and Rest. The enormous park lay along the sea. Here all was quiet, forsaken. It was especially quiet down below, at the bottom of the precipice by the sea frozen to the horizon. Silence as thick as a wall lay over the sea. A few big stars twinkled above the white branches of the trees. The light blue beam of a searchlight slid among the stars.

She walked along the broad asphalt pathway. On the left was the very same stadium where they had all gone together for the Odessa-Kharkov match. Beyond the wreckage of the stadium was the sea. It wasn't visible in the dark, but one could sense it right away from the silence. The park stretched out to the right. The broad asphalt pathway glittered like emery paper in the starlight. As the woman walked along she noted the different species of trees. Here were catalpas with their long pods hanging almost to the ground like strings. And here were pyramidal acacias, plane trees, thuyas, vinegar trees. Covered with heavy frost, they melted together and bent down to the ground like clouds. She took a deep breath and walked more slowly along the endlessly long row of empty benches. But on one of the benches someone was sitting! She walked by with a pounding heart. The black figure, its head leaning on the back of the bench, didn't move. The woman noticed then that the person was half covered with frost, like a tree. Above the black cupola of the observatory which rose up among the white clouds of the park twinkled the cut-glass stars of the Big Dipper. It was very quiet and not at all frightening here. Maybe it wasn't frightening because the woman was so tired.

And the next morning, before it was completely light, trucks drove through the city picking up the bodies of people who had frozen during the night. One truck drove slowly along the broad asphalt pathway in the Shevchenko Park of Culture and Rest.

The truck stopped twice. It stopped first at the bench where a frozen old man was sitting. It stopped a second time by the bench where a woman and a little boy were sitting. She was holding the boy by the hand. They were sitting side by side. They were dressed almost identically. They wore quite good coats made of artificial monkey-fur, soft leather boots and gaily colored wool mittens. They were sitting as if alive, only their faces, covered with frost during the night, were completely white and fluffy, and a fringe of ice hung from their eyelashes. When the soldiers picked them up they didn't straighten out. The soldiers swung around and threw the woman, her legs still in a sitting position, into the truck. She knocked against the old man like a piece of wood. Then the soldiers swung around and lightly threw in the boy, his legs still in a sitting position. He knocked against the woman like a piece of wood and bounced back a little.

As the truck was rolling away, a rooster began to crow from the loudspeaker of the public address system, heralding the beginning of a new day. Then a gentle childish voice repeated with angelic tones:

"Good morning! Good morning! Good morning!"

Then the same voice, slowly, with great feeling, recited the Lord's Prayer:

"Our Father Who art in heaven, hallowed be Thy name, Thy kingdom come . . ."

Translated by Marie Winn

VENYAMIN KAVERIN

THIS MORNING

The last ten-spot on which he put his last hope flew up on the rake and, flashing its white wings, vanished in the air.

Skalkovsky wiped his forehead, glanced at his sweaty hands, sighed, and came out of his daze.

Everything was finished. He had to make an effort to take his eyes off the irretrievable horizon of the green gaming fields. Yes, everything was finished. He had lost everything, he was ruined. He sank, catching at his own eyeglasses. In his stead a small, downcast wretch, his head all a-sweat, cringed in his chair.

"Hold the place for me, croupier," he muttered, getting up and drawing a cigarette case out of his pocket. "I'll be back in around fifteen minutes."

Swinging like a pendulum he made his way into the lobby and stopped, folding his hands behind his back.

"So that's that," he reflected vaguely. "Yes, that's the way it is."

But this time there was nothing behind those habitual, empty expressions, behind the "that's the way it is." Instead, a certain memory which he was vainly trying to dispel throbbed in his temples with the persistence of a savage.

The memory of his wife with upraised arms and pale face throbbed there. What, after all, is a loss? . . . It's nothing, the end of an unlucky day, that's all! He wouldn't even have been in this smoke-filled club, had he not this morning . . .

"I'm not lucky . . . neither in love nor at cards," he muttered gloomily. "Still, another ten, another five rubles and . . . I'd win it all back. I know, I'm convinced I'd win it back."

He crossed the lobby several times, crushing his dead, sweaty cigarette into a lump. Everything was gloomy, hostile, mean. Only one thing was clear: he must flee. But how could he flee when the last ten-spot on which he had put his last hope . . . ?

"So now," he continued to reflect, "now I must . . . I must tell. . . . But no, I must win back what I lost. Now . . ."

Only then did he notice some sort of confusion and commotion in the lobby. A woman in an orange-colored hat who had been standing at the lottery table suddenly sat down on the floor and began to rummage about with her hands. She looked like someone who had been executed or was about to be executed. Mechanically waving her arms, she abruptly got off her knees and shouted something.

Skalkovsky came closer, glanced at her distractedly and hastily jumped back. The sullen mouth of the woman in the orange-colored hat was shouting about him, Skalkovsky. Unbelieving, he understood that she was accusing him of theft, and with a trembling hand he began to adjust his eyeglasses.

"You must be crazy, God help you, you must be crazy," he muttered in dismay and unwittingly began to make his way quickly toward the exit.

"But what am I doing!" flashed through his mind. He dashed aside and ran out of the club.

The empty, slushy street came full against him, against his burning face and hands. "I mustn't turn around," he muttered and turned. Motley figures of clowns with red triangles on their cheeks and livid foreheads rushed at him from the posters. The crowd in front of the club was going off in various directions, and an ever-present policeman's cap flashed above the yellow blotches of faces.

Skalkovsky shuddered, took a step backward and convulsively swallowed his saliva. He was still under the impression that he was walking along unhurriedly in the street trying not to attract any attention, but for a minute or two now he had

been running full speed, his head buried in his shoulders, his
hand on his eyeglasses.

Without looking back—something now prevented him
from looking back—he raced up to the corner. They were
running after him, he clearly heard the sound of boots on the
pavement; they shouted something. They were running after
him, they were catching him, another ten minutes and he
would be standing before an examining judge or public prosecutor, and the judge or prosecutor would question him not
about the theft, no, not about the theft . . . Rather, why the
upraised arms and pale face of his wife throbbing in his
temples, and whether he, Citizen Skalkovsky, pleaded guilty
to what happened this morning?

The policeman's cap again flashed behind him. He tore
ahead and a greenish, rectangular square, empty like a theater in the morning, suddenly appeared in front of him near
the edge of the bridge he had just left behind.

And in this square a covered automobile with red crosses
on its sides moved slowly.

The automobile turned up before Skalkovsky's eyes the
way an unlucky card turns up, the four of clubs, on which he
lost almost everything that he had lost this evening. It turned
up on the greenish square as on a gaming table, and just as it
was impossible to set oneself against the verdict of the unlucky card, so it was impossible not to hurl oneself toward the
cross-covered automobile.

"Especially," he thought vaguely, "since no one will think
of looking for me in an ambulance . . . It's empty, I'll go no
more than a block. . . ."

He caught hold of the handrail, jumped onto the running
board, but stumbled and hit his face against the cold side of
the vehicle.

Something quickly tinkled on his face, on the running
board, on the cobblestones, and the whole world confined
within the rectangular square foundered before him, impetuously losing its outline.

"Broke my glasses," he said confusedly and bent down,
but the ground—the wet cobblestones, the tracks, the thaw-
ing snow—was already speeding away from under his feet
and slowly stuck to the tires.

With an uncertain hand he threw open the door of the automobile and stuck in his head. He saw almost nothing: a dull, frosted glass seemed to loom and dissolve before his eyes.

A sudden jolt almost made him fall off the running board. He got a firmer grip on the handrail, turned on his heels and fell back into the ambulance. No, he did not merely imagine that he had seen a frosted window: he could reach it with his hand.

Like a street urchin, the street light played about in the frosted window, and the round, blank ceiling rocked up there, on top, like a shaky, faltering sky.

"The door, shut the door!"

Skalkovsky raised himself to his knees and looked around with careless persistence.

"I must have been hearing things, there is no one here," he thought and sat down on the stretcher.

"Shut the door! It's cold, there's a draft. . . ."

A green light with feverish eyes appeared beneath the frosted window and, moving up and down, settled on Skalkovsky's face. He shrank back, raised himself, slammed the door.

"What's the matter with you?"

"I'm all right," muttered Skalkovsky.

"Then you must be the doctor. Or are you an orderly?"

"No, I'm an orderly. Yes, I'm the doctor," answered Skalkovsky and decided that the man talking to him had raised himself on his elbows, that he was helplessly shaking his head, that he was not over twenty, that he was gravely ill.

"The fact is, I've been killed," complained the sick man, "I was shot. And it seems very strange to me, Doctor, but I was shot by accident."

"By accident?"

Painfully straining his eyes, Skalkovsky stood up and brought his face as close as possible to the face of the sick man. The green light finally disappeared and he caught sight of a pale, hook-nosed, young face stuck into the wretched wall of the ambulance. A surreptitious glance from chin to foot revealed to Skalkovsky a bandaged chest, coat torn off one shoulder, legs wrapped in a blanket.

"You were shot?" he asked again sullenly. "Perhaps it's nothing, only a scratch? And you say by accident?"

"I'm convinced of that, Doctor. No, it's more than a scratch; no, I've been properly shot!"

The automobile jerked, leaned to one side and turned with a gentle motion. But where? To the left? To the right?

"Where is it taking me?" Skalkovsky thought intensely.

"You don't know, Doctor, what sort of woman she is," muttered the sick man. "Whatever you might say, it's not that; it's something else, certainly not that!"

Skalkovsky reached for his cigarette case but shoved it back at once.

"Are you crazy?" he asked indifferently.

"Sure, sure, that's right. Certainly not that, something else. I'm convinced that he aimed . . ."

"Aimed at whom?"

"At her," muttered the sick man and fell back helplessly on his back. "And what luck that he missed the mark!"

"Nevertheless, it's a nasty story," muttered Skalkovsky gloomily.

"The story is coming to its end," said the sick man sadly. "At least for me. I can already see the shore. It'll be a green shore with a name, a patronymic, a family name and dates of death and birth. And the funniest thing is that I saw that man for the first and last time."

"What man?"

"The man who shot me. But I've already seen you somewhere."

"Unfortunately I broke my glasses," said Skalkovsky gloomily. "Anyway, I recognize your voice. Yes, we met—at the University."

"At the Institute, sure, sure," corrected the sick man joyfully. "You can't imagine how glad I am to have met you. I live alone, absolutely alone, I don't have anyone here. My mother lives in Voronezh. She's in dire need, so I wasn't shot inopportunely."

"So you say that we met. . . ."

"We met, I'm convinced of that." The sick man stretched out his arm and touched Skalkovsky's shoulder affectionately. "My head is spinning now, I lost a lot of blood during the day, I can't recall too well where, but we met. I think at a party at the Institute."

"Quite possible," said Skalkovsky slowly. "I seem to recall that we played lottery, drank wine, and I ended up owing you something."

"No, not lottery, we had no lottery," declared the sick man, and Skalkovsky decided that he was rubbing his forehead with his fingers, that he was trying to recall. "But we did indeed drink wine and I became indebted to you and not you to me. I owe you five or six rubles."

"You're mistaken."

"Not at all," said the sick man emphatically. "I'm not mistaken, I'm not yet altogether out of my mind, I remember everything excellently. I'll pay you back the money now. . . ."

"Throw it away, I won't take it," muttered Skalkovsky with annoyance. "I don't think I met you at the Institute party at all. I simply said so without thinking."

"No, you'll take it," repeated the sick man obstinately. "If you want me to die in peace. All the more . . . all the more, since I no longer have any use for the money. Perhaps it will still come in handy for you."

Skalkovsky opened his hand—a ten-spot, its white wings twitching, lay in his palm.

"I'll take it in order not to upset you," he said, smiling forcedly. "When you get well I'll send you the money. Tell me your address."

The sick man smiled.

"My address," he said sadly, "is the Volkovo cemetery, third row from the chapel, fourth grave on the right. I said this at random, Doctor. But our post office is very efficient. They're sure to find me, don't hesitate to send it."

Two hours later he was sitting behind the very same table which he had left in order to pursue, through the empty and slushy streets, an ambulance which, like an unlucky card, was covered with funeral crosses. He sat behind the very same table and played, painfully straining his eyes, overcoming by force of will the hopeless absent-mindedness of an extremely nearsighted person. He invariably staked everything, both singly and in league with any partner. Within two hours more money came into his hands than during his entire past and future life. He tossed it back on the table and, like a boomerang, it came back into his hands with profit. One would have thought that he possessed a hanged man's rope and that the rope of a hanged man actually brings luck . . . The entire club gathered around him and in solemn silence celebrated his game like a Catholic mass.

And finally the last ten-spot on which the banker had put his last hope, flashing its white wings, swooped down like a swallow and, whirling in the air, fell at his feet.

Then he wiped his forehead, lifted his damp hands to his eyes, sighed, and slowly wrapped his money in newspaper. He went out into the lobby and came back a few minutes later.

"Citizens, comrades and brothers," he said quietly, walked up to the table, and with difficulty focused his thoroughly fatigued eyes on the crowd. "This morning I killed a man. I shot him. However, that's not the point. The point is that I played with his money. But it's seven o'clock in the morning now, and I must assume that he has already reached his shore with the name, patronymic, family name and dates of birth and death. Therefore all that I won now belongs to his mother. She lives in Voronezh and is in dire need. I wired her the money. They will find her. Our post office is very efficient!" He fell on the table with his face, arms and chest.

Sure arms lifted him by the shoulders, seated him in an armchair and brought a glass of water close to his face.

He caught sight of the familiar cap, the same persistent cap that had flashed above the yellow blotches of faces under the circus posters. He drank the water and smiled.

"The boy was right," he said simply. "I aimed at her, and what luck that I missed."

Translated by Ira Goetz

LEONID LEONOV

THE WOODEN QUEEN

I

And really, of course, there is nothing strange about this.
. . . One night Vladimir Nikolayevich was sitting at a small
table and relaxing at chess—he was repeating Staunton's
king's gambit of the early period, which had been printed as
far back as the '70s in *Palamède*. On the table behind him the
landlady's defective samovar was singing a copper song.

. . . December was then flurrying outside the window,
and like a whirlwind, the white snow horses of the fine snowstorm were carrying the blue sleighs of dream around the
town. And it was as though someone were playing the flute,
and as though the flute were playing itself.

This game, played in Avignon about seventy years ago,
was, perhaps, Staunton's most brilliant. The attack of the
white knights after the sudden assault of the black queen was
as measured, efficient, and careful as a mathematical formula
where the signs so well and wondrously interlace with one
another. . . . But the very center of the game, when Black
corrects his disarrayed pawns and the black rook, using the
confusion of the enemy's flank, sails from QKt1 to QKt5 and
takes away the white knight—is this not a Wagnerian leitmo-
tif, the angry copper of which blossoms above one's head as
an unexpected and ringing flower?

The samovar heaved its cleaned out chest, quieted down

for a brief moment, and then the quiet little song of samovar grief began to creep sleepily around the room again. At such a pause, Vladimir Nikolayevich moved the rook and pondered over the queen. Staunton departed here into an obscure maze of attack by the knight and with incomprehensively wild persistence forced his way with the knight from KB3 to Q4, and then developed an excellent combination on his left flank. . . . Vladimir Nikolayevich clearly imagined another variant to himself: the queen goes from Q4 to QR4, as Andersen subsequently played against Kizeritsky, and from there—risking a catastrophe, it is true—it was possible to threaten the white center directly. . . . Vladimir Nikolayevich decided to work out this variant, and, having lit a cigarette, he stared out the window.

. . . There the inaudible flight of the wind's hoofs pierced the icy blue depth of the night. They sped away . . . and new ones ran by. And all this snowy torrent was like a flute. And someone's strong hands held a laughing flute high above the houses.

The samovar purred. Vladimir Nikolayevich's attention was centered upon a white pawn—in it lay the cause of several complications and obscurities, but now things had already become clear: QB4 took KB2, but the Blacks' KKt2 . . .

This was the reason that Vladimir Nikolayevich stared fixedly into the night, and then quite unexpectedly heard the quiet whistle of a snow flute luring him into the plains of December. . . . And it so happened that this recalled the letters of the slender girl, Mariannochka, who had once tenderly run past his heart wearing a violet shawl. Vladimir Nikolayevich clearly pictured to himself both her eyes and her lips, which were precisely the lips of a snow flute.

But immediately after the sweet lips of Mariannochka, he for some reason recalled the very shrewd variant of Murphy, and then Izvekov with one mocking smile wiped away all this rosy sediment from his soul, like a puddle off the sidewalk, while Staunton, on the advice of the infallible Murphy, urged his horse forward and threateningly raised him up on his hind legs right under the nose of the dumfounded king.

And again the flute started singing. And, submitting to

something which was once but had now gone, Vladimir Niko-layevich went up to the window and started staring out.

. . . Between the houses—yellow eyes swollen by the storm gazed into their first and second stories—rushed snowy herds of horses, spraying blue flakes to the sides and drawing the topsy-turvy bishops gaily into the icy sediment of the starless night. . . . Then, turning endlessly, all patterned, like a cube of snowy lace, a tower crept under his very window. And again someone gentle invitingly raised his arms above the head of this snowstorm, fixing his bloodless lips to the flute.

Suddenly it became exceedingly pleasant—was that not because the copper purring of the samovar had suddenly broken off? . . . And, instead, its quiet little woman's laugh was running about the room and into Vladimir Niko-layevich's ear and hiding in his very heart. It was clear that he had turned around—but what he had seen was not at all clear. He noticed on the chessboard, at that moment enlarged into all . . . but the flute was still singing. A white hand ran across it forwards, ran back. . . .

He clearly saw how, having crossed to QKt2, the black queen wished to hand a little white note to a strange officer, while behind a fretted tower the black king bent forward his bald crowned head over a reddish, plump woman of whom there are always eight stupid and lonely examples on a chessboard. . . . Then he saw that everything had petrified, and behind the silk folds of the queen's dress was fearfully hidden her precise and fine hand—it moved, shivered, and then froze still.

. . . With a flourish of white hands behind the window the flute broke off, and again the samovar stretched forth its downcast and lonely, intermittent song. Vladimir Niko-layevich remembered only two things then. The first: the eyes of his queen—swift, the eyes of a snow tempest in which no matter how many continually different eyes, equally close to one's heart there are, still, in the middle of them, one. . . . And the second: the figures on the board seemed arranged precisely. . . . Why, yes! This was extraordinary—Vladimir Nikolayevich with his own eyes clearly saw what Steinitz had not dreamed about and Andersen had not dared to suggest. This was more unexpected than the very scintillating, sudden—like a waterfall—gambit of Evans. This was a yet unknown situation in play of the officer and the queen. . . . It was easy to recall: the queen on Q7 and next to her, one move away, the alien officer—a knight. . . . The pawns, indissoluble as an anchor chain, run to the attack—two fall—but in only three moves that same officer who hid the love note places the befuddled king in check.

And again . . . and again the flutes.

. . . With a frightened glance Izvekov felt both the four walls greatly enlarging and this samovar swelling into a copper grief. Yes—he, Vladimir Nikolayevich Izvekov, was standing on the chessboard, one move of the knight from the queen, and she extended to him a note folded in four. He took it, and when that note lay quite comfortably in the triangular, flapped pocket of his velvet robe, all this suddenness and its strangeness suddenly became clearly evident. . . . This brought him to a state of indescribable fear and even terror. Yes—he had become the black left flank officer of the wooden king.

Another moment and his consciousness began to grow cold in him, and his own hand glittered on a level with his eyes like lacquered wood. It was raising his cap to wipe away the perspiration of fright. With a last frenzied leap of his petrifying will, five wooden words burst from him: "No, I don't want . . . no . . ."

. . . Somewhere quite near, the snow flute sounded loudly, like a hunting horn. Then something shifted, and the sharp angle became dull and disappeared—it was crushed on a straight line into nothing; it wavered like a flower; and again, that unexpected square became a triangle.

The samovar returned from somewhere and became audible, and Izvekov found himself sitting in a three-legged armchair (the fourth was the landlady's bucket), and it seemed as though he had even been drowsing. He rubbed his eyes, recollected, and started to smile at the dream which had come upon him so ornately, but . . . on the board was that unique situation out of a billion when the black queen and an enemy bishop in the name of the most brilliant of goals mutually tie themselves together with the fine threads of a chess pattern.

The snowstorm subsided—the little clock ticked away on the little wall. The street lantern stared at Vladimir Niko-layevich's back with its glassy, frozen eye through glass taut with light icy lace. The snowstorm subsided, but the mercury hid lower and lower in its little glass ball. And on the floor near his very legs from where it had fallen, the note showed white. In it were the simple words:

> Darling, I want to be with you always. My whole self yearns for your heart from my wooden checkerboard. I have only you—all the rest around are wooden. . . .

II

Boris Viktorovich Kolomnitsky was, in the first place, a musician, also, in the first place, a passionate lover of all chess oddities, and in the second place, a jolly man, but a little too talkative. In the third place, he was, because of his friendship, the sole and patient custodian of Izvekov's few secrets.

It was already late. Boris Viktorovich lay in bed and held a piece of the paper right in front of his nose, waiting for yesterday's soup to heat on the kerosene stove.

It was late—it was already twelve. Through the leaded pane of insuperable drowsiness, Kolomnitsky was trying to pierce the secret meaning of several words on that scrap of paper: . . . *extra fine* . . . *22.10* . . . *fully good fare* . . . *19.10* . . . Of course—if it were not for this very drowsiness —undoubtedly he would have been able to understand instantly that this was quite simply a report of cotton goods' prices for July. But drowsiness moved these words and figures far, far off—about twenty versts, and there they swelled with unfathomable rapidity and effrontery and rushed toward his weary eyes, sinister in form like apocalyptic beasts. . . . But it was still too early to go to sleep.

And just at that point Vladimir Nikolayevich came in. The apocalyptic beasts then fearfully shrank in an angry fist and took flight into a dark, dusty corner where a cello protruded its yellowish-red belly.

"I've come to see you, Borya."

"Eh heh—I understand! . . ."

"Oh, no, I myself have money: I got it today . . . I've brought that little book you were talking about."

"You bought it?"

"I did."

"And when you were buying it—" Kolomnitsky looked sternly at Izvekov, but behind his serious look there pranced gaily the green and yellow devils of uncontrollable laughter —"didn't the clerk ask you: isn't Kolomnitsky planning, now, to get married?"

Izvekov clapped his hands: "This is what comes of leaving you alone! But you were completely out of your mind at my place, old man!"

Kolomnitsky sat on the bed and wiped his eyes with his fists. "Oho, it's indecent, my friend, to live alone! Every young, properly constituted man is obliged, you see, to fall in love sometime. What's a man without love?"—Kolomnitsky drew the forefinger of his right hand to the side—"A two-legged amphibian or a stupid, arch-procrastinator!"

Kolomnitsky lowered his protruding, laughing eyes and sighed heavily. "The thing is, Volodya, do you know what sort of gossip the children have been spreading about me in the conservatory? One would think I was having an affair with my cello! . . . Do you get the point? . . . There's this girl there, intelligent—absolutely nothing personal, but don't worry, I won't introduce you before the marriage!"

Vladimir Nikolayevich became sullen: "Where are your chessmen, tarantula?"

"In the corner. The landlady knocked my chess table over yesterday, the pieces scattered like cockroaches. . . . But you look for them if you need them!"

Vladimir Nikolayevich crawled around the floor, swept his hand under the couch, drew out a knight, and began to set up the figures.

"But, Borya, one of your pawns is missing."

"White?"

"White."

"It's in a state of continual and obscure absence. Don't get upset, use this glass stopper instead . . . no matter!"

Vladimir Nikolayevich began from a Muzio gambit, knocked out a bishop, gave up a knight, and castled. . . . Kolomnitsky hummed, flashed a vigilant glance around the board, and then came close to it and began to stare.

Izvekov had led skillfully. Bang—the rook jumped overboard straight into a puddle of yesterday's spilled tea. One, two, three—the white bishops penetrate the right flank of the blacks deeply, the king again returns from Q2 to Q1 and again performs his sacred kingly dance of revenge to the wry lashes of the hostile knights. . . . Two more moves—K4 takes KKt4—the bishop tramples a pawn in the path of the queen, and then . . .

. . . Kolomnitsky was dumfounded. More than that, he was overwhelmed and looked into Izvekov's eyes with an almost canine sweetness.

"Listen! But this just can't be! Wait, the bishop takes KKt5. . . . Yes, but you well know, Filidor himself took to the air at that point with his entire household! . . . But it's all the same, whether you discover Venus . . . or invent a locomotive!" Kolomnitsky was beside himself—his delight seemed to transfix him.

. . . A quiet snowstorm began to ripple, and still the moonlight spread all over outside the windows, boundlessly and broadly—and, like islands in an icy lunar flood, the snowclouds stood out in the black sky.

"There you are, Izvekov! I've striven for just this for four months. . . . I've long been persuaded that there must be in chess, too, the situation when a woman is unfaithful just for the sake of being unfaithful, in which there is a secret and an unusual magic. . . . But wait, were you dreaming or something? . . . I don't think it was lack of skill. . . ."

He could have related everything clearly and simply, hiding the part about the note—and then nothing would have happened, but Vladimir Nikolayevich preferred to show this very note, from another plane, from the wooden chessboard. He stretched out his open hand to him, as he had been extending his heart in the course of these three years, and he took it.

Then Kolomnitsky grew completely pale, his lower lip seemed to tremble, and, smiling hostilely and with vexation, he asked: "Have you known her long?"

"Whom?"

"Anka . . ."

"Who?"

"You."

"I? But I simply don't know any Anka. . . . Why are you frowning so?"

Kolomnitsky interrupted Izvekov, and his voice trembled unpleasantly: "You? You, of course, have nothing to do with it! The whole point is . . . that my fiancée wrote this note . . . the one I described to you a little while ago. . . . Even her initials are here at the bottom: A. and R., and it's her handwriting. Personally, of course, I confess . . ."

Izvekov stared dully at his friend, hardly understanding what was happening, but something was beginning to irritate him. Then he guessed what it was, and, while Kolomnitsky silently chewed his cigarette, he began—hotly, but confusedly—to describe and explain to his friend how tenderly the flute had sung in yesterday's snowstorm and how the black queen from the chess fields had dropped him the note, and so on, and so on . . . He spoke sincerely, spoke without concealing a word, spoke for an entire half hour. But, when the pot on the kerosene stove suddenly began to sputter, Kolomnitsky stood up, breaking off the disorderly torrent of Vladimir Nikolayevich's talk.

He yawned and said: "I don't believe you because I don't believe in witches and fairies and evil eyes, I don't believe in any miracles. Besides that, I'm going to eat now, and then I'm going to lie down and sleep."

Vladimir Nikolayevich was a very good man. He stayed a minute more out of politeness, then put on his overcoat, sighed quite deeply, and went out without saying good-by.

. . . In the alley, lunar shadows slid down from snow peaks on gaily crackling snow slides. It was very cold and pleasant. It seemed as though the moon had penetrated his overcoat and was pressing closely to his back—this too was pleasant. And it really is good when your steps make a crunching noise and your shadow like a faithful dog runs on in front of you, with its head poking each bend in the road.

But a man's thoughts are not good when he is returning after an offensive unpleasantness to his empty, unsheltering lair.

III

. . . Several times more, in evenings marked by snow-storms, Vladimir Nikolayevich saw how his black queen, who had placed her tender two initials A. and R. on that little note, came to life. And each time, when by the knight's gambit, he stood on the chessboard beside her, he managed to catch only one quick and tender glance from the queen. And if his heart suddenly began to wish that this wooden happiness would go on, the supernatural square became a triangle in lightning speed and one of its angles was flattened out into nothing: 180° this way and 180° that—and the secret link fell out of the chain. And he awoke from his dream into our, into this plane, and floundered in the thick murky mess of the unsatisfying present . . .

And then love, large like a seven-towered house, came to Vladimir Nikolayevich. And his soul began to dwell in this house and was very happy there.

. . . By day he ran around giving lessons. Sometimes in the evenings when there was a snowstorm, he would place his wooden queen on his outspread palm and wait to see whether this wood would blossom under his burning stare with vermilion and blue flowers, like Aaron's rod.

But all was silent, and her wooden soul in the chiseled folds of the piece did not awaken. And the evening would pass, and he would write in his soul with a violet-inked pen; "Nothingness."

Everything in Kolomnitsky had burst by itself, he believed neither in witches nor the evil eye, but Izvekov—it turned out —did. From ten mouths, one heard that he drank; from eight, that he was working out some sort of unbelievable chess strategy; from four, that he had changed greatly and had become still redder. . . . Then everything fell silent.

. . . While the samovar on the table sang out, now in a

deep-voiced baritone, now in a delicate copper tenor, he sat by the window, and, when the shadows of white, dappled snow horses began to sprinkle the snow banks and the flute began to sing, he was still waiting to see if that secret angle of intense happiness—which Kolomnitsky had likened to a witch and the evil eye—would suddenly taper off out of nothing, if the link of the queen's awakening would bind itself into the chain of the familiar and hellishly boring circles.

But on one of these evenings a great misfortune happened: the queen disappeared. She could be found nowhere —neither here nor there, nor any place else. . . . That night Vladimir Nikolayevich flew into the kitchen like a bomb—the fat witch Natalya lived there.

"She left here, have you seen her?" asked Vladimir Nikolayevich his head reeling.

The witch jumped back from her trough and could only mumble:

"No-o-o . . . no one's gone out . . . no-o-o . . ."

Vladimir Nikolayevich knew how to talk to witches:

"Has anyone been here?" Izvekov almost dislocated her arm.

"That red-headed friend of yours was here . . . then he went away. He left you a letter pinned to the wall. . . ."

"Was he tall?"

"Yes, about your size. . . ."

"Red-haired?"

"I think so. . . ."

Now, of course, this was Kolomnitsky—and it was he who had carried off the little piece of wood where the queen's soul was sleeping. Then Izvekov groaned, groaned in a manner peculiar to him, and, all hunched over, he rushed into the room to find the note. It was hanging on the wall, stuck to the wallpaper with a rusty pen:

"I'm leaving with her. I'll explain everything. Don't look for me—don't lead me into temptation."

Vladimir Nikolayevich seized his head four times; then, twice, he had a single stupid idea, which his despair had brought forth; and then grabbed his hat. He flew straight out onto the street with Natalya's speed, leaving behind him the jarring of an overturned glass, the quiet moaning of Natalya the witch who was holding her side where there remained, very likely, a good trace of Izvekov's elbow, and the frantic screech of the cat caught by its tail in the door.

. . . The damp, slightly warm dusk had a favorable but slow effect upon him. For an hour and a half he wandered aimlessly up and down side streets, immersed in solving some problem—chess, of course—the meaning of which suddenly had become the meaning of his whole existence on earth. This murderous perplexity did not leave him right up to the moment when he raised his hat in apology after having collided with a lamp post. When he observed what he had done, he laughed out loud, and headed home.

. . . And night crept up like a black cat, unseen and unheard, but very close. Low clouds spread out in the sky—puffy and gray like cats' tails. Cats scraped at his soul . . . Right by the doorway an emaciated black cat ran across the road. Vladimir Nikolayevich spat after it—again, such a foul gloom filled his soul that he wanted to sink his teeth into a streetcar bumper and to howl so that the pavement trembled. . . .

He entered the room—Natalya pouted maliciously and offensively—rushed to his bed, grabbed the pillow with his teeth, and gnawed through the new pillowcase. There was no limit to his grief, no end to his gloom, and his teeth were sharp.

IV

And then it began.

The good old woman, who, in her letters, caressed her dear and only Volodya as best she knew how with old, uncomplicated words would not have recognized him now: his face had grown hollow, his nose stood out, his eyes had become suspicious and sharp, and a sudden abundance of hair on his chin made him look as though he were covered with a dull, gray film.

. . . In the evenings he raced about in the twilight, searching and staring into the dark faces of those he met. He peeked into strange windows, searching. . . . The snowy flakes of the storm, without success, sought to sheathe him.

. . . The frost tried to freeze his heart, but it beat as before: poorly and uneasily.

Quite recently, four days ago, Vladimir Nikolayevich had met the one he had been seeking. There was a snowstorm then—it whirled in the side streets like white phantom columns, and the columns passed by in succession, and each column had eyes: take your pick! . . . She walked by, and two officers, one on each side, walked with her. One, of course, was Kolomnitsky. The other was that docktailed chess piece which had been lost at Izvekov's about three weeks before.

Pressing himself to the wall, he followed with bewildered eyes, listened, as the resounding flakes of the queen's laughter fluttered down upon his heart and melted in a twisting column, saw her wooden face—one of the two. They walked as though they were swimming . . . and from the vacillating, gray hills resting upon trembling roofs, there came to him then the sound of the far-off, singing flute. . . .

When he heard it, he rushed in pursuit, but the stinging wave of wet flakes, blending into a transparent avalanche, closed up his eyes and ears. . . . He came to and again rushed forward, but before his very eyes the storm reared up, more blue and more shrill, its sharp snow claws reaching out high above the houses.

. . . Later he saw her on the street. By a store window, reflecting a black silhouette in the mirrored glass, she was adjusting her hat.

. . . Then once, late at night, she was crossing the street—painfully close—on the arm of a tall old man, and her laugh was like a porcelain bead against a gay piece of silver.

At that time automobiles, with their shrill and icy horns, frightened the dawdling old folk at intersections, and there were streetcars going, wild bulls of the evening city. And then: precisely a certain group of fifty people of various calibers, on precisely this streetcar, at precisely this hour, had to go to the very same section of town. . . . Then the milky spheres of arc headlights wavered on the broad street amidst the whirling spheres of the snowstorm. And it was clear to each and everyone on this evening that strewn along the broad, snowy street were many pieces of worn-out hearts.

v

On this very evening, a new thought came to Izvekov. He clearly pictured the chess situation when the queen, playing with the officer alone, does not notice the other knight also on the move. He then understood that this other one was indeed Kolomnitsky.

. . . Izvekov ran home, by waving his arms casting off shadows on the way, the frightened smiles of passers-by, and the animate waves of wind which met him. . . . He finally halted in his doorway, wiped his forehead with his sleeve, ran in, and sat down at the chessboard.

In place of the queen on the queen's square, there stood a worn water stopper; in place of Kolomnitsky, a wax candle stub. . . . The pieces were in their places. Izvekov smiled wryly at someone unknown standing by the wall, blinked, and coughed. . . . Play began.

. . . Again it was snowing in the alley. The window clouded over with an icy curtain on the outside, but it was at once all swept away when the black wool of the shadows being borne on the snowstorm brushed against it. To all appearances, here was a remote alley, but in the alley there was a little house with two little windows, and in the house sat a disheveled man, and the paw of his soul was crippled, and his eyes were the eyes of a snowstorm. . . .

. . . The alley was swept with sharp, granular snow just as it had been in the very beginning.

The white knight moved forward. The wax candle stub moved back and placed an awkward check on the worn, glass stopper, QR1 made a leap to QR4, and the white bishops approached. . . . The queen took a pawn from the board. The knight took another pawn and then another and another. . . .

Vladimir Nikolayevich could not restrain himself—leaning against the door frame he quietly whispered to the invisible being standing by the wall:

"Listen—this is not a game, it's a slaughterhouse. . . . Be a little more decent!"

. . . It had become obvious: the queen had to be isolated

and Kolomnitsky knocked off the board with a well-aimed blow.

He started perspiring and threw his overcoat off his shoulders, but his head functioned more and more effectively. If one had been listening, he who had a good ear could have heard how one after another the small gears interlaced with their clever teeth and moved the large, heavy wheel.

And the flute began to sing. . . . And the snowstorm did not abate. And it seemed someone was dancing, raising the whistle of the singing flute into the smoky sky. And it seemed the flute itself was dancing. . . .

Vladimir Nikolayevich was exerting himself to the very utmost—something in him might burst . . . twenty-two . . . twenty-three . . . And then, on the twenty-fourth move, the white knight moved with precision to Q6, while, on the twenty-fifth move, the black chess rook, as slow as Charon's,* threatening the hiding king, knocked off Kolomnitsky and . . . everything was over; the three-move checkmate was clear,—a primitive Filidor! . . .

. . . He leaned back heavily in his armchair, and at once his soul became like an empty green bottle, and his eyes closed as though someone weighing a hundred-weight had set upon his eyelids. Then the two different paths came together and an angle was formed . . . and around his very ear hovered the close whistle of the flute. Then everything changed, and in this move the barely audible soft laughter of a woman appeared from *there*. . . .

. . . He turned about in such a way that all three armchair legs squeaked, opened all his hundred thousand pairs of eyes, and a sadness of intolerable sweetness upon his transfer there to the queen immersed him in a cold sweat from head to foot.

She was sitting nearby, all in black—so many times wished for and won, but never attained—her snowstorm eyes resting on him. Someone drew him to her, and he rushed and grasped her hand and kissed her dear, chiseled palm and fingers. He stared into her eyes, repeating in his mind all his brilliant part by heart. He recited her given name—"Anna"

* In Russian *ladya* means both (poet.) a boat and (chess) a rook.

—the same from either end—and everything melted and was borne away, and it seemed that the walls had become like doors . . . and everything all around became cloudy and whirled with the snowy dust of not one, but a thousand fine snowstorms.

And he whispered dear sweet nothings to her, and the words, like flakes of snow, danced above and below them. And he endlessly kissed her chiseled hand which had opened the door to supernal happiness for him. . . . And thousands of harmonious flutes came out of it toward the two of them.

. . . He was not at all himself. And he inadvertently looked at her face with a loving eye and with a keenness which was necessary where the dejected samovar was singing near the three-legged chair (the fourth was a garbage pail), and he saw that the lacquered wood of the queen's pale face was glittering in a light that was not from ordinary lamps. And everything became azure blue. And tenderness poured into his empty green bottle like burning wine. But he at once felt how they two were being clothed with folds of merciless wood. . . .

With a burst of ebbing consciousness, he threw out his hands to the sides and moved the right angles apart. . . . Somewhere behind this wall which had suddenly appeared, the departing flute burst out in wooden laughter. It moved forward and straightened out, painfully striking him on the back of the neck.

Vladimir Nikolayevich opened his eyes, blinked, extended his arm and opened his fist—there lay the wooden queen, warm from his own warmth, a wooden chess piece.

The pieces showered about the floor. The snowstorm and the landlady's defective samovar sang in harmony, like a blind man with his leader.

. . . The snow rushed down, but it was warm, and instead of becoming smooth surfaces of piled-up snow, it entrusted itself to dirty, cold, melting puddles.

The fat witch, Natalya, came into the room:

"That red-haired man is here to see you. . . ."

Translated by Andrew Field

ANATOLY MITROFANOV

FIRST LOVE

Tonya had scarcely reached her fifteenth year when I fell in love with her.

It was her golden hair which captivated me. We apprentice bookbinders and stockboys had to have our hair close-cut with clippers. We dreamed of a haircut like the polite printer Savka had. He wore a cap with crossed hammers and thought of himself as a technician. The bosses gave us a five-kopeck piece for a haircut, and the mincing apprentice barbers would give our heads a haphazard clipping. Perhaps that was why Tonya's golden hair, which she wore loose over her shoulders, struck me so.

"I know who you're sweet on, you scruffy brat," said Fedya Sachok. He took me by the arm, led me to his room and pushed me into a chair. On the table in front of me he spread out in a fan some pornographic cards.

"Hot stuff?" he asked.

I folded my arms in front of me and looked him straight in the eye without blinking. Fedya Sachok didn't like me, and made fun of me because I was studying English and used tooth powder. In the morning when I was washing up at the rusty wash basin, he would come out of his room, motioning for Agniya to follow him. Agniya was the forty-year-old prostitute who was keeping him that month. I was gargling, with my head back. I felt helpless.

"Get the little song bird," said Fedya about me, and winked at Agniya.

I should mention that it was hard for me to take humiliation: I was writing a novel about a certain Captain Wainwright, which was called *The Icy Volcano*. And besides that, a year before they had kicked me out of the Home because Vera, a college girl and daughter of the directress, used to come to my room in the evenings to kiss. When I was depressed, I would pick up the magazine which described how Amundsen discovered the South Pole. This always made me feel better.

Fedya Sachok had the lean face of an actor, black wavy hair and a haughty nose with curly nostrils.

"A beautiful man," the prostitutes called him.

He was tight-fisted, and it pained him when I wasted money on the movies, or when he saw anyone give more than a kopeck to a beggar, or even when Agniya lit a candle in church for his, Fedya's, health.

He was cruel to women because there was only one Fedya and there were many beautiful girls. Minor civil servants and high-school students hovered around them. Instead of paying the girls the agreed sum and going away, they sometimes fell in love, insisted on bridling them and restraining their receptiveness to approach.

Sachok—to us, who lived near Bolshaya Gruzinskaya Street, that meant "the lover." In this word was a touch of malice and of his humiliating disregard for women.

On Trinity Sunday, I woke late, put on my cheap gray jacket and went out into the courtyard.

Next to the stable, some little girls were playing school. Tonya came out of her wing and went up to them. She thought herself already grown up, and that the little girls, really arguing over the game, could never be friends of hers. After disrupting the progress of the game, she hopped around a little on one foot—simply to show her superiority. Her hair leaped about her shoulders, first covering then uncovering her small ears.

Noticing me, she put her head back and carefully, as though blind, took a few steps. Her face became expressionless and blank, and her hair hung down her back as though it was going to flow on to the ground. A little girl with a big black eye folded her arms behind her and was looking straight into her face.

I leaned against the stable doors and closed my eyes. The horses were rubbing against their stalls and snorting. I felt as if I were dying.

"Hey, stupid," said Fedya Sachok, as I dragged myself home. "Take her off to the movies, and then—into the stable, so that her mom and daddy don't see anything."

I was startled. I reached into my pocket for something and dropped a ten-kopeck piece, and couldn't find it for the life of me.

Agniya, who laughed at me only because it pleased Fedya, said mockingly, "There it is, little Shura, right beside your tippy-toe."

I shoved open my door, which was made of planks and papered over with newspapers, and went to my cot.

In the room, besides me, there lived the landlady, the widow Matryosha with her two children, a pockmarked working woman for the "Ducat" plant, and Regina, a young girl who slept during the day and in the evening went out onto Naryshkin Boulevard.

I got some ink, sat down at the table and set about making a final copy of The Icy Volcano. I held strictly to the rules I had read on the last page of The Russian Morning: "Manuscripts must be presented typed, or written in a clear, legible hand, with margins, on one side of the paper." But this time, the procedure of recopying couldn't calm me.

I gave up trying to write, and began thinking about the U.S.A.; for a long time, I'd been planning to run away to the United States, across the Bering Strait. Toward this end I had acquired the A. I. Konovalov edition of English Self-Taught, and had saved up thirteen rubles.

I undressed and went to bed. I looked out the window and whispered to myself:

"O, my pretty girl!"

Fedya shoved his head, in a new velvet cap, inside the door.

"Playing with yourself?" he asked.

His own words struck him so funny that I could hear him sniggering over them that night as he romped with Agniya.

The next day, I learned from Tonya's brother that the evening before Tonya had put on his jacket and said: "Look at me now—just like Shura."

I left the courtyard right away. I was afraid of seeing Tonya.

That night, my father came. Tall and stout, in a tussore coat and black cotton trousers, he sat down facing me directly. His huge cap, which reminded me somehow of a ship, rested on his knees. His big meaty face, with its sparse but bristling mustache, was serious. He spoke sparingly, moved little, and the collar of his snow-white shirt cut into his bull neck. It had been three months since he had taken a drink, and he was living in a kind of dream: he put money by in a savings account, took a bath every Saturday, and changed his shirts often—each more snow-white than the next. In the evenings, he drank twelve glasses of tea in Tikhomirov's tavern. His immobility, his devotion to cleanliness and thrift scared me—I knew how gay and how terrible he could become when he started to drink.

He looked at me with exaggerated conscientiousness; perfect sobriety shone in his eyes. I was his only son, and he had come to admonish me, kiss me on the cheek and give me a twenty-kopeck coin on taking his leave.

Matryosha, with whom I boarded, complained to my father that I wrote, and that I ate a lot, and my father added a ruble over what was agreed upon for my monthly keep.

Fedya Sachok came in. He sat down at the table without removing his cap and palmed his pack of cigarettes. He trembled when he found out that my father had a hundred twenty rubles in his account.

"A military tailor is not just anybody," he said enviously, and he lit a cigarette, even though Regina was in the room and might have asked for one.

My father worked at Surin's, on Tverskaya Street, and he was proud of it. Military men from all corners of the Empire sent their orders to Surin's.

Fedya disappeared and suddenly began shouting loudly in the corridor, as though he were out in the open:

"Yegor Feoktistych, your little Shura is careless with his money; he chases girls, loves the movies, God knows what.

. . . You're his father; it's your duty to have a little talk with him." He burst into the room with the program of the Eclair movie theater which he had stolen from me and hidden until just the right time. My father focused on the narrow strip of paper. On top was printed *"The Three of Hearts.* Drama in six serials; each serial in five parts." And below: "In the foyer, the salon orchestra is under the direction of that public favorite, the Rumanian virtuoso, M. Shcherbonescu."

My father, by the way, didn't know how to read. He began to give me a talking to. Without particular heat, he preached a few aphorisms, such as: one ought to save money, movies spoil children, etc.

Then he got up, awkwardly thrust twenty kopecks into my hand and kissed me. I smelled the formidable scent of cleanliness and of the birch switches used in the bathhouses; his mustache pricked my cheek.

We went out into the corridor. The door to Agniya's room was open. Agniya, half-dressed, was sitting crossways on the bed and was pulling on a stocking. She raised her leg up high, as though she were trying to touch my father's chest with the tips of her toes.

My father laughed darkly and tipped his cap to her. I knew that no later than the day after tomorrow my father would start drinking again.

That night I had a dream. I was lying on my bed, with my arms crossed under the blanket, stretched out as though I had died. Outside the window, on the ground, there was a steamship, bulky and ramshackle like the tavern. On board there was a crooked sign, with the word *Orinoco* in big gray letters.

Tonya came into the room. She walked very quietly, on tiptoe. She took my jacket from the chair and started to put it on. Very slowly, she lowered herself into the chair at my bedside. One after another, she fastened the buttons with her slim fingers. She whispered, "Shura, Shura." She didn't see me. Without moving, I said, also in a whisper: "She is golden-haired, golden-haired." I looked at the blanket under which my body lay stretched out, with my arms crossed on my chest. She squirmed, because the jacket was squeezing her under the arms.

I was awakened by a shout. Fedya was arguing with Half-John. He was standing at the window, looking into the room.

"You old beggar-woman! Parasite!" Fedya shouted enviously. "Probably on All Saints' Day everybody will just be waiting to give you something. How many kopecks did you scrounge from the good Orthodox yesterday?"

"Seventeen kopecks," Half-John quietly answered.

Half-John had once been a wood-turner in the furniture shop at Muir & Merilies. A year before, he had fallen under a streetcar, and his right leg was cut off at the knee, and his left hand was crippled. He was a non-drinker, and the whole block was overwhelmed at the misfortune. Then people began to get used to the idea that he was a cripple, and when his wife left him, they named him Half-John, and looked on him as though he had always been poor.

The proprietor of the shop, glad that the accident had happened in the street, sent him ten rubles.

Half-John was broad-shouldered, with a well-developed chest. He had gray eyes and an eagle beak. He shaved his head. In his day, he'd been a big, strong guy, and despite himself, he used to look down on people. After the accident, he provided himself with crutches high enough so that he could still look down at the world from his former height.

He didn't know how to beg: moving into a crowd on his crutches, he would stand facing away, and would look somewhere off to the side with his eagle-like eyes. He was given little, especially because he reddened darkly and dropped his head when he took the alms.

He hung on his crutches, his eyes cast aside, and without a word he listened to Fedya Sachok curse him. Finally, Fedya got out of breath, and Half-John went away; small change clinked in his jacket pocket and his crutches scraped on the pavement.

Out of the funds intended for my flight to America, I took two half-rubles and wrote a note to Tonya, trying to be as witty as possible:

Miss Tonya:

Today, at the moving-picture theater, the Eclair, the second episode of the picture *The Three of Hearts* is being shown. I propose that you and your brother accompany me to the showing at 8:30. Run a comb through your magnificent hair, and let's go.

                                        L. Y.* Shura

P.S. *O, my pretty girl!*

                                                    S.

After the show, during which I could glance at her only rarely, the three of us stood on the steps and chatted. Until I had decided to write her a letter, I had not seen her for whole days at a time. During those days, she came to me in my dreams, and this only increased my longing. During those days, I searched for her several times on the banks of the Orinoco, whence I had gone from the United States; I saved her from the flames of a conflagration just at the instant when the fire threatened to catch her hair. I threw her across my saddle, and cutting across the savannahs, I saved her from the Iroquois—and it moved me just to see her standing there on the creaking step, telling us just how she had heated the iron, put on her dress, combed her hair.

"You have beautiful hair," I said proudly, with a shaky voice. "You don't even have to comb it. I'll call you . . ."

In an attempt to repress the trembling which had seized me, I ran my palm over my shaven head.

"I shall call you . . . 'golden-haired.' "

An idea came into Tonya's head to buy gloves the following week, and she fluttered her fingers, inspected her hands, brought them up to her face as though they were already in gloves.

When I had worked up enough courage to call her "golden-haired," she ran her fingers through her hair, and turning her head, she tried to examine it.

"Oh, to heck with it," she cried, tossing her head.

Afterward, I went into my wing to get some apples.

Tonya had easily deciphered the letters "L. Y.," but the sentence in English stumped her. When I came back with the

---

* Of course, Tonya was meant to guess that these letters signified: "Loving you." (Author's note.)

apples, Tonya had folded my note so that only *"O, my pretty girl!"* could be seen, and showed it to me.

"What's that?"

I gave her an apple.

"Close your eyes, and then we'll translate this sentence which puzzles you." I was trying to be smart.

She obeyed.

"No, *Miss,* you're peeking."

She turned her back to me. She was treating me as she would have the clever playmate with whom she often played. I understood, and covered her eyes with my hands. Her eyelashes tickled my palm. Bending over, I saw the freckles on the bridge of her nose, the well-ironed white ribbon which lay on her shoulder, and I whispered the three words in her ear.

"So, it's English," she said, and began to breathe again.

Her brother, a fifteen-year-old good-for-nothing, condescendingly accepted an apple from me. Sympathetically, he pronounced from time to time a bass "mai prretti gerl!" His pronunciation was even more terrible than mine.

"Papa used to work in Lodz, and he says that there all the Polish girls go to high school. He wanted to send me to high school, but we don't have the money. Soon, they'll send me to a linen workshop as an apprentice seamstress. Do you know what? I can already cut out from a pattern now."

Her brother left and we were alone. I tried to put my arms around her, but stumbled and almost fell. Tonya laughed, without parting her lips, and her eyes became apprehensive.

I put my left arm around her shoulders; I stopped breathing. She wasn't laughing any more, and she looked down.

"My pretty girl," I thought, and only after that could I breathe again.

Tonya raised her head. At first her hair barely touched my hand, then covered it, then wrapped around it.

We looked at each other tensely. Actually, we wanted to kiss, but it had never entered our heads that it would be difficult, or that one would feel so sad doing it.

We began to meet more often. Now, when she was helping her mother bleach the linen or heat up the iron, she would drape the window with muslin so that I could then cross over under the windows. We would walk along the Bolshaya Gruzinskaya, Tonya beside me with her gloves in her hand. We counted the trees along the edge of the walk, stopped in entrance ways, read the posters, chatted, or didn't talk. Sometimes she would wait for me in the stable, and when we met we would smile at the horses, which snorted and rubbed against their stalls.

I was a constant source of amazement to Tonya. I embodied for her that whole mysterious race of boys, whose members smoked on the sly and dreamed of running away to America, who bragged how they "used" their employers, how they "took them over," and who summoned each other with piercing whistles to a fist fight.

"You boys are all hooligans," she teased. "How can you do it, you devils, jump onto a streetcar when it's moving?"

"We just jump."

She brought the palm of her hand to my nose, and listening with her eyes half-closed, she asked dreamily, "What does it smell of?"

"Mignonette, I think."

"It's violet, little boy!" she shouted, as though out of her mind, and slapped me lightly with her gloves.

And wasn't she a riddle to me, too? When she left me, didn't I imagine, my eyes closed, that I, too, was growing long, golden hair? If earlier I had been moved almost to tears just by the word "Orinoco," now I was prepared to fall on my knees at the very mention of the simple words "linen workshop." It seemed to me something big and white, like a hospital ward; a room where ten girls sit, all of them redhaired and similar to Tonya. On their knees are piles of linen and batiste. They sew, their hair tumbling into their foreheads. The strict senior seamstress pinches them and makes them sing, and she herself sings along with them to the beat of the Singer treadles.

Tonya taught me to be a man. I began to see that it was my duty to protect her here, around Gruzinskaya Street, in the muddy courtyard of Building #5, next to Kazakov's bakeshop and the Eclair movie house, and not on the banks of the mighty Orinoco.

What could I do? I read about herds of bison, Tonya was

sent off to work in a sweatshop, and Fedya bragged that he was going to throw Agniya over and would soon become Regina's "Sachok."

At the end of June, Tonya disappeared. A week later, on Sunday, she came back with a new girl friend from the linen workshop.

"Look at me, a full-fledged seamstress," she said.

She had become thinner and had done her hair in a new way, close to her head.

Her friend, thin like Tonya but with a black braid, shook her head and laughed. "Her, a seamstress? That's a good one!"

They sat down on the porch in front of me, laughing and gossiping.

A clock in the neighboring wing struck five.

I knew that it would attract their attention.

"Five o'clock," said Tonya, and started to laugh. They would exchange significant looks, then would fall on each other's necks and put their heads together, then quickly turn away—it seemed like Tonya was trying to catch her friend's braid.

Chufeyev, the former policeman for the local beat, passed by in civilian clothes.

"The local cop," snorted Tonya's friend.

"The local cop," said Tonya meaningfully, and began to laugh.

"Hey, watch out for the horse!"

"Yes, look out: a horse!"

About two hours later, Tonya's girl friend left. She had been allowed to spend the night at home, with her family. Tonya had to return to the shop; there was some rush work to be done that evening.

We walked around the court and came to my wing. Half-John was standing at his window, looking at the fence. Things were going from bad to worse for him.

I told Tonya that I missed her when she was away and asked what had happened to her gloves.

I thought she was going to break down and cry. She looked right into my eyes, and her lip trembled.

It struck six. We looked at the empty court, at the stables.
"Will you walk me back?" asked Tonya.

"I'll walk you to the end of the world, if you like," I answered, and went to get my cap.

Tonya stayed with Half-John.

In the room, I ran into Fedya. He was courting Regina,
despite the fact that Agniya was giving him money; he was
even proud of this. He was sitting on Regina's cot, squeezing
his pimples before her little hand mirror. He was singing a
Petersburg crooks' song through his nose: "I'm loading up
my guns and I'll leave you holding the bag. . . ."

Seeing Tonya from the window, he winked at me and put
the mirror down.

"She's filling out," he said. "In a couple years . . ." His
gestures showed what could be done with Tonya in a couple
years.

For the first time, I was seized with an intense, real hatred.
Only the day before, I had been reading in a book:

> In vain will our young reader ride across stifling Louisi-
> ana in hopes of coming across a herd of wild bison or
> buffalo. And with no hope at all, finally, will our young
> traveler look off into the distance, anxiously trying to
> catch sight of an Iroquois or a low-down Dakota sneak-
> ing through the grass.
>   . . . The immense forests have long since been cut
> down, and the meager remnants of impassable woods
> are now constrained into a pedantic order. Almost ana-
> logical is the fate of the primordial rulers of the land: the
> Indians, whose remnants lead a pitiable existence. And
> only from time to time, in the parks and music halls of
> the big cities, is shown "a real chief."

My father had already been drinking for two months. The
day was not far off when he—having left his last pawnable
item with the pawnbroker—would come to me in a dirty shirt
and beg from me, Agniya or anybody "at least a little something." Fedya sat on Regina's cot as though he owned it.
Tonya's gloves had been taken from her. And our building,

with its tavern and courtyard where the cabbies loafed, was not at all like America. On the contrary, the drunks called the tavern "Africa" for some reason.

"My pretty girl!" I muttered between my teeth.

I dropped to my knees in front of my trunk, and knocked the lock off with my fist. I moaned in hatred, and felt an insupportable burden being piled upon me. I took the America money, twelve rubles and fifty kopecks, all in half-rubles.

I went over to the window, and in a hoarse whisper called to Half-John. I poured all the money into his big palm. He understood, and took it. His swarthy face blazed.

"You scruffy kid, you're out of your mind!" Fedya shouted. "You, cripple, give the boy back his money right away."

"Bastard!" I answered him. "You're worse than a thief. They ought to slap bums like you in the face and shoot them down like mad dogs."

Regina came back with a guest, and they remained in the doorway.

"What's going on here?"

Matryosha woke and sat up in her bed. Over Regina's shoulder, Agniya looked into the room, raising her compact over her head.

Fedya moved toward me, but I snatched a knife from the table.

"My pretty girl!" I shouted, as though I had been wounded, and I struck my fist on the table. The teapot and dishes jumped.

Tonya was waiting for me on the porch. It was seven o'clock in the evening, July, 1917.

I took Tonya's arm and led her first across the yard, then to the market place, past the Eclair where the third episode of *The Three of Hearts* was playing, past the bakeshop and the whorehouse to Tverskaya Street. Prostitutes came toward us, sometimes looking us over; officers and ladies walked quickly and carefully along the Bolshaya Gruzinskaya as though they were afraid of being spattered; hooligans, builders, cadets, rogues.

But there were people like us, too, in the stream of people moving against us: seamstresses, printers, plumbers. Some passed in front of us, jostling against us, with their tools in their hands or on their shoulders.

Translated by Sam Driver

Nikolai Nikitin

The Forest

"It could be that that forest is my love . . ."
N. Gumilyov

I

I love her, who runs from me, my fleeing love. And when I possess her entirely—she leaves again.

So my love is like a Russian swing.

But I also love the world, grasses and my art.

Everything in my life is necessary. And I enter carefully as into a bath made ready.

On a very barren and intoxicating day I write this story for my run-away love.

I would like the words to be as blood-thick as my anguish.

II

In the earth's hollows are rusty brews. On the hillocks, reddish, mossy grasses. The earth body is overgrown with red hair, warts, pools.

It is bare, unkempt, awkward—and mists wash the morning.

And the evenings wash the mists.

It is dull.

Emptiness lies like a hide, without end, without thought.

And in the sky only scanty dawns, promising nothing.

Whether it rains or not—steam hangs over the deep pools; and a worm crawls out to a rock, twisting its body-flesh into a ring. Moving its meaty sharp face, it sniffs.

But solitude is all around—quieter and more terrible than a pit. My bride, my endless earth—how shall you live?

III

In the mornings glimmer scanty dawns. Their wings and legs are like a lazy snipe's.

The indolent dawns struggle with the mists, but the mosses—gray and coarse—await something else. They wait for strength, so that hair would thicken and the earth would grow strong, chasing off the rust, and fill the pools with crystal. In the mornings it is colder and harder than stone; and such a stone is clear—our fate—tragic.

From the swamps and wastes spreads a rust:

"My bride . . . will you?"

There, from the blue swollen fields which sometimes drop damp and perspiring rains, and sometimes, drying up, stretch tighter and redder than worm's skin—from there came a voice:

"She will. . . ."

This is the sun—a kind red beast hurling warm grains into the earth, burning the pools and hillocks.

And, moving its paws, tears up the virgin soil, rips the earthen hide, shoving in grains. And the grains are light and molten, like gold. And the earth is warm, like pus.

In July the beast gathers the clouds like grains and squeezes them like a bear squeezing stones.

Blue swords burn in the sky—July storms; the earth is watered by rains.

So began the sun.

And having watered its work, beginning with the holy day, already wrapped it in soft white cloths. Becoming tired, it went over the edges where the ends of the earth are and where clouds lie which are like boundary stones on the furrows.

And all the long time of Russian frosts, the wind crackling

from the cold, the sun slept there, tucking its hot, able paws under its belly.

IV

Spring always comes to us unexpectedly, like love. On St. John's Eve the days are clear and light like the quiet of fields. In the pools the water is filmed over by flowering green lymph. And under the lymph the water denizens will sin in green, gentle dusk. No one disturbs—no one will lift the green canopies. There is love and birth. Because the prime strength, unholy strength is born immediately in the water.

In these light, field days, the kind beast awoke in the sky. It yawned well, licked its paws and put them out to dry in the soft spring wind. And while its paws, damp from the winter, were drying—the beast laughed. And because the beast laughed, along the ravines and dales the waters tumbled down.

The beast stroked the land, rumpling it with its paw. Barely touching it with its claws, it lifted the earthen crust—looked at the shoots under the crust.

And said to them simply—

"Well, kids, come out. . . ."

And the coming out took place this way:

The grains warmed up and burst and the shoot, salty as a tear and gay as a red dawn, spreading the shell with its body, came out and looked about.

And seeing the bare pools, pits and rusty still water in the puddles, swayed.

And another swayed.

And a third.

They look about. . . .

A force of them had run out on the waste, a glory of them had run out on the pits.

The hillocks are in verdure, in green nets. A bumblebee flew here in order to hum, in order to drink new and green honey.

This was the first bumblebee in the waste, in the solitary pits. He hummed because there was much room and much honey. And the bumblebee's humming gaily flew from the pools to the red sky, stretched like a skin.

There the beast sprawled, thinking—how much more work there was. . . . And carefully grasping the tendrils, pulled them up higher.

From that time on it nursed like an attentive nanny, warmed things in its hands with its breath, sifted the earth near by, dried mosses.

V

Thus the beast labored for years; and the years were tens of ours, and not one decade, but two, three, four—maybe seven. . . .

VI

In June, new grass grew. Cranberry—a pale pink and bell-like flower. In the dales, fragrant savory. By the pools, blades of grass, sharp as swords. And on the plump forest meadows, bright blue bluebells, slyer than a maiden's eye. Bluebells are a dangerous and bitter flower. But the more bitter bluebells are, the better. This grass is like a woman's love.

VII

The sun worked.

Forest upon forest evened out of the shoots and saplings. And in June and in July, the color of their skin was the same as the windy evening sky's—red.

And the forest had birds. For example—the cuckoo—a simple bird. And the cuckoo had lice.

From the prickly pine needles the ant came to life in order to build a kingdom for itself, to work. The ant's paws were as strong as the sun's, and its odor was just as thick and strong, and in perseverance the ant was equal to the sun. After all, the ant grew out of the pine and the sun.

VIII

In May—happiness, in June—joy, in July—strength, in August—intoxication, in winter—rest.

Thus lived the forest. And when it couldn't love, the sun guarded it—a kind red beast.

The years went by like water, true as ice, blessed in the shallows and exuberant in the inundation, in the floods.

And the beast in the sky knew exactly when and what to dry, when to gather clouds, when to water, when to dry.

IX

Again the waters came, and with the water, years.

Pink, white—the forest wedded by candlelight. In the sky the kind breast, red as copper, shouted. The beast beat a copper gong. And amidst the ringing the trunks whispered—pink, white, clear, just like the month of May, the month of June—joyful melodies.

The waters, years and ringing went on; and the cuckoo counted the years. And the birds sang wedding choruses. And life seemed to have no end. Thus thought the cuckoo.

X

The sun then decided—it will. . . .

And the trees decided—we will. . . .

And removing their bridal capes, they loved.

The wind brought them together on the peripheries. Crushed the green lace and tore the tight, virgin, fruit-bearing buds. Fever and wind strolled through the forest, and the bluebell grass breathed a bitterness. From her comes love. The wind carried the kisses.

The trunks swelled, matured and became heavy due to passion, springs, summers, windy years and quite quiet ones. And fate furrowed the bark. The trees grew, became heavy, multiplied—that is life.

Because there is strength in the branches, power in the leaves and pine needles, and because there was desire, the

saplings ran along the meadows; because of all this the forest
lived mightily.

And in the evenings, swinging on the resilient branches,
the sun thought: "All is good."

The bark was washed by rains—this made the skin golden;
the snows silvered it. Profuse wrinkles strengthened it—this
is also life.

Years, decades, a century . . . Possibly another. This century was aromatic, constant, joyful, like the ant who built a
kingdom for himself. And there grazed in the valleys the
pouchy, foolish forest cattle, and the grouse pecked at the
cranberry and the gamecocks fought at mating time.

It seemed to everyone that the house was good and true.
And in this house all wanted to live comfortably.

XI

Thus the forest grew up dark and well fed, stronger than
stone and richer than earth.

XII

Once, some unknown people came from afar, from the
swamps where the rusty still-water is and the rotten, wilted,
intestine-like grasses grow.

And the talk of these unknown people was rusty.

"Who are you?"

"Vanka Torban's son!"

"Then you're a relative."

"Is everything okay?"

"Everything's okay. . . . My son is a bit ill—no legs or
arms. Ma ran away from Pa, my brother Vaska they decided
to . . ."

"What?"

"By the throat."

"Stupid, I didn't ask that. . . . For what reason?"

"A lousy business. The court was miserable. . . . He
robbed a church, stole a chasuble and an incense burner, and
ripped the headdress off the Virgin Mother."

"That's nothing."

They chopped a fence and surrounded the forest with it. They cut down the raw saplings which don't burn at the root at all. While they were cutting them down, the saplings squeaked and cried. They piled them into a heap to dry. And the saplings dried. Then they set fire to the fence.

The fire was picked up by the wind and carried along the heaps of saplings and in the heaps thick golden water hissed and the spray flew like gold dust and the smoke smelled like dew at hay-mowing.

The fire boils and pours from the heaps into the forest. At first the roots burn slowly, then the clots of sap flare up like earrings. And now on the branches the incense burners smoked as on an altar during holidays, and along the tops of the pines, insane flaming squirrels galloped in herds.

Suddenly the wind, flames and beads shuddered. The trunks burst louder than cannons. Shooting and crumbling. Red smoke (because there is blood in trees) burned the sky. It bubbled; and together with the grasses, the dangerous bluebells, and the sharp vines, the earth cooked hard and light like an egg.

All in black blisters.

And for a week, if not longer, burned pus smoked from the blisters.

XIII

There is neither a forest nor grass—only ashes and dust.

And in the dust, not even a worm lives. The very same one which has a sharp, meaty snout.

The peasants, returning from the rusty swamps, calmly looked on.

"It's nothing. Plow up the earth; the ashes will do it good. . . ."

It happened the way the peasants thought it would.

In the first year, the earth, plowed with the oily, fat-like ashes, gave birth to wealth.

They didn't even know what to gather it with, where to store it.

And the peasants walked in a fog of happiness. And in the second year too. Out of the rye gaily scented bread was

baked and beer was brewed. They were even amazed—
"What luck we've had!" And the women, sent for by the
peasants, showed off their flaming new skirts.

This life is drunken and wasteful.

XIV

And then?

The next year they waited, but the earth bore only straw—
and little of that. The former harvests had eaten up all her
strength. The earth was completely impoverished. And now,
after drunkenness and wastefulness, instead of a forest and
field there is now an unkempt and bare waste.

Again an empty anguish and an empty wasteland, more
silent and blacker than a pit.

On the rugged bald hillocks mists entwine themselves in
the mornings.

Mists in the evenings.

Meager emptiness before the eyes—without end and without thought.

The same thing that was three hundred years ago. The
same rusty still-water in the pits and the former old dawns
glimmer in the sky.

Thus one day, when they lit the fire and looked long for
wealth in the ashes, thus on that unhappy day they squan-
dered the work of three centuries.

My bride, my earth—how and with what shall you live?

But there is no one. Only a worm crawled out to the rock.
It sniffs.

XV

There is!

There is that, of course! The most powerful.

It may be called life.

It may be called a kind, red beast.

The sun said firmly:

"All right . . . We shall start anew."

And harnessed itself to work, to greased boots, to the
earth, to sweat—in order to return.

The earth believed, because everything in the world is good and clear, except man, and of man there can be no doubt—all stupidity is in him.

And again the meadows began to perspire with warm, live steam.

XVI

The end.

This story is about what comes and goes, like a swing—about my love. Tonight I saw her in a dream, as if she were leaving me, and I cried with terrible tears. This means, according to an omen, that tomorrow she will return to me after the separation, as always—in new anguish, with new caresses. And I know that I cannot escape from woman's love, as the earth cannot not bear the bluebell grass, as people cannot get rid of their stupidity.

Translated by Natalie Bienstock

YURY OLESHA

THE CHERRY PIT

On Sunday I went to visit Natasha at her country place.
There were three other guests besides me: two young girls
and Boris Mikhailovich. The girls took off for the river to go
boating with Natasha's brother Erastus. We—that is, Natasha, Boris Mikhailovich and I—went for a walk in the
woods. In the woods we stretched out in a bright sunny
clearing. Natasha raised her head and suddenly her face
looked to me like a shiny porcelain plate.

Natasha treated me as an equal, but she played up to Boris
Mikhailovich as to an older person. She knew this made me
unhappy, that I'm jealous of Boris Mikhailovich, and so
whenever she said something she kept squeezing my hand
and asking:

"Right, Fedya?"

That is, as if to beg my pardon in a roundabout sort of way.

We heard a silly birdcall from the thicket and that started
us talking about birds. I said that in all my life I had never
seen a thrush, for example, and I asked: "What's a thrush
like?"

A bird flew out of the thicket. It flew above the clearing and
sat on a protruding branch just over our heads. It didn't sit,
actually, but stood there on the swaying branch and blinked.
And I thought to myself that bird's eyes are very ugly—they
have no eyebrows but very prominent eyelids.

"What's that?" I asked in a whisper. "A thrush? Is that a thrush?"

Nobody answered me. I had my back turned to them. Without my greedy eyes following them, they reveled in being alone. I looked at the bird. Then I glanced back and saw that Boris Mikhailovich was stroking Natasha on the cheek. His hand was clearly thinking: *Let that fellow with the chip on his shoulder keep looking at the bird!* But I couldn't watch the bird any more—I had to eavesdrop. I heard the sticky sound of a kiss. I didn't turn around, but they knew they were caught: they saw me give a start.

"Is that a thrush?" I asked.

The bird was gone. It had soared away, high through the treetops. It flew away with difficulty, brushing the leaves with its wings.

Natasha offered us some cherries. I kept one cherry pit in my mouth, an old childhood habit. It rolled about in my mouth until it was sucked clean. I took it out—it looked as if it were made of wood.

I left the country place with the cherry pit in my mouth.

Now I travel through an invisible country.

I'm walking, returning from the country to the city. The sun is setting, I'm walking to the east. But I'm making a double journey. My first journey is clear to everyone: a passer-by sees a man strolling through a deserted, verdant countryside. But what's going on with this peaceful pedestrian? He sees his own shadow going before him. The shadow moves along the ground far ahead of him; it has long, pale feet. I come across a wasteland, and the shadow climbs a brick wall and suddenly loses its head. This the passer-by cannot see; this I alone can see. I enter a passageway between two buildings. The buildings are endlessly high, and the passageway is filled with shadows. The soil here is decayed and crumbly, as in a garden patch. A wild dog comes running along the wall to meet me. We pass each other—I look around—the doorstep, left behind, is shining. There on the doorstep the dog is suddenly surrounded by a flash of sunlight. But he manages to escape and runs into the wasteland; only then can I define its color—reddish.

All this took place in the invisible country, for in the land of normal observation something quite different occurs: simply, a traveler meets a dog, the sun sets, the wasteland is green. . . .

The invisible country—that's the land of observation and imagination. Here the traveler is never lonely, for two sisters go at his side, leading him by the hand. One sister is called Observation, the other Imagination.

Well, what does this all mean? Does it mean that in defiance of everyone, in defiance of order and society I may create a world which is controlled by no laws at all other than the illusory laws of my own personal sensation? But what does this mean? There are two worlds: the old and the new. But what sort of a world is *this*? A third world? There are two paths; but what sort of a third path is *this*?

Natasha made a date with me but didn't show up.

I arrived half an hour early.

A public clock is hanging above the intersection. It reminds you of a small barrel, doesn't it? Two clock faces—two bottoms. Oh, empty barrel of time!

Natasha's supposed to come at three-thirty.

I wait. Oh, of course she's not coming. It's now ten after three.

I'm standing at the trolley stop. Everything's moving around me, only I am motionless. People who have lost their way spot me from a distance. And now it all begins. . . . A strange lady comes up to me.

"Excuse me," says the strange lady. "Can you tell me if Twenty-Seven will take me to Kudrinskaya?"

No one has to know that I'm waiting for a girl. Let them think instead: *This young man who smiles so broadly came to this very corner to help everyone; he'll explain everything, he'll arrange everything, he'll comfort us . . . to him! . . . to him!*

"Yes," I answer, quite exhausted from so much courtesy. "Twenty-Seven will take you to Kudrinskaya."

Then I suddenly remember and rush after the lady.

"Oh no, I'm sorry! You have to take Sixteen."

Oh, let's forget about the date. I'm not in love. I'm the good genie of the street. To me! To me!

A quarter after three. The hands of the clock have come together, making a single horizontal line. Seeing this I think: *It's a fly twisting its feet. The restless fly of time.*

Stupid! What kind of a fly of time can there be?

She hadn't come. She wouldn't come.

Now a soldier comes up to me.

"Tell me," he asks, "where's the Darwin Museum?"

"I don't know . . . that way, I think . . . just a minute . . . just a minute . . . no, I don't know, comrade, I don't know. . . ."

Next! Who's next? Come on, don't be shy. . . .

A taxi making a turn pulls up to me. Just see how scornfully the driver looks at me! Not that he'd stoop to scorning me wholeheartedly, oh, no! He scorns me with his gloves! Comrade driver, believe me, I'm only an amateur, I can't tell you where to turn your car . . . I'm not standing here to give directions . . . I have my own things to do . . . my standing here like this—I have to, it's pathetic! I'm not smiling from good-naturedness—my smile is forced . . . just look!

"Which way to Varsonofevsky?" the driver asks over his shoulder.

Flustered, I explain: "That way, that way, and then that way . . ."

Come to think of it, why shouldn't I stand in the middle of the street and really take the job seriously since they're foisting it on me?

A blind man's coming toward me. Oh, this one's simply crying out at me! he nudges me with his cane. . . .

"Is Number Ten coming?" he asks. "Eh? Ten?"

"No," I answer, almost caressing him. "No, comrade, this isn't Ten. It's Two. But here comes Ten."

Natasha's already ten minutes late. Why wait any more? But maybe she's somewhere, hurrying, flying to me . . . *Ah, how late I am, how late!*

The lady's already rolled away on Sixteen; the soldier's walking in the cool rooms of the museum; the driver's already honking away to Varsonofevsky; the blind man's already mounting the front platform, irritably and selfishly holding his cane in front of him.

They're all satisfied! All happy! And I'm just standing here, smiling idiotically.

And again, people come up and ask things: an old woman, a drunk, a group of children carrying a flag. And soon I begin to wave my arms about wildly. I don't just nod my head any more like an ordinary person asked something—no! I'm reaching my arm out, palm edgewise . . . another minute and a night stick will rise up out of my fist. . . .

"Back!" I'll shout. "Stop! To Varsonofevsky? Turn around! Old woman, to the right! Stop!"

Oh, look! There's a whistle hanging between my lips . . . I'm blowing it . . . I have the right to whistle . . . children, envy me! Back! Hoho . . . look! Now I can stand in the middle of the street between two lines of traffic. Just look at me—I'm standing there, one leg forward and my hands behind my back, propping up my shoulder blade with my crimson night stick.

Congratulate me, Natasha. I've turned into a police-man. . . .

Then I notice Abel standing a little way off and watching me. (Abel—that's my neighbor.)

Natasha won't come, that's obvious. I call Abel:

I: Did you see that, Abel?

Abel: I did. You're crazy.

I: Did you see, Abel? I turned into a policeman.

(Pause. One more glance at the clock. Damn! Ten to four.)

Abel: Your invisible country—that's all idealistic delirium.

I: And you know what's the most amazing thing, Abel? The most amazing thing is the fact that in this magic country I figure as a policeman. . . . You'd think that I ought to walk about it peacefully and majestically like a sovereign, a prophet's flowering staff shining in my hand . . . but now look—instead of that, a policeman's night stick. What a strange crossing of the practical and the imaginary worlds. And what's even stranger is that the premise which turned me into a policeman was undivided love.

Abel: I don't understand any of this. It's all some sort of Bergsonism.

* * *

I decided to bury my cherry pit.

I picked a spot and buried it.

Here, I thought, a cherry tree will spring up, planted in honor of my love for Natasha. Perhaps some day, perhaps five years from today in the springtime, I'll meet Natasha by this new tree. We'll stand on each side of it—cherry trees aren't very tall: if you stand on your toes you can shake the highest blossoms. The sun will be shining brightly but the spring will be somewhat empty, for it will be that time of spring when sewage gutters lure children out, when this imaginary tree will burst into bloom.

I'll say:

"Natasha, the day is bright and clear, the wind is blowing gently, making the day even brighter. The wind is shaking my tree; its lacquered branches creak. Each blossom rises and falls so the tree is sometimes pink and sometimes white. It is the kaleidoscope of spring, Natasha. Five years ago you offered me some cherries, remember? I remember to this day: your palm was purple from the cherry juice, and you made it into a tube, pouring the berries out for me. I took a cherry pit away in my mouth and I planted a tree in memory of the fact that you didn't love me. It's blossoming now. There, you see it. I was ridiculed then. Boris Mikhailovich was manly and he won you, but I was dreamy, infantile. I was looking for a thrush in the world while you were kissing. I was a romantic. But just look now: a hard, virile tree has grown from the seed of the romantic. A cherry blossom, you know, is the soul of a man—that's what the Japanese believe. Take a look: here stands a small, strong, Japanese tree. Believe me, Natasha, romanticism is a manly thing, and not something to be laughed at. You see, everything depends on how you approach it. If Boris Mikhailovich had met me squatting in the wasteland and burying a childish cherry pit, he would have again felt his victory over me—the victory of a man over a daydreamer. But at that very time I was hiding the kernel in the ground. It burst and let out a blinding explosion. It was a family that I hid in the ground. This tree is my child from you, Natasha. Bring me the son Boris Mikhailovich gave you.

I'll take a look and see if he's as healthy, as clean, as unrelated as this tree, fathered by a childish daydreamer."

I came home from the country. Straight away Abel popped into my room. Abel's a skilled laborer. He's short, has on a short paper-covered shirt, sandals, blue socks. He's clean-shaven but his cheeks are black. No matter what, Abel always looks unshaven. His face seems to be made up not of two but of only one cheek—a black one. Abel has an aquiline nose and one black cheek.

Abel: What's going on with you? On my way out to the country today I saw you squatting down on the ground, digging the earth with your hands. What's going on?

(I am silent.)

Abel (pacing up and down the room): A man squatting on his heels, digging in the ground. What's he doing? Who knows. Is he making an experiment? Or is he having an attack? Who knows. Are you subject to attacks?

I (after a pause): You know what I was thinking, Abel? I was thinking that daydreamers ought not to have children. Of what use to the new world are daydreamers' children? Let daydreamers make trees for the benefit of the new world.

Abel: That's not provided for in the Plan.

The land of Observation begins at the head of the bed, on the chair which you've pulled toward your bed while getting undressed before going to sleep. You wake up early in the morning, the house is still asleep, the room is full of sunshine. Quiet. Don't stir, don't destroy the stillness of the light. A pair of socks lies on the chair. They're brown. But in the stillness and brightness of the light you suddenly observe that the brown wool has separate, multicolored strands curling through the air: crimson, blue, orange.

Sunday morning. I tramped once again along the familiar path to visit Natasha. I was writing a book as I walked entitled *Journey Through an Invisible Country*. If you want, here's a chapter from *Journey* which ought to be called: *The Man Who Hurried to Throw a Stone*

There were shrubs growing at the bottom of the brick wall. I walked along the path bordered by the shrubs. I noticed a niche in the wall, and I felt an impulse to throw a stone into the niche. A stone was lying at my feet, I bent down to pick it up . . . and then I saw an ant hill.

The last time I had seen an ant hill was twenty years ago. Oh, of course I had stepped on ant hills many times in the course of these twenty years—how many times! And certainly I had noticed them, but noticing them, I didn't think: I'm stepping on an ant hill; no, simply the word "ant hill" flashed into my mind, and nothing more. In an instant the living image was obligingly pushed out by the appropriate term.

And then it all came back to me: ant hills are discovered by glancing down unexpectedly. One . . . Oh! There's another! and then—look! There's still another! That's what happened now. One after another I discovered three ant hills.

I couldn't really see the ants from my height; my sight caught only a certain agitation of forms which could easily be made to seem motionless. And my sight readily accepted the illusion; I looked and agreed to think that these weren't ants swarming around their ant hills, but ant hills themselves, crumbling like sand dunes.

Stone in hand, I stood about four steps from the wall. The stone had to land in the niche. I swung my arm. The stone flew off and hit the bricks. A cloud of dust rose up. I had missed. The stone fell to the foot of the wall, into the shrubbery. Only then did I hear the cry of the stone, uttered even before I had opened my palm to throw it:

"Wait!" cried the stone. "Look at me!"

And really, thinking it over, I should have given the stone a looking-over. Why, without a doubt, it was a remarkable thing in itself. And now it lay in the shrubbery, in the overgrowth—gone! And I, having held this thing in my hand, don't even know what color it was. Maybe it was purplish. Maybe it wasn't monolithic, but made up of several different materials. Maybe there was some sort of fossil in it—the remains of a beetle or a cherry pit. Maybe the stone was porous. And finally, maybe I hadn't picked up a stone at all, but a petrified bone!

I met a group of hikers on the road.

Twenty people were walking across the wasteland where my cherry pit reposed. Abel was leading them. I stepped aside. Abel didn't see me, or rather, Abel saw me but didn't realize that he saw me; like any fanatic, he swallowed me without waiting for my agreement or resistance.

Abel detached himself from his flock, turned to face them (his back toward me) and exclaimed with a mighty wave of his arm:

"Right here! Right here! Right here!"

A pause. Silence.

"Comrades from Kursk, there!" Abel shouted. "I hope you have some imagination. Use it, don't be afraid!"

Oh! Abel is trying to break into the country of Imagination. Could he be trying to show his hikers the cherry tree blossoming in honor of undivided love?

Abel is looking for paths to the invisible country. . . .

He's walking. He's stopped, shaking his foot. He shakes it again and again, trying to free himself from some sort of a curling plant which had gotten tangled around his foot as he walked.

He stamped his foot again, the plant crackled, and little yellow balls rolled away. (How many plants in this story, how many trees and shrubs!)

"Here's where the giant I told you about will come up."

. . . Dear Natasha, I've lost sight of the most important thing: the Plan. I acted without consulting the plan, but the plan exists. In five years time, at this very spot, where now there's only wasteland, ditches and useless walls, a concrete giant will be erected. My sister Imagination is a rash person. They'll begin to lay the foundation in the spring—and then what will become of my stupid cherry pit? Someday, in the invisible country, the tree dedicated to you will still start blossoming. . . .

The hikers will come here to see the concrete giant. They won't see your tree. Is it really impossible to make the invisible country visible? . . . .

This is an imaginary letter. I never wrote it. I could have written it if Abel hadn't said what he did.

"The structure will be laid out in a semicircle," said Abel.

"The whole interior of the semicircle will be taken up by a garden. Have you any imagination?"

"Yes," I answered, "I see, Abel. I see clearly. The garden will be here. And on the very spot where you're standing a cherry tree will grow."

Translated by Marie Winn

BORIS PASTERNAK

THE CHILDHOOD OF LUVERS

THE LONG DAYS

I

Luvers was born and grew up in Perm. Just as her toy boats and dolls were once drowned in shaggy bearskins which filled the house, so, later on, were her recollections. Her father managed the Lunevsky mines and had a large clientele among the factory-owners of Chusovaya.

The skins were luxurious gifts, dark reddish-brown in color. The white she-bear in her nursery resembled a huge chrysanthemum scattering its petals. This was the skin acquired for "Zhenichka's room"—selected, haggled over in the store and sent home by messenger.

During the summer they lived in a *dacha* on the far shore of the Kama River. In those days Zhenya was sent to bed early. She could not see the lights of Motovilikha. But once, frightened by something, the Angora cat stirred abruptly in its sleep and awakened Zhenya. Then she caught sight of the adults on the balcony. The alder hanging over the balustrade was thick and iridescent like ink. The tea in the glasses was red. Cuffs and cards—yellow, the cloth—green. It was like delirium, but this delirium had its own name, known even to Zhenya: card-playing.

On the other hand, it was in no way possible to determine

what was happening on the opposite shore, far in the distance; it had no name and had neither distinct color nor precise outline; in its undulations it was dear and familiar and not like delirium, like that which rumbled and tossed about in the puffs of tobacco smoke, casting fresh, breezy shadows on the reddish beams of the gallery. Zhenya burst into tears. Her father entered and explained. Their English governess turned to the wall. Her father's explanation was brief. It is Motovilikha. Shame on you. Such a big girl. Sleep. The little girl understood nothing and contentedly licked off a tear rolling down her cheek. She requested only one thing: to find out the name of the incomprehensible—Motovilikha. That night this name explained everything, because that night the name still possessed a complete and soothing significance for the child.

But in the morning she began to ask questions about what it was—Motovilikha, and what happened there at night, and she found out that Motovilikha was a factory, a government factory, and that pig iron was made there, and from pig iron . . . but this no longer held her attention or interested her, and she wondered whether there were special countries called "factories" and who lived there; but these questions she did not ask and, for some reason, intentionally kept them to herself.

That morning she left the state of infancy in which she had been just the night before. For the first time in her life she suspected the existence of certain things which a phenomenon keeps for its own use or reveals only to those people who know how to shout and to punish, who smoke and bolt doors. For the first time she, like this new Motovilikha, did not say everything she thought, and the most essential, necessary and perturbing things she kept to herself.

Years passed. The children, from birth, had become so accustomed to the departures of their father, that in their eyes fatherhood was reduced to a special quality of rarely dining and never supping. More and more frequently, they played and squabbled, drank and ate in completely empty and solemnly uninhabited rooms, and the cold lectures of their English governess could not replace the presence of a mother who filled the house with the sweet distress of obstinacy and a quick temper, like a familiar electric current. The quiet northern day streamed through the curtains. It did not smile. The oaken sideboard appeared gray-haired. The silver was piled up gravely and sternly. The hands of the English girl, bathed with lavender, moved over the tablecloth: she never gave anyone too small a portion and possessed an inexhaustible supply of patience; she maintained a sense of fairness which was as peculiar to her nature as the constant need to have her room and books clean and orderly. The maid, having served one dish, remained standing in the dining room, and only went back to the kitchen for the next course. Everything was comfortable and agreeable, but terribly sad.

Because these were years of suspicion and loneliness for the little girl, years of guilt-feeling and what one would like to call *christianisme* in French, because it is impossible to call it Christianity, she sometimes felt that nothing could ever, or would ever, improve due to her depravity and impenitence; that everything was exactly as it should be. Meanwhile—but this never reached the consciousness of the children—on the contrary, their entire bodies quaked and fermented, confused at their parents' attitude toward them whenever they were at home, when they entered the house rather than returned home.

In general, their father's rare jokes were unsuccessful and often not quite apropos. He felt this and sensed that the children understood his feelings. A certain cast of sad confusion never left his face. When irritable, he would become an absolute stranger; a complete foreigner at the very moment when he lost his self-control. A stranger touches no one. The children never answered back to him rudely.

However, for some time the criticism coming from the nursery and solemnly expressing itself in the eyes of the children, found him insensitive. He did not notice it. Invulnerable to everything, somehow unrecognizable and pitiable —*this* father was terrifying as opposed to the irritable father, the stranger. He affected the little girl more than the son. But their mother confused them both.

She showered them with caresses and loaded them with gifts and spent long hours with them when they least of all wanted to be with her, when their childish consciences were overwhelmed by a sense of undeserving, and they did not recognize themselves in all those endearing pet names which her instinct extravagantly poured over them.

And often, when a rare, limpid peace entered their souls, and they no longer felt like criminals, when their consciences were relieved of all the secrecy which shuns detection like fever preceding a rash, they saw their mother as a quick-tempered stranger who avoided them and who became angry without cause. The postman arrived. The letter was taken to the addressee, to mama. She accepted it without a thank you. "Go to your room." The door slammed. They silently hung their heads and, feeling miserable, yielded to a lengthy, despondent feeling of bewilderment.

At first, when this happened, they cried; later on, after one especially sharp outburst, they became frightened; then, as years passed, this fear changed into a smoldering, ever more deeply rooted enmity.

Everything that passed from parents to children, came inopportunely, indirectly, not provoked by them, but by some extraneous reason, and everything emitted a sense of remoteness, as always happens, and a sense of mystery, as at night the whimpering beyond the gates when everyone lies down to sleep.

These circumstances reared the children. They were not conscious of this for there are few, even among adults, who are aware of, or able to discern, what it is that creates, harmonizes and stitches them together. Life lets very few into the secret of what she will do with them. She loves her cause too well, and only speaks about her work with those who wish her success and who are fond of her workbench. No one has the power to help her; anyone can hinder her. How? In this manner. If one entrusted a tree with the care of its own growth, the entire tree would become all branch or disappear completely into roots or lavish itself on one leaf, because it would forget about the universe which must be taken for a model and, having produced one thing out of a thousand, would begin to produce that very same thing by the thousands.

And so that there shall not be dead branches in the soul, so that its growth shall not be retarded, so that man shall not involve his small mind in the creation of his immortal essence, many things have been instituted to deflect his vulgar curiosity away from life, who does not like to work in his presence and avoids him in every way. Hence all respectable religions and all generalizations and all people's prejudices and the most brilliant of them all, the most amusing—*psychology*.

The children no longer remained at the stage of pristine infancy. Concepts of punishment, retribution, rewards and justice had already penetrated their childlike souls and deflected their consciousnesses, letting life do with them whatever she considered necessary, exigent and beautiful.

II

Miss Hawthorn would not have done it. But in one of her fits of irrational tenderness toward the children, Madame Luvers spoke sharply to the English governess about a most trivial matter, and she disappeared from the house. Soon afterward her place was imperceptibly filled by a consumptive French girl. Later on, Zhenya could recall only that the French girl resembled a fly, and that no one loved her. Her name was completely lost, and Zhenya could not have said among what syllables and sounds one could stumble upon this name. She remembered only that the French girl had shouted at her first, and later, picked up the scissors and cut away that place in the bearskin stained with blood.

It seemed to her then that everyone would always be shouting at her, that her headache would never pass and she would be sick indefinitely, and that never again would she be able to understand that page in her favorite book which stupidly began to blur before her, like a textbook after dinner.

That day dragged on for a terribly long time. Her mother was not home that day. Zhenya was not sorry. She even felt that she was glad at her mother's absence.

Soon the long day was buried in oblivion amid forms of the *passé and futur antérieur*, watering hyacinths and strolling along the Sibirskaya and Okhanskaya. It was so well forgotten that she noted and sensed the length of the other day, the second one in her life, only toward evening, while sitting by the lamp reading, when the slow-moving story aroused in her hundreds of the most idle thoughts. Much later, when she recalled that house in the Osinskaya where they lived, it always appeared to her as she had seen it on that second long day as it was drawing to a close. It was a long day indeed. Spring was outside. Spring in the Urals, brought to fruition feebly and with great difficulty, burst forth wildly and tempestuously, in the course of a single night, and then tempestuously and wildly flowed onward. The lamps only set off the vacuous quality of the evening air. They did not reflect light, but swelled from within like diseased fruit, from the light and lusterless dropsy which dilated their bloated shades. They were absent. One encountered them where they were supposed to be, in their places in rooms, on tables and hanging from sculptured ceilings, where the little girl was accustomed to see them. But all the while the lamps maintained fewer points of contact with the rooms than with the spring sky, toward which they seemed to be moving, like a drink toward the bed of a sick man. Their souls were out on the street, where the servants' gossip in the damp earth crawled, and where drops of melting snow congealed for the night. It was there the lamps vanished for the evening. Her parents were away. However, it seemed that her mother was expected that day. That long day or the next. Probably. Or, perhaps, she would arrive unexpectedly. That too was possible.

Zhenya began to prepare for bed and found that that day had been long for the very same reason as the day before, and at first she thought of getting the scissors and cutting away those places on her nightgown and on the sheet, but later decided to take some powder from the French governess and rub the spots white; and just as she took the powderbox in her hands, the French girl entered and slapped her. Her whole sin was concentrated in the powder. "She powders herself. Only that was missing. Now she finally understood. She had noticed it long ago." Zhenya burst out crying because of the slaps, because of the scolding and because she was offended; because, knowing she was innocent of the crime of which the French girl suspected her, she also knew she was guilty—she *felt* it—of something else, something far worse than what her governess suspected. It was necessary—she felt this to the point of insensibility, she felt it in her temples and in the calves of her legs—it was necessary to conceal it, not knowing how or why, but somehow, in any possible way. Her joints moved painfully as if executing a fading hypnotic suggestion. And this suggestion, agonizing and exhausting, was the work of the organism which concealed from the little girl the significance of everything that was happening to her; the organism, behaving like a criminal, forced her to see in her bleeding a disgusting, heinous, wrong. *"Menteuse!"* She was compelled merely to make denials, after having stubbornly refused to speak about that which was more odious to her than anything else, and she found herself somewhere in the middle, between the shame of illiteracy and the disgrace of a street scandal. She began to shiver, clenching her teeth, and choking back her tears, she pressed herself against the wall. It was impossible to jump into the Kama because it was still cold and the last vestiges of ice were floating down the river.

Neither she nor the French governess heard the sound of the bell. The excitement which had flared up vanished into the depths of dark reddish-brown bearskins; and when her mother entered it was too late. She found her daughter in tears, the French girl—blushing. She demanded an explanation. The French girl told her bluntly that—not Zhenya, no— *votre enfant*—she said, *her daughter* was powdering herself, that she noticed it and had suspected it for a long time—the mother would not let her finish—her terror was not pretense —her little girl was not yet thirteen. "Zhenya, you? My God, what are we coming to?" (At that moment the mother felt that her words meant something, as if she, too, had known for a long time that her little daughter was disgracing and degrading herself, and that she had failed to deal with the situation in time—and now she found her Zhenya falling lower and lower.) "Zhenya, tell me the whole truth . . . it will be worse . . . what were you doing . . . with the box of powder?" is probably what Madame Luvers intended to say, but she said "with this thing" and seized "this thing" and brandished it in the air. "Mama, don't believe Mademoiselle, I never . . ." and she burst into tears. But her mother heard only wicked sounds in her weeping where none were present. She felt herself to be at fault and she suffered an inner terror; it was necessary, she thought, to remedy everything; it was necessary even to contradict her maternal instincts—"to rise to pedagogical and judicious measures." She resolved not to yield to compassion. She was determined to wait until this flood of tears, profoundly tormenting her, would cease to flow.

She sat down on the bed, gazing quietly and vacantly at the edge of the bookshelf. From her body came an odor of costly perfume. When her daughter had calmed down, she began to question her again. Zhenya stared out the window, her eyes red from weeping, and whimpered. Ice was drifting and, probably, making noise. A star was shining. The empty night harshly black, wrought and cold but lackluster. Zhenya turned her eyes away from the window. In her mother's voice she heard a threatened impatience. The French girl stood by the wall, all seriousness and concentrated pedagogy. Her hand in an adjutant-like position, rested on the ribbon of her watch. Zhenya stared at the stars and the Kama River once more. She made up her mind. In spite of the cold, in spite of the ice. She plunged in. Enmeshed in her own words, she inaccurately and fearfully told her mother all *about this thing*. Her mother let her talk herself out only because she was stunned by the emotional intensity expressed in her child's confession. Understand; she understood everything from the first word. No, no: from the moment the little girl swallowed deeply before beginning her story. The mother listened in ecstasy, loving and burning with tenderness for this slender little body. She wanted to throw herself at her daughter's neck and weep. But—pedagogy: she rose from the bed and lifted the coverlet off the bed. She called her daughter to her and began to stroke her hair slowly, slowly, tenderly. "You're a good girl . . ." The words tumbled from her lips. She walked to the window, noisily, and turned her back on them. Zhenya did not see the French girl. Tears and her mother completely filled the room. "Who makes the bed?" The question had no meaning. The little girl trembled. She felt

sorry for Grusha. Then something unfamiliar was said in
French: angry words. And then again in a different voice,
"Zhenichka, go into the dining room, sweetheart. I'll come
there in just a minute and tell you about the marvelous *dacha*
papa and I have taken for you this summer."

The lamps became themselves again, as in winter, at home,
with the Luvers—warm, zealous, friendly. Her mother's sa-
ble frisked about the blue woolen tablecloth. "Won. Am
holding to Blagodat wait end Passion Week unless—" it was
impossible to read the rest since the edge of the telegram was
folded. Zhenya sat down on the edge of the sofa, tired and
happy. She sat down unpretentiously and comfortably, exactly as she sat down six months later in the corridor of the
Ekaterinburg school on the edge of a cold, yellow bench
when, having received a five for her answers in the Russian
language, she learned that she "could enter."

The next morning her mother told her what to do when
this happened; she said it was nothing, and that one must not
be afraid since it would happen again. She called nothing by
name and explained nothing, but added that now she, herself, would prepare her daughter's lessons because she
would never go away again.

The French girl was fired on grounds of negligence, after
only a few months with the family. As she was coming down
the stairs on the day that the coachman came to fetch her, she
met the doctor coming up from the landing. He answered
her greeting very coldly and said nothing about her departure; she suspected that he already knew everything, scowled
and shrugged her shoulders.

The maid was standing in the open doorway, waiting to
admit the doctor, and that is why in the vestibule where
Zhenya was, the din of footsteps and the reverberation of
ringing cobblestones echoed longer than usual in the air.
And in this way the story of the first stage of a girl's maturity
was imprinted in her memory: the full echo of chirping
streets in the morning, hesitating on the stairway, and freely
pervading the house; the French governess, the maid and the
doctor, the two criminals and the one initiate, cleansed,

disinfected by the light, the fresh air, the sonority of shuffling footsteps.

It was a warm, sunny April day. "Feet, feet, wipe your feet," the bare bright corridor echoed from end to end. The bearskins were put away for the summer. The rooms arose clean, transfigured, and sighed with pleasure and relief. All day long, all that wearisome adhesive day without sunset, in all the corners and spaces of the rooms, in the mirrors and in panes of glass leaning against the wall, in tumblers of water and in the blue air of the garden, blinking and preening themselves, the bird cherry laughed and raged, and the choking honeysuckle washed itself; everything was insatiable, unquenchable.

The tedious chatter of the courtyards continued around the clock; the passing hours announced that night was dethroned and repeated throughout the day, gently and incessantly, in roulades acting like a sleeping draft, that evening would never come again and they would let no one sleep. "Feet, feet!" but they burned; they arrived drunk from the air with ringing ears and because of this they failed to understand the sense of what was being said and they strove to chew and swallow as quickly as possible so that, having pushed back their chairs with a scraping noise, they could run right back into this day which was breaking through into evening, this day in which the tree drying in the sun cracked sharply, the dark blue sky chattered stridently and the earth glistened greasily like rendered fat. The boundary between the house and courtyard was obliterated. But the rag did not wash away the last trace. The floors were covered with a dry and shining dust and they crackled.

Her father brought home sweets and miracles. Everything became wondrously pleasant in their house. With a moist rustle precious stones announced their appearance from under the colored tissue paper which became ever more transparent as layer after layer was removed from these soft, white gauze-like packets. Some of the stones resembled droplets of almond milk; others, splashes of blue watercolor, and a third group resembled solidified tears of cheese. Some were blind, sleepy and dreamy, others had a playful sparkle like the frozen juice of blood-oranges. No one wished to touch them. They were perfect on the frothing paper which secreted them, like a plum secreting its lusterless juice.

Their father was unusually gentle with the children; also, he often accompanied their mother to town. They would return together and they appeared joyful. But most important, both were calm, even-tempered and affable; and when their mother would gaze at their father, from time to time, with an air of playful reproach, it seemed as if she elicited this peace from his small and homely eyes, and then poured it from her own which were large and beautiful, onto her children and those surrounding her.

Once her parents arose very late. Then, no one knows why, they decided to take lunch on the steamer standing by the wharf and they took the children with them. Seryozha was allowed to taste cold beer. They enjoyed everything so much that they decided to take lunch on the steamer again. The children did not recognize their parents. What had happened to them? The little girl attained a state of perplexed, blissful happiness and it seemed to her that everything would always be as it was then. They were not saddened by learning that they would not be going to the *dacha* that summer. Their father soon went away. Three huge, yellow traveling trunks with solid metal rims appeared in the house.

III

The train left late at night. Mr. Luvers had moved a month earlier and now wrote that the apartment was ready. Several cab-drivers set off for the station at a trot. Its approach was announced by the color of the pavement. It became black, and the street lamps lashed at the brown railroad ties. At that moment, as they crossed the viaduct, a view of the Kama was revealed, and below them ran a soot-black pit, crashing along heavily and terribly. It ran off, swift as an arrow, and then, far in the distance, at the farthest point, it took fright, gathered momentum and began to quake and quiver amid the twinkling beads of distant signals.

It was windy. Silhouettes flew down from houses and fences, like chaff from a sieve; they tossed about and were frayed in the pitted air. There was an odor of potatoes. Their cab-driver pulled his horse out of the line of jolting baskets and carriage-backs in front and began to overtake them. From a distance they recognized the cart carrying their luggage; they caught up with it; Ulyasha yelled something to her mistress, but the rattling of wheels concealed it, and she shivered and shook, and her voice jolted.

The little girl did not notice any sadness in the novelty of all these night sounds and darkness and fresh air. Far, far in the distance something blackened mysteriously. Beyond the warehouses of the wharf, lights were dangling from the shore and from boats—the town rinsed them in the water. Then many more appeared and they began to swarm thickly, greasily, blind like maggots. On the Lubimovsky wharf, funnels, roofs of warehouses and decks shone a sober blue. Barges stood by, gazing at the stars. "Here's a rat-hole," thought Zhenya. White porters surrounded them. Seryozha jumped down first. He glanced about and was very surprised to find that their baggage cart had already arrived; the horse threw back her head, raised her collar and reared up like a cock; she pressed against the rear of the carriage and began to back-step. Seryozha had been preoccupied throughout the journey by how far behind them their luggage cart would remain.

The boy stood there in his white school uniform, intoxicated by the prospect of the trip. The journey was a novelty for both of them, but he already knew and loved the sounds of the words: "depot," "locomotive," "siding," "through-train," and the association of sounds: "class," seemed to him to have a sour-sweet taste. His sister was also attracted by all this but in her own way, without the boyish systematization which distinguished her brother's enthusiasm.

Suddenly their mother appeared next to them, as if she had arisen out of the ground. She had the children taken to the buffet. From there, wending her way through the crowd like a peahen, she went directly to the person called, as loudly and threateningly as possible, "the stationmaster"—a name to be mentioned often thereafter, in many places, with variations, among different crowds.

Yawns overpowered them. They sat down by one of the windows which were so laden with dust, so stiff and so vast that they appeared as institutions made of bottle-glass wherein it is impossible to remain if one is wearing a hat. The little girl saw not only a street beyond the window, but also a room; however, it was more severe and depressing than the picture on the decanter nearby; and steam-engines slowly entered this room and stopped, carrying darkness with them; but after they left the room and it was empty, it seemed not to be a room any more because the sky was visible behind the columns, and on the other side a rolling meadow and wooden houses and people were walking there, moving farther away; perhaps over there cocks were crowing, and perhaps not long before the water carrier had spilled pools of water.

It was a provincial railway station without the glow and commotion of the capital; where travelers gathered early, away from the city shrouded in darkness; where there was long waiting, silence and wanderers who slept on the floor among hunting dogs, suitcases, engines wrapped in straw and unprotected bicycles.

The children lay down in the upper berths. The boy fell asleep immediately. The train was still standing in the station. Gradually, it dawned on the little girl, it grew clear to her, that the carriage was clean, blue and chilly. And gradually it became clear—but she was already sleeping.

He was a very fat man. He was reading a newspaper and swaying. Looking at him, the swaying became evident; everything in the compartment was saturated and inundated by swaying, as if by the sun. Zhenya examined him from above with that lazy precision with which one thinks about something or views something when he is fully and freshly awake, remaining in bed merely because he is waiting, because the decision to get up will come itself, without outside help, clearly and naturally, like his other thoughts. She examined him and thought: where did he enter their compartment, and when did he manage to wash and dress? She had no conception of the time of day. She had just awakened, consequently it was morning. She examined him but he could not see her; her upper berth was well inclined into the wall. He also did not see her because he rarely glanced from his newspaper—

and when he did raise his head toward her berth, their eyes did not meet, and either he saw just the mattress or . . . but she quickly tucked bare legs under herself and pulled on her scanty stockings. Mama was in the other corner. She was already dressed and was reading a book, Zhenya decided reflectively as she studied the look of the fat man. But Seryozha was not below. Where was he? And she yawned sweetly and stretched. It was terribly hot; only then had she realized it, and she turned from the heads to peer out the small partially opened window. "But where is the earth?" she exclaimed in her heart.

What she saw defies description. The vociferous hazelnut forest into which the serpentine train was pouring them became a sea, a world, anything you wish, everything. The forest ran on, brilliant and grumbling, along the gently sloping plain, and then becoming smaller, contracting, and growing misty, it broke off abruptly, almost entirely black. And what arose there, on the far side of the break, resembled something huge, all in curls and ringlets, a pale yellow-green storm cloud, pensive and dumfounded. Zhenya held her breath and immediately sensed the speed of that limitless, oblivious air, and simultaneously realized that the storm cloud was some other country, some other place bearing a stentorian, mountainous name which rolled all around and was flung into the valley below with rocks and sand; that the hazel-nut forest alone knew about this and whispered, whispered it; here and there and way, way over there; whispered it alone.

"Is this the Urals?" she asked of the whole compartment, leaning forward.

She spent the rest of the journey by the corridor window, unable to pull herself away. She clung to it and was continually leaning out. She was greedy. She discovered that looking backward was more pleasant than looking forward. Her majestic acquaintances became hazy and vanished into the distance. After a brief separation from them, in the course of which she was accompanied by the perpendicular roar of grinding chains, a draft of cold air would sweep across her neck and right before her eyes a new miracle would appear,

and again she would begin to search. The mountainous pan-
orama expanded and everything grew and spread. Some became black, others were refreshed, some were obscured, and
others obscuring. They clustered together and separated,
descended and achieved new heights. All this happened in a
sort of slow circular process, like the rotation of the stars,
watched over by the solicitous discretion of giants, within a
hair's breadth of catastrophe, anxious about the preservation
of the earth. These complex movements were directed by an
equable, powerful reverberation, beyond human ears, and
omniscient. It watched them with an eagle eye, mute and
invisible; it held them under its gaze. And so the Urals are
built, built and rebuilt.

She returned to the compartment for a moment, screwing
up her eyes against the glaring light. Mama was chatting with
the unknown gentleman and smiled. Seryozha was fidgeting
with the crimson plush and clinging to some kind of leather
wall strap. Mama spit the last seed into her hand, brushed off
her dress and bending over nimbly and directly, threw the
rest of the rubbish under the seat. Contrary to her expectations, the fat man had a husky, cracked voice. He evidently
suffered from asthma. Her mother presented Zhenya to him
and offered her a tangerine. He was funny and probably kind,
and as he spoke, would continually raise his plump hand to
his mouth. His breathing troubled him and, suddenly becoming short of wind, he would often interrupt himself. It
turned out that he was from Ekaterinburg and often traveled
through the Urals and knew them well; and when he took his
gold watch out of his vest pocket and raised it to his nose and
put it back again, Zhenya noticed what good-natured fingers
he had. Like all fat people he picked up things with the
movement of one who gives things away, and his hands
sighed all the while as if proffered for a kiss, and they jumped
gently through the air as though bouncing a ball on the floor.
"Soon, now," his eyes squinting, he looked away from the
boy, although he was talking to him alone; and he smiled
broadly.

"You know the signpost they talk about, at the border of
Asia and Europe, with 'Asia' written on it," Seryozha blurted
out, slipping off the seat and running out into the corridor.

Zhenya understood nothing, and when the fat man had explained what it was all about, she also ran out to the side of the corridor where the signpost was to appear, afraid that she had already missed it. In her enchanted mind, the "frontier of Asia" assumed a kind of phantasmagorical barrier-like shape, similar to railings placed between the public and a cage of pumas, frightening bars, black, like night, fraught with evil-smelling danger. She awaited the signpost like the raising of the curtain on the first act of a geographical tragedy, about which she had heard rumors from witnesses, triumphantly excited because this would happen to her and because she would soon be seeing it all with her own eyes.

But, meanwhile, what had earlier compelled her to go back into their compartment, to the adults, monotonously continued: the gray alders, through which they had been moving for half an hour, did not anticipate any conclusion, and nature was not making any preparations for what awaited her. Zhenya became annoyed at tedious, dust-laden Europe which was languidly avoiding the approach of a miracle. And how amazed she was when, as if in answer to Seryozha's unrestrained shriek, something like a small gravestone flashed by the window, moved to one side and ran off, withdrawing into the alders which were pursuing it, the long awaited legendary name! At that moment a multitude of heads, as if by agreement, poked out the windows of every carriage, and the train, carrying clouds of dust down the slope, became animated. Already more than a score of milestones had been counted in Asia, but kerchiefs still fluttered on the heads flying out the windows, and people, both bearded and shaven, exchanged glances, and everyone flew on, in clouds of whirling sand, everyone flew on, flew past those dusty alders which were Europe just recently and were long since Asia.

IV

Life began anew. Milk was not carried to the house, to the kitchen, by a milkmaid; Ulyasha brought it each morning in two pails; and there were special loaves of bread, not like that in Perm. The sidewalks here were made of something like marble or alabaster with a wavy white sheen. The flagstones were blinding even in the shadows, like icy suns which avariciously devoured the shadows of spruce trees spreading out, melting on them and liquefying. It was quite different to step outside on these streets which were wide and luminous and planted with trees, as in Paris—Zhenya repeated after her father.

He said this the first day of their arrival. Everything was fine and spacious. Her father had a light meal before meeting them at the station and did not partake in the dinner. His place setting remained clean and bright, as at Ekaterinburg, and he only unfolded his napkin and sat sideways and spoke about things in general. He unbuttoned his vest, and his shirt-front curved crisply and vigorously. He said it was a beautiful European town and rang the bell when it was necessary to clear the table and serve something else; and he rang and continued talking. From along unknown passageways, from still unknown rooms, a noiseless, white maid entered, a brunette, all stiff and starched; they spoke to her with the formal "you," and she—this new maid—smiled at her mistress and at the children as if she were an old acquaintance. She was then given certain orders pertaining to Ulyasha who was at that time in the unfamiliar, and probably very, very dark kitchen, where there was certainly a window through which something new could be seen: some church steeple or other, or a street, or birds. And Ulyasha, dressed in her oldest clothes so that she would later be ready to do the unpacking, immediately began to question the new girl; she asked questions, familiarized herself with everything and stared about her: in which corner was the stove—in that one, as in Perm, or elsewhere?

The boy learned from his father that the school was not far away—in fact, it was right nearby—and they could not avoid seeing it as they drove past. Father drank his seltzer, swallowed, and continued: "Didn't I show it to you? From here we can't see it but from the kitchen, perhaps." He weighed it in his mind. "But perhaps only from the roof. . . ." He drank some more Narzan and rang.

The kitchen turned out to be fresh, bright, exactly as it had seemed a minute ago to the little girl, as she had guessed beforehand when imagining it in the dining room—the stove tiled in blue and white, and the two windows in the new positions she had expected. Ulyasha threw something over her bare arms, the room became filled with children's voices; people were walking along the roof of the school and the topmost scaffolding jutted out. "Yes, it's being repaired," Father said, when they filed into the dining room, one after another, noisily chatting, and made their way along the already well-known but as yet unexplored corridor, which she would have to visit again the following day, after she had unpacked her notebooks, hung her washcloth on its hook, in a word, finished thousands of little tasks.

"Marvelous butter," Mother said, sitting down; and they went to visit the classroom which they had seen before, when they had just arrived and were still wearing their hats. "What makes all this Asia?" she thought aloud. But Seryozha, for some reason, did not understand what would have been understood perfectly at another time: up to now they had lived in unison. He sidestepped toward the map hanging on the wall and moved his hand across it from top to bottom, along the Ural range, looking at his sister who was overwhelmed, so he thought, by his argument. "They agreed to trace a natural boundary-line, that's all." And she thought back to the noon of that same day, which was already so long. It was unbelievable that a day, containing all this—this very day, now in Ekaterinburg and still here—was not complete, had not yet ended. At the thought of all that had passed, while preserving its breathless order, into its prescribed distance, she experienced a sensation of amazing mental fatigue, similar to what the body feels at night after a hard day. It was as if she had participated in pushing back and shifting those ponderous majesties, and had strained herself. And for some reason, confident that *they*, her Urals, existed *over there*, she turned and ran through the dining room into the kitchen where there was less crockery, but where there was still that marvelous iced butter on damp maple leaves and the strong mineral water.

The school was being repaired, and the air like cotton cloth on the teeth of a seamstress, was torn apart by shrill martins; and below—she had leaned out the window—a car-

riage glistened near the open coachhouse and sparks flew up
from the grinding wheel; and there was an odor of already
eaten food, much better and more interesting than when it is
being served, a long-lasting and melancholy smell, as in a
book. She forgot why she came running into the kitchen and
did not notice that her Urals were not in Ekaterinburg; but
she did notice how it gradually grew dark everywhere in
Ekaterinburg, and how they were singing below, underneath
her, while performing simple tasks—probably washing the
floor and spreading bast with warm hands—and how they
splashed water from the kitchen-pails and although they
were splashing downstairs, how quiet it was all around her.
And how the faucet babbled: "Well, there, young lady," but
she still avoided the new girl and did not want to listen to her,
and how—she pursued her thoughts to the very end—everyone below them knew, and probably were saying: "Look,
now there are people in Number Two." Then Ulyasha entered the kitchen.

The children slept soundly that first night, and they woke
up: Seryozha in Ekaterinburg, Zhenya in Asia, as it crept into
her thoughts again, strangely and deeply. On the ceiling,
alabaster flakes were playing once more.

This had begun while it was still summer. She was told that
she would be entered in school. This was not unpleasant at
all. But she was told. She did not call the tutor into the
schoolroom, where the sun's colors adhered so closely to the
painted walls that evening succeeded in ripping off the adhesive day only with bloodshed. She did not call him, when
accompanied by Mama, he came in to make the acquaintance
of "his future pupil." She did not give him the absurd name
"Dikikh." And was it she who wanted the soldiers to be
taught every day at noon from then on, stern, puffing and
perspiring like the reddish convulsions of the faucet when a
waterpipe rusts; and that a lilac-colored storm-cloud would
squeeze their boots, a cloud which knew the import of guns
and wheels far better than the white shirts, white tents and
very white officers? Did she ask that now there would always
be two things: a small wash basin and a napkin, uniting like
carbon rods in an arc-lamp, which would instantaneously

evoke a vaporized third thing: the idea of death, like that signboard at the barbershop where this had first happened to her? And was it with her consent that the red road signs reading "No Loitering" became the site of certain town secrets forbidding loitering; and that the Chinese became something terrible, something related to Zhenya and horrifying? But not everything, of course, lay so heavily on her soul. There were many pleasant things, like her approaching entrance to school. But, like everything else, she was *told* about that too. Ceasing to be a poetical caprice, life began to ferment like a harsh, black fable—in so far as it became prose and was transformed into fact. Bluntly, painfully and insipidly, as if in a state of eternal sobriety, the elements of day-to-day existence entered her newly awakening soul. They sank to its very depths, real, solid and cold, like sleepy pewter spoons. There, deep within, this pewter began to melt, fusing into lumps, and dripping with fixed ideas.

v

The Belgians often came to tea. That's what they were called. Her father called them that, saying: "The Belgians will be here today." There were four of them. The one without a mustache rarely came and was not very talkative. Sometimes he came alone, by chance, on a weekday, choosing an unpleasant, rainy day. The other three were inseparable. Their faces resembled cakes of unbroken soap, fresh from the wrapper, fragrant and cold. One of them had a thick, downy beard and downy, chestnut hair. They always appeared in the company of their father, returning from some meeting or other. At home everyone loved them. When they spoke, it seemed as if they were pouring water on the tablecloth: noisily, freshly and immediately, sometimes to one side, sometimes where no one expected it, with long-drying traces of their jokes and anecdotes, always understood by the children, always thirst-quenching and clean.

Noise encircled them, the sugar-bowl glistened, the nickel coffeepot, the clean, strong teeth, the stiff linen. They joked courteously and politely with Mother. As Father's colleagues, they were very subtly skilled in restraining him whenever, in reply to their swift innuendos and references to business or people at the table known only to them—to the professionals —Father would begin seriously but in very poor French, speaking diffusely and hesitatingly about contractors, about *références approuvées*, and about *férocités*, i.e., *bestialités, ce que veut dire en russe*—embezzlement at Blagodat.

The one without a mustache had been attempting to study Russian for some time, often testing himself in his new venture, but so far with little success. It was disrespectful to laugh at her father's French phrases, although all his *férocités* were positively annoying; but just because of this situation, the laughter which drowned Negarat's attempts seemed fully justified.

His name was Negarat. He was a Walloon from the Flemish districts of Belgium. They recommended Dikikh to him. He wrote down his address in Russian, absurdly transcribing the more complicated letters like Ю, Я ѣ. They appeared from his hand double, uneven, and with straddling legs. The children took the liberty of kneeling on the leather cushions of the armchairs and placing their elbows on the table—everything was permissible, everything was confused; the 10 was not a 10, but a sort of ten; shrieks of laughter encircled them. Evans banged his fist on the table and wiped away his tears; Father, trembling and blushing, paced the room and repeated: "No, I can't," and crumpled his handkerchief. *"Faîtes de nouveau."* Evans blew on the fire. *"Commencez,"* and Negarat opened his mouth slightly, slowly, like a stutterer who stands wondering how he will ever manage to give birth to those Russian sounds of "bl," still unexplored, like colonies in the Congo.

"Dites: 'uvy, nevygodno,' " father suggested in a hoarse voice, spitting out the syllables.

"Ouivoui niévoui."

"Entends tu?—ouvoui, niévoui—ouvoui, niévoui—oui, oui— chose inouïe, charmant," the Belgians burst out laughing.

Summer departed. Examinations were passed successfully, and some even brilliantly. Cold, transparent noises poured forth from the corridor as from a fountain. Everyone knew each other here. In the garden, leaves turned yellow and gold. The classroom windows languished in the bright, dancing reflections. Partially lackluster to begin with, they clouded over and shook from the base. The small sliding panes were unhinged by blue convulsions. And bronze-colored maple branches made furrows in their frigid clarity.

Luvers did not know that all her worries would be transformed into such a light-hearted joke. To divide so many yards, so many inches by seven! Was it worth her while to go through all those fractions, grams, ounces, pounds and poods? Or grains, drams, ounces and pounds advoirdupois —which always seemed to her like the four ages of the scorpion? Why, in the word "useful," must one write "e" and not the Russian equivalent. She worked hard over her answers only because all her reasoning power was concentrated in a single effort: to imagine troublesome reasons by which the word "useful" would one day spring up, wild and shaggy, from the page. She had no idea why they did not send her to school, then although she had been admitted and enrolled, and already owned a coffee-colored uniform which had been cut out and fitted on her for several hours, covetously and possessively; and her room already contained such horizons as a handbag, a pencil-case, a lunch-basket and a remarkably loathsome eraser.

THE STRANGER

I

The girl was covered from head to knees by a thick woolen shawl, and was running about the courtyard like a pullet. Zhenya wanted to go up to the Tatar girl and talk to her. At that moment a window was flung open noisily. "Kolka," shouted Aksinya. The child who resembled a peasant bundle into which felt shoes had been hurriedly jammed, scurried swiftly into the gatekeeper's lodge.

To take her homework into the courtyard always meant having pondered a footnote to a rule until it lost all significance, and afterward, going upstairs to her room and beginning all over again. From the threshold, the rooms of their house immediately chilled one with a peculiar semidarkness and freshness, and with a special ever-unexpected familiarity which the pieces of furniture, having once and for all assumed their appointed places, retained. It was impossible to predict the future. But one could catch sight of it entering the house. Here, there was already evidence of its plan, of the order to which the future submitted, although insubordinate to everything else. And there was no dream blown in by the motion of the air outdoors which could not be quickly shaken off by the brisk and fatal spirit of the house, suddenly rushing in from the threshold.

This time it was Lermontov. Zhenya crumpled the book, folding it inside out. In the house, if Seryozha had done this, she would have revolted against such a "shocking habit." But outdoors, it was another matter.

Prokhor laid the ice-cream freezer on the ground and went back into the house. When he opened the door into the passageway, the roaring, devilish barking of the general's short-haired dogs came pouring out. The door slammed shut with a short ringing sound.

Meanwhile, Terek, bounding up like a lion with a shaggy mane on his back, continued to howl as he thought fit and Zhenya began to have doubts, but only about whether it was the back or the spine to which all this referred. She was too lazy to check her book, and the golden clouds, from distant southern lands, had hardly time to follow him to the north, for they had already reached the threshold of the general's kitchen, pail and bast wisp in hand.

The general's servant laid the pail on the ground, bent down, and having dismantled the ice-cream freezer, began to wash it. The August sun broke through the arboreal leaves and settled firmly in the soldier's sacrum. Reddening, it rooted itself in the cloth of his faded uniform and then, like turpentine, greedily soaked through to the soldier underneath.

The courtyard was large, complicated and overwhelming, with many intricate and secret places. Paved in the center, it had not been repaved for a long time, and the cobbles were thickly overgrown with flat, curly headed grass which in the early afternoon emitted a pungent medicinal odor such as one smells on a sultry day walking near a hospital. At one end, between the gatekeeper's lodge and the coachhouse, the courtyard bordered on somebody else's garden.

Zhenya made her way in that direction, beyond the wood-pile. She propped up a ladder from below with some small flat logs in order not to slip on the shifting wood, and then sat down on one of the middle rungs, uncomfortable but interested, as if playing a game. She soon stood up, climbed higher and placed her book on the broken top rung, intending to start reading *The Demon;* but then, realizing she had been more comfortable before, climbed down again, forgot her book on top of the woodpile and did not remember it at all, because, once below, she began thinking only about the other side of the garden which she had never before imagined to exist, and she stood gaping, stockstill, like someone enchanted.

There were no bushes in the other garden, and the ancient trees, bearing their lower branches upward into the leaves, as into some dark night, denuded the garden below, although it stood continuously in the solemn and airy shadows, and never stepped out of the shade. Forked, lilac in a storm, covered with a gray lichen, they allowed one to see very well the deserted, rarely frequented by-street onto which the garden opened at the other side. A yellow acacia grew there. Now it was parched; it writhed and dropped its leaves.

Transported from this world to another by the somber garden, the mute by-street shone brilliantly like events kindled in a dream; that is, very sharply and painstakingly illumined, and very noiseless, as if the sun, wearing glasses, was rummaging through the buttercups.

What exactly was Zhenya gaping at? At her own discovery which interested her more than the people helping her to make it.

Then, there must be a small shop there? Behind the wicket-gate in the street. In such a street! "The happy ones," she envied the unknown women. There were three of them.

They were all in black, like the word "nun" in the song. Three smooth napes, under their circular hats, were bowed so that it seemed as if the last one, half-hidden by a bush, was asleep, leaning her elbows on something, and that the other two were also asleep, pressed up closely against her. Their hats were a dark dove-gray, and like insects, glittered and died out in the sunlight. They were covered in black crepe. At that moment the unknown women turned their heads to the other side. Evidently something at the far end of the street attracted their attention. They gazed at the far end for a minute as one gazes in summer, when a second is dissolved by the light and lengthened, when one is forced to screw up one's eyes and shade them with one's hand—for such a moment they gazed, and once more fell into their former state of harmonious somnolence.

Zhenya was about to go home, but suddenly missed her book and could not immediately recall where it was. She came back for it, and, having returned to the woodpile, she noticed that the unknown women had risen and were moving away. They passed through the gate one after another, in single file. A short man followed along behind them with a rather strange crippled gait. Under his arm he carried a huge album or atlas. So that was what they had been doing, peering over each other's shoulders—but she had thought they were sleeping. The neighbors moved about in the garden and were hidden behind the out-buildings. The sun was already going down. On reaching for her book, Zhenya shook the woodpile. Its very depths awoke and began to move, as though alive. A few logs slid down below and fell on the grass with a light tap. This served as the signal, like striking the clapper of the watchman's bell. Evening was born. A multitude of sounds were born, soft and misty. The air began to whistle something of old, something from beyond the river.

The courtyard was empty. Prokhor had finished. He had withdrawn beyond the gates. Out there, very close to the ground, the strumming of a soldier's balalaika resounded, softly plucked and melancholy. And just above this, whirling and dancing, rising and falling, sinking off into the air, and then falling and sinking even lower, and finally without touching the earth, a fine swarm of midges climbed upward. But the strumming of the balalaika grew ever softer and more tenuous. It sank to the earth below the midges, and without becoming dust-covered, more delicately and airily than the swarm, rushed up again to new heights, shimmering and falling, in cadences, slowly.

Zhenya returned to the house. "Lame," she thought, pondering over the unknown man with the album—"lame, but a gentleman, without crutches." She entered by the back door. There was an odor of camomile in the yard, cloying and persistent. "For some time now, Mama had collected a whole apothecary shop, a collection of blue phials with yellow stoppers." She climbed up the stairs, slowly. The iron railing was cold, the steps creaked in answer to her shuffling feet. Suddenly, something strange came to mind. She skipped two steps and lingered on the third. What had suddenly entered her head was a realization that recently there was some kind of incomprehensible resemblance between her mother and the gatekeeper's wife. Something completely elusive. She stopped. Something like—she thought for a moment—what people have in mind when they say: we are all people . . . or we are all tarred by the same brush . . . or fate pays no heed to birth—she pushed away a rolling phial with her foot, the phial flew down the stairs and fell into a dusty straw bag without breaking—something, in a word, that is very, very common, common to all people. But then, what about between herself and Aksinya? Or Aksinya and, perhaps, Ulyasha? This seemed even more strange to Zhenya because it would be difficult to find any more dissimilar people: in Aksinya there was something earthy, as in a garden, something recalling swollen potatoes or the earthen color of a rabid pumpkin. Whereas her Mother . . . Zhenya smiled at the thought of such a comparison.

And meanwhile, it was Aksinya who set the tone of this imposed comparison. She played the leading role in the analogy. The peasant woman did not gain anything from it, but the lady did lose something. For a moment Zhenya imagined something wild: that something of the common people had taken root in her mother, and that her mother said *"shuka"* instead of *"shchuka,"* and *"rabotam"* instead of *"rabotayem"*; but suddenly it struck her that the day might come when her mother would enter in a new silk dressing gown without a girdle, like a ship, and would even blurt out some heavy peasant greeting.

There was an odor of medicine in the corridor. Zhenya
went in to her father.

II

The furnishings were refurbished. Luxury appeared in the
house. The Luvers acquired a carriage and began to keep
horses. The coachman's name was Davletsha.

Rubber tires were very new then. When they went for
drives all things turned around to follow the carriage with
their eyes: people, fences, churches, cocks.

They did not open the carriage door to Madame Luvers for
a long time; and when the carriage moved off at a slow pace,
out of respect for her, she would call after them: "Don't go
too far, just to the highroad and back, be careful on the
hills"; and the whitish sun which reached out to her from the
doctor's doorstep, moved farther down the street and having
stretched out toward Davletsha's thickset, freckled and ruddy
neck, it warmed and shriveled it.

They drove to the bridge. The conversation of the girders
resounded cunningly, roundly and harmoniously, sturdily
constructed to last forever, tightly incised into the ravine and
remembered by it always, day and night.

Vykormysh, clambering up the hill, started to attempt the
steep, unyielding flint; he pulled, he could do nothing, and
suddenly in his clambering resembling a creeping grasshop-
per, he took on the characteristics of the insect which by
nature flies and jumps, and became unexpectedly beautiful
in the humility of his unnatural efforts; it seemed as if he
could no longer endure remaining in that position, and that
he was about to flash his wings angrily and fly away. And, so it
happened. The horse pulled, kicked up his forelegs, and with
a swift leap bounded over the wasteland. Davletsha began to
pull at him, tightening the reins. An old shaggy dog began to
bark at them sadly. The dust looked like gunpowder. The
road veered sharply to the left.

The black street ran up to the red fence of a railway depot
like a blind alley. It was striped. The sun beat through the
bushes at a slant and shrouded the crowd of strange figures
in women's cloaks. The sun drenched them with a gushing

white light which seemed to spout up from a capsized bucket resembling a boot, spout up like slaked lime bursting forth in waves over the earth. The street was striped. The horse moved at a walk. "Turn right," Zhenya ordered. "There's no road," Davletsha answered, indicating the red fence with his whip-handle—"a blind alley." "Then stop, I want to look." They were our Chinese. "I see." Davletsha, realizing that his young mistress was not inclined to talk to him, slowly chanted "Whoa," and the horse, his whole body swaying, stood as if rooted to the ground; then, Davletsha began to whistle softly and appropriately, interrupting himself every now and then to make sure the horse was doing what was necessary.

The Chinese ran across the road, carrying huge rye loaves in their hands. They were dressed in blue and resembled peasant women in trousers. Their bare heads ended with a knot at the parietal bone and seemed to have been twisted out of handkerchiefs. Some of them loitered. One could easily discern them. They had pallid, earthy faces which grinned. They were swarthy and dirty, like copper oxidized by poverty. Davletsha took out his tobacco pouch and began to roll a cigarette. Meanwhile, several women appeared from the corner toward which the Chinese were headed. They were probably also coming for bread. Those on the road began to roar with laughter and approached the women stealthily, sidling up to them as if their hands were behind their backs. Their swaying motions were particularly emphasized by the fact that from shoulders to ankles they were dressed in a single piece of cloth, like acrobats. There was nothing frightening about them; the women did not run away, but stood still and laughed among themselves.

"Hey, Davletsha, what's wrong with you?"

"The horse is pulling! He's pulling! Can't stand still, can't sta-and!" Meanwhile Davletsha struck Vykormysh repeatedly with the reins, first tugging at them and then letting loose.

"Quietly, you'll overturn the carriage. Why do you whip him?"

"I must." And only after he had entered the field and quieted the horse which was about to panic, did that wily Tatar, carrying his young mistress like an arrow from the shameful scene, switch the reins to his right hand and put away his tobacco pouch which had remained in his hands all that time.

They returned by another road. Madame Luvers caught sight of them probably from the doctor's window. She came out on the front steps at the very moment when the bridge, having completely told its tale, began all over again under the weight of the water-carrier's cart.

III

At one of her examinations Zhenya made friends with the Defendov girl, with the girl who had brought a rowan berry branch, plucked along the way, to school. The daughter of a sacristan was re-taking a French exam. Luvers, Evgenia was seated in the first empty place. And so they made each other's acquaintance, sitting over the same sentence:

"*Est-ce Pierre qui a volé la pomme?*"
"*Oui, c'est Pierre qui vola*" etc.

The fact that Zhenya was to study at home did not put an end to the girls' friendship. They continued to meet. Their meetings, due to her mother's opinions, were one-sided: Liza was allowed to visit them, but Zhenya was forbidden, for the time being, to visit the Defendovs.

Such irregularity in their meetings did not prevent Zhenya from quickly becoming attached to her friend. She fell in love with the Defendov girl, that is, she assumed a passive role in the relationship, as if she were its barometer, vigilant and burning with anxiety. All Liza's references to classmates unknown to Zhenya evoked in her a feeling of emptiness and bitterness. Her heart sank: these were the attacks of first jealousy. For no reason, by the force of her anxiety alone, Zhenya was convinced that Liza was playing her false, outwardly sincere, but in her heart laughing at everything in her peculiar to the Luvers, and at home or in the classroom, as soon as she was out of sight, Liza would make merry over all this. Zhenya accepted everything, however, as being as it should be, as something in the very nature of their attachment. Her feelings were aroused as much by the accidental choice of a subject, as in answer to the powerful demands of instinct which, disinterested in self-love, knows only how to suffer and consume itself in the glory of a fetish when it feels for the first time.

Neither Zhenya nor Liza decisively influenced the other, and Zhenya remained Zhenya, Liza—Liza; they met and separated—one with deep feeling, the other without.

The father of the Akhmedyanovs traded in iron. During the year intervening between the birth of Nuretdin and the birth of Smagil, he unexpectedly grew rich. Then Smagil became Samoyla and it was decided to give the sons a Russian education. Not a single peculiarity of the free seigneurial mode of living was omitted by the father, and in ten years of hurried imitation he overshot his mark in every way. The children succeeded marvelously, that is, they followed the pattern taken by their father, and the rapid strides of his willfulness remained in them, noisy and destructive, like a pair of flywheels, revolving and rebounding by virtue of their inertia. The brothers Akhmedyanov were the most genuine representatives of the fourth class in the fourth class. They consisted of chalk broken into tiny pieces, cribs, pellets of gun-shot, the crash of desks, obscene swear-words and red-cheeked, snub-nosed cocksureness which peeled off like scales in sub-freezing weather. Seryozha made friends with them in August. By the end of September the boy had no face left. This was in the order of things. To be a typical school-boy, and later even something more, meant to be at one with the Akhmedyanovs. And Seryozha wanted nothing so much as to be this schoolboy. Mr. Luvers did not impede his son's friendship. He did not see the changes in him, and even if he had noticed something, he would have written it off as part of adolescence. Besides, he had other things to worry about. For some time he had suspected that he was ill, and that his illness was incurable.

IV

She was not sorry for him, although everyone around her spoke only about how ill-timed it was and how unpleasant. Negarat was too subtle even for their parents, and everything

felt by the parents in connection with the foreigner was also
vaguely communicated to the children, as to spoiled domestic animals. Zhenya grieved only because nothing would now
be the same as it was, and only three Belgians would remain,
and there would never again be such laughter.

She happened to be present at the table the evening when
he explained to her mother that he had to return to Dijon for
some kind of military service. "How young you must
be . . ." said her mother and was at once stricken with great
pity for him. But he just kept sitting, his head lowered. The
conversation flagged. "Tomorrow they're coming to putty
the windows," her mother said, and asked him whether she
should close them. He said it was not necessary, the evening
was warm, and in his country windows were not puttied even
in the winter. Soon her father came in. He also indicated his
sympathy at the news. But before he began to deplore the
situation, he raised his eyes and asked, rather amazed: "To
Dijon? But aren't you a Belgian?"

"Belgian, but a French subject."

And Negarat began to tell the story of his "old folks'"
emigration so amusingly that he seemed to be relating it
from a book about foreigners. "Excuse me for interrupting,"
her mother said. "Zhenya, close the window, anyway. Vika,
tomorrow they're coming to putty the windows. Well, continue. But, that uncle of yours was a fine old roughneck. Is
that true, *literally*, would you swear by it?"

"Yes." And he resumed the interrupted story. Then he
turned to his affairs, the papers he had received the evening
before from the consulate; he sensed that the little girl understood none of this and was straining to understand. So he
turned to her and began to explain what his military duty
was, attempting not to show his purpose so as not to offend
her pride.

"Yes, yes. I understand. Yes. I understand, I understand,"
the little girl asserted, gratefully and mechanically.

"But why go so far? Be a soldier here; *learn* where everyone
does," she corrected herself, clearly imagining the meadow
which could be seen by the hill of the monastery. "Yes, yes. I
understand. Yes, yes, yes," the little girl repeated again; but
the Luvers who were sitting there doing nothing and think-

ing only that the Belgian filled the child's head with useless details, interjected their own fuzzy and simplified comments. And suddenly a moment came when she began to pity all those who a long time ago, or just recently, were Negarats in various far-away places, and who set out along unknown roads which seemed simply to have fallen from heaven, in order to become soldiers here in Ekaterinburg, in a strange land. So well did this man explain everything to her. No one had ever made anything so clear to her before. The thin coating of callousness, the startling coating of clarity, fell from her picture of white tents; regiments faded away and became groups of individual men in military uniform whom she had begun to pity at that moment, while their significance animated them, exalted them, brought them nearer to her and discolored them.

They took leave of each other. "I'll leave some of my books with Tsvetkov. He's the friend I've spoken about so much. Please, make use of them in the future, Madame. Your son knows where I live; he often visits the landlord's family; I'll give my room to Tsvetkov. I'll tell him."

"Tell him to visit us—Tsvetkov, did you say?"

"Tstvetkov."

"Tell him to visit us. We'll be glad to meet him. When I was much younger I knew the family . . ." and she looked at her husband who was standing in front of Negarat, his hands lying on the edge of his tightly fitting coat; he was waiting rather absent-mindedly for a convenient opening in which to make final arrangements with the Belgian for the next day.

"Tell him to visit. Only not now. I'll let him know. Yes, take it, it's yours. I haven't finished. I was reading it and crying. The doctor advised me to give up reading in general. To avoid the excitement." And she looked at her husband again; he was standing, his head lowered, crackling his collar and puffing, pondering over whether he had boots on both feet, and whether they were well cleaned.

"Well now. So. Don't forget your walking stick. We'll see each other again, I hope."

"Oh, of course. Until Friday, then. What day is today?" He was frightened, like anyone who departs under such circumstances.

"Wednesday. Vika, Wednesday? . . . Vika, Wednesday?
Wednesday. *Ecoutez.*" Father's turn came at last: "*De-
main . . .*" and they walked down the stairs together.

V

They walked and talked, and from time to time she had to
break into a slight run so as not to lag behind Seryozha and
to keep step with him. They walked very briskly, and her coat
fidgeted on her because she worked her hands to help her
move forward, and she kept her hands in her pockets. It was
cold; the thin ice burst musically beneath her galoshes. They
were going on an errand for Mama, to buy a present for their
departing guest, and they were talking.

"So they were taking him to the station?"

"Yes."

"But why did he sit in the straw?"

"What do you mean?"

"In the cart. All of him. From his feet up. People don't sit
like that."

"I already told you. Because he's a criminal—a prisoner."

"Are they taking him to a prison camp?"

"No, to Perm. We have no prison here. Watch your feet."

Their route led them across the road, past the coppersmith's shop. Throughout the summer the doors of his shop
stood wide open, and Zhenya was accustomed to associate
the crossroads with the warm friendliness and sense of animation imparted by the wide-open jaws of the workshop. All
through July, August and September carts would stop, and
block up the exit; peasants, mainly Tatars, would congregate
in crowds; pails rolled on the ground and pieces of gutter-
piping, broken and rusty; and there, more than anywhere
else, having transformed the crowd into a gypsy camp and
having painted the Tatars as gypsies, vivid and terrifying sun
sank into the dust, at just that hour when chickens' throats
were being cut behind the neighboring wattle-fence; and
there, the detachable cart-fronts and the polished plates of
their coupling bolts, just released from under the chassis,
were plunged deeply into the dust by their shafts.

Now, however, the very same pails and scraps of iron lay

scattered about and powdered with a light frost. And the doors were tightly shut, as on a holiday, against the cold, and the crossroads were deserted; but through the circular venthole came the familiar smell of musty fire-damp which Zhenya recognized; it poured forth with a roaring screech, and striking one's nostrils, precipitated on the palate like cheap pear-flavored soda pop.

"And there's a prison in Perm?"

"Yes. The central offices. I think we should go this way. It's closer. It's in Perm because that's the capital of the province, but Ekaterinburg is only a district capital. It's very small."

The road running past the private homes was faced with red brick and framed by shrubbery. On it traces of the weak, lusterless sun could be distinguished. Seryozha determined to walk as noisily as possible.

"If one tickles a barberry with a pin, in spring when it flowers, it will flutter its leaves quickly like a live being."

"I know."

"And are you afraid of being tickled?"

"Yes."

"That means you're . . . nervous. The Akhmedyanovs say that if one is afraid of being tickled . . ."

On they walked, Zhenya running, Seryozha walking with unnatural strides, and her coat fidgeted. They saw Dikikh at the very moment when the wicket gate, revolving like a turnstile on a shaft, moved across their path and detained them. They saw him from a distance: he was coming out of the very store toward which they were headed, still a half block farther on Dikikh was not alone; following him was a short man attempting to conceal his limp. It seemed to Zhenya that she had seen him somewhere before. They passed each other without a greeting. The others turned obliquely. Dikikh did not notice the children; he wore high boots and frequently raised his hands with outspread fingers. He did *not agree* and with all ten fingers demonstrated that his companion . . . (But where had she seen him? Long ago. But where? Perhaps, in Perm, *in her childhood.*)

"Stop!" Something was annoying Seryozha. He dropped on one knee. "Wait a second."

"Did it catch?"

"Well, yes. Idiots, they can't even knock a nail in right!"

"Well?"

"Just a second, I can't think where. I know that cripple. Well, there. Thank goodness."

"Is it torn?"

"No, it's all right, thank goodness. But this tear in the lining is an old one. I didn't do it. Well, let's go. Stop, I just want to brush off my knee. Well, all right, let's go."

"I know him. He's from the Akhmedyanovs' house. Negarat's friend. Remember, I told you: people gather there, they drink all night long, there's a light in the window. Remember? Remember when I spent the night there? On Samoyla's birthday. Well, he's from there. Remember now?"

She remembered. She had made a mistake. If that were so, she could not have seen the cripple in Perm as she first imagined. But she continued to feel otherwise; and reticent to disclose such feelings, sifting through her memories of Perm, she followed certain movements of her brother: she grasped something, crossed over something, and looking all around her, found herself in the half-light of counters, small boxes, shelves, fastidious greetings and service—and Seryozha was speaking.

The title, for which he asked the bookseller who also dealt in all sorts of tobacco, was not to be found; but he assured them, certain that the promised Turgenev had been sent from Moscow and was already on its way, and that he had only just this moment—well, a minute ago—spoken about this very same book with Mr. Tsvetkov, their tutor. His shiftiness and his error concerning Tsvetkov set the children giggling; they took their leave and went home empty-handed.

As they were leaving, Zhenya turned to her brother with the question: "Seryozha! I always forget. Tell me, do you know that street which can be seen from our woodpile?"

"No. I've never been there."

"That's not true. I saw you myself."

"On the woodpile? You . . ."

"No, no, not on the woodpile, but on that street, behind the Cherep-Savvichs' garden."

"Oh, you mean that! Oh, certainly. When we pass by I'll show you. Behind the garden, in the back. There are some sheds there and firewood. Wait a second. So that's our court-yard? That courtyard? Ours? How clever! Whenever I went there I used to think how nice it would be to go as far as the woodpile, and from there to the attic. There's a ladder there. So that's really our courtyard?"

"Seryozha, show me the way there?"

"Again? Indeed, the courtyard's ours. What's there to show? You yourself . . ."

"Seryozha, you still don't understand. I'm talking about the street and you're talking about the courtyard. I'm talking about the street. Show me the way to the street. Show me how to get there. Will you show me, Seryozha?"

"But I don't understand. Why, we walked by it today . . . and soon we'll pass it again."

"Really?"

"Yes. And the coppersmith? . . . At the corner."

"Then it's that dusty one . . ."

"Yes, that very one you asked about. But the Cherep-Sav-vichs' is at the end, to the right. Don't stand still or you'll be late for dinner. Lobsters today."

They began talking about something else. The Akhmedya-novs had promised to teach him how to tin a samovar. And in answer to her question concerning "solder" he told her that it was a certain kind of metal, in a word, an ore like tin, a dull metal. Tin boxes are soldered with it and earthenware pots baked from it, and the Akhmedyanovs knew all about this.

They had to run across the road or a line of carts would have detained them. So they forgot—she, her request about the unfrequented side street, Seryozha, about his promise to point it out to her. They passed by the very door of the shop, and there, while inhaling the warm tallow fumes which were produced along with the scourings of copper candlesticks and fixtures, Zhenya momentarily recalled where she had seen the crippled man before and the three unknown women, and what they were doing; and in the next instant she understood that this Tsvetkov, of whom the bookseller had spoken, was that very same crippled man.

VI

Negarat left in the evening. Father went to see him off. He returned from the station late at night and his appearance at the gatekeeper's house aroused a great commotion which was not calmed down very quickly. People came out with lanterns, others called out. Rain was falling and the geese, which had been let out, cackled at someone.

Morning arose, gloomy and trembling. The damp, gray street bounced like rubber, the foul rain idled and splashed up mud; carriages jolted and splattered people in galoshes as they crossed the pavement.

Zhenya returned home. Echoes of the night's commotion still resounded in the courtyard that morning: she was refused a carriage ride. She set off for her friend's house after saying she would go to the store for hempseed. But halfway there, convinced that she could not find the road from the shopping district to the Defendovs' all alone, she turned back. Then she remembered that it was too early anyway, and Liza was still in school. She was soaked through and shivering. The weather broke; but still it had not cleared up. A cold, white glitter flew along the street and like a leaf, stuck fast to the damp flagstones. At the end of the square, behind the three-armed street lamp, turbid clouds scurried away from the town, jostling each other capriciously, in frenzied agitation.

The man changing his lodgings was probably a very slovenly person or without principles. The furnishings of his scanty study were not loaded but simply placed in the dray exactly as they had been standing in his room, and the casters of the armchairs which looked out from under white dust covers, slid along the boards as if on a parquet floor, every time the cart jolted. The dust covers were snow-white in spite of being drenched right down to their very threads. They struck the eye so sharply that one look caused everything around them to assume the same color: the cobbles gnawed by bad weather, the freezing water under the fences, the birds flying from the stables, the trees flying after them, pieces of lead, and even the fig tree swaying in the tub, bowing awkwardly from the cart to all the passers-by.

The cart load was absurd. It called attention to itself quite involuntarily. A peasant walked along beside it and the dray, careening from side to side, moved at a walking pace, brushing against the road posts. And floating above everything, in croaking tatters, was the damp and leaden word "town," giving birth to a multitude of ideas inside the young girl's head; these ideas were winging past like the cold October glitter, which was flying through the street and dropping into the water.

"He'll catch cold unpacking his things," she pondered a moment over the unknown owner. And she imagined a man —*just any man, unsteady on his feet, lacking co-ordination in his movements,* arranging his belongings in various corners. She vividly imagined his mannerisms and movements, especially how he would take up a rag and, hobbling around the tub, begin to wipe the leaves of his fig tree clouded over by the freezing drizzle. And then he would catch cold, with shivering and fever. Definitely catch cold. Zhenya imagined all this. Very vividly. The cart load began to rumble down the hill towards Iset. Zhenya had to make a left turn.

It probably arose from someone's heavy footsteps behind the door. The tea in the glass on the table by the bed rose and fell. A piece of lemon in the tea rose and fell. Sunny stripes on the wallpaper were swaying. They were swaying in pillars, like columns of syrup in the shops behind signboards, on which a Turk is smoking a pipe.

On which a Turk . . . is smoking . . . a pipe. Smoking . . . a pipe.

It probably arose from someone's footsteps. The patient fell asleep again.

Zhenya fell ill the day after Negarat's departure; on the very day when she learned, after her walk, that Aksinya had given birth to a boy during the night; on the day when she decided, upon seeing the cart load of furniture, that the owner would contract rheumatism. She was in a fever for two weeks, a fever densely sprinkled with sweat, like a painful red pepper which burned her and clung to her eyelids and the corners of her lips. The perspiration fatigued her and a feeling of hideous obesity was mingled with the stinging sensation. It seemed as if the flame causing her to swell up was poured into her by a summer wasp. As if its sting, as fine as a gray hair, remained within her although she wanted to pull it out, more than once and in more than one way. Now from her purplish cheekbone, now from her inflamed shoulder, aching underneath the nightgown. Meanwhile she was convalescing. A feeling of weakness manifested itself in everything.

For example, this feeling of weakness gave way, at its own risk and peril, to a certain strange geometry of its *own*. One became slightly giddy and nauseated from it.

Having begun, for example, with a certain episode on the blanket, the feeling of weakness began to build upon it rows of gradually increasing empty spaces which quickly took on incredible proportions as twilight attempted to assume the shape of a square which lay at the basis of this confusion of space. Or else, moving away from the pattern on the wallpaper, stripe by stripe, it drove the widths in front of the little girl's eyes as smoothly as oil, substituting one for another, and also acted like all these sensations, harassing her with a regular, gradual increase in its dimensions. Or it tormented the patient with depths which descended endlessly, having betrayed from its very inception, from the first trick on the parquet floor, its fathomlessness; it permitted her bed to fall into the depths, silently, silently; and along with the bed— the little girl. Her head felt like a sugar-lump tossed into a gulf of vapid, shocking empty chaos, and it dissolved and vanished within.

It arose from the heightened sensitivity in the labyrinths of her ears.

It arose from someone's footsteps. The lemon rose and fell. The sun on the wallpaper rose and fell. At last she woke up. Her mother entered, and having congratulated her on her recovery, produced on the little girl the impression of someone reading strange thoughts. She had already heard something similar as she was waking up. These were the congratulations of her own hands and feet, elbows and knees, which she accepted as she stretched herself. Their greetings even awakened her. And Mama was there also. The coincidence was strange.

All the servants entered and exited, sat down and stood up. She asked questions and received answers. There were things which had changed during her illness, and there were other things which remained unchanged. She did not touch on the latter, the former she did not leave in peace. Mama obviously had not changed. Her father was completely unchanged. Changed were: she herself, Seryozha, the distribution of light in her room, the silence of all the rest, and something more. Had snow fallen? No, it fell lightly, melted, the ground froze; one could not quite make it out; it was quite bare outdoors, without snow. She hardly noticed whom or what she was questioning. Answers flew at her, vying with each other. Healthy people came in and left. Liza came. There was arguing. Then they remembered that measles do not come twice, and Liza was allowed to enter. Dikikh visited her. She hardly noticed what answers came from whom. When everyone had left for dinner and she remained alone with Ulyasha, she remembered how they had all laughed at her stupid questions in the kitchen. Now she took care not to ask similar ones. She would ask an intelligent and practical question in an adult voice. She asked whether Aksinya was pregnant again. The maid tinkled a small spoon as she removed her glass, and turned away. "Darl—ling, let her rest. She can't be pregnant always, Zhenichka . . ." and she ran out, leaving the door ajar and the whole kitchen roared as if shelves of dishes had tumbled to the floor, and the laughter became a howl, and passed into the hands of the charwoman and Halim, and blazed beneath their hands, and crashed swiftly and vigorously, as if beginning a fight after a quarrel; then someone approached and closed the forgotten door.

She should not have asked this question. It was still more stupid.

VII

Will it ever thaw again? It would mean that today they could go for a drive: was it still impossible to harness the sleigh? Zhenya stood for hours by the little window, her nose growing colder and her hands shivering. Dikikh had gone out a short while ago. He had previously been dissatisfied with her.

How can one study here, when the cocks are crowing in the yard, and the sky droning, and when the ringing gives out the cocks again begin their song. The clouds were shabby and mud-spattered like balding lap rugs. The day poked its head against the windowpane, resembling a calf in his steaming stall. Is it not yet spring? But since lunchtime the air was being intercepted, as if by a hoop, by the dove-gray frost, the sky was hollowed out and gradually sucked away, the clouds were breathing, audibly, with a whistling sound; and meanwhile, from the north, toward wintry dusk, the fleeting hours abruptly snatch the last leaves off the trees, shear the lawns, break through crevices, cut through the breast. Behind the houses muzzles of northern storms blacken; they are aimed at the courtyard and charged with the immensity of November. But still it is October only.

But it is as yet only October. No one can recall such a winter. People say winter crops have perished, they are afraid of starving. As if someone were waving his wand, encircling all the gutter pipes, roofs and starling nests. Smoke shall be there, snow there, here hoarfrost. But still neither one nor the other has appeared. Deserted, sunken-cheeked dusk languishes after them. It strains its eyes, and the earth aches from the early street lamps and fires in the houses just as the head aches from the eye's wistful fixation during the lengthy hours of expectation.

Everything is strained and expectant; the firewood is already stacked in kitchens, the clouds have for two weeks been brimming over with snow, the air is pregnant with darkness. But when will he, the magician, who has encircled everything visible to the eye within magic circles, pronounce his magic incantation and conjure up winter, whose spirit is already at the door?

And yet, how they neglected it! True, no one paid any attention to the calendar in the schoolroom. They were busy with their own. But just the same! The twenty-ninth of August! Neat!—as Seryozha would have said. A red-letter day. The Decollation of St. John the Baptist. It was easily removed from its nail. Nothing better to do, she busied herself by tearing off the leaves. Acting out of boredom, she soon ceased to understand what she was doing, but from time to time she repeated to herself: thirtieth, tomorrow is the thirty-first.

"It's already the third day she hasn't been out of the house. . . ." These words, echoing in the corridor, aroused her from her reverie, and she noticed how deeply engrossed she had been in her work. She had even passed the Annunciation. Her mother touched her hands. "Say please, Zhenya . . ." the rest of the sentence vanished as if unspoken. Interrupting her mother as though in a dream, the daughter asked Madame Luvers to pronounce "The Decollation of John the Baptist." The mother repeated the words, puzzled. She didn't say "Dec*a*llation." Aksinya said that.

The very next moment Zhenya was seized with amazement at what she had done, and came back to herself. What was it? Who made her do it? Where did it come from? Did she, Zhenya, ask that? Or, could she have thought that Mama . . . ? How fantastic and implausible! Who invented all that? . . .

Her mother was still standing there. She did not believe her ears. She looked at her daughter, her eyes wide-open. This prank stupefied her. The question appeared as mockery; meanwhile tears welled up in her daughter's eyes.

Her dim forebodings were realized. While out for a drive, she heard clearly how the air was growing softer, how the clouds were growing pulpy and the ring of horses' hoofs becoming gentler. Fires had not yet been lit when dry, grayish flakes began twirling about, roaming freely through the air. But just as they crossed the bridge, individual snowflakes disappeared and a solid, coagulating mass of snow began to fall. Davletsha slid down from the coachman's seat and raised the leather roof. It became dark and close for Zhenya and Seryozha. She wanted to rage about like the foul weather raging all around her. They noticed that Davletsha was driving them home because once again they could hear the bridge beneath Vykormysh's hoofs. The streets became unrecognizable; there were simply no streets. Night came on almost immediately and the town, having lost its senses, moved countless thousands of thick, pale lips. Seryozha leaned out the window and, sitting on his knees, requested to

be driven to the industrial school. Zhenya became petrified
with excitement, as she recognized all the secrets and charms
of winter in the way Seryozha's words resounded through the
air. Davletsha shouted back that they had to return home so
as not to tire the horses; his master and mistress were going
to the theater and would have to go by sleigh. Zhenya remembered that her parents were going out and that they
would be left alone. She decided to sit up very late at night,
very comfortably with a lamp and a copy of the *Tales of Kot-
Murlyka*, a book which was not for children. She would have
to take it from Mama's bedroom. And chocolate. And she
would read, sucking chocolate, and listen to the wind sweeping through the streets.

The storm had already arrived, there could be no doubt
about it. The sky shook and white kingdoms and countries
tumbled down from above; they were innumerable, mysterious and terrifying. It was evident that these territories, falling
from no one knows where, had never heard about the earth
or life. Northern and blind, they covered the earth unseeing,
unknowing.

They were ecstatically terrifying, these kingdoms; completely, satanically ravishing. Zhenya became enraptured
gazing at them. The air reeled, grasping whatever fell its way,
and far in the distance, experiencing extreme pain, fields
began howling as if they had been lashed. Everything became
confused. Night rushed at them, growing furious at a mean
gray hair which had become loose and blinded her. Everything split apart with a screech, disregarding the road. A cry
and an echo vanished without meeting; they perished, borne
in a whirlwind up above the rooftops. Storm.

They stamped for a long time in the foyer, shaking the
snow from their white sheepskin coats. And how much water
flowed from their galoshes onto the checkered linoleum!
There were many egg shells scattered on the table, and the
pepper pot, taken out of the cruet stand, had not been put
back, so pepper was sprinkled over the tablecloth and the
spilled egg yolk and on the tin of unfinished sardines. Their
parents had already finished supper but were still sitting in
the dining room hurrying their dawdling children. They did
not blame them; they had eaten earlier so they could get

ready for the theater. Mother was hesitant, not knowing whether to go or not, and she just sat there in low spirits. Looking at her, Zhenya remembered that, strictly speaking, she was not in such a joyous mood herself—she finally managed to undo that nasty hook—but on the contrary, she was rather melancholy; and walking into the dining room, she asked where they had taken the hazelnut torte. Then Father looked at Mother and said that no one was compelling them to go and they had better stay home. "No, what for? We're going," Mother said. "We must have a change; even the doctor allowed it."

"We must decide."

"But where's the torte?" Zhenya interrupted again, and she heard in reply that tortes would not run away, that one must also eat what precedes the torte, that it was in the cupboard; as if this were the first time she had come to him and did not know their routine—so her father answered; and turning again to Mother, repeated, "We must decide."

"It's decided. We'll go." And sadly smiling at Zhenya, Mother went to get dressed. But Seryozha, tapping a spoon on his egg, and looking businesslike and preoccupied so as not to miss it, warned his father that the weather had changed—a snowstorm, and that he should take this into consideration, and he began to laugh; something ugly was hanging from his nose which had begun to drip; he began to fidget and took out his handkerchief from the pocket in his tight-fitting uniform trousers; he blew his nose just as Father had taught him "without harming the eardrums." He picked up his spoon and staring straight at his father, ruddy and washed clean from their drive, said, "On our way we saw Negarat's friend. You know him?"

"Evans?" his father asked absent-mindedly.

"We don't know the man," Zhenya retorted hotly.

"Vika" was heard from the bedroom. Father got up and went to answer the call. In the doorway, Zhenya bumped into Ulyasha bringing a lighted lamp in to her. Soon an adjoining door slammed. It was Seryozha going to his room. He had been superb today; his sister loved it when the friend of the Akhmedyanovs became a boy, when it could be said of him that he was in his school *uniform*.

The doors were heard. They stamped out in high galoshes. *They* had gone at last. The letter said that she "up to now was not selfish and that if they wanted something, to ask as before"; but when the "dear sister," overburdened with greetings and kind regards, went to distribute them among her relatives, Ulyasha, who became Juliana at those moments, thanked her mistress, turned down the lamp and went out bearing her letter, a small bottle of ink, and the rest of the greasy octavo paper.

Then she picked up her homework again. She did not confine the decimals within brackets. She continued the division, writing down decimal after decimal. There was no end in sight. The fraction in the quotient grew and grew. "What if measles suddenly returned," flashed through her mind. "Today Dikikh said something about infinity." She ceased to understand what she was doing. She felt that something just like this had happened to her earlier that day, and she also wanted to sleep or cry, but she could not think when it was or what it was exactly, because to reason clearly was not in her power. The noise outside the window quieted down. The snowstorm gradually abated. Decimals were completely new to her. There was not enough space on the right. She decided to begin all over again, to write smaller, and to check each link. Outside there was complete silence. She was afraid that she would forget the number she had taken down from the next figure, and that she would not be able to retain the product in her mind. "The window won't run away," she thought—continuing to pour threes and sevens into the fathomless decimal— "but I'll hear them in time; silence everywhere; they won't come up immediately; in fur coats, and Mama pregnant; but here's the thing, 3,773 keeps repeating, one can simply write it down or cancel it." Suddenly, she recalled what Dikikh actually told her that day, that *"it's not necessary to go on and on, simply throw them away."* She stood up and walked to the window.

It had cleared up outside. A few snowflakes came sailing out of the black night. They sailed up to the street light, swam around it, wriggled about and fell out of sight. New ones swam up into their places. The street glistened, paved with a snow-white carpet for sleighing. It was white, it spar-

kled, it was sweet, like treacle cakes in fairy-tales. Zhenya
stood for a while by the window, watching the rings and
figures which the Hans Christian Andersen silvery flakes designed by the street lamp. She stood there for a while and
then went to her mother's room for *Kot-Murlyka*. She went in
without a light. Everything was still visible. The coachhouse
roof gave the whole room a mobile sheen. Under the sigh of
that huge roof the beds became frozen and glittered. Scattered moiré silks lay about in disorder. Tiny blouses emitted
a close and oppressive smell of calico and armpits. There was
an odor of violet and the wardrobe was raven-black, like
night in the courtyard and like that dry, balmy darkness in
which all this frozen glitter was stirring. One metal knob on
the bed sparkled like a single bead. The other was extinguished by a shirt tossed over it. Zhenya screwed up her eyes,
the bead detached itself from the floor and swam toward the
wardrobe. Zhenya remembered why she had come. Book in
hand, she walked toward one of the bedroom windows. The
night was full of stars. Winter had come to Ekaterinburg. She
glanced out into the courtyard and began thinking about
Pushkin. She decided to ask her tutor to have her write a
composition about Onegin.

Seryozha wanted to have a chat. He asked, "Have you put
on perfume? Give me some, also." He had been very nice to
her all day. He was very ruddy. She thought there could
never be another evening like this one. She wanted to be
alone.

Zhenya turned into her own room and took up the *Tales*.
She read one story and began another, holding her breath.
She was completely carried away and did not hear her
brother going to bed on the opposite side of the wall. A
strange game took possession of her face. She was not conscious of it. Now her face spread out like a fish; her lips
parted and the pupils of her eyes, grown numb with fright,
rooted to the page with terror, refused to rise, fearing to find
that very same thing behind the wardrobe. Now, her head
suddenly began to nod in sympathy with the print as if ap-
plauding it, as one applauds a good deed, and rejoices over a
happy turn of events. She slowed down when reading descriptions of lakes but charged ahead at breakneck speed into

the very darkness of night scenery holding onto a burning
coal of a Bengal fire on which the whole illumination depended. In one passage the lost hero cried out intermittently, listening for an answer, but could only hear the echo
of his own cry. Zhenya was forced to clear her throat, a muted
cry settled in her own larynx. The non-Russian name
"Mirra" lifted her out of her stupor. She put the book down
and began to think. "So that's how winter is in Asia. What are
the Chinese doing now, on such a dark night?" Zhenya's eyes
fell on the clock. "It must be really terrifying to be with
Chinese in the dark." Zhenya looked at the clock once more
and became frightened. Her parents might appear at any
moment. It was already twelve o'clock. She unlaced her
shoes and then remembered she had to replace the book.

Zhenya jumped up. She sat up in bed staring straight
ahead. It was not a thief. There are many of them, and they
stamp around and talk loudly, as in the daytime. Suddenly,
someone let out a shriek, like a knifed animal and something
was dragged along knocking over chairs. It was a woman
screaming. Little by little Zhenya recognized everyone; everyone except the woman. An incredible confusion arose.
Doors began to bang. When one of the far doors started
banging, it sounded like a woman who was being choked. But
it swung open again and the sound scalded the house with a
burning, welting scream. Zhenya's hair stood on end: the
woman was her mother; she had *guessed*. Ulyasha was wailing
and after once catching her father's voice, she heard it no
more. They were pushing Seryozha somewhere and he was
shouting, "Don't dare lock it!" Just then, Zhenya, bare-
footed, wearing only a nightgown, rushed out into the corridor. Her father nearly knocked her over. He was still in his
overcoat and as he ran, shouted something to Ulyasha.
"Papa!" She saw him running back from the bathroom with a
china pitcher. "Papa!" "Where's Liza?" he yelled in a frenzied voice, still running. Splashing water on the floor, he
vanished behind the door, and when he appeared a moment
later, in his shirtsleeves and without a vest, Zhenya found
herself in Ulyasha's arms; she did not hear the words uttered
in that deep, despairing, heart-rending whisper.

"What's the matter with Mama?" Instead of an answer, Ulyasha repeated the same things over and over again, "Don't, Zhenichka, don't, darling, sleep, go to sleep, close your eyes, lie on your side, ah-ah . . . My God! darl-ing! Don't, don't," she repeated, covering her like a baby, and getting ready to leave; don't, don't—but why? She did not speak and her face was damp, and her hair disheveled. The lock clicked behind her as she passed through the third door-way.

Zhenya lit a match to see how soon it would be daylight. It was exactly one o'clock. She was startled. Had she slept for less than an hour? But the noise in her parents' room had not lessened. Anguished cries burst forth—hatched, then shot out. Then for a brief moment a vast, ageless silence fell. Scurrying footsteps and guarded, private conversations broke into it. Then a bell rang. Then another. Then words, quarrels, orders—there were so many that it seemed as if the rooms were blazing with voices, like tables set under thousands of dying candelabras.

Zhenya fell asleep. She fell asleep with tears in her eyes. She dreamed that they had guests. She counted them and always made a mistake. There was always one too many. And every time she recognized her mistake she was seized by that very same terror she had experienced on realizing it was not just anyone, but Mama.

How could one not rejoice at such a fine, clear morning! Seryozha imagined games in the courtyard, snowballs, battles with the children in the yard. Tea was served in the classroom. They were told the floor polishers were in the dining room. Father came in. It was immediately evident that he knew nothing about the floor polishers. He told them the true reason for the changes. Mother had been taken ill. Silence was necessary. Crows flew over the street shrouded in white, the air resounding with their familiar croaking. A small sleigh passed by, drawn by a small mare. She was not yet accustomed to her new bit and kept losing her step. "You will go to the Defendovs', I've already made arrangements. And you . . ."

"Why?" interrupted Zhenya. But Seryozha guessed why

and anticipated his father, "So you won't catch the infec-
tion," he explained to his sister. But the street would not let
him finish. He ran up to the little window as if he were being
beckoned. A Tatar, walking along in his new clothes, was as
spruced up and smart as a pheasant. He was wearing a sheepskin cap. The bared sheepskin shone more brightly than
Moroccan leather. He walked with a waddling gait, swaying
to and fro, since the crimson pattern on his white boots had
nothing to do with the structure of a human foot; so freely
were these designs scattered about that little care was given
to whether they were feet or teacups or the tiles on a porch
roof. But what was most remarkable—at that moment
moans, carrying weakly from the bedroom, increased, and
Father went out in the corridor, forbidding them to follow
him—but most remarkable of all were the footprints which
he drew with the clean narrow toes of his boots along the
smooth field. The snow seemed even whiter, more satiny
compared to those neat, sculptured marks. "Here's a letter.
You will give it to Mr. Defendov. Himself! Understand? Well,
get dressed. Everything will be brought to you. Go down the
back stairway. And the Akhmedyanovs are waiting for you."

"Waiting, really?" the son asked scoffingly.

"Yes. You'll dress in the kitchen." He spoke distractedly,
and, without hurrying, accompanied them to the kitchen
where their coats, hats and mittens were found lying in a pile
on a stool. From the stairs came a rush of winter air.
"Aiyokh," the frozen cry of passing sleighs hovered in the
air. They hurried and could not get their arms into the
sleeves. From their clothes came the odor of trunks and
sleepy furs. "What's the fuss?" "Don't put it on the edge. It'll
fall. Well, any news?" "Still moaning," the maid tucked up
her apron, and, bending down, threw some logs under the
flames of the sighing stove. "This isn't my job," she was
indignant and went off once more on her round of the
rooms. A battered black pail was piled up with broken glass
and yellowed prescriptions. Towels were soaked with bloody
streaks and clots. They were inflamed. They wanted to be
trampled on like smoldering flames. Water was frivolously
boiling away in saucepans. White beakers and mortars, all
wondrous shapes, were seen standing about the room, as in

an apothecary shop. The slight figure of Halim was chopping ice in the passage. "Was much left over from summer?" asked Seryozha. "Soon there'll be new ice."

"Give me some. You're chopping it for nothing."

"Why for nothing? It has to be chopped up. For the bottles."

"Well, are you ready?"

But Zhenya was still running about the house from room to room. Seryozha went out to the stairway and, as he waited for his sister, began drumming one of the logs against the iron banisters.

VIII

They sat down to supper at the Defendovs'. The grandmother, having crossed herself, fell back into her armchair. The lamp burned with a dull glow and smoked; one moment they turned it too high, the next moment, too low. The dry hand of Mr. Defendov often stretched forth toward the screw, and, while slowly drawing it back from the lamp, he let himself drop slowly into his seat; his hand shook with a vibrating motion not at all like that of an old man, but as if he were raising a wineglass filled up to the brim. The ends of his fingers trembled, down to his fingernails.

He spoke with a distinct, even voice, as if he did not form his speech from sounds but composed it from letters, and he pronounced everything, including the special Russian hard sign.

The swollen neck of the lamp was ablaze, overcome by tendrils of geraniums and heliotrope. Cockroaches ran out toward the warmth of the glass and the hour hand advanced cautiously. Time crept past as in winter. Here it festered. In the courtyard it grew numb, fetid. Outside the window it scurried, pranced, doubling and trebling through the will-o'-the-wisps.

Mrs. Defendov placed some liver on the table. The dish was steaming, seasoned with onions. Mr. Defendov said something, often repeating, "I recommend this," and Liza was chattering incessantly, but Zhenya did not hear them. For two days now the little girl had felt the need to cry, now actually craving tears as she sat in the blouse sewn according to her mother's instructions.

Mr. Defendov knew what was wrong with her. He attempted to amuse her. But he started out talking to her as to a small child, and very soon attained results completely opposite to what he had intended. His joking questions frightened and embarrassed her. He fumbled around blindly reaching out for the soul of his daughter's friend as if asking her heart how old it was. He conceived his plan, having *unmistakably* detected one of Zhenya's characteristics which he intended to play upon in order to help the child forget about her own home, but his questioning only reminded her that she was among strangers.

Suddenly she could no longer contain herself; she stood up, childishly confused, and muttered, "Thank you. I've had enough, really. May I look at the pictures?" Then, blushing deeply at the sight of general perplexity around her, added, nodding in the direction of the adjoining room, "Walter Scott. May I?"

"Go, go, darling!" murmured the grandmother, raising her eyebrows to keep Liza in her seat. "Poor child," she turned to her son, when the wine-colored curtains of the portière had closed behind Zhenya.

A very grim series of magazines *The North* caused the bookshelf to slope somewhat, while below stood a complete set of Karamzin giving off a dim golden glow. A rose-colored lamp hung down from the ceiling, ignoring the pair of shabby armchairs left without light, and the rug which vanished into total darkness came as an unexpected surprise to her feet.

Zhenya imagined herself going in, sitting down and bursting into tears. Tears welled up in her eyes but her grief did not break through. How to dispel this melancholy which lay on her chest like a heavy beam since yesterday? Tears alone could not help her, to raise the beam was not within their power. To help them she began thinking about her mother.

For the first time in her life, as she was preparing to spend the night among strangers, she measured the depth of her attachment to the dearest, most precious being in the world.

Suddenly she heard Liza laughing behind the portière. "Eh, what a fidget, what an imp, you are . . ." her grandmother coughed out, swaying gently. Zhenya was struck by the thought that she could have loved that girl once, that girl whose laughter sounded so close to her, but who was so far away, so unnecessary. And something within her turned over, giving her the power to cry just at the very moment when her mother entered her consciousness: her mother still suffering, still remaining amidst the multitude of yesterday's events, like someone still standing in the crowd which had come to see people off, left behind, as the train of time carried Zhenya away.

But actually it was that piercing glance, so completely unbearable, which Madame Luvers had fixed on her yesterday in the schoolroom. It was engraved in her memory and refused to leave. Everything Zhenya now experienced was connected with it. As if it were something which ought to be taken with her, something very precious to her which had been forgotten and disregarded by her.

This sensation was likely to cause one to lose his head, its drunken, mischievous bitterness and inconsolability kept whirling about with such intensity. Zhenya stood by the window and cried noiselessly; tears flowed, and she did not wipe them away: her hands were busy although she was holding nothing. They were held erect, vigorously, impetuously and obstinately.

A sudden thought took her by surprise. All at once, she felt a terrible resemblance to her mother. This feeling was combined with a sensation of vivid certainty, imperious enough to turn fantasy into fact if it were not yet evident, and to liken her to her mother through the singular force of a remarkably sweet state of mind. This feeling was transpiercing, so sharp that it caused her to moan. *It was the sensation of a woman, perceiving both from within and without, her own appearance and charm.* Zhenya could not be fully aware of herself. She was experiencing this for the first time. In one thing she was not mistaken. Thus excited, Madame Luvers had once turned away from her daughter and the governess, and stood alone by the window biting her lips and striking her lorgnette against her gloved palm!

She returned to the Defendovs drunk with tears and brightened, and she did not enter in her own way but in a changed step, broad, dreamily disconnected and novel. At the sight of her approaching, Mr. Defendov realized that the conception of the girl which he had conceived in her absence was in no way applicable. He would have to draw up something new when he was not distracted by the samovar.

Mrs. Defendov went into the kitchen for a tray, placing the samovar on the floor; all their glances were fixed on the gleaming copper as if it were a living thing whose mischievous capriciousness would end the moment it was again placed on the table. Zhenya took her place. She made up her mind to enter into conversation with them. She vaguely felt that the choice of topic was now up to her. Or else she would be forced back into her previous isolation, for they would not notice that her mother was now present, here with her, and within her very self. And their lack of understanding would be painful to her, but even more painful to her mother. And as though encouraged by this last idea—"Vassa Vasilevna"—she turned to Mrs. Defendov who was lowering the samovar onto the edge of the tray with great difficulty. . . .

"Can you give birth?" Liza did not answer Zhenya immediately.

"Shh, quiet, don't shout. Well, yes, like every girl." She spoke in intermittent whispers. Zhenya did not see her friend's face. Liza fumbled about the table but did not find a match.

She knew much more than Zhenya about such things; she knew *everything;* as children know, learning from strange words. In such cases those natures which are selected by their creator, rise up, revolt and become wild. One cannot pass through this experience without exhibiting pathological traits. It would be contrary to nature, for childish madness at this age is only a seal of deep normality.

Liza was once told about various passions and vile actions in whispers, in a corner. She did not choke over what she heard but carried everything in her brain through the streets and brought it all home. On the way she lost nothing of what had been said, and even preserved all the trash. She found out everything. Her organism did not burst into flame, her heart did not begin beating an alarm, and her soul did not strike blows at her brain since it had dared to find out something on the sly, apart from her, not from her own lips, her own soul, without asking permission.

"I know." ("You don't know a thing," thought Liza.) "I know," repeated Zhenya. "I'm not asking about that. But about whether you feel that . . . you take a step and suddenly you give birth, well . . ."

"Do come in," replied Liza hoarsely, overcoming her laughter. "You've found some place to yell. They can overhear you on the threshold!"

The conversation took place in Liza's room. Liza spoke so softly that it was possible to hear the water dripping in the wash basin. She had already found the matches but was slow in lighting them, feeling incapable of expressing any seriousness through her radiant cheeks. She did not want to hurt her friend. But she spared her ignorance because she did not think that one could discuss such matters other than with those expressions which could not be mentioned here at home, before an acquaintance who was not going to school. She lit the lamp. Luckily, the pail was full to overflowing, and Liza rushed to wipe up the floor, concealing a new fit of laughter in her apron, in wringing out the cloth, and finally having found a real excuse, burst out laughing: she had dropped her comb into the pail.

All that time she knew only that she thought about her family and awaited the hour they would send for her. And during the days, while waiting, after Liza had gone off to school and the grandmother alone remained in the house, Zhenya would get dressed and go outside for a walk by herself.

Life in the district little resembled life in the places where the Luvers had always lived. Here, the greater part of the day was bare and tedious. There was nothing for the eye to revel in. Whatever it encountered or gazed upon was completely useless except, perhaps, for a birch rod or broom. Coal lay scattered about. Dirty dishwater was poured into the street and immediately grew white, turning to ice. At certain hours the street was full of ordinary people. Factory workers crawled through the snow like cockroaches. Tearoom doors were opened on pulleys and billows of soapy steam poured forth as from a laundry. It was strange, as if it had become warmer in the street, as if it had turned to spring, when steaming shirts ran past, round-shouldered, and felt boots flashed by on skinny legs. The pigeons did not fear these crowds. They flew along the road to find some food. Was there a bit of millet, oats, or dung-seed scattered in the snow? The pieman's stall was shining from the grease and warmth. This luster and heat fell into mouths rinsed with raw brandy. The grease inflamed their throats. And then it escaped along the road from their palpitating chests. Was it this that warmed the street?

And then suddenly it became deserted. Twilight fell. Peasant sleighs drove past empty, low sledges moved along swiftly carrying long-bearded men drowned in fur coats, who jokingly pulled the furs over their backs, hugging them bearfashion. From the sleighs there fell tufts of dullish hay and the slow, sweet thaw of distant bells. The merchants vanished at the turning, beyond the birch grove, which at that distance resembled a paling pulled apart.

The very same crows who scudded past over her own home, croaking freely, were now flying in her direction. Only here they did not croak. Here, shouting and flapping their wings, they hopped along the fences and then, suddenly, as if at a given signal, threw themselves up into the trees and in unison, nudging each other, took their places on the bare branches. Ah, how one felt then the lateness of the hour— how late it was in the whole world! So late, ah, so very late, later than any clock could show!

So one week passed, and toward the end of the second week, on Thursday at dawn, she saw him again. Liza's bed was empty. As she was waking up, Zhenya heard the wicket gate banging behind her. She got up and without lighting a lamp, went over to the little window. It was still completely dark. But she felt that very same oppressive quality as she had experienced the evening before, in the sky, in the branches of the trees and in the dog's movements. The weather had been overcast for three days so far and there was no strength left to remove it from the friable street, like a cast-iron kettle from a loose floorboard.

Across the street a lamp burned in the window. Two bright stripes, cast beneath a horse, lay on its shaggy pasterns. On the snow shadows moved, the arms of a phantom wrapped in a fur coat moved, a light in the curtained window moved. The horse stood motionless, dreaming.

Then she saw him. She immediately recognized him by his silhouette. The cripple raised his lamp and started off into the distance with it. Behind him both bright stripes moved, becoming distorted and lengthening, and behind the stripes the sleigh which quickly flashed by and then even more quickly plunged into the darkness, moving slowly behind the house toward the porch.

It was strange that Tsvetkov should continue to cross her field of vision, even here in the district. But Zhenya was not amazed by this. It made little impression on her. Soon the lamp reappeared, drifting smoothly across the curtains; it began to back up again, until suddenly it found itself right behind the curtain right at the very spot on the window ledge from which it had been removed.

This happened on Thursday. And on Friday they finally sent for her.

IX

Ten days after her return home, after more than a three-week interval, her studies were resumed, and Zhenya found out the rest from her tutor. After dinner the doctor packed his things and left and she asked him to greet the house in which he had examined her that spring, and all the streets, and the Kama. He expressed the hope that it would no longer be necessary to summon him from Perm. She accompanied him to the gate—the man who had made her tremble so that first morning after her trip home from the Defendovs', while Mama was sleeping and no one was allowed to see her, and who, in answer to her question concerning her mother's illness, began with recollections of the evening her parents went to the theater. And how at the end of the play they went out and their stallion . . .

"Vykormysh?"

"Yes, if that's his name . . . yes, Vykormysh began to

stamp, began to struggle; he reared up, and he struck down and crushed a person who happened to be passing by. . . ."

"What? To death?"

"Alas!"

"And Mama?"

"And Mama suffered a nervous breakdown. . . ." He smiled, barely able to adapt his own Latin *partus praematurus* to the child's language.

"And then my dead brother was born?"

"Who told you . . . ? Yes."

"And when? In front of everyone? Or was he found already dead? Don't answer. Oh, what a terrible thing! I understand now. He was already dead or I would have heard him. You see, I was reading. Till very late at night. I would have heard. But when did he actually live? Doctor, is it true, do such things really happen? I even went into the bedroom! He was dead. Absolutely!"

How fortunate that she had observed him only yesterday, at dawn, from the Defendovs' window, whereas the terrible accident at the theater happened three weeks ago. How fortunate that she recognized him. She dimly imagined that had she not seen him at all during this period, she would now, after hearing the doctor's words, have believed for certain that the crippled man was run over at the theater.

And now, having remained with them for such a long time, and having become one of the family, the doctor was going away. In the evening her tutor arrived. It was wash day. In the kitchen, linen was rolled through the mangle. The hoarfrost descended from the window frame and the garden came right up and touched the window; then becoming entangled in the lace curtains, it came right down to the table. Short rumbling sounds from the mangle roller burst into the conversation. Dikikh, like everyone else, found that she had changed. And she noticed a change in him.

"Why are you so sad?"

"Am I? Anything's possible. I lost a friend."

"So you have a sorrow, too? So many deaths—and all so sudden—" she sighed.

But he had only begun to relate what he knew when something inexplicable occurred. Suddenly, the little girl linked together her other thoughts concerning the number of deaths, and evidently having forgotten which arguments could be deduced from seeing the lamp that morning, she asked excitedly, "Wait a moment. You were at the tobacconist's shop the day Negarat left; I saw you with someone else. Him?" She was afraid to say, "Tsvetkov?"

Dikikh sat in silent perplexity as these words were pronounced; he searched his memory and at last recalled that they had actually gone there for some paper and asked about a complete set of Turgenev for Madame Luvers; and in fact, he had been with the dead man. She shuddered and tears gathered in her eyes. But the most important thing was still to come.

When, having related his story—interspersed with the uneven squeaking of the mangle—about the kind of youth he had been and from what a good family he was descended, Dikikh lit a cigarette, and Zhenya realized, terrified, that only this delay now separated her tutor from the repetitions of the doctor's story; and when he made an attempt to say a few words, among which was the word "theater," Zhenya uttered a frenzied scream and rushed out of the room.

Dikikh listened. Except for the mangle, not another sound was audible throughout the house. He stood up like a stork. He stretched his neck and raised one foot, ready to go to her aid. He searched hurriedly for the girl, deciding that no one was at home and she had lost consciousness. But meanwhile, as he fumbled about in the dark, knocking against the mysteries of wood, wool and metal, Zhenya sat in a corner crying. He continued to search and grope about but in his thoughts he was already raising her, half-dead, from the carpet. He shuddered when a tearful voice from just behind his elbow loudly proclaimed, "I'm here. Watch out for the cupboard over there. Wait for me in the schoolroom. I'll come in a minute."

The curtains fell to the floor, the starry winter night outside the window leaned over and also dropped down the floor, and outside, up to their waists in snowdrifts, dragging the glittering reticula of branches through the deep snow, massive trees strolled along toward the bright light in the window. And somewhere behind the wall, tightly drawn together by the sheets, the steady rumble of the mangle sounded, back and forth, back and forth. "What can explain this abundance of sensitivity?" pondered the tutor. "Obviously the girl had some special concern for the dead man. She's greatly changed. Repeating decimals had been explained to a child; however, the person who sent him into the schoolroom just now . . . And this happened in a month? Obviously the dead man had somehow produced an especially deep and indelible impression on this young woman. There is a name given to impressions of this kind. How strange!" He had been giving her lessons every other day and had noticed nothing. She was *extremely kind,* and he was desperately sorry for her. "But when will she cry herself out and finally come into the schoolroom? Everyone else is probably away." She was to be pitied from the depths of the soul. A remarkable night!

He was mistaken. That impression which he attempted to name had nothing to do with this situation. He was not entirely mistaken, however. The impression which lay concealed behind all this *was* indelible. It was much more than he thought, it went much deeper. It lay beyond the girl's control because it was vitally important and significant, and its significance rested in the fact that it was the first time *someone else* had entered her life, a third person, completely indifferent, nameless and even lacking an accidental name, neither provoking hatred nor inspiring love, *but the one whom the commandments bore in mind,* when addressing people in name and consciousness, they said: Thou shalt not kill, thou shalt not steal and so forth. They said: "Thou who art singular and alive, shalt not commit *against the common and nebulous* that which thou, the singular and alive, doth not want done unto thee." Dikikh blundered even more in thinking that there is a name for such impressions. They have no name.

But Zhenya was crying because she considered herself guilty in everything. Indeed, it was *she* who introduced him into the life of the family on that day when, noticing him in the strange garden, and noticing him needlessly, purposelessly, thoughtlessly, she began to meet him at every step, continuously, directly and obliquely, and even as on the last occasion, in defiance of all probability.

When she saw which book Dikikh was taking from the shelf, she winced and said, "No. I won't be able to answer questions on this today. Put it back. I'm sorry. Forgive me, please."

And without further words Lermontov was squeezed by the same hand back into the tilting row of classics.

Translated by Jane Gary Harris

KONSTANTIN PAUSTOVSKY

MOSCOW SUMMER

I

A break was called. They stuck their skis into the snow. The sun was reflected in the broad bends of the skis like an amber fruit. The wind with delicate clouds blew overhead very low, just above the tips of the fir trees. Then the clearing began to drift over, and the sun turned into a gray spot.

The architect Hoffman, called "the pocket skier" because of his small stature, wiped off his skis with his mittens. He got a mirror-like shine. The wood was warmed from the vigorous rubbing, and its shine merged with the odor of varnish and pine needles.

A compass lay in Lyolya's palm. Its timid arrow trembled for a long time. The compass was lost in the snow-drifted underbrush and wastelands. Then it pointed firmly to the south with its white needle, a little to the left of the sun. In that direction was Bear Mountain. Hoffman checked it on the map. On the faded green stain indicating forest, there was a notation in black: "Monastery, burned by the French." The compass showed true.

Beyond the monastery, overlooking a ravine on Bear Mountain which bristled with spruce, stood the still uncompleted rest home, the "Fifth Day." It could easily be approached from the Bryansk road, but the skiers were coming from the north, from Golitsin, through the thick woods. Hoffman was building the house.

Of the five skiers, only one—Mett, a feature writer—had

come with a practical goal. He wanted to describe the "Fifth Day." The others had come along for the snow and the winter woods.

Mett knew about the "Fifth Day" only from short articles in the newspapers. They said that a famous French architect considered Hoffman's project a work of genius. Among the graduate students at the Communist Academy, arguments grew up around the "Fifth Day." It was said that the building was cylindrical, and almost completely constructed of glass. Hoffman answered Mett's questions briefly and obliquely. He reviled the new buildings in Moscow, called them "American trash," and had suggested that Mett go with him on skis to the "Fifth Day."

In the coach of the suburban train, Mett had thought about the "Fifth Day." In the forest, however, he forgot all about it. He breathed deeply. A kind of spring passed over the snows. Mett thrust his ski poles into the crusted snow and looked around—the snow had a clean, sharp smell. Wind smells like that, and ice melting in the mouth, and youth.

Great layers of sea air lay over the land around Moscow. The match in Mett's hand—he had lit a cigarette—didn't go out for a long time. Its flame didn't even flicker in the wind.

From behind, with a measured whishing, Luzgin moved up.

"Oho!" he shouted, frightening the rabbits and running onto Mett's skis. Luzgin wanted to talk, but Mett couldn't make out what he was saying.

He took off his leather cap and finally could hear Luzgin's words, which came to him in separate shouts.

". . . It was six in the morning . . . dark . . . I was walking to the station, and in front of me, block after block was being turned out."

"What do you mean, turned out?"

"The street lights were being turned out. Click—and the whole ring of boulevards is thrown into darkness! Click—and all Tverskaya Street, from Sadovaya to the Arch of Triumph goes out! It was wonderful."

On the bushes lay small caps of snow. Lyolya stopped, took off a glove and carefully touched them with her cold fingers.

"Just like white sparrows!"

Lyolya's husband, the reporter Danilov—taciturn and nearsighted—had been behind the whole way.

Luzgin was counting the rabbit tracks. The rabbits, running from the skiers, had made tangled loops in the snow.

A low sun shone through the frozen branches. Transparent shadows lay on the snow, untouched by anything, even by the wind. You had to look closely even to notice them.

It was getting dark. The woods sloped broadly downward, toward the ravine. Hoffman turned around and shouted, "Bear Mountain!"

They stopped. Across the ravine, the brush-covered mountain rose triumphantly, like a lump of antique silver.

Lyolya cried out. She was the first to see the "Fifth Day" on the mountainside. Over the wall of transparent trees hung the moon. It looked like a pinkish cloud, carried up to a dizzying height.

II

Mett thought for a little while, squinted and looked out of the window where the stars and snowy branches created a painting of a winter night. He struck the piano keys. The grand piano, stiff from the cold, resounded dully. Mett struck the keys a second time, a third, and finally the piano began to sing in a full voice:

> A beautiful name is a great honor.
> The township of Granada is in Spain.

When the wind came up, Mett frowned. The howling of the wind muffled the music. The wind passed in and out freely through the walls, as it does through Venetian blinds. A gust of wind will pour fresh air into all corners of the room, like water into a glass, and tobacco smoke will rise evenly.

Hoffman was nodding over a cold cup of tea. When Mett struck the keys hard, he opened his eyes, looked at Mett in astonishment and fell asleep again. Lyolya, beside him, slept sitting up in a chair.

Danilov had moved the kerosene lamp right up to his nose

and was nearsightedly writing, keeping one eye on what he had already written.

The building is cylindrical. Bowed windows of plate glass (frameless) occupy all the wall space. Semicircular rooms. Main hall circular. Walls very thin and admit sounds from outside. In the walls are arranged narrow apertures, which close automatically with planks of semirough pine. The planks can be positioned at any angle.

Three floors are connected by a wide spiral stairway of marble. The stairway rises next to the wall. It cuts unexpectedly through floors and ceilings. There is no lighting as yet. All the lights will be tungsten lamps, which do not retard ultraviolet rays. Hoffman maintains that there will be eternal summer in the building, the climate of Algiers. In winter, the convalescents will be able to tan as they would in summer at the beach.

A round stone column, like a mast, cuts through the center of the building, from the foundation to the roof. In general, there is something of a lighthouse about the building. Hoffman grew up near the seashore. In his youth, according to him, he had even sailed on schooners carrying cherries from Kherson. As a watchman for the "Fifth Day," he took on Grishin, a Komsomol member, who had been released from the Baltic Fleet.

In any case, there is something lifeless about the building, something of the crematorium. It is not yet furnished, and not completed.

There is no enclosure around the building. It stands in a thicket above the ravine. Below is the forest and a wooded stream which is frozen over. It has a very strange name: "Dar'inka."

Danilov wrote "Dar'inka, Dar'inka, Dar . . ." and fell asleep. The stars raced by outside, scribbling over the windows with their greenish tracks.

Mett was playing more and more softly, picking out the keys like strings.

Luzgin went down to the boiler room for some matches.

He felt like smoking. Grishin was not there—he had gone to Moscow. The janitor Nikifor was sitting beside the furnace, drying out his wet felt boots. Nikifor was old; his eyes were watery.

"Well, Pop, have you gotten used to this building?" asked Luzgin.

Nikifor thought for a little while and looked inside his boot.

"The building is, of course, a bit roundish. The wind blows around it from all sides; there's nothing to hinder it. It's a practical thing."

It was Nikifor's conviction that buildings begin to fall apart at the corners. He had become used to the house. Something else was on his mind.

"Do you know what? The other day Grishin," he said, becoming more animated, "shot a rabbit with a revolver. Never saw the like, although I'm a hunter myself. Would you believe it—shooting a rabbit with a revolver?

"This house is one beautiful building," sighed Nikifor, apparently forgetting about the rabbit. "When they were putting this building up, there was an order not to cut down a single little bush. Look around: even the road they put through is narrow, so as not to cut down extra trees. And how did it used to be? They'd uproot trees for acres around, they dried up the streams, destroyed the wild life. Some of the animals went toward Meshchovsk, others toward Rzhev. They emptied the forests. The last time Hoffman came, we got to talking. 'We,' he said, 'are going to make the whole area into a preserve, otherwise what kind of rest will people get here? Let everything grow as it is.'"

Luzgin went back upstairs. Everyone was already sleeping. Lyolya was curled up on the couch. Mett and Danilov were asleep on the floor. Hoffman was stretched out solemnly on a camp cot, flat on his back, like the corpse of a general. His sharp nose cast a gigantic shadow on the wall.

Luzgin admired the shadow for a minute, then put out the lamp and lay down beside Mett. Dreams swam toward him with a distant roar; in the roar was the sound of train whistles, the howl of the wind over the ravines. The piano settled and resounded softly. Luzgin fell asleep.

Nikifor, in the boiler room, alone stayed awake, ruminating over his drying boots.

Mett opened his eyes. He sensed a warm freshness; his head felt surprisingly light—he'd had a good sleep. A heavy snow was falling outside the window. Mett did not see it. He noticed only the individual snowflakes, flying away from the glass.

"Beautiful!" Mett said loudly, and lit a cigarette. With its light he looked at his watch. It was 4:30.

"What's beautiful?" Hoffman asked from his cot. He had wakened before Mett.

Mett was silent for a while.

"I want to write about this building; you'll sob with ecstasy over your own work. Not a single architect in the world has been worthy of such a study. Let's arrange an interview."

"To hell with you," growled Hoffman. "Go ahead and ask now what you want to know."

"Tell me in your own words."

Hoffman thought a little.

"Of course, experts will write about the building. That's important for me, but nobody else needs it. I suppose that the 'Fifth Day' can be best described only by a perfect ignoramus about architecture, like, let's say, you or Danilov. It would be like the ordinary reader's opinion of something new in literature."

"Thanks a lot," said Mett.

"Cities have outlived their time. If you, Citizen Mett, think that's not true, then Engels would have thought otherwise. In every governmental system, there are inherent its own forms of settling people. Socialism needs no cities. Cities are created by man's limitations, his inability to distribute raw materials, labor, manufactured goods and cultural advantages. They dump all this together in a heap and gather a million people around it."

"That's a weak argument. You're denying the collective basis."

"Radio, telephone, air lines and transmitting images over long distances allow us to refuse the necessity of gathering millions into one place. The collectives will be smaller in number, that's all."

"Let's assume that, then."

"What is a house? For a man, it is what a shell is to a turtle or snail. It should be constructed so as to make our physical and psychological life easier, to create a milieu in which it can develop. The house must be efficient, must conform strictly to its purpose, and be pleasing to the eye. Contemplation of beautiful things calls up the creative mood. This is a powerful factor in the business of building Socialism and creating the well-developed personality."

"They don't accept that."

"Who doesn't? Dilettantes? Philistines?" Hoffman said angrily. "Who said that only an idiot could dislike Pushkin?"

Mett said nothing.

"You're a slob, not a writer. You don't know even that much. From what I've said, all the details of the 'Fifth Day' are understandable."

"I don't understand a thing."

"How can you not understand? I just said that a building must answer its purpose. You go to the woods for a rest, not to Moscow. Right? Then the rest home must be inseparable from nature. Hence its form. Restful lines are needed. The most restful line is the circle, not a sharp angle. Hence, rounded rooms. The walls admit sound, and you wrinkled your brows when you were playing the piano. This was done with a conscious purpose. The sound of the trees and wind is master inside the house as well as outside. Instead of exterior walls—glass. You are awakened not by the front door slamming, but by the sunrise.

"In the walls are apertures. Just set the planks at a certain angle, and the whole building is filled with fresh air, yet at the same time there is perfect quiet in the rooms. The roof is divided with barriers at all points of the compass. One can sleep there, shielded from any wind. The ceilings are not high. The apertures in the walls make high ceilings unnecessary. The height of the rooms must conform to the average height of the people, otherwise the rooms become repulsive, like a skinny man who is tall as a giant. Enough?"

"Enough for now."

Mett looked out of the window for a long time, hoping to catch sight of that delicate touch of blue which heralds the coming of morning, but he couldn't wait; he fell asleep.

As soon as it began to be light, Luzgin woke Danilov. Both of them had to return to Moscow that morning. They came out of the forest on their skis at Aprelevka, on the Bryansk road. The night turned from black to blue, then to gray. The frosted treetops shone with yellow fire; the sun came up beyond the woods.

Heavy steam rose from the station, the engines, the cars. Crows cawed desolately. Weatherbeaten trains, stuffy and smelling of cheap cigar smoke, ran to Moscow. They snuffled along like a wild animal, a dark spot among the deep, silent snows. Smoke and steam also rolled up from Moscow, but Moscow's smoke was grim and majestic. It was like the smoke of history, of revolutions, the smoke of eternity. So thought Danilov, being inclined to poetic metaphor and a slightly hysterical type.

"I didn't like Hoffman's building," he said to Luzgin in the restaurant of the Bryansk station, where they were drinking tea. "You can see the calculation behind every tiny little thing. Is such ferocious efficiency necessary?"

"What's the matter with you? Born yesterday?" Luzgin growled sullenly. "Why do you talk such nonsense?"

Danilov was insistent.

"In every building, there should be a certain amount of useless things. In every building, there should be at least one mistake."

"Why?"

"To give it life. A smooth speech without any mistakes is terribly boring. A mistake is a sign of life; faultlessness is deadly. Hoffman's house is dead."

Luzgin shrugged his shoulders.

"There are all kinds of mistakes," he said, putting on his knapsack. "A Tatar oil magnate built himself a palace in Baku. The architect made a mistake and didn't put a bathroom in the palace. When the guests and owners had to go, they had to run out into the yard. I don't think they'd share your views."

* * *

Lyolya, Hoffman and Mett returned to Moscow that evening. In the streetcar, a button from Lyolya's fur coat was torn off in the crowd. The passengers shoved and trampled each other unbearably. Truck-drivers rolled down Pyatnitskaya Street, spitting out curses.

Danilov wasn't home. The primus stove in the kitchen hissed. Lyolya sat down at the table and, pulling off her gloves slowly, began to cry. . . . In answer, a broken-down streetcar rumbled maliciously, like a mean dog.

III

Luzgin arrived at the factory two hours before work started. He was that sort of man—he took his rest at the factory. He would make a round of the shops, stand for a long time at the machines, and leave the workers with a joke.

Talk about how factories are not picturesque and are not material for painters made him angry. Even now, through the thick March fog, the windows of the blacksmith shop breathed with torn flames; violet, unbearably bright stars from the cutting torches hissed in the yard; in empty shops black movable cranes rolled along high up in the blue smoke from welding; light broke its way through the thick lenses of safety glasses; steel machines, champing dreamily, cut through tarnished golden brass.

Despite the signs in the information shack about not looking at the flame, the eyes were very much drawn to it. Looking at it, one recalled memories of an ocean never seen, of a lilac-colored smoky sun, of cities in silent coastal nights scattered with bunches of street lights, as the sparks cut with a cruel grinding noise from the T-beams were scattered in the darkness. Luzgin stood longest of all next to the welders.

The factory hummed day and night, but Luzgin's hearing, used to the din, noticed a growing, higher and higher tone. The factory was putting on speed, exceeding the winter pick-up. Life at the factory went on in a calm rush, through the efforts of the hard-working shock brigades.

The brigades worked silently, without shouting, without banter. It was not at all like what the bright young men in knitted vests wrote pompously about the factory in the newspapers. They supercharged their reports with a lot of noise and familiarity with regard to the brigades. The brigades didn't like this. There crept into the reports not the productive, not the workers' approach to the work, but a slightly bragging one. The brigades, however, put up with it—"Let them write what they want; we'll do our jobs."

Luzgin fought with the reporters. He tried to instill in them the necessity of writing about work at the factory clearly, simply, without breathlessness and without panic. The reporters agreed, but did things their own way. One day they would report ecstatically: "The factory moves brilliantly toward catching up with the plan." And the next day they would sound the alarm: "Danger signal. The factory is not measuring up to its March production. Insufficiency in planning is the decisive factor in lags at the plant." Both reports would be equally exaggerated.

Luzgin went into the workers' reading and recreation room. The workers were already gathering. Almost all of them were from the hot shops—dry men, burned out from the heat, with sharp, bronzed profiles.

Luzgin prepared his talks painstakingly. He had worked out a simple and perfected language. He spoke slowly, even haltingly, but after each stop a new paragraph began, shedding light on the subject from an unexpected quarter. He thought in images and involuntarily constructed his talk according to them, developing them to the necessary expressiveness.

The workers went willingly to hear Luzgin's talks.

Luzgin paid close attention to the make-up of his audience. More than anything, he was pleased by the presence of old men. Among the factory workers, the conviction reigned that it is impossible to shake up the oldsters; that the old men are stubborn as mules. Luzgin secretly rejoiced: more and more old men appeared each time.

This time, he was giving a talk on events on the Chinese-Eastern Road. He peppered it with quotes from letters of Red Army men, told about the Far East, where he had spent two years in the Red Army. He mentioned in passing the famous researcher Arsen'ev of the Ussuri Region, and advised them to read his book, mentioning Gorky's comment on it.

Luzgin's talks were encased in the flesh of everyday life, with people, characteristic details, even landscape. Luzgin noticed that this method, removing the abstractness from the theme, created a pleasant mood among the workers. The method was correct, and Luzgin hit his mark exactly.

IV

Evening came on, with all the splendor that a Moscow summer is capable of. Toward five, the day acquired the dull color of badly filtered white wine. Hoffman lay on a couch and looked at the fountains in the dark gardens, ready any minute to burst into a bright shower. From the window could be seen the Vorobyov Hills.

He was tired. It had been necessary to debate a great deal, to find forcible arguments quickly, and to prove that which, in his opinion, did not need to be proven.

The "Fifth Day" was completed and open, but somebody had to start all over again the pointless debate over this building. The debate went on in the Construction Committee. Hoffman received a summons. It stated: "The Report of Comrade Ivanitsky on the Inadvisability of Constructing Buildings of the Type of the 'Fifth Day' "—and at the end: "Your presence is obligatory."

Hoffman was afraid of public appearances. He didn't know how to speak. His small stature made him, in his own eyes, less authoritative. He was depressed by the successful, respectable engineers in their narrow-cut English suits, who stated unhurriedly laconic and seemingly incontrovertible truths. He was persecuted by a few graduate students of the Construction Institute, who gave the building of the "Fifth Day" an almost universal but negative significance. They plastered their speech with a multitude of "isms," and Hoffman was amazed: one "ism" caught onto the next with the precision of gear teeth. With all his being, Hoffman knew they were wrong, but he couldn't prove it.

At the meeting, the "Fifth Day" was utterly obliterated. The graduate students said that Hoffman had committed many errors, and had demonstrated an unnecessary functionalism in his construction. They said that the building was constructed like a machine—only of working parts, in a utilitarian manner, in the American manner—in other words, dry and efficient to the point of boredom. One of the graduate students called the "Fifth Day" a silo. Hoffman blew up and said some harsh words. He was convinced that the graduate students were ascribing to him what they themselves were struggling against.

The engineers listened to the graduate students respectfully, but absent-mindedly. In their opinion, it was much more important that the "Fifth Day" cost a lot and required many construction materials. The engineers considered the construction of such buildings a waste. The representative of the RKI also joined in with them.

"You see, dear Comrade," said Engineer Rosenblit through his nose, squeezing a squeaking yellow briefcase between his knees, "you see, there is one thing I don't understand. In the winter, the convalescents will be sleeping with the planks open. That seems to be the case, doesn't it? In other words, the building will be turned into a sieve for the night. At the same time, it is necessary, I submit, that the room temperature not fall below a fixed norm. In other words"— Rosenblit placed his briefcase on the table like a border between Hoffman and himself—"in other words, there should always be fresh but warm air in the rooms. Consequently, they must be heated. Given the condition of perforated walls, that is tantamount to"— Rosenblit got up and put his briefcase under his arm, preparing to leave—"tantamount to trying to heat the grove at Sokol'niki Park."

"In the first place," answered Hoffman, "when it is not much below freezing, the heat can be cut off. The convalescents sleep in sleeping bags. When it is really cold, heating is necessary, but the planks will be shut periodically, and when they are open, they will be adjusted in such a way that the temperature will not fall below a certain limit."

Rosenblit gave a short laugh and left. In the next room, he said loudly to someone, "I have a lot of work to do today, and I don't feel like listening to conversationalists."

Now, lying on the couch, Hoffman remembered Rosenblit; he reddened and growled, "The idiot! The arrogant fool!"

Only one man, in heavy shoes and a stiff new jacket who kept making notes on something, supported Hoffman.

"Even if there is a shortage of materials," he said, "that doesn't mean we have to build trash. You can even build a house on your thumb, if materials are that short. I lived in that building, and had such a rest there as I never had in the Crimea. It's a remarkable building; I can't say it strongly enough."

"From what organization are you?" the chairman asked him.

"I'm a workers' correspondent from *Workers' Moscow;* I'm going to write an article on it."

The decision reached was vague—to recognize the question of constructing buildings of the type of the "Fifth Day" as open.

"You open it and we'll close it," said the workers' correspondent; he gathered up his notes and left. His puzzling sentence brought strained smiles to the faces of the engineers.

The day of the meeting with the Construction Committee was Hoffman's last day in Moscow. The next day he was leaving—more precisely, flying—on vacation. He was to fly to Kharkov, and from there was planning to go to his home town: the little port of Skadovsk on the shore of Karkenitsky Bay.

His things were packed and there was nothing to do. Hoffman decided to go back to Usachyovka on foot. He passed by the narrow, Asiatic Zaryad'e and came out onto the quay. Gulls skimmed over the water, which looked blue from exhaust fumes. From the black throats of the chimneys of the Moscow Electric Plant rolled a greasy smoke. At Kamenny Bridge, old men were fishing in the green, filthy water. In the water, a pink Kremlin floated. It was a fairy-tale reflection, but the old men spat indifferently on it, and inhaled approvingly the dank coolness exuding from under the arches of the bridge.

Hoffman turned off into the Prechistenka. In this area of Moscow, the sunlight was free of dust. The yard-keepers poured water on the roads. The gray asphalt was turned into black, shining pools. It smelled like rain.

"How hot it is!" Hoffman recalled that flights are unpleasant during a heat wave; there are so many air pockets.

Above the deserted Usachyovka, little boys were chasing pigeons. At home, Hoffman lay down, remembered the meeting for a long time, then under his closed eyelids red and violet spots began to race around, and he fell asleep.

He was awakened by someone banging at the door. Lyolya and Mett had come to say good-by. Lyolya was laughing on the other side of the wall. The most delicate ripples of clouds, like fish scales, were shining golden over the city.

Mett smiled with his eyes. He could not laugh. Lyolya, in an unusual dress—short, thin and shining—would now laugh, now fall to thinking and stare into space. Her pupils were unnaturally widened, and in the whites of the eyes sparks caught fire—a reflection of the evening, filled with heat and light. It was like the reflection of waves playing back and forth on the white side of a ship.

The room was stifling. They went down to the river.

"Friends," said Hoffman, "if we could only go to the seashore together. How wonderful it would be!"

An accidental conjunction of several unimportant facts called up a burst of fantasy in Hoffman. The lazy summer day, the short but deep sleep, were enough to bring on the state which Hoffman now experienced. He called this state a "dry drunk."

He vaguely imagined acacias rustling in the darkness, waves lapping, the sands, and the steppes from which a dry wind blows.

"How wonderful it would be!" he repeated with regret.

"Everybody gets his vacation at a different time," complained Lyolya. "How idiotically everything is set up."

Mett was busy with calculations. "For two hundred eighty-one days in the year," he said precisely, "you sit in some dirty room. We haven't yet learned to work in a civilized way. By the end of the working day, the air is green with smoke."

"It's awful!" answered Lyolya.

Hoffman's mood did not survive their complaints. The attack of his "dry drunk" gave way to irritation.

"It's stupid," he said. "You're an intelligent man, Mett, but your mind is moldy. You've decided that skepticism will save you from reality. You live in it, like infusoria in a culture medium. In the depths of your soul you know yourself that this is the wrong attitude toward your environment, but you are lazy and a sensitive type, and therefore you swim along with the current."

"Very interesting," Mett said caustically. "Please go on."

"You take the course of least resistance, and are guided by your feelings, not your mind. Of course, that's the easy way."

"You mutter that at me every day," Mett said evenly.

"Force yourself to think. Imagine a situation like this: we are surrounded by friends, not enemies. No one badgers us, or bristles at us with bayonets. Imagine the victory of the Soviet order if not in the whole world, then at least in Europe. You first conclude agreements with the publishers and rush off to Turkey, Greece, Italy. You will write magnificent books, and your life will acquire a fullness as never before. You'll grow ten years younger. Then, I hope, you will understand what the words 'cultural revolution' mean. You'll be one of its partisans. Its values will live within you, like the whole complex of your thoughts and moods. Don't think that it will be a sweet, idyllic time. People will die and struggle then also—on expeditions, in laboratories—everywhere that living human thought exists."

"That's not clear, but rather attractive," said Mett.

"What is the Five-Year Plan?" asked Hoffman. "The supreme effort to bring the future closer, not by the dreamy tempos of biological life, but by the tempos which we need as human beings who don't expect to live for two hundred years. The Five-Year Plan is heroic impatience, corraled within the limits of numbers. In this is its significance and uniqueness, young man."

Mett said nothing.

"Would you agree to leave the USSR right now, forever?" asked Hoffman.

Mett stopped smiling.

"Never," he answered sharply.

"Then why do you act like such a fool?"

Lyolya burst out laughing.

They came out onto the river at the bridge on Okruzhnaya Road. The transparent twilight was green in the river's reflection. Hoffman rented a boat.

Lilac quicksilver dripped from the raised oars. Each drop was saturated with the string of lights shining in the Park of Culture and Rest. The water slept under the dense, heavy lindens.

Hoffman brought Lyolya and Mett almost to Boloto. Here they said good-by. Pulling out toward the middle, Hoffman watched Lyolya walking slowly along the quay. Mett stopped to light a cigarette and fell behind.

"Oh, my friends," Hoffman sighed, and turned the boat. With short strokes, he drew it toward the noisy darkness of Neskuchny Park.

v

In July, Luzgin's father died, suddenly, of a heart attack.

The next day, Luzgin sent the body to the crematorium, and went himself by bus. There was no one but Luzgin in the crematorium. A very polite man in a surgical smock walked around carefully, and the organ sobbed in bass tones.

Luzgin felt relieved. With the death of his father, the past was gone; he could exclude it from his mind forever.

From the Donskoi Monastery, Luzgin crossed over to Kaluga Street. It swept toward the Vorobyov Hills, within a belt of parks and hospitals. It was four o'clock. The drought had reached the point where colors are burned away. Leaves on the trees, buildings, even the sky faded to a grayish color. The wings of the Petroleum Institute shone white, as though coated with salt.

Luzgin knew that Lyolya worked as a typist in the Petroleum Institute. He entered the courtyard, which was like a parade ground for military drill. He opened the door, and the cool bright quiet of the concrete rooms and corridors struck him like an unexpected shower.

The room was pointed out to him. He went in. Outside the window, the motley Zamoskvarech'e area smoldered. Lyolya was taking dictation. She jumped up, moved a chair over for Luzgin and asked him to wait—she still had a page to finish.

An inconspicuous man in a gray Mostorg suit dictated haltingly and tonelessly; it embarrassed Luzgin. He was dictating a report on rejuvenating petroleum areas in the Groznensky oil fields.

Lyolya typed in spurts, her lips compressed. The machine clicked in time with her confused thoughts:

"Why did he come? . . . so unexpectedly . . . how nice that he came, anyway . . . I'm ashamed—I complained to him about my work, and it's nice here today, nicer than it has ever been—everything is bright and clean, Myatlikov is dictating an interesting report . . . does he know that Hoffman has flown to Kharkov? . . . he must have come for some reason . . . people don't come so far for nothing . . . why am I upset . . . why, why, why?"

Lyolya didn't have time to answer this question in her thoughts. Myatlikov said: "That's all," and waiting unassumingly while Lyolya removed the finished page, he took the report and, saying good-by, he quickly left. He was afraid of keeping Lyolya an extra minute, or being in the way. Lyolya was amazed by the kindness and perception of scientists in affairs far removed from oil. She had thought about it, but found no explanation. One could only assume that in scientific books, among incomprehensible formulae and integers, were spontaneously generated the tiny bacteria of respect for mankind, which took root in the consciousness of the scientist and there lived out their modest life.

"Well, what's up; what brings you here?" Lyolya said hurriedly, coming up to Luzgin. "How did you ever find me here? You came just at the right time. I haven't been myself today, not since this morning. I feel so rotten, as though I were alone in all Moscow."

Luzgin could see that Lyolya regarded his coming as a turning point in her life. He had dropped in accidentally, but listening to Lyolya, he realized that some sort of decision to meet her had been in his mind, unnoticed by himself, ever since the ski trip to Bear Mountain. This meeting had come closer, like a storm cloud—in disturbed rustling of the leaves, in sudden gusts of wind, in the vagueness of his mood. He felt like crying out, as though he had just been awakened and slightly startled.

"I had some business not far from here," said Luzgin, reddening. What sort of "business" he did not say. He realized that that would be impossible now. Lyolya wouldn't even hear words about death; they wouldn't reach her consciousness. The storm raging inside her would muffle them; her sudden confusion would make a jumble of them, and push them aside.

She needed to hear something quite different, and Luzgin said, "I came for you. Let's go down to the river."

"Yes, shall we go?" Lyolya asked joyfully, as though she'd been waiting for this for a long time.

In her eyes, Luzgin caught the wide, intense shining which had struck Hoffman not so long before. "It's going to rain; aren't you worried?"

"On the contrary. It's nice by the river in the rain. Do you have a raincoat?"

"Yes," Lyolya sighed deeply. "I'll be right with you."

While she was putting on her hat, Luzgin looked out the window. Smoke stretched upward from Dorogomilova. The smoke of railroad engines rose in white, sinister columns toward the sky. Beyond the Bryansk Station, over the dust and din of the suburbs, a gigantic blue cloud was growing.

They ran down to the river through Neskuchny Park and stopped for lunch at a pavilion near the pond. The approaching thunderstorm had scared off the strollers; the park was empty.

Lyolya ate nothing. She told Luzgin about her morning. She had had a fight with Danilov that morning.

Danilov, drying his hands with a towel, had said, "You know, I've printed my article on the 'Fifth Day.'"

"Well, so what?" Lyolya had been irritated since the evening before—July was ending, and she hadn't been out of the city once. The summer languished in the stagnant air of the rooms and the streets.

"Nothing special. After that article, a committee was appointed to ascertain whether it is worthwhile to construct such buildings at all."

"I heard about it. Show me what you wrote."

Danilov held out the newspaper. Lyolya quickly found the article and laughed drily. Danilov had written that the "Fifth

Day" was a specimen of formalistic pursuits quite foreign to the proletariat, and that to construct such a building now, when construction materials are needed for industry, is a criminal waste of resources.

"You halfwit!" Lyolya threw the paper onto the table. "All your life you've swum along close to the surface, and you'll still be small fry when you die. Why the editors believe in you I don't know. A wonderful building, the future caught in it, there is talent and thought in it—and you write such a scabrous article."

"We don't need such buildings," Danilov answered icily.

"Who doesn't need them, who doesn't?" Lyolya shouted. "Mama's boys, shopkeeper's sons?" (Danilov's father had been a merchant.) "How dare you talk that way? Talented people irritate you. It's disgusting, do you hear me, disgusting to listen to you. Get out!" Lyolya broke a pencil in two and threw it into a corner. "Get out right now; I don't want to look at you! How can I ever face Hoffman, Mett, anybody?"

"You hysteric!" Danilov began quickly tying his necktie. "You quarrelsome, crazy old woman! Your Hoffman is a braggart and a hack. Everybody's talking about it; only you can't see it at all."

"I told you—get out!"

Danilov left, slamming the door. Lyolya fell onto the couch and sobbed. She was late for work. The graduate students, seeing her eyes red from weeping, went into the next room at once. One of them unexpectedly brought her an orange from the snack bar. Lyolya looked at him, smiled, and the tears dropped quickly onto the keys of her Underwood. The graduate student disappeared immediately.

Luzgin listened to Lyolya, blushed and coughed a little. Then, making up his mind, he said, "Yes, he is rather shallow. The thing is that those who lack talent—" Luzgin halted, but the words had already burst out, and therefore he repeated them. "Those who lack talent slander people with fresh ideas, like Hoffman. Hoffman's a character, of course, but we need characters like him. We should never exchange them for the most sensible people."

The river was deserted. Over the blind, leaden water, a hot wind blew in gusts. The gardens were disturbed, and exchanged anxious opinions with their dusty foliage. Luzgin rowed quickly. He wanted to reach Noevsky Park before the rain. Signs on the bank could already be seen: "Do not anchor—water supply siphon." Yellow dust swirled up with the gusts above Khamovniki.

"We won't make it," said Lyolya.

Iron-gray ripples hurried from bank to bank, and dust mixed with leaves blinded Luzgin. He turned the boat toward the bank and, in the middle of the river, saw a wall of water sweeping toward Lyolya. The rain came down, and in that moment, they could smell the wild smell of wet grass and river mud.

The boat struck the bank. Luzgin leaped ashore and pulled it up. Lyolya jumped out, bumping hard against Luzgin's shoulder.

"Up!" Luzgin ordered, jerking violently at the oars which were stuck in their locks. Lyolya ran up the rotten wood stairs. Luzgin, with the heavy wooden oars over his shoulder, took the steps two at a time behind her. Above them stood a boarded-up summer house. From far off, Luzgin had caught sight of a covered terrace, protected from the rain.

Lyolya, laughing, ran onto the terrace. Shining linden leaves, knocked down by the storm, stuck to her shoes.

The downpour drummed steadily, spreading a solid sheet of linen over the river. Lightning flashed with liquid fire, thunder rumbled and the rain fell even more heavily.

Luzgin smiled, not knowing himself at what, and wiped the large drops of rain from his face. The rain set in. It began to sweep over the terrace, and forced Lyolya and Luzgin into a corner, the only place it could not reach. Enjoying the dryness of the brambles under the terrace floor, mosquitoes began to sing.

Lyolya and Luzgin stood close together.

"Lyolya, you know what's going on in here," said Luzgin, pointing to his forehead.

"Yes," Lyolya answered quietly, "and ahead of us there are so many things. . . . So many worries, we can't talk about it at all. You can't talk about anything, when it happens."

She emphasized slightly the word "it."

"How untrue it is." She continued, beginning to laugh,

"how stupid people are who think that to love means to love one man, that the whole world revolves around him. It's just not so, not so. Just think—here is the storm, the wet leaves, you, Hoffman's building, friendship, arguments, everything —all this is love, not one man."

"Yes, you're right," said Luzgin.

He listened to the even drumming of the rain on the prickly nettle bushes and the quick beating of Lyolya's heart next to him.

"There are unforgettable things," he said. "We know very well that there is nothing which lasts forever, but there are unforgettable things. They exist without any dependence on what might happen to us later."

They returned to Moscow late. The rain had passed, but the wind still blew in gusts until morning. Moscow rustled with leaves. Droplets flew from branches into the open windows of streetcars.

Lyolya did not sleep that night. Danilov was not at home— distraught, he had gone to a friend's summer house. Twice, late that night, Lyolya quietly called Luzgin on the telephone, and his soft, muffled voice answered immediately from the receiver. Lyolya scolded herself for being a fool and brushed away her tears when she heard him joking and laughing.

The windows were open. The raw night air came in. From the direction of the Kremlin came the majestic chiming of the tower clock. Lyolya had never noticed its ringing before.

VI

Mett received a letter, written in the trembling hand of an old man. The letter was dated August 10.

> My son, Victor Borisovich Hoffman, mentioned your name several times, calling you a friend. In his notebook I found your address. Therefore, I consider it my sad duty to inform you of the terrible news—Vitya drowned on the second of August.
>
> The children from the kindergarten here [the hand-writing continued, and its trembling grew more

marked], were taken for an outing on an island by motorboat, three kilometers from Skadovsk. Toward three, the boat was to have returned, but at three a hurricane blew up and there was a cloudburst; the ground swells were getting bigger and there could be no question of the children's return. Anxiety grew in our little town, because the children were sent off in light clothes, and naturally could have caught cold. Besides, they had to spend the night on the island, where there is no shelter at all, except for a ramshackle shed for drying nets. Toward evening, the storm reached the proportions of a gale.

The fisherman, Koval'chenko, and Vitya were called out in a sailing sloop to deliver warm clothing and provisions to the island for the children. They took a tarpaulin from the port authority in order to erect some semblance of a tent.

My Vitya was a man used to the sea, and therefore I let him go, not being too apprehensive about the consequences.

According to Koval'chenko's story, they crossed the sound successfully, piloting on the lights of Skadovsk. On approaching the island, however, they were caught in a powerful backwash. Vitya and Koval'chenko jumped into the water in order to pull the sloop up. A wave knocked Vitya over; he fell, and apparently the wave struck his head with great force against the keel, or else the keel pinned him against the bottom—it's hard to say, but he disappeared. Only after ten minutes did Koval'chenko find his body in the surf. Attempts to return him to life were unsuccessful.

He was buried in Skadovsk. The whole town gathered for the funeral. Everyone here loved him very much, especially the fishermen; they were even proud of him as someone from their home town. They read in the newspapers about his splendid buildings.

I still have one son in Tashkent, but he can't compare with my Vitya. About how I feel now, about how the days pass, I shall not write, for I know it is hard to comprehend the grief of an old man. If you should have the desire and the occasion to spend a little time in Skadovsk, you would give me great pleasure. I don't live in a very rich fashion, as befits a retired port official, but I think you will excuse that.

                                        Respectfully,
                                           B. Hoffman

"Is this some kind of joke?" Mett smiled crookedly.

He went to the window, timidly opened the letter and read it a second time. Perspiration stood out on his forehead.

"How can it be?" he said hoarsely. He put on his hat and went out onto Ostozhenka. "How can it be?" he kept repeating, bumping into passers-by.

He stopped and looked for a long time at a pink poster. From a way off, it would have seemed that Mett was carefully reading it. But he wasn't reading; he was listening closely: inside him a steel string was being stretched, twanging and quivering. It was from this that his heart hurt so. Mett was waiting until the string would reach its breaking point, and his heart would burst with it.

The string stopped quivering. It stretched tight and drew his heart to his throat. Mett winced and gave a small cry. The string had broken, but his heart did not burst. It began to beat joyfully and quickly, and Mett walked staggering away from the poster.

"I've got to see Luzgin," he decided. He remembered that it was Luzgin's day off. Where could he be? Of course, at the river. Then Mett seemed to see the poster in front of which he had been standing, printed with gigantic white letters against a fresh, blue sky. The letters ran together into words:

> At the "Dynamo" River Landing
> August 14—The Moscow–Leningrad
> Crew Races

Mett turned off toward the Krymsky Bridge, toward the "Dynamo" landing. The motley colors, the flags, the flashing water, the shining sky, and the hubbub of the swimmers calmed him a little. He saw Luzgin in blue trunks on the referees' tower. Luzgin yelled, jackknifed from the tower and swam breast-stroke, spitting and splashing the water aside with his head.

Mett came down to the landing raft and hailed Luzgin.

"Take off your clothes, old man!" Luzgin shouted, swimming up to the raft—but then he frowned, climbed out and, shaking the water off himself, came up to Mett.

"You look like there's something wrong," he said seriously.

"You see, I got a letter. . . ." answered Mett, not looking at Luzgin. "Hoffman, it appears, has drowned."

"No!"

"Here is the letter."

Luzgin didn't take the letter; his hands were wet.

"God knows," he said, "what nonsense you're talking."

Mett told him about Hoffman's death; Luzgin listened while he dressed.

"Well," he said, after a silence, "it's hard to take. But that's not the thing. You've got to go on living. Let's go; have some black coffee and calm down."

On a pleasant terrace, similar to a ship's deck, some girls in bathing suits were giggling and rowers with numbers sewn on their chests were arguing. Luzgin and Mett sat down near the railing. Mett was silent and looked down toward the boat landing. A naked little boy was running around on it, joyfully slapping his wet feet on the hot boards. Mett, with the sharp-sightedness that comes with any radical change in circumstances, inspected his sunburned hands and the tablecloths blue from the sky; he listened to the excited shouts of the children.

"When are the races?" asked Mett.

"Not for a while. It's only ten now."

Mett was surprised. It had seemed to him much later.

"I'm going to Lyolya right away." Luzgin was embarrassed. "She is resting at the 'Fifth Day.' She must be told."

Mett nodded his head.

"Yes," he continued, "a great prophet has died. Well, you're right, we must go on living."

They said good-by. Mett stayed to watch the races, and Luzgin went to the Bryansk station.

It was difficult to get to the "Fifth Day," and Luzgin arranged to meet Lyolya on the road in the forest, beside a road marker.

It was a hot summer.

Over the timbered clearings and dried-up swamps hung the smell of smoke. The roads smelled of dust and tar. In the woods, the birches were already turning yellow. Luzgin took a shortcut through a clearing.

He saw Lyolya in the woods, among the yellowing birches. She was walking toward him. Shadows ran over her face and her softly rustling dress. She came closer quickly. The heat broke. Lyolya brought with her a freshness, a vague happiness, a breath of autumn, of open spaces and of the excitement of their recent love. She seemed to have come from the land where clouds disperse.

Luzgin stopped, overwhelmed.

"Well then," Lyolya came up to him quickly and pressed Luzgin's hands.

"Lyolya," Luzgin said hurriedly, "Hoffman . . ."

"Yes, I know." Lyolya looked calmly into his eyes. "He died. I received a card from his father. What is there to do? Since his death I cannot get rid of very light thoughts—I don't understand why. He died well. He taught me not to fear life."

Luzgin, listening to her, looked up at the clouds. It seemed to him that out beyond the layer of smoke he could make out an immense land—the one from which Lyolya had just come —a land transparent with air and sunshine. Our wild and dreamy ancestors must have imagined the golden age to be like that.

Translated by Sam Driver

BORIS PILNYAK

THE HUMAN WIND

I

Ten years of a human life—looking back over a decade—it all seems as if it were yesterday: everything is remembered right down to details, to the little wrinkle around the eyes, to the smell of a room. But during every decade one-fifth of all the people living on earth depart from life on the earth, ten million people go into the ground to rot, to feed the worms. However, in those same ten years millions of people come to life, are born, grow up, live, go to new lands, multiply, behave wildly in the spring of their youth, teem in summer, rest peacefully in the untroubled days of Indian summer, burn out with the red winter sunsets. And every period of human life, every land, every city, every house, every room has its own smell; just as every man, every family, every race has its own smell. Sometimes the decades cross and fuse, and very often—over and above the ages, transcending the events of cities and countries—the wrinkles around the eyes and the smell of a room are for him, this given man, more essential, more significant than the events of the ages.

Over every land blow its own winds.

For him, for this man, Ivan Ivanovich Ivanov, life was filled with a town of wooden sidewalks, wooden fences along the streets, a gate leading into a yard choked with weeds, the heavy smell of a lodging house in the entryway and low, narrow rooms. Over his life blew that wind which smelled of a man's dwelling. In his room stood a broken-down leather sofa; for ages cigarette butts had collected behind the sofa. The books on the table in his room rarely changed. The tablecloth was never changed: this was the desk; the ashes had changed the color of the tablecloth from green to yellow, and it was impossible to blow the ashes off the table. And outside in the garden beyond the low windows grew wild weeds, nettles, burdocks and henbane. Over his life blew that wind which smelled of a man's dwelling—and that wind pervaded and remained in his room.

And, here, over the years, there had always been the memory of a foul, autumn evening permeated with a stifling human smell: that was the evening when he had thrown his wife out. Before that there had been the wild grasses of dawn, the spring floods in the fields and nights with the words, "I love, I love you, forever, forever!" There were the avalanches of daybreak when in the dawn-awakening world there was the sun, world and lake of her eyes in which one might drown the world and the sun—she encompassed the universe. Then a child was born of their joy—new Ivan. In the twilight the mother's eyes were beautiful with all the beautiful motherhood of the world; in the twilight he went to her to kiss her pale hand. The child slept then, the new Ivan. All this was in the past. And then there was that horrible evening, the kind of an evening when it is lonely and terrifying on earth because of the suffocation of human flesh.

It was not evening: it was midnight. An autumn rain poured down outside, and inside he had to throw it all in her face. A candle burned on the table and dripped wax on that same tablecloth which was never changed. Her eyes swelled, and there were little wrinkles around her eyes. He stood next to the table, she next to the door.

She said:

"Ivan, try to understand, it's all a lie, forgive me. It was an obsession. After all, we've had great happiness, we really loved each other."

Ivan Ivanovich bent over the candle and for the hundredth time spelled out the words on the scrap of paper which she had written: "Nikolai, it's an obsession, but I cannot be without you. My husband will not be home today, the gate will not be locked. Come at eleven, when everyone is asleep. . . ."

Ivan Ivanovich put the scrap in his pocket, turned away from the flame and, pronouncing every word, said slowly:

"There is nothing to forgive here. The word has no meaning here. I'm not concerned about obsessions. And obsession has nothing to do with it. You simply lay naked in my bed with a naked man. Get out!"

"Ivan! We have a baby. We have a son! . . ."

Ivan Ivanovich mimicked her derisively:

"We have a b-a-b-y.* Quite so, but I don't have to let you have stallions. Get out!"

And then the little wrinkles disappeared from around her eyes, leaving only eyes full of hatred, contempt and outrage. She whispered to him, also pronouncing every word:

"W-r-e-t-c-h! I love and love him—I love him and not you!"

Momentarily at a complete loss, Ivan Ivanovich said nothing in reply. She turned abruptly and slammed the door. He did not go after her. On the other side of the door it was quiet. He stood motionless. Probably a quarter of an hour went by. Then he rushed to the door. On the other side of the door it was empty, the baby's bed was empty, a candle was burning on the table next to the bed. The outside door was open. He dashed into the passageway, into the heavy smell of the lodging house. The door to the courtyard was open. He rushed out into the yard in the rain. The street gate was open. Then he screamed helplessly, very humiliatingly and pitifully:

"Alyonushka!"

No one answered him. The street disappeared into the gloom and rain.

In the morning a woman brought a note: "Ivan Ivanovich would you be so kind . . . !" In the note he was asked to send her and their son's belongings with the messenger. He gathered up all the things, collected them all day long; the

---

* The wife said, *"Ivan!—u nas zhe rebenok"*; the husband turns it into a bitter pun: *"U nas zherebenok,"* meaning "We have a foal."

woman helped him with it. Twice the woman left to eat, at tea and dinner. He did not think about food for himself, and, when she went off, he wrote a long letter.

Toward evening the woman carried the things off on a hand-cart and the letter next to her breast. Ivan Ivanovich helped her take the hand-cart out to the street where he shook her hand and asked her not to forget to bring back an answer. The woman felt awkward shaking hands, and, with-drawing her hand, she said soberly:

"I'll bring back what I'm told; after all, I've got my own two feet." There was no answer that day, nor the next, nor the day after. But on the day after he learned that his wife had left town and gone somewhere by train with all her things, prob-ably for good. And, indeed, she had left for good. Ivan Iva-novich never saw her again. A year later he found out that she was living somewhere in Moscow—three years later he learned that she had had a new baby, a boy, named Nikolai. The boy's last name was his—was Ivan Ivanovich Ivanov's—Nikolai Ivanov.

The cigarette butts piled up behind the broken-down leather sofa.

II

She, the mother of these two children, the wife of Ivan Iva-novich, understood love the way very many women under-stand it when they follow a man's every step and want to know his every thought. Actually, women interfere with a man's living, get in the way of his thinking and working, when, losing their virtue first thing, they lose everything. Such love inevitably fails, because even the slavery of love is slavery, and there is no creation in it. Every human life and every human love may be represented by an image: in the years after she had left her husband, this woman's life was like a very bright, gay, red kerchief, like a gypsy shawl which has been twisted around the hand, has swirled and whirled nightly around the outlying houses, the candles and the dull dawns. This shawl smelled of many tobaccos and perfumes, but from days of old the smell of human flesh had been concealed in its scent. Then this shawl unwound, fell and sank into an extremely filthy Moscow suburb, into a stifling trash heap. Son Ivan lived with a sister in the provinces. Son Nikolai lived at first with his mother, then she put him in an orphanage. Seven years after his birth son Nikolai suffered the anguish of epilepsy, there in the hollow corridor of the stone orphan asylum. Only then the mother found out that his father, the one who did not give even his name to their son, was nothing but a wretch, because only wretches would beget sick children. However, for a long time the mother had considered herself a wretch too for having borne the child. (No one passes harsher judgment than a man does upon himself.)

And then the mother died. She died with dignity, after having been able to leave in the children—both in Ivan, who lived far away and was healthy, and in Nikolai, who lived nearby behind the asylum walls and was ill with epilepsy— she was able to leave in both of them love and respect for herself. She died from some kind of typhus, but the great significance of her death was that she had outlived everything through what she had brought into life.

The children did not know each other. And only years later a letter came for Nikolai at the asylum from brother Ivan in the provinces. The brother wrote that they ought to become acquainted and re-establish their brotherly relations. Nikolai answered him. Brother Ivan wrote about the river on which he lived, about the hayloft in the courtyard, his comrades at school, the birds and the field. Brother Nikolai wrote about his corridors, his industrial school, the daily dormitory life. After many letters, brother Nikolai wrote to brother Ivan about his sickness. Both of them wrote a great deal about their mother; each told the other in detail everything he remembered about what was sacred for them—about her.

And when in his provincial home Ivan turned fourteen, and his aunt told him about his father, Ivan wrote to Nikolai that their father was still alive. This news had a strange effect on Nikolai (or, perhaps, just exactly the effect one might expect): Nikolai dreamed about his father. Deep in a heart which had learned to hide in the asylum dormitories, Nikolai

hid his dreams and thoughts about his father: the cherished
memory and the tenderness. Ivan wrote to the father, and the
father answered him affectionately and at length. Ivan sent
the father's letter on to brother Nikolai. Nikolai wrote to Ivan
Ivanovich Ivanov—but the latter never answered him.

III

Ten years of a human life is not a long time. And ten years in
a human life is an enormous amount of time!

At Ivan Ivanovich Ivanov's the pile of cigarette butts grew
ever larger and larger behind the broken-down leather sofa
—and, just as before, the town lay there with the wooden
sidewalks, the wooden fences along the streets, the gate into
the yard, the heavy smell of the lodging house in the little
passageways and the weeds along the windows. It is not
important who Ivan Ivanovich was or might have been,
whether a teacher at the high school or a rural statistician:
over his life there blew that wind which smelled of a man's
dwelling. . . . And there, across the years, Ivan Ivanovich
recalls the letter from son Ivan. It had been brought to him in
the morning, and the first line went: "Hello, my dear Papa,"
and on that day Ivan Ivanovich became ten years younger,
remembered the sun, and recalled the wild weeds of the
dawns, the floods of the summers—and just barely remembered the terrible night, that moment when he went from
one open door to another, to the gate, when he cried out into
the gloom on the street: "Alyonushka,"—and on that day he
constantly wanted to cry out like that again, only loudly,
joyfully and in forgiveness. Then he answered his son with a
long, happy letter. And then there soon came another letter
from Nikolai, and it began with the very same words as Ivan's
letter: "Hello, my dear Papa,"—and with all the fierceness,
all the hatred, all that whole foul night smelling of human
flesh, he wanted to cry out, again and again: "Get out! Get
out! Go to your stallions! I don't want any mongrels!"

. . . And there was the autumnal twilight when, from the
rains, the smell in the little passageways was especially stifling and when the candles had to be lit very early. The gate

in the yard creaked; someone with a cane noisily climbed the little steps of the small entrance. The door into the hall opened, and from there someone softly inquired:

"Would you be so kind as to tell me, does Ivan Ivanovich Ivanov live here?"

"Yes, I'm here," answered Ivan Ivanovich.

Into the room there came a short man leaning on a cane with a rubber knob, such as those carried by cripples. His shoulders were hunched. In the darkness his face with its thin string-like mustache seemed very pale, very tired. That is the way Ivan Ivanovich remembered this person. He, this man, stepped into the room and irresolutely and joyfully stopped on the threshold. He said:

"You are Ivan Ivanovich? . . ." and began to cry, stretching out his arms in front of him, the cane falling to the floor. "Papa, it's me . . . your . . . your son Nikolai!"

Ivan Ivanovich was standing next to the table, the very same table on which the cloth had changed its color. He did not offer his hand, he turned away from Nikolai—he felt as if *that* night had entered the room from out of the past. He said softly:

"Sit down. What can I do for you?"

Nikolai said nothing in reply and submissively, hastily, sat down on a chair next to the door.

"What can I do for you?" Ivan Ivanovich asked more loudly.

Nikolai did not understand the question, and could not answer.

"What can I do for you!" Ivan Ivanovich shrieked out.

"Excuse me, I don't understa . . ."

Ivan Ivanovich dragged an armchair from the table across the floor and sat down opposite Nikolai, resting his arms on those of the chair. He picked up the cane and gave it to Nikolai. Nikolai took the cane. Ivan Ivanovich stared intently at Nikolai and squinted.

"Excuse me, I don't know your patronymic," Ivan Ivanovich began in a whisper, squinting more and more. "I don't know your patronymic," he repeated more loudly. "Excuse me. We must have a real talk to clear up a misunder-

standing. You're using my last name out of some misunderstanding. I don't know who your . . ." Ivan Ivanovich interrupted himself and took his cigarettes out of his pocket.
"Excuse me, do you smoke?—No? . . . I see!—Excuse me,
I haven't the honor of knowing who your . . . father
is!"

Nikolai rose from his chair; Ivan Ivanovich also got up.
The cane fell down again; Ivan Ivanovich hastily handed it to
Nikolai. Ivan Ivanovich's eyes were squinted.

"Yes, yes, excuse me! I haven't the honor! I've nothing to
do with it! . . . I haven't the honor! . . . I haven't the
honor of knowing with whom . . . with whom your mother
slept to get you!"

Nikolai did not listen any further. He left the room, leaving
hurriedly, limping on his right leg, the cane held in his right
hand, and his right shoulder was hunched up just as it is with
very sick people.

"Yes, yes, I haven't the honor! I haven't the honor!" Ivan
Ivanovich kept shouting after him.

. . . The brothers Nikolai and Ivan had arranged to meet
in the town where the father lived. Nikolai had arrived several hours earlier than Ivan. From the station Ivan went to
the hotel. He learned that his brother was already there.
They had never seen each other. In the room a candle was
burning on the table when Ivan came in, a tall healthy fellow
in the military uniform of a regimental commander. He asked
the porter, "Where's my brother?" The porter replied, "He
hasn't gone out anywhere, sir." Then Ivan saw a man on the
floor behind the table. The man was clinging to the back of a
chair. Ivan, though entangled in the sword and revolver
straps, lifted him in his strong arms.

"Nikolai, old boy, what's happened to you?" he asked anx-
iously. "A fit?" Nikolai calmly replied:

"No, no fit. I'm fine. I was . . ." Nikolai was pained by the
words. "I was at Ivan Ivanovich Ivanov's, at your father's. He
told me that our mother was . . . that he doesn't know who
my father was, with whom, as he put it, my mama slept to get
me."

"What? . . . Our mama—"

A candle was burning on the table in the room. The strong man held the weak one by his shoulders. Outside, the streets sank into the gloom. Cigarette butts lay on the table next to the candle. Before long the strong man was sitting on the floor next to the weak one: this was the first time the two brothers had met, two men who had never seen one another, but who, from the first days of their conscious childhood, had known everything about each other. They talked about Mama, whom one of them remembered. And for that man who lived in this town to which they had traveled they had only one word—*wretch*—a wretch who had dared to sully the memory of their mother.

. . . In district towns, wooden sidewalks serve not only for people to walk along them through the mud; the sidewalks also carry around all the district news. And it befell him, Ivan Ivanovich Ivanov, the man whose life was filled with the smell of human flesh, once more to relive a night like that other when all the doors were opened: it was a night of obsessions, of those obsessions which, once, years ago, had taken his wife from him. The streets disappeared into the gloom, the earth wept with rain and Ivan Ivanovich stood waiting at the gate for his son Ivan, who was across the alley at the hotel "Moscow." And Ivan Ivanovich cried out into the darkness, "Ivanushka!" Son Ivan did not come to his father. In the morning father Ivan saw his son for the first and last time—at the railroad station. He, the father, was standing in the crowd. Two men passed by him: one, leaning on a rubber-knobbed cane, and this lame man was being led by a tall, healthy army commissar, harnessed in saber and revolver straps, a blond, ruddy, healthy, quiet fellow. And the father saw that his eyes were extraordinarily like his mother's, like those lakes in which he at one time had drowned the earth and sun. . . . The train departed very soon, whistled, let off steam, thundered away. The father went along the wooden sidewalks of the town along the wooden fences. The wind blew gustily through the streets. . . . Through the streets along the wooden sidewalks walked a decrepit, gray-haired man—

At home the narrow passageways smelled of human flesh.

IV

No one passes harsher judgment than a man does upon
himself.

Translated by Thompson Bradley

MIKHAIL PRISHVIN

THE MARSH

I know there are few people who would sit in the marshes in early spring waiting for the gathering of the blackcock at mating time, and I can hardly find words even to intimate all the magnificence of the birds' concert in the marshes before sunrise. I have often noticed that the curlew strikes the first note in this concert long before the very first hint of dawn. It is a very delicate trill completely unlike the well-known whistle. Afterward, when the willow-ptarmigans cry out, the blackcocks begin to chuff-chuff, and the leader, sometimes right next to the blind itself, begins his mutter. Here, for a time, the curlew is forgotten, but then at sunrise, at the most triumphal moment, you always turn your attention to the curlew's new, most joyful, and dance-like song: this dance-song is just as necessary for greeting the sun as the crane's cry.

Once I watched from the blind as a gray curlew, a hen, settled down on a hillock amidst a black mass of cocks; a male flew to her and, sustaining himself in flight by the sweep of his large wings, touched the hen's back with his talons and sang his dance. Here, to be sure, the air fairly quivered from the singing of all the marsh birds, and, I remember, in the total calm, a pool was entirely rippled by the scores of insects awakened on it.

The appearance of the curlew's long and crooked bill always directs my imagination to that time long past when man did not as yet exist on the earth. . . . And then, everything in the marshes is so strange; the marshes have hardly been studied and have been completely ignored by artists. In them one feels as if man had not yet begun to live on earth.

One evening not long ago I went out into the marshes to walk the dogs. It was very sultry after the rain before a new shower. The dogs ran around with their tongues hanging out and from time to time lay down in the marsh pools on their bellies like pigs. Evidently the young had not yet been hatched and moved from the dense forest into the open, and in our parts, which are chock full of marsh wildlife, the dogs could not for the time being catch any scent and in their idleness even grew excited over crows flying past. Suddenly a large bird appeared. It began to cry out in alarm while describing large circles around us. And then another curlew flew up and also began to circle around with a cry. A third, obviously from another family, cut across the circle of these two, calmed down and disappeared. I needed to get a curlew's egg for my collection, and, reckoning that the birds' circles would for certain decrease if I were to approach the nest and increase if I moved away, I began, as in a game of blindman's buff, to wander through the marsh following the sounds. So, little by little, when the low-lying sun grew enormous and red in the warm, heavy marsh vapors, I sensed the nearness of the nest: the birds cried unbearably and flew so close to me that against the red sun I saw their long, crooked beaks opened for the incessant, alarmed cry. Finally, both dogs caught the scent in the air and pointed. I followed the direction of their eyes and noses and straight away saw two eggs lying without any support or cover right on a dry yellow strip of moss next to a tiny bush. Ordering the dogs to lie down, I glanced around with joy: the gnats bit unmercifully, but I had gotten used to them.

How fine I felt to be in the inaccessible marshes—what prehistoric ages breathed from these great birds with long, crooked beaks, traversing the crimson disk of the sun on curved wings!

I was just about to bend down to take one of those beautiful large eggs, when suddenly I noticed in the distance a man coming through the marsh straight toward me. He had neither a rifle nor a dog, not even a walking stick with him. There was no path anywhere a person might take from here, and I knew of no one like myself who would take delight in wandering through the marsh in a swarm of gnats. I had an unpleasant sensation, as if, while combing my hair before a mirror and in the process having made some funny face, I suddenly noticed the reflection of some strange attentive eye. I even moved away from the nest and did not take the egg so that this person might not ruin for me with his questions what I felt to be a precious moment of being. I ordered the dogs to get up and led them over to a small rise. There I sat down on a gray stone so thickly covered with yellow lichen that it was not even cold sitting there. As soon as I moved away, the birds widened their circles, but I could no longer follow them with any pleasure. Anxiety had grown in my heart over the approach of this stranger. I could already make him out: elderly, very thin, he walked slowly, closely observing the birds' flight. I felt easier when I noticed that he changed direction and went over to another hillock where he sat down on a stone and also became frozen still. I even had the pleasant feeling that there sat a fellow, just like myself, reverently listening to the evening. It seemed that we understood each other perfectly without a single word, and that no words were needed. With redoubled attention I watched how the birds traversed the red disk of the sun; at the same time my thoughts curiously turned on the immense eons of the earth and the very short history of mankind—how, indeed, everything had quickly passed.

The sun had set. I glanced over at my companion, but he was no longer there. The birds had calmed down and had evidently settled back on their nests. Then, ordering the dogs to go back stealthily, I began to approach the nest with silent steps: I wondered if I might not see these interesting birds up close. By the bush I knew exactly where the nest was and was very surprised how close the birds allowed me to approach. At last I stealthily made my way up to the bush and stopped dead in astonishment: there was nothing behind the bush. I felt the moss with my hand; it was still warm from the warm eggs which had been lying on it.

I had only glanced at the eggs, but the birds, fearing a human eye, had hastened to hide them farther away.

Translated by Thompson Bradley

PANTALEIMON ROMANOV

WITHOUT BIRD-CHERRY BLOSSOMS

I don't think there's ever been a more beautiful spring than this one.

And I'm feeling so sad, dear Vera.

Sad, sick at heart, as if I've spoiled forever something unique in my life. . . .

There's a broken-necked bottle on my window in the dormitory with a small crumpled branch of bird-cherry blossoms in it. I brought it home yesterday. . . . And for some reason or other I feel like crying when I look at this bottle.

I'll brace myself and tell you everything. Not long ago I met a man who's in another department of my University. I'm far from being sentimental, as he likes to say; far from any regrets for my lost virginity; and especially from feeling remorse for my first "fall." But still there's something that's eating away at me, dimly, vaguely and relentlessly.

I'll tell you in a minute, completely frankly and "shamelessly," how it all happened. But first I'd like to ask you a few questions.

When you went with Paul for the first time, didn't you want your first love to be something special, didn't you feel that the days of this love should be different, somehow, from other, ordinary days?

And didn't it strike you that it was degrading somehow, in

this first special time of the spring of your life, to go around with your shoes unpolished, to wear a dirty or torn blouse?

I'm asking because all the people of my own age around here look at it quite differently than I. And I don't have enough courage to think and act as I feel.

Surely it takes a great effort to go against what's accepted by the environment you live in.

Around here everyone believes in behaving with some sort of an arrogant defiance toward everything beautiful, toward any sort of neatness or grooming or trying to live in pleasant surroundings.

Here in the dormitory, everywhere you look there's dirt and litter, disorder and rumpled beds. Cigarette butts clutter the windowsills, torn posters announcing meetings dangle from the flimsy plywood partitions, and not one of us even attempts to fix the place up. And the fact that there's a rumor that we're going to be moved to another dormitory has brought out the very worst in everyone, and what's more, has encouraged deliberate damage and destruction.

In general, it's as if we were ashamed to have anyone see us spend any time on such stupidities as trying to make a clean beautiful place to live in, a place full of healthy fresh air. And it's not that we haven't a moment of free time left because we have such important things to do; but because we feel obliged to detest any sort of concern for beauty. I don't know why we feel this way.

It's even stranger when you consider that our government, our proletarian government, spends a great amount of money and energy to make everything beautiful: we have beautiful squares with flowerbeds such as we never had under the rule of the capitalists and landlords who boasted about their love for a refined, beautiful life. All of Moscow gleams with cleanliness, even the old plaster houses. And our University, once an eyesore under the old system, has turned into the most handsome building in Moscow.

And we feel proud, despite ourselves, that the University is so beautiful. Meanwhile, within these walls made clean and beautiful by our government, our inner lives are governed by dirt and disorder.

All our young men and women act as if they were afraid

they might be suspected of having good manners. They purposely talk in an impertinent, vulgar tone of voice, using the worst gutter slang, the coarsest words they can find for their conversations.

The dirtiest words are given the place of honor in our vocabulary. And if some of our young girls happen to grow indignant at this, it's even worse, because then someone will set about to "teach them their native tongue" in the lowest possible way.

Only a vulgar, cynical, licentious manner is considered acceptable. You might try to explain it by saying that we're poor students, unable to buy beautiful clothes and therefore we pretend that we don't give a damn about such things. Or you might say that children of the revolution such as we are have no business with sentimentality or pretty manners. But after all, if we're children of the revolution, then we should, after all, take an example from our government which strives to make life beautiful for its people, not merely for the sake of beauty alone, but also for the sake of health and cleanliness. And so you'd think it's about time for us to drop this exaggerated, devil-may-care, uncouth manner.

But do you know, the majority of us like to act this way? And not only the men; our girls like it too because they have more freedom and they don't have to bother with their appearance.

And finally it pervades our most intimate moments, this hatred of anything beautiful or clean or healthy; even at those times you find the same informality and vulgarity and a certain dread of revealing any human gentleness or delicacy or considerateness.

And all of this comes from the fear of not conforming to the unwritten moral code we've set up for ourselves.

Everything's different at your Conservatory. I'm often sorry I transferred to the University. And I often wonder what would happen if my mother, a country midwife who worships me and looks up to me almost as to a superior creature, heard the sort of language we use and saw the filthy way we live—what would she think?

We don't believe in love, only in sex, because we class love

contemptuously under the heading of "psychology" and we
believe only in physiology.

The girls go off casually with the men, for a week, for a
month, or sometimes just for a night. And anyone who looks
for something more in love than physiology is laughed at and
considered pathetic and rather feeble-minded.

II

What kind of a person is he? An ordinary student in a blue
shirt opened at the collar and high boots, always swiping his
hair back carelessly with his hand.

My attention was first attracted by his eyes. I felt a great
seriousness and tranquillity in him when I saw him going
somewhere in the halls or when he was alone. But as soon as
he met up with some other people, it seemed to me that he
became overly noisy, impertinent, rude. He was confident
with the girls because he was good-looking, and with his
friends because he was clever. But he seemed, somehow, to
be afraid of not living up to their expectations of him as a
leader.

It was as if he were split into two persons: the one made up
of a great firmness of mind, a moral fortress, and the other
characterized by a banal, annoyingly affected effort to defy
those things that other people value, and a constant striving
to appear more vulgar than he really is.

Yesterday at dusk we went out together for the first time.
The evening hush was already settling over the city, that time
when all sounds grow softer, the air seems fresher and a
breeze from the park brings with it a smell of damp earth.

"Let's go to my place," he said, "I live right around here."

"No, I don't want to."

"Not proper?"

"That has nothing to do with it, in the first place. And in
the second place it's so nice outdoors."

He shrugged his shoulders.

We went down to the river and stood by the railing for a
while. A girl passed by, selling branches of bird-cherry blossoms. I bought a branch and had to wait a long time for the
change, while he stood and watched me with a slight frown.

"Can't you survive without cherry blossoms?"

"Yes I can, but life's better with cherry blossoms than without cherry blossoms."

"I never have cherry blossoms, and my life's all right, not so bad," he said, laughing somewhat unpleasantly.

Two girls were standing ahead of us. A group of students passing by made a grab at them and when the girls tore themselves away the students laughed and continued walking, turning back every few steps to shout something back at the girls.

"They spoiled the girls' mood," my companion said, "they went up to them without cherry blossoms and the girls got frightened."

"Why do cherry blossoms bother you so much?" I asked.

"Don't you know that it will all turn out the same, with cherry blossoms . . . without cherry blossoms . . . so why should I waste my time?"

"You only say that because you've never been in love."

"What's the use of that?"

"Well then, what else do you want a woman for?"

"In the first place, don't be so damn formal and use the familiar form with me—and in the second place, there's certainly something else I need a woman for."

"I won't use the familiar form with you," I said. "If I used it with everyone, there wouldn't be anything special about it."

We walked by some lilac bushes. I stopped and began to fasten a sprig of cherry blossoms to my blouse. Then, suddenly, he took a quick step toward me and tilted my head back to kiss me.

I pushed him away.

"You don't have to if you don't want," he said calmly.

"Well, I don't," I said. "If you don't believe in love, then it makes absolutely no difference to you which woman you kiss. If there were someone else with you now, you'd want to kiss her too."

"Quite right," he replied, "but women, you know, are the same way. We had a little party a while ago, and the fiancée of a friend of mine kissed me with the same pleasure as she kissed him. And if someone else had come up she would have kissed him as well. And mind you, they're marrying for love, getting a license and all that rubbish."

Everything boiled in me as I listened to him go on. It had seemed to me that I wasn't just like any other woman for him, that his eyes had always searched me out, even when I was in the midst of a crowd at the University. Why did he have to spoil this beautiful spring evening that cried out for soft, gentle words, with rude and arrogant ones?

I hated him. But just then we passed a bench where some lady was sitting in the semidarkness. She sat with one silk-stockinged leg crossed high over the other, watching everyone who went by.

My companion gave her a long look. She looked back at him. Then, after we had walked a bit farther he glanced back at her again. Suddenly I felt a certain pang.

"Let's sit here," he said, going up to the next bench. I realized that he wanted to sit there so he could look at her.

For some reason I suddenly felt so bad I wanted to cry. Without even knowing the reason, I got up and said, "I don't feel like staying with you. I'm going. . . ."

He stopped, obviously taken aback.

"Why? Did I upset you by speaking so frankly? Would you rather have me tell lies and show off?"

"I feel sorry for you that you have nothing at all to show off."

"What are you doing," he said as if he hadn't understood me at all, and then, "well, why not. In that case good-by. Only . . . it's a shame . . ." he added, holding my hand, "a shame," and he dropped my hand and walked away toward his house without looking back.

I hadn't expected this. I hadn't thought he'd really leave.

I stood on the corner and looked around. It was one of those May nights when everything around you seems new and unique.

There was a full moon surrounded by light cottony clouds in the warm, foggy-yellow sky. Even the occasional street lights were blinded, as it were, by the light of the moon, by the half-light that lit up the rooftops of houses and palaces and towers.

And everywhere—in the dark shadows of the trees and in

the bright squares in the park—merry groups of young people, all paired off, were sitting on the latticed garden benches beneath the clipped trees and lilac bushes.

I could hear them talking and laughing. I could see the flashing little fires of their cigarettes, and it seemed that all these people were charged, somehow overwrought by the exciting warmth of this night, sensing that they had to breathe in its essence rapturously, without losing a single moment.

And when one has nothing to reply to such a night, when there is only emptiness inside, and terrible loneliness, when everyone else is together with someone and only you are alone—then no one can be more miserable than you.

Just a few minutes before I hadn't cared whether he was there or not. But from that moment when I saw him look at the woman on the bench I was filled with a sort of pain and uneasiness, on the verge of tears, without any will power at all. And nothing else mattered, suddenly, except to be with him again.

You can't blame me—I couldn't bear feeling myself an outcast from this symphony of springtime and nature, expelled from the universal chorus.

Hardly aware of what I was doing, I turned around and walked quickly in the direction of his house.

III

I walked faster and faster, with one thought alone running through my head: I'd get there too late—he'd be gone and I'd be alone. But the main thing was that our date had ended so abruptly and I had rejected him almost rudely without making any attempt at all to see his good side.

It occurred to me that in making no effort at all to get to know him I was behaving in just the same way as everyone else here who doesn't try to make his room more beautiful. Just like everyone, I was trying to get the best of everything without making the smallest effort for it.

I walked into the dark entranceway of the old stone house where he lived. Even on this warm May night the walls still smelled of winter. To this day Moscow is full of such entranceways: the dusty glass doors unwashed for many years, covered with scraps of old announcements; the dirty, worn staircases covered with dust, cigarette butts and penciled scribbles.

He was definitely not expecting to see me. It looked as if he were getting ready to begin his work. A narrow table knocked together out of thin boards stood against the wall; it looked something like a painters' step-ladder. An electric lamp on a cord running along the ceiling from the center of the room hung above the table, fastened to a nail on the wall.

"Oh, you're a character!" he exclaimed. "Thought it all over, did you? So much the better."

He came up to me and took my hand, giving a little laugh. It looked as if he wanted to kiss it or caress it but he did neither.

"I felt bad that we had a fight," I said, "I wanted to set it straight."

"What's there to set straight? Wait—I'll go hang a sign on the door—some people might drop in."

He wrote out a sign at the table and went out; alone in the room, I looked around.

The room gave the same effect as the staircase: unswept cigarette butts, scraps of paper and dirt tracked in from the outside on the floor; telephone numbers and doodles scribbled on all the walls; rumpled, unmade beds, dirty dishes, empty bottles, egg shells, tin teapots on the windowsill—just as in our dormitory.

I felt uncomfortable. I couldn't think of anything to tell him when he came back, and to say nothing was worse since that might give my visit an altogether different meaning.

And then a thought suddenly struck me: why, as a matter of fact, had he gone to hang a sign on the door? Why shouldn't anyone drop in?

All at once I realized why. A wave of blackness came over me and my breath quickened. Straining to listen, my heart pounding, I went to the window. I started to clear the bottles and cigarette butts from the windowsill so that I might sit down. My hands were shaking but I cleared everything off and leaned my elbows on the windowsill.

My heart thundered and my ears were alerted to catch

every sound behind me. I was agitated and expectant in a way
that I had never felt before.

But I found it hateful to think that this, perhaps my first
day of love, my first happiness, the finest moments of my life,
should be spent surrounded by these dirty, bespattered walls
and plates with remains of yesterday's dinner.

That's why when he came back I began to beg him that we
go outside into the fresh air.

A look of surprise and then annoyance flashed across his
face.

"Why? You were just out there."

And then he added hastily, his voice taking a new tone:

"I just fixed it that no one would come here. Don't be so
silly. I won't let you go anywhere."

"I don't like it here."

"So, now it starts all over. . . ." he said almost angrily.
"Well, what's the matter? Where are you going?"

He spoke quickly, unevenly, and his hands shook as he
tried to hold me back.

My hands too were shaking and my heart pounding so hard
I could hardly see. And all the while I was torn by two somehow contradictory emotions: on the one hand the excitement
mixed with dread that came from the awareness of being
alone in the room with him and the knowledge that no one
would come, and on the other the feeling that everything was
wrong—his sly, hurried whispers, his impatience and loss of
his usual self-control. It seemed as if he were thinking of only
one thing, to *get it over with* before his friends arrived. And at
the slightest resistance on my part a flash of anger and impatience came across his face.

We, and women in general, never look at *facts* in a very
straightforward manner, especially when we're in love. For
us, the facts are always the last consideration; we place above
all our love for the person himself, for his intellect, his talent,
his soul, his tenderness. At the beginning of an affair we
always look for something else beyond a physical satisfaction. And when this something else isn't there and a woman
gives way nevertheless, momentarily carried away by an intoxication of the emotions, then she feels no happiness or
fulfillment, but only disgust with herself. She feels herself

degraded, together with a sharp hatred for the man, the insensitive person who subjected her to a loathsome, unclean sensation; and the man himself feels repelled afterward, for participating in something unclean.

Everything upset me now: the unmade beds and the egg shells on the window and the dirt and his distorted face and the knowledge already certain in my mind that all this would end wrong.

"I can't stay here," I said, almost crying.

"What do you want? Nicer furniture? More poetry? Do you think I'm some sort of aristocrat? . . ." he answered, fairly bursting with irritation and anger.

Evidently my face must have shown how this exclamation affected me, because he hastened to add, as if trying to tone down what he had said:

"Now come on . . . really . . . someone might come soon."

I knew positively that I had to leave. But inside of me, as in him, was that desire that came from the awareness of being alone in the room with him. And I didn't leave, deceiving myself, thinking that somehow something might change. . . .

"Wait, I'll show you some poetry now," he said and turned off the light.

This made everything better, it's true, because I didn't have to see the beds, the bottles and the butts on the floor. Blindly, with a beating heart I went over to the window and stood with my back to him.

He was silent, as if he didn't know what to do. My heart was thumping so loudly it echoed in my ears, while I waited, agitated and strained, for something to happen.

At last he came up to me. He stopped just behind me and put his hands on my neck and then just stood there, apparently looking out of the window too. I couldn't see his expression without turning around, but I felt grateful to him for touching me. I wanted to stand like that for a long, long time, feeling his hands on my neck.

But soon he grew urgent.

"Well, what do you say, are you just going to stand there like that?" he asked, obviously thinking that his friends might come back soon and I was wasting time standing by the window.

He pulled me by the hand in the direction of the bed. But I pulled away from him in fright.

"Well, come on, let's go here, let's sit down."

I stood with my back to him as before and shook my head to his attempts to get me away from the window.

He walked away from me. For a short time we were both silent. Without turning around I stood and waited for him to kiss me on the back of my neck or on my shoulder. But he didn't kiss me. Instead, he came up to me again and began to pull me away from the window even more persistently and impatiently.

"Well, what do you want?" I asked, taking a step in the direction he was pulling my hand. I asked this question without really expecting an answer, but as if trying by words to draw his and my attention away from the fact that I had taken a step in the direction he wanted to go.

"I don't want anything, but let's just sit here instead of standing."

I stopped and looked silently, in the half-dark of the empty room, at his flashing eyes and his parched lips. Thanks to the darkness I no longer saw the shabby, threadbare room. I could imagine that my first happiness came to me in a place worthy of such happiness. But I needed some human tenderness, some kindness. I needed to feel him near and to be loved, to stop feeling him a stranger. Then everything else would become possible.

I covered my face with my hands and stood without moving for a time.

"Really, what's the use of talking, we're only wasting time. . . ."

I was mortified by these words and moved away from him. But then he grabbed me firmly and angrily by the hand, saying:

"Really, why must you make such a damn fuss!"

And he quickly caught me by the hand and dragged me to the nearest rumpled bed. It occurred to me then that it might not even have been his own bed, but simply the nearest one at hand. Desperately I tried to tear away his hand, to get up, but it was already too late.

When we rose, before anything else he turned on the light.

"We don't need the light!" I cried in pain and fright.

He looked at me with amazement and turned the light out again, shrugging his shoulders. Then without coming near me he began quickly to fix the bed, saying:

"We'd better fix Vanka's bed or he'd know right away what went on. . . ."

I walked away without a word and looked out of the window without thinking or feeling anything.

He kept doing something by the bed, crawling on his hands and knees, obviously looking for something. Then he came up to me. A deep sigh escaped from me and I turned my head toward him in the half darkness, trying with all my strength to dispel something disturbing and oppressive inside me. I stretched out my hand toward him.

"Here are your hairpins," he said, putting them in my outstretched hand. "I had to crawl all over the floor in the dark looking for them. Why do we have to sit in the dark? . . . Well, anyhow, it's time for you to go, the gang will be here any minute," he said. "I'll walk you to the side door. The main entrance is locked at this hour."

I began to put on my jacket. He stood next to me and waited for me to finish so he could show me the way to the side exit.

We didn't say a word to each other and avoided looking at each other for some reason.

When I got outside I walked along the street for some time, mechanically, blindly. Then, suddenly I felt something metallic in my hand; a wave of fear and horror and loathing came over me, but instantly I remembered that it was only the hairpins he had put in my hand. I stopped and looked at them and they were really only hairpins, nothing more.

Holding the hairpins in my hand I dragged myself home, walking unevenly, like an invalid. And still pinned to my blouse, crumpled, was the sprig of bird-cherry blossoms. And around the sleeping city was the very same night as two hours before. And above the massive stone houses stood the moon, surrounded by light, smoky clouds, and the same misty, foggy distance beyond the innumerable rooftops of the city.

And the same scent of apple blossoms, cherry blossoms and grass in the air . . .

Translated by Marie Winn

MIKHAIL SHOLOKHOV

A FAMILY MAN

On the outskirts of the Cossack village the sun still lay in patches on the sickly green of the brushwood. It was late afternoon. I was on my way from the village to the ferry landing on the Don. The moist sand beneath my feet smelled rotten, like a water-logged tree. A road tangled with sorrel slipped through the brush. Swollen and purple with strain, the sun dropped down behind the village cemetery, leaving blue wreaths of dusk in its wake.

The ferry was moored to the landing; lilac water lapped against its hull with a croaking sound. Dancing and bobbing, the oars groaned in their oarlocks.

The ferryman was scraping the mossy bottom with a scoop, bailing the water out. Raising his head slightly, he looked at me with his yellowish slit eyes and muttered ill-naturedly:

"Want to get across? Let's get going then. Undo the rope!"

"Do you want me to row too?"

"You'll have to. Here it's almost night now, and people still come up wanting to be taken across."

Rolling up his pants, he again looked at me and asked:

"You don't come from around here—not one of us, are you? . . . Where do you hail from?"

"Just passing through on my way home from the army."

The ferryman threw off his cap. With a jerk of his head he

tossed back his hair, which was like Caucasian silver shot with niello. Winking at me, he showed his rotted teeth in a grin:

"Going home on leave or just sneaking off for a spell?"

"Demobilized. Let out before my year was up."

"Well, things are pretty quiet now. . . ."

We sat down at the oars. Capriciously the Don drew us toward a flooded grove of willows just off the opposite bank. The water scratched drily against the rough bottom of the ferry. The ferryman had his bluish feet braced against the crossbar, and tense bands of muscle stood out on his bare blue-veined legs. His hands were long and bony, his fingers gnarled at the joints. He was tall and narrow-shouldered, and rowed in an awkward stooped position; but after each stroke his oar lay flat on the crested backs of the waves and then bore deeply into the water again.

I heard his slow steady breathing; his knit woolen shirt smelled of acrid sweat, tobacco and fresh water. Suddenly he threw down his oar and turned to me:

"Looks like we're going to get stuck in the grove! Bad break, son, but nothing we can do about it!"

In the middle of the river there were strong rapids. The ferry was swung back and forth and zigzagged crazily in the direction of the grove. Half an hour later we were stuck among the flooded shoots. The oars broke off. In the oar-locks the jagged stubs rattled back and forth resentfully. Water oozed in slushily through the drain hole. We moved onto a nearby willow tree to spend the night. The ferryman sat next to me on a branch with his legs tucked up under him. He puffed on a clay pipe, listening to the sound of geese flying through the clammy darkness overhead.

"You're going home to your family. . . . Your mother's probably waiting there for you: her son and provider is coming home to warm her old age. Every day she's been pining for you, crying her heart out at night, but how much does that matter to you? . . . You sons are all alike. . . . Until you have children of your own you can't understand a parent's sufferings. But how much suffering should a parent have to bear?

"Sometimes a woman will crush the bile when she slits open a fish; you eat your chowder and it has a funny bitter tang. That's the way it is with me: I'm alive, but everything in my life has the same bitterness to it. There are times when you suffer so much your heart cries out: 'Life, Life, how can you bring such misery?'

"You're a stranger to these parts. . . . Listen and tell me if it isn't enough to make a man want to hang himself to the nearest tree!

"I have a daughter, Natasha, who'll be seventeen this year. One day she says to me:

" 'I can't stand sitting at the same table with you, Dad. Every time I look at your hands I remember that with those hands you killed my two brothers; and then I feel like vomiting from the bottom of my soul. . . .'

"And that little bitch can't even understand that I did it all for their sake, for the sake of her and the other children!

"I married young; my wife happened to be fertile and foaled me eight kids, but on the ninth one she faltered. She gave birth all right, but five days later she was carried off by fever. . . . I was left alone, like a woodcock in a swamp, but God didn't see fit to take any of the kids, no matter how hard I prayed. . . . The oldest was Ivan . . . looked like me, swarthy and handsome. . . . He was a fine Cossack and a conscientious worker. I had another son four years younger than Ivan. This one was the image of his mother: short, on the stout side, hair so fair it almost was white, and brown eyes —he was my dearest and most cherished son. Danila was his name. . . . The other seven were girls and very young children. I married Ivan off, gave him some farmland of his own, and in due time they had a child. Danila also wanted to get married, but then came a time of trouble. There was an uprising in our village against the Soviets. On the second day Ivan came running to me:

" 'Dad,' he says, 'let's go join the Reds. By Christ our Lord, I beg you! We've got to stick by them; it's our only hope for a just rule.'

"Danila also insisted. For a long time they kept at me, until I finally said:

" 'Go ahead, I won't stand in your way; but I'm not going anywhere. Besides you I have seven hungry mouths to feed!'

"Then they disappeared from the farm, and the rest of us

Cossacks were called to arms. I was put with the Whites and given front-line duty.

"At the meeting I said:

" 'Elders, you all know I'm a family man. I have seven small children at home. If I'm killed, who will take care of my family?'

"I tried everything—nothing worked! They took me and sent me to the front anyhow.

"The fighting was going on just below our farm. Then on Easter Eve nine prisoners were herded into the farm, and Danila—my darling son—was among them. . . . They led them through the square to the battery Commander. The Cossacks poured out onto the street shouting:

" 'Beat the hell out of those crawling reptiles! Get 'em when they're brought out from questioning!—Let's cut 'em up ourselves!'

"I stood among them with my knees shaking, but I didn't let on that I felt sorry for my son Danila. . . . I looked around and saw the Cossacks whispering among themselves and nodding in my direction. . . . Then Sergeant Arkashka came up to me and asked:

" 'How about you beating up the Commies, Mikishara?'

" 'All right, the dirty swine! . . .'

" 'Take the bayonet and get up there on the porch!'—He hands me a bayonet and grins:

" 'Don't forget we'll be watching you, Mikishara . . . Look out, or it'll be bad for you!'

"I stood on the steps thinking: 'Holy Mother of God, am I going to have to kill my own son?'

"I heard a shout from the Commander. They brought the prisoners out, and in front was my Danila. . . . I looked at him and felt a chill in my heart. . . . His head was the size of a bucket—all bloodied up like a slaughtered animal. He had his gloves on top so they wouldn't hit him on a bare spot. . . . The gloves were soaked with blood and matted to his hair. . . . They had beaten the prisoners on the way up to the farm. . . . Danila came down the corridor, swaying. He looked at me and stretched out his arms. . . . He tried to smile, but his eyes were bruised black and blue, and one of them was swimming with blood. . . .

"Then I realized: 'If I don't beat the life out of him, the Cossacks will kill me and my small children will be left orphans. . . .' He came up alongside me:

" 'Dad,' he says, 'my own father, have pity! . . .'

"Tears washed the blood down over his cheeks. My arm was already raised. . . . I was frozen with terror. . . . But I gripped the bayonet as hard as I could and hit him one with the rifle end—right over the ear I caught him. . . . God, how he yelled—kept trying to shield his face with his palms and then fell down off the steps. . . . The Cossacks roared with laughter:

" 'Thrash 'em, Mikishara! What are you favoring your Danila for! Let him have it good or we'll make hash out of you! . . .'

"The Commander came up on the porch swearing, but there was a grin in his eyes. . . . Then they began to stick them with bayonets, and my heart sickened. I ran out in the street, and when I looked back I saw them rolling my Danila along the ground. Then the Sergeant drove a bayonet in his throat, and he just went *kr-r-r.*"

Below us the boards of the ferry creaked under the pressure of the rushing water; the willow we were sitting on shuddered and groaned. The stern of the ferry stood up out of the water; Mikishara touched it with his leg and knocked a yellow flurry of sparks from his pipe:

"Our ferry's sinking, tomorrow we'll have to spend till noon here on the willow. Guess we're just out of luck! . . ."

He was silent a long while; then he began to speak again in a low dull voice:

"Because of this business with Danila they made me a Senior Sergeant. . . .

"A lot of water has flowed through the Don since then, but even now at night I sometimes think I hear someone gurgling and choking—like Danila while I was running away. But it's just my conscience acting up, fit to kill. . . .

"Till spring they kept me at the front fighting the Reds; then General Sekretyov joined us, and we chased the Reds across the Don to the Saratov district. I was a family man, but I had sons with the Bolsheviks so they didn't give me any dispensation from service. We came to the city of Balashov. I

didn't see hide or hair of Ivan, my oldest son. The Cossacks
—blast them!—managed to learn that Ivan had left the Reds
and joined the thirty-sixth Cossack battery. The men from
our village threatened: 'If we find out where Vanka is, we'll
beat the life out of him!'

"Then we occupied a certain village, and the thirty-sixth
was there. . . .

"They found my Ivan, tied his arms behind his back, and
brought him to our battery Commander. The Cossacks from
our village beat him to a pulp, then told me:

" 'Take him over to regimental headquarters!'

"Headquarters was nine miles from the village where we
were. The Commander gave me a paper and said without
looking me in the eye:

" 'Here's a paper for you, Mikishara. Take your son over to
headquarters; with you he'll be safe—he won't try to escape
from his own father!'

"And then I saw the light: they had chosen me for convoy
because they thought I would let my son escape—then they
would catch him and kill me. . . .

"I went to the hut where they were keeping Ivan under
arrest and said to the guard:

" 'Give me the prisoner, I'm supposed to take him over to
headquarters!'

" 'Go ahead,' they said, 'we're not sorry to see him go!'

"Ivan threw his coat over his shoulders, but he kept twisting his cap in his hands and finally tossed it upon a bench. We
got as far as the hill outside the village, neither of us saying a
word. I kept looking back to see if we were being followed.
But we reached the halfway point, passed the chapel, and I
still couldn't see anyone behind us. Then Ivan turned to me
and said in a pitiful voice:

" 'Dad, sure as anything they're going to kill me at headquarters. . . . You're taking me to my death! Doesn't your
conscience bother you about that?'

" 'Sure, Vanya,' I say, 'my conscience bothers me plenty!'

" 'But don't you feel sorry for me, Dad?'

" 'I do feel sorry for you, son—deathly sick at heart.'

" 'If you really feel sorry for me—let me go. . . . I'm still
too young to die!'

"He fell down in the middle of the road and bowed to me till his head touched the ground three times. I said to him:

" 'We'll go as far as the gullies up ahead, son. . . . Then you start running, and for appearances' sake I'll shoot after you twice!'

"When Ivan was very small—you were probably the same way—I could never get a tender word out of him; then all of a sudden he'd throw himself on me and start kissing my hands. . . . Well, we went on a little over a mile together without talking. Then we came to the gullies and he stopped:

" 'Let's say good-by now, Dad. If I stay alive, I'll take care of you till you die, and you'll never hear a harsh word from my mouth!'

"He embraced me, but my heart was bleeding for him.

" 'Run, son!' I told him.

"He ran to the gullies, looked back and waved to me.

"I let him run about twenty-five yards, took up my rifle, braced it on my knee so my hand wouldn't tremble, and let him have it . . . in the back."

Mikishara took out his tobacco pouch. Striking two flints together, he tried to light his pipe; after sucking on it a long time, he finally got it lit. The tinder glowed in the hollow of his hand; his cheekbones moved convulsively; but the ferryman's slit eyes looked hard and impenitent under his swollen lids.

"Well . . . He jumped up and hot-footed it about fifteen yards, clutching at his belly; then he turned toward me:

" 'What'd you do that for, Dad!' he said, and fell, his legs jerking.

"I ran up and bent over him, but his eyes were rolling and there were bubbles of blood on his lips. I thought he was dying, but he suddenly raised himself up and spoke, putting his hand in mine:

" 'Dad, I have a wife and child. . . .'

"He dropped his head on one side and fell back again. Then he put his hand over the wound, but the blood kept gushing through his fingers. . . . He groaned, lay down on his back and looked at me sternly, but his tongue was already numb. . . . He wanted to say something, but all he could get out was: 'Dad—Da . . . Da . . . d.' Tears came to my eyes, and I began to speak to him:

" 'Take the martyr's crown from me, Vanyushka. You have a wife and child, but I have seven to take care of. If I let you go—the Cossacks would kill me, and my children would have to go begging.'

"He lay there a while, then died, still holding my hand. . . . I took his coat and shoes off him, covered his face with a handkerchief, and went back to the village. . . .

"I suffered so much grief for the sake of those children that my hair turned completely gray. Even now I work day and night to earn a living for them, but they . . . even my daughter Natasha says: 'I can't stand sitting at the same table with you, Dad.'

"Tell me, my friend, I want to ask you—how much should a man have to suffer for the sake of his family? . . ."

Hanging his head, Mikishara the ferryman looked at me with a serious steady gaze. Behind his back turbid dawn clouds had begun to furl up. On the right bank, from within a black tuft of ragged poplars, the noisy quacking of ducks was broken by a cold, sleepy shout:

"Mi-ki-sha-ra-a! Da-a-amn! . . . Bri-i-ng the fer-r-ry! . . ."

Translated by Richard Ravenal

YURY TYNYANOV

SECOND LIEUTENANT SALSO

I

Emperor Paul was dozing by the open window. In the afterdinner hour when food slowly wrestles with the body, any kind of disturbance was forbidden. Sitting in a high-backed chair surrounded on three sides by a glass screen, Pavel Petrovich dozed, dreaming his usual postprandial dream.

He was sitting in his own little formal garden at Gatchina, and the round Cupid in the corner was staring at him as he dined with his family. Just then a screech sounded in the distance. It came jolting along, jumping monotonously. Pavel Petrovich espied a three-cornered hat, a horse's leap, shafts of a gig, dust. He hid himself under the table; the three-cornered hat was a courier. They were galloping all the way from Petersburg to get him.

"Nous sommes perdus . . ." he hoarsely shouted to his wife from under the table, beckoning her to join him.

He was suffocating under the table, and the screech was already there; the gig, shafts and all, crawled over it.

The courier peered under the table, found Pavel Petrovich there, and told him:

"Your Highness, Her Highness, your mother, is dead."

But just as Pavel Petrovich began to crawl out from under the table, the courier hit him on the forehead and shouted, "Help!"

Pavel Petrovich brushed aside a fly and caught it.

There he was sitting, his gray eyes open wide, staring out the window of the Pavlovsky Palace, choking from food and boredom, with a buzzing fly in his hand, listening for something.

Under his window someone was shouting, "Help!"

II

At the office of the Preobrazhensky regiment a military clerk had been punished and banished to Siberia.

A new clerk, still quite young, sat at the table writing. His hand trembled because he was behind time. He had to finish copying the order for the regiment at exactly six o'clock so that the adjutant on duty could take it to the palace where the adjutant of His Highness, after combining it with others exactly like it, could present it to the Emperor at nine. Tardiness was a crime. The regiment clerk had risen early but had ruined the order and was now writing out a second one. In the first copy, he made two mistakes: he had written Lieutenant Sinyukhayev as "deceased" because Sinyukhayev came right after deceased Major Sokolov; and he had permitted a preposterous spelling error—instead of "Second Lieutenants, also, Stiven, Rybin and Azancheyev are appointed . . . ," he wrote "Second Lieutenant Salso, Stiven, Rybin and Azancheyev are appointed . . . ." An officer had entered just as he was copying "Second Lieutenants," and he had had to stand up and salute, stopping on "t"; then when he sat down again to his order, he became confused and wrote: "Second Lieutenant Salso."

He knew that if the order were not completed by six o'clock the adjutant would shout "Take it away," and it would be taken. Therefore his hand would not move, and he copied ever more slowly; then, all of a sudden a blot, big and beautiful like a fountain, spurted up and landed on the page.

Only ten minutes remained.

Tossing back his head, the clerk looked toward the clock as if it were a living person, and then with fingers seemingly separated from his body, moving at their own will, he began to shuffle through papers for a clean sheet although there were no more clean sheets there at all; they were lying in the cabinet in a big, neat pile.

But then, already in despair and rummaging about only out of a last sense of duty, he froze a second time.

Another, no less important paper, also contained some mistakes.

In accordance with the Emperor's proclamation #940 which prohibited the use of certain words in reports, one was not supposed to use the word *to survey* but *to view*, not supposed to use the word *to execute* but *to fulfill*, not to write *sentinel* but *guard*, and never, under any circumstances, to write *detached force* but *detachment*.

For civil codes there was additional limitation, that one should not write *rank* but *class*, and not *society* but *assembly*, and instead of *citizen* use *tradesman* or *burgher*.

But this was written in very small script, below the main paragraphs of ordinance #940 which hung there on the wall right before the clerk's very eyes, and which he had not read, but he had studied about the words *to view* and so forth on the very first day and remembered it well.

In the same paper prepared for the signature of the regiment commander and directed to Baron Arakcheyev, there was written:

> *Having surveyed,* at your Excellency's request, the *detached forces* of the *sentinel,* especially assigned to the performance of local duties in St. Petersburg and its environs, I am honored to report to you that everything has been *executed.* . . .

And that was not all.

The first line of a dispatch recently copied by himself, went as follows:

> *Your Excellency Dear Sir.*

Even a small child knew that a salutation written in one line indicated an order, whereas in dispatches of a subordinate, and especially one addressed to a personage like Baron Arakcheyev, it was only proper to write two lines:

>   *Your Excellency*
>   *Dear Sir*

which would show both subordination and courtesy.

If in the writing of *having surveyed* and so forth, one could blame him for not being alert and not paying attention in time, in the copying of *Dear Sir* he had simply gotten mixed up.

And no longer conscious of what he was doing, the clerk sat himself down to correct this paper. In recopying it, he momentarily forgot about the order even though it was much more urgent.

So, when the orderly came for the adjutant's document, the clerk glanced at the clock and at the orderly and suddenly held out to him the sheet with the deceased Lieutenant Sinyukhayev.

Then he sat down, and still trembling, wrote: *excellency, detachment, guard.*

III

Exactly at nine o'clock a bell rang out in the palace; the Emperor pulled the cord. Exactly at nine o'clock His Highness' adjutant entered with the usual report for Pavel Petrovich. Pavel Petrovich was sitting in the same position as the night before, next to the window, walled in by a glass screen.

However, he was neither sleeping nor dozing, and the expression on his face was also different.

The adjutant knew, as did everyone else in the palace, that the Emperor was angry. But he also knew that the anger was seeking reasons, and the more it found the more inflamed it became. Thus the report could by no means be omitted.

He stood at attention facing the glass screen and the Emperor's back, and delivered the report.

Pavel Petrovich did not turn around to the adjutant. He was breathing heavily and slowly.

The whole of the preceding day they had not been able to discover who had shouted "Help!" beneath his window, and twice during the night he had awakened in anguish.

"Help" was an absurd outcry, and at first Pavel Petrovich

was not very angry but acted like one who has had a bad dream and is interrupted before finding out its conclusion: for a happy ending to a dream signifies all is well. Then there was the curious mystery: who was shouting "Help" right under the window, and why? But when nobody in the whole court, now swept by great fear, could find that person, his anger increased. Things happened this way: in the palace itself, the after-dinner hour was a time when anyone could cause a disturbance and remain undetected. Thus no one was able to discover the reason for shouting "Help." Perhaps this was a forewarning of a repentant trouble maker. Or, perhaps, down there in the bushes, already searched three times, a man had been gagged and suffocated. It was as if he had been swallowed up in the earth. It was necessary . . . But what was necessary if that person were not found?

It was necessary to augment the guard. And not only here.

Pavel Petrovich, still not turning around, was staring at the rectangular green bushes which were almost like those of the Trianon. They were clipped. But no one knew who had been in them.

Not even glancing at the adjutant, he let his right hand drop down behind him. The adjutant knew what this meant: in times of great anger the Emperor did not turn around. He deftly placed the order concerning the guards of the Pre-obrazhensky regiment in his hand, and Pavel Petrovich began to read it attentively. Then the hand was again thrust behind him, and the adjutant adroitly and noiselessly picked up the pen from the desk, dipped it in the inkwell, shook it off, and placed it gently in the hand, having first blotted off the excess ink. All this took a moment. Almost immediately the signed paper flew at the adjutant. So the adjutant began to present other papers, and these papers, signed or simply glanced at, came flying at the adjutant one after another. He was already becoming accustomed to this business and hoping it would soon end, when the Emperor jumped up from his raised armchair.

Taking tiny steps, he ran up to the adjutant. His face was red, his eyes dark.

He came up very close to the adjutant and sniffed him. The Emperor did this when he was suspicious. Then with two fingers, he fiercely clutched at the adjutant's sleeve and pinched him.

The adjutant stood up straight and held the papers in his hand.

"You don't know your job, sir," said Pavel hoarsely, "you enter from behind."

He pinched him once more.

"I'll knock that spirit of Potemkinism out of you. Get out." And the adjutant backed out the door.

As soon as the door was silently closed, Pavel Petrovich quickly unwound his neckerchief and quietly began to tear the shirt off his chest, his mouth distorted and his lips trembled.

The *great anger* began.

IV

The Emperor angrily revised the order concerning the guards of the Preobrazhensky regiment which he had previously signed. The words: "Second Lieutenant Salso, Stiven, Rybin, and Azancheyev are appointed," the Emperor corrected: after "Lieutenant" he placed an enormous "s," the following word he crossed out, and inserted above: "Second Lieutenant Salso to guard duty." The rest met with no objections.

The order was given.

When the commander received it, he thought for a long time trying to recall what second lieutenant had the strange last name Salso. He immediately took up the list of all the officers in the Preobrazhensky regiment, but an officer with such a name was not to be found. Nor was he even listed among the ranks. It was incomprehensible how this had occurred. Only one clerk in the whole world really understood, but no one questioned him and he told nobody. Meanwhile, the Emperor's order had to be executed. But nothing could be done, for nowhere in the regiment was there a Second Lieutenant Salso.

The commander wondered whether he should turn to Baron Arakcheyev. But he immediately dismissed the idea.

Baron Arakcheyev was living in Gatchina, and not only that, the outcome was dubious.

But as usual, when in a predicament, one is able to turn to relations, and so the commander quickly considered his relative Sablukov, His Highness' adjutant, and galloped off to Pavlovskoye.

There was great confusion at Pavlovskoye and at first the adjutant did not want to receive the commander at all. But afterward he listened to him with disgust, and just when he wanted to tell him to go to hell and enough of this business, he suddenly frowned, glared at the commander, and just as suddenly altered his expression: he became excited.

The adjutant slowly said:

"Don't inform the Emperor. Consider Second Lieutenant Salso among the living. Assign him to guard duty."

Not even glancing at the dumfounded commander, he left him to the mercy of fate, drew himself up and walked off.

v

Lieutenant Sinyukhayev was an impoverished lieutenant. His father was doctor to Baron Arakcheyev, and the Baron, as a reward for the pills restoring his strength, quietly slipped the physician's son into the regiment. The Baron liked the son's straightforward and stupid countenance. He was not in with anyone from the regiment, but he also did not avoid friends. He was not very talkative, loved tobacco, did not chase women and took pleasure in playing the oboe (not quite the activity for a brave officer).

His equipment was always spotless.

When the order was read to the regiment, Sinyukhayev was standing as usual, stiff at attention, thinking about nothing at all.

Suddenly he heard his name and his ears trembled, exactly like those of a pensive horse after an unexpected crack of the whip.

"Put Lieutenant Sinyukhayev, who died of a fever, on the service casualty lists."

Just then the commander, having read the order, involuntarily glanced at the place where Sinyukhayev always stood, and his hands dropped from the paper.

Sinyukhayev was standing in his place as usual. Nevertheless, the commander began to read the order again, but more briskly—true, no longer so precisely—he read about Stiven, Azancheyev, Salso and continued to read on to the end. The guard parade began, and Sinyukhayev had to march with everyone else in the drill figures. But instead, he remained standing.

He was accustomed to regarding the words of all orders as special words, not resembling human speech. They had no meaning, no significance, but had a special life and power of their own. It was not a matter of an order being executed or not executed. Somehow the order was changing the regiment, streets and people, even if it was not being executed.

When he heard the words of the order he just remained standing in his place like a deaf man. He pondered over the words. Then he ceased having any more doubts. These words were about him. And when his column moved, he began to doubt whether he was actually alive.

Sensing his hand lying at his sword-hilt—a certain uneasiness from the lightly strapped sword-belt, and the weight of the annoying braid that morning—he felt as if he were alive, but at the same time, he knew that something was not right, something was irreparably spoiled. Never once did he think there was a mistake in the order. Quite the contrary, it seemed to him that he was alive due only to a mistake, due to negligence, and that due to carelessness he had not noticed this or communicated it to anyone.

In any case, he ruined all the drill figures by standing like a pole on the field. He did not even think of moving.

As soon as the drill ended the commander flew at the lieutenant. He was crimson. It was very fortunate indeed that the Emperor was not present at the guard parade during this feverish period, but had remained resting at Pavlovskoye. The commander felt like bellowing: "To the guardhouse"—but needed more of a booming sound for the full expression of his anger, and he also felt like letting his *rr*s roll "Under arrest"—but suddenly his mouth snapped shut, as if the commander had captured a fly in it accidentally.

Then, having recoiled as if stricken by the plague, he went his own way.

He remembered that Lieutenant Sinyukhayev, being deceased, was discharged from duty, but he restrained himself from immediate action, not knowing how to speak to such a person.

VI

Pavel Petrovich walked back and forth in his room, halting every now and then.

He listened.

Since the day when the Emperor, in his dusty boots and street cloak, clanked his spurs and slammed the door of the bedchamber in which his mother still lay dying with a rattle in her throat, people had observed that his large anger developed into a great anger, and a great anger reached its peak after about two days, turning then into fear or tenderness.

Wild Brenna made the chimeras on the staircases of Pavlovskoye, but the ceilings and walls of the palace were done by Cameron, a lover of delicate colors, which caused everyone to stop dead before them. On the one hand— gaping mouths of anthropomorphic lions poised to spring; on the other hand—elegance and refinement.

In addition to this, two lanterns were hanging in the palatial chamber, a gift from the days just preceding the beheading of Louis XVI. He had received this gift in France when still traveling under the name of Count Severny. They were of the finest craftsmanship: their sides were so constructed that they softened the glare. But Pavel Petrovich refrained from lighting them.

There was also a clock, a gift from Marie Antoinette, which stood on a green jasper table. The hour hand was golden Saturn with a long scythe, and the minute hand—Cupid with an arrow. When the clock struck midday and midnight, Saturn bowed his scythe to Cupid's arrow. This meant the time was ripe for love. However, no matter what anyone tried to do, the clock could not be wound up.

Thus, one could see Brenna in the garden, Cameron on

the walls, and overhead in the sub-ceiling spaces a lantern of Louis XVI, swinging.

During the periods of great anger, Pavel Petrovich even acquired a certain external resemblance to one of Brenna's lions.

Then, out of a clear sky, cudgels fell upon whole regiments; in the black of night, by torchlight, heads were cut off along the Don; soldiers recruited by accident, and clerks, lieutenants, generals and governor generals all marched on foot to Siberia.

The usurper of the throne,* his mother, was dead. He had knocked out the spirit of Potemkinism, as Ivan the Fourth in days gone by had knocked out the boyars. He swept away the Potemkin bones and leveled his grave. He blotted out the very taste of his mother. The taste of an usurper! Gold rooms spread with Indian silks, rooms spread with Chinese porcelain, with Dutch stoves, and the room of blue glass—the snuff-box! Buffoonery. He ordered the Roman and Greek medals of which she boasted melted down for the gilding of his castle. But for all this, her presence haunted him. He could sense it all around him, and perhaps that is why Pavel Petrovich had the habit of sniffing his interlocutors.

And overhead a French gallows-bird, the lantern, was swinging.

And the fear came on. The Emperor began to choke. He was not afraid of wives or older sons each of whom might recall the example of his joyous grandmother, or mother-in-law, and stick him with a fork and mount his throne.

He was not afraid of the suspiciously gay ministers nor of the suspiciously melancholy generals. He was not afraid of anyone from the multitude of fifty million which populated the hills, swamps, sands and steppes of his empire, and which he could not even imagine. He was not afraid of them, taken separately. Together, however, they formed a sea, and he drowned in it.

Consequently, he ordered his Petersburg palace surrounded by earthen trenches forming a moat, and by outposts; he had a drawbridge constructed which could be

* Catherine the Great [Trans.]

raised or lowered by chains. But even the chains were unreliable—guards stood watch over them.

And when the great anger became the great fear, the Bureau of Criminal Action got to work and someone was hung by his hands, while someone else had the floor removed from under his feet as torturers awaited him below.

Therefore, when from the Emperor's chamber there sounded at first small, then dragging and suddenly great stumbling steps, everyone sadly exchanged glances, and rarely did anyone smile.

The great fear was in the room.

The Emperor was pacing about.

VII

Lieutenant Sinyukhayev was standing in the very same place where the commander had flown at him to upbraid him, had not upbraided him and had suddenly halted. There was no one around him.

Usually after drill he stretched, relaxed his military stance, let his hands go limp and walked voluntarily toward the barracks. Each limb freed itself and became individualized.

At home in the officers' barracks, the lieutenant unfastened his uniform and played his oboe. Then he filled his pipe and gazed out the window. He saw a large piece of cleared land, now desert, called the Tsarina's meadow. There was no variety or green in the field, but tracks of soldiers and horses were preserved in the sand. He liked smoking and everything that accompanies it: stuffing tobacco, pressing it into his pipe, inhaling, and the smoke. While smoking, a man is at a loss for nothing. This was completely satisfying, since evening was coming soon and he would then go out to visit friends or simply take a walk.

He loved the politeness of simple folk. Once when he sneezed, a merchant told him: "A knitting needle in the nose is small compared to a finger."

Before he went to sleep he played cards with his manservant whom he taught to play pam and napoleon, and if the servant won the lieutenant would punch him in the nose, but if he himself won he refrained. Finally, he inspected his equipment, polished by his manservant, curled his own hair, braided it, and went to bed.

But this time he did not stretch, his muscles were flexed, and no more breath was noted passing through the lieutenant's tightly closed lips. He began to stare at the exercise field, and it seemed unfamiliar to him. At least, previously, he had never noticed the eaves on the windows of the red government building and the musty windowpanes, and the round cobblestones of the pavement did not watch each other.

The military quarter of St. Petersburg stood in perfect order, in gray regularity, next to the wastelands, the rivers and the musty-eyed pavement, a rather unfamiliar city.

Then he understood that he was dead.

VIII

Pavel Petrovich heard the footsteps of his adjutant; like a cat he stole toward his armchair standing behind the glass screen, and sat down so resolutely that he appeared to have been seated there all the while.

He recognized approaching steps. Sitting with his back to the doorway, he discerned the shuffling footsteps of the reliable, the bouncy steps of the fawning and the light airy steps of the intimidated. He never heard forthright steps.

This time the adjutant walked confidently; he made his obeisance. Pavel Petrovich turned his head halfway.

The adjutant went up to the center of the screen and bowed his head.

"Your Highness. Second Lieutenant Salso shouted 'Help!' "

"Who is he?"

His fear subsided somewhat as he heard the name.

The adjutant did not expect this question and took one step back.

"A second lieutenant who is assigned to guard duty, Your Highness."

"Why did he cry out?" The Emperor stamped his foot. "I'm listening."

The adjutant was silent.

"Out of foolishness," he murmured.

"Hold an inquiry and after having him lashed, send him on foot to Siberia."

IX

So began the life of Second Lieutenant Salso.

When the clerk copied the order, Second Lieutenant Salso was a mistake, a slip of the pen, no more. It could not have been noticed and would have been drowned in the sea of papers, and since the order was not in any way peculiar, later historians would hardly have been expected to uncover this mistake.

The captious eyes of Pavel Petrovich extracted it however, and with the simple addition to the spelling, gave him a dubious life—a slip of the pen became a second lieutenant without a face, but with a name.

Later on, from among the intermittent musings of the adjutant, a face was acquired—actually, one was just beginning to form, as in a dream. It was he who had shouted "Help" beneath the palace window.

Now this face was hardening and growing: Second Lieutenant Salso seemed to be a trouble maker who was condemned to the rack, or, more specifically, to a mare for lashes and then to Siberia.

This was reality.

Up to now he was just the distress of the scrivener, the perplexity of the commander, and the windfall of the adjutant.

From now on the mare, lashes and the trip to Siberia were part of his personality.

The order had to be executed. Second Lieutenant Salso had to walk out of the military department, cross over to the justice department and from there follow the green highroad to Siberia.

And that is what happened.

The commander of the regiment in which Salso was enlisted, called out the name of Second Lieutenant Salso before the formation of the guards in a stentorian voice pitched especially for those occasions when a soldier was missing.

A mare stood to one side already prepared, and two guards began to whip her with straps, on the head and legs. Two guards from each side lashed a smooth tree with a cat-o'-nine-tails, a third counted, and the regiment looked on.

Like the tree which had been polished previously with thousands of lives, so the mare's back did not seem quite bare. Although there was no one on her, it seemed as if someone were. The soldiers, knitting their brows, watched the silent mare, while the commander flushed toward the end of the flogging, and his nostrils distended as usual.

Then the straps were untied and it seemed as if someone's shoulders were set free on the mare. Two guards approached and awaited orders.

They moved off along the highroad in step, rifles high on their shoulders, and from time to time they would glance out of the corner of their eyes, not at each other, but at the distance preserved between them.

A young soldier stood in the guard formation, one who just recently had his first shave. He watched the flogging with great interest. He thought that everything which was taking place was very ordinary and often occurred in the military.

But in the evening he suddenly turned over in bed and softly questioned the older guard lying beside him: "Say, Uncle, who's our Emperor?"

"Pavel Petrovich, stupid," answered the old man in a frightened voice.

"You've seen him?"

"Yes," growled the old man. "And so will you."

They were silent. But the old soldier could not fall asleep. He turned over. About ten minutes passed.

"But why do you ask?" the old man suddenly turned to the youth.

"I don't know," volunteered the young man, "they talk and talk: Emperor, but who he is—no one knows. Perhaps, it's only talk. . . ."

"Stupid," retorted the old man and turned to one side. "Be quiet, wooden head."

Ten more minutes passed. It was dark and silent in the barracks.

"He exists," the old man suddenly said in the young man's ear, "only he's a substitute."

x

Lieutenant Sinyukhayev attentively inspected the room in which he had been living.

The room was low-ceilinged, spacious, and contained a portrait of a middle-aged man in glasses, his hair in a braid. This was the lieutenant's father, doctor Sinyukhayev. He lived in Gatchina but, glancing at the portrait, the lieutenant did not feel certain of this. Perhaps he was living, perhaps not.

Then he looked over the things which belonged to Lieutenant Sinyukhayev: an oboe in a small wooden case, curling irons, a small jar of powder, a box of sand, and these things all looked at him. He answered their look.

He stood this way in the middle of the room, expecting something. It is doubtful that he was waiting for his man-servant.

Meanwhile his servant cautiously entered the room and stopped, facing the lieutenant. He opened his mouth slightly and stood, staring at his master.

He probably always stood this way, awaiting orders, but the lieutenant just looked at him as if this were the first time he had seen him and lowered his eyes. Death ought to hide temporarily, like crime.

Toward evening a young man entered the room, sat down at the table on which the case containing the oboe was standing, took the oboe from its case, blew into it and, not obtaining a sound, placed it in the corner.

Then having called the manservant, he ordered a drink. He did not once glance at Lieutenant Sinyukhayev.

Finally the lieutenant asked him in an embarrassed voice: "Who are you?"

The young man, sipping his drink, answered with a yawn: "A student of the government Junker school," and then ordered the manservant to make up the bed for him. Then he began to undress, and Lieutenant Sinyukhayev stared for a long time, watching how adroitly the student pulled at his boots and pushed them off with a thud, unfastened his uniform, covered himself with a blanket and yawned. Finally, having stretched out comfortably, the young man suddenly gazed at Lieutenant Sinyukhayev's hand and drew a linen handkerchief out of the cuff of his shirt. After wiping his nose he yawned again.

Lieutenant Sinyukhayev finally found his tongue and half-heartedly stated that all this was counter to regulations.

The student replied rather flippantly that, on the contrary, everything was according to regulations, and secondly, that he was acting like the late Sinyukhayev—"like the one who died"—and that the lieutenant should take off his uniform which to the student seemed too decorative and that he should put on a uniform more suitable for off duty wear.

Lieutenant Sinyukhayev began to remove his uniform, and the student helped him, explaining that the late Sinyukhayev was "not able" to do this himself.

Then the late Sinyukhayev put on a uniform not quite suitable for duty, and stood for a moment fearful lest the student would take his gloves. He had a pair of long, yellow gloves with tapered fingertips for formal attire. He heard that to lose these gloves led to dishonor. A lieutenant in gloves, no matter what else he might be, remained a lieutenant. Therefore, having pulled on his long gloves, the late Sinyukhayev turned and went out.

All night long he wandered through the streets of St. Petersburg, not even attempting to go somewhere. By morning he was tired and sat down on the lawn of someone's home. He slept for a few minutes, then suddenly jumped up and walked on, not glancing to either side.

Before long he crossed the city limits. A sleepy clerk at the highroad absent-mindedly jotted down his name.

He never returned to the barracks again.

XI

The adjutant was sly and did not tell anyone about Second Lieutenant Salso or his own task. Like everyone else he had many enemies. Therefore he told only one certain person that the man who shouted "Help" had been found.

But this produced strange activity in the female quarters of the palace. Near this edifice built by Cameron, with its lofty columns like thin fingers moving up and down a clavichord, two wings were constructed, rounded like the feline paws a cat employs when she plays with a mouse. In one wing, Nelidova, the First Lady-in-Waiting, managed the whole establishment.

Often Pavel Petrovich, having escaped somewhat sheepishly from his bodyguard, made his way to this wing, but once his guards saw the Emperor leave there rather hastily, his wig awry, and a feminine slipper flying at his head.

Although Nelidova was herself a lady-in-waiting, she too had ladies-in-waiting. And when the news reached the female quarters that the one who shouted "Help" had been found, one of Nelidova's ladies-in-waiting fainted briefly.

Like Nelidova, she was curly headed and thin, like a shepherdess.

During Elizabeth's reign, the brocade of the ladies-in-waiting rustled, their silks crackled, and exposed nipples made frightened appearances from inside them. Such was the fashion.

Amazons who admired men's clothing and who wore velvet appliqués of sea horses and starfish on their breasts, vanished with the usurper of the throne. At this time, ladies were shepherdesses with curly locks, and so it was that one of them collapsed in a brief faint.

Lifted from the floor by her patroness, and brought back to consciousness, she told everyone that she had had an assignation at that very hour with the officer. She could not, however, leave the upper story, and suddenly as she glanced out the window she had caught sight of the passionate officer who, forgetting all precaution and perhaps not realizing it, was standing below the Emperor's very window and making signs to her up above.

She waved him away, made frantic signs with her eyes, but her lover understood all this only to mean that she was in serious trouble, and plaintively shouted "Help."

At that very moment, without losing her head, she flattened her nose with her finger and pointed below. After this snub-nosed gesture, the officer was stupefied and vanished.

She saw him no more and, due to the swiftness of the love affair which had taken place the evening before, did not even know his name. And now he had been found out and exiled to Siberia.

Nelidova grew pensive. Her affair was on the wane, and even though she did not wish to acknowledge this to herself, her slipper could no longer fly.

She was cold toward the adjutant and did not want to appeal to him. The Emperor's condition was unpredictable. At such times she turned to an individual who was powerful although not connected with the court, Yuri Alexandrovich Neledinsky-Meletsky.

So she wrote him a note and sent it with her footman.

The stalwart footman, who had delivered more than one such message, was always amazed at the poverty of this powerful personage. Meletsky was a singer and a state secretary. He was a singer of "Swift-flowing Waters" and was passionately addicted to shepherdesses. He was of very slight build, with a sensual mouth and thick eyebrows. But he was capable of great cunning all the same, and gazing over the footman's shoulders he said:

"Tell her there should be no disturbance. Let her wait. Everything will be resolved."

But he was somewhat fearful himself, not quite knowing how all this would be resolved, and when one of his young shepherdesses, formerly Avdotya, now Selimena, poked her head through the door, he raised his eyebrows fiercely at her.

Yuri Alexandrovich's servants were, in the main, young shepherdesses.

XII

The guards walked and walked.

From crossing to crossing, from watchpost to fortress, they walked straight ahead and cautiously observed the safe distance set up between them.

This was not the first time they had accompanied an exile to Siberia, but never had they led such a criminal. When they crossed the city limits, they had some doubts. There was no sound of chains and they did not have to chase him with rifle butts. But later on they recalled that this was a government affair and that they had an order with them. They conversed little because it was forbidden.

At the first outpost, the warder looked at them as if they were crazy, and they became confused. But the senior guard showed the order which stated that the secret convict had no face, and the warder quickly led them to a special room with three plank beds for the night. He avoided conversation and so ingratiated himself that the guards involuntarily felt their own importance.

They approached the second, large outpost with confidence, with an air of silent importance, and the senior guard simply threw the order down on the commander's desk. And the latter began to ingratiate himself and hurry through the necessary procedures exactly like the warder at the first outpost.

Little by little they began to understand that they were escorting an important criminal. They became accustomed to it and spoke significantly between themselves of "he" or "it."

And so they entered the depths of the Russian empire along that direct and much traveled Vladimirsky Highroad.

And the space so carefully maintained between them changed: it was evening, dusty, and they were in the fatiguing, oppressive heat of late summer.

XIII

Meanwhile, along that very same Vladimirsky Highroad, an important order went in pursuit of them from outpost to outpost, fortress to fortress.

Yuri Alexandrovich Neledinsky-Meletsky had said to wait, and in that he was not mistaken because Pavel Petrovich's great fear was slowly but surely changing into self-pity, into compassion.

The Emperor turned his back on the animal-like bushes in the garden and having paced about in the empty chamber, turned to the elegance of Cameron.

He had reduced to servile obedience the generals and governors who had served his mother and had them confined to their estates. He had had to do so. Why? A great emptiness was forming all about him.

He hung a box for complaints and letters in front of his palace because he alone, and no one else, was father of the fatherland. At first the box remained empty, and this distressed him for the fatherland must converse with the father. But finally, an anonymous letter was found in the box, in which he was threatened and called "Old Daddy Snub Nose."*

After that he took a good look at himself in the mirror.

"Snub nose, my dear sirs, really a snub nose!" he wheezed and ordered the box removed.

He then undertook a journey throughout this strange fatherland. He banished to Siberia a governor who dared build new bridges in his province expressly for the Emperor's trip. The trip was not a parlor tour: everything had to be just as it really was, not dressed up for the occasion. But the fatherland was silent. In the Volga region the peasants started gathering around him. He sent one fellow to draw some water from the middle of the river so that he could drink clean water.

He drank it and told the peasants in a husky voice:

"Look, I'm drinking your water. Why are you staring at me?"

And everyone deserted him.

He did not travel any farther on his journey and, instead of a complaint box, he put armed guards at each outpost, but he did not know whether or not they were loyal, and so did not know whom he had to fear.

All around him there were treason and emptiness.

He found the secret of how to avoid these, and he instituted firmness and complete submission. Bureaus began to function. He was supposed to have taken over only executive power. But somehow his executive power confused all the bureaus, and this only led to further treason, emptiness and cunning insubordination. He pictured himself as a lone swimmer raising empty hands amid violent waves—he had seen such an engraving in the old days.

---

* Portraits of Emperor Paul vividly portray his snub nose [Trans.].

And besides, he felt that after many long years he was the only lawful autocrat.

And he was weighed down by a desire to lean on his father, even though the latter was dead. He had had dug out of his grave the German halfwit killed by a fork who was considered his father, and had had his coffin placed next to the coffin of the usurper of the throne. But this was done mainly to revenge his dead mother during whose life he had lived as a prisoner continually condemned to death.

And was she really his mother?

He knew vaguely something about the scandal of his birth.

He was a man without kith or kin, deprived even of a dead father and a dead mother.

He never thought about all this and would have ordered anyone who might have suspected him of such thoughts shot by cannon fire.

But at such moments even small pranks and the little Chinese cottages of his Trianon pleased him. He became a great lover of nature, and in return wanted everyone's or just anyone's love.

This desire came on like a fit, and in such periods coarseness was considered frankness, stupidity—directness, cunning—kindness, and the Turkish orderly who blacked his boots was called Count.

Yuri Alexandrovich had a special flair for invariably sensing the change.

He waited it out for a week, and then detected it.

He tiptoed around the glass screen with soft but gay steps and suddenly, pretending simplicity, related to the Emperor everything that he knew about Second Lieutenant Salso, except, of course, details about the sign for snub nose.

Then the Emperor burst into boisterous laughter with a barking, husky, broken laugh, as if he were frightening someone.

Yuri Alexandrovich became uneasy.

He wanted to bring good news to Nelidova who was his palace friend, and show, in passing, his own importance—for, according to a German proverb then popular, *"umsonst ist der Tod"*—death alone is free of charge. But such a laugh could immediately reduce Yuri Alexandrovich to a secondary role or even be a sign of his destruction.

Perhaps this was sarcasm?

But no, the Emperor broke down, exhausted from laughter. He extended his hand for a pen, and Yuri Alexandrovich, having raised himself slightly on tiptoe read the Emperor's hand:

> Second Lieutenant Salso, banished to Siberia, is to return, to become First Lieutenant, and to marry that lady in waiting.

Having written this, the Emperor walked about the room inspired.

He clapped his hands and started to sing his favorite song and whistled:

> *Little fir grove, my little fir grove,*
> *My own little birch grove . . .*

while Yuri Alexandrovich joined in with a fine and very soft voice:

> *Liushenki-liuli.*

XIV

A badly bitten dog likes to run away into the fields and cure himself there with bitter herbs.

Lieutenant Sinyukhayev went on foot from St. Petersburg to Gatchina. He went to see his father, not to ask for any help, but perhaps out of a desire to ascertain whether or not his father still lived in Gatchina. He said nothing in response to his father's greeting, took a look around and then and there decided to leave, like an embarrassed and even affected youth.

But the physician, having observed his son's appearance, sat him down and began to question him:

"Did you lose at gambling or were you fined?"

"I'm not alive," the lieutenant suddenly blurted out.

The doctor felt his pulse, said something about leeches and continued to question him. When he found out about his son's situation, he became excited and for a whole hour wrote and rewrote a petition, forced his son to sign it and the next day went to Baron Arakcheyev in order to hand it in with the daily report.

He was too embarrassed, however, to keep his son at home, and put him in the hospital and wrote on the plaque above his bed: *Mors occasionalis* (accidental death).

xv

The idea of the state alarmed Baron Arakcheyev.

Therefore his personality defied definition; he was elusive. The Baron was not spiteful, he was sometimes even indulgent. During the telling of some sad story he would weep like a child and, after a pleasant walk, give a kopeck to the girl who took care of the garden. Later, having noticed that the paths in the garden were not well swept, he would order the girl beaten with birch rods. Then, after the flogging, he would hand out five-kopeck pieces to the children.

In the Emperor's presence he experienced a debility similar to love.

He admired cleanliness, it was the emblem of his morality. But he was pleased precisely when he found cleanliness and order lacking, and if such instances did not turn up, he was secretly grieved. He always ate salted beef instead of fresh roasts.

He was as absent-minded as a philosopher, and it is a fact that scholarly Germans found a similarity between his eyes and those of the then celebrated philosopher Kant: they were of a wishy-washy, indefinable color, and covered with transparent scales. But the Baron would have been insulted if someone had told him of this resemblance.

He was not only miserly but also liked to shine and to show off everything to its best advantage. For this he would go into the most minute household details. He would sit for hours over projects for chapels, medals, icons and the dinner table. He was fascinated by circles, ellipses and lines which, intertwining like a belt with three tails, formed a figure specially designed to deceive the eye. And he loved to deceive visitors or to deceive the Emperor, and he feigned not to see when someone cunningly tricked him. Of course, it was difficult really to trick him.

He had a detailed list of the things belonging to each of his servants, beginning with the valet and ending with the cook, and he checked every hospital list.

In the construction of the hospital in which Lieutenant Sinyukhayev's father worked, the Baron himself had decided how to place the beds, where to put the benches, where the consulting table had to stand, and even the type of pen to be used, that is, a bare, tuftless reed like a Roman *calamus*. For a pen sharpened with a tuft, the doctor's assistant was sentenced to five birchings.

The idea of the Roman state alarmed Baron Arakcheyev.

Therefore he absent-mindedly listened to Doctor Sinyukhayev, and it was only when the latter handed him the petition that he read it through attentively and then admonished the doctor that the paper was signed in an illegible hand.

The doctor excused himself saying his son's hand had trembled.

"Aha, look at that, my friend," answered the Baron with a satisfied air, "his hand was trembling."

Then, having glanced at the doctor, he asked him:

"And when did the death occur?"

"The fifteenth of June," the doctor answered somewhat dumfounded.

"The fifteenth of June," added the Baron gathering his thoughts, "June the fifteenth . . . And today is already the seventeenth." He suddenly said in the doctor's face, "Where was the dead man for the two days?"

Grinning at the doctor's countenance, he wryly stared at the petition and said:

"There are some mistakes. Now, good-by, my friend, be off."

XVI

The singer and State Secretary, Meletsky, would act on impulse, he would take risks and often win because he did everything in a delicate manner, as befits the colors of Cameron, but winnings turned into losses, as in the game of quadrille.

Baron Arakcheyev was of another sort. He never risked anything, never guaranteed anything. On the contrary, in his reports to the Emperor he pointed out an abuse and then asked for orders by which to abolish it. The denigration which Meletsky risked, the Baron actually sought. However, a great victory was often the final result, as in a game of faro.

Yuri Alexandrovich drily informed the Emperor that the late Lieutenant Sinyukhayev had made an appearance in Gatchina where he had been put in the hospital. He seemed to be alive and had presented a petition for reinstatement in the lists. Such a petition was dispatched and solicited a further decree. By this paper he wanted to show submissiveness, like a zealous steward who asks his master about everything.

The answer was received immediately, concerning both the petition and the Baron.

The following resolution was drawn up regarding the petition:

> To the late Lieutenant Sinyukhayev, withdrawn from the lists because of death, request denied for that very reason.

And to Baron Arakcheyev the following note was sent:

> Sir Baron Arakcheyev.
> I am astounded that, being a general, you do not know the code of regulations, and that you have referred directly to me the petition of the deceased Lieutenant Sinyukhayev, referred it to someone who is not even in your regiment. It should have been sent directly to the

regimental office to which this lieutenant belongs, and not have been addressed to me.

Nevertheless, I remain your devoted

Pavel

But he had not written "eternally devoted."

And Arakcheyev shed a few tears since he did not want to receive the death sentence. He went to the hospital himself and ordered the immediate discharge of the deceased lieutenant, giving him some underclothes and an officer's uniform which indicated resumption of duty.

XVII

When Lieutenant Salso returned from Siberia, many people already knew about him. He was that very same lieutenant who had shouted "Help!" under the Emperor's window, had been punished and banished to Siberia, and had then been pardoned and made a first lieutenant. Such were the distinguishing features of his career.

The commander no longer felt any embarrassment with him, and simply assigned him to positions as orderly or guard. When the regiment left camp for maneuvers, the lieutenant left with him. He was a superb officer because it was impossible to notice whether he did anything wrong.

The lady-in-waiting whose short fainting spell had saved him, at first rejoiced, thinking they would marry her to her surprise lover. She put a beauty mark on her cheek, and tightened the uncomfortable laces of her underclothes. Then, at church, she noticed she was standing alone, but that over the empty place next to her an adjutant stood holding a marriage crown. She again felt like fainting, but as she kept her eyes lowered and saw her own waist, she thought better of it. Many people enjoyed the unique mystery of a ceremony in which the bridegroom was absent.

And after a certain time a son was born to Lieutenant Salso; rumors have it he was very much like his father.

The Emperor forgot about him, having much to do.

Cunning Nelidova was dismissed and her place occupied by plump Gagarina. Cameron, the Swiss cottages, and even

Pavlovskoye were forgotten. In its brick precision lay the
squat soldiers' quarters of St. Petersburg. Suvorov, whom
the Emperor did not like but tolerated because he had fought
the late Potemkin, was aroused from his rural isolation. A
campaign was approaching, since the Emperor had plans.
These plans were numerous, and one often followed on the
heels of another. Pavel Petrovich grew in girth and settled
down. His face attained the color of brick. Suvorov again fell
into disfavor. The Emperor laughed less and less.

Sifting through the regimental lists, he once stumbled
upon the name of Lieutenant Salso and appointed him captain and, another time, colonel. The lieutenant was a superb
officer. Then the Emperor forgot him again.

The life of Colonel Salso flowed on unnoticed and everyone became reconciled to it. At home he had his own study;
in the barracks his own room; and sometimes dispatches and
orders were sent there, and carried away again, not too surprising in the absence of the colonel.

He now commanded a regiment.

The lady-in-waiting, in her huge double bed, fared best of
all. Her husband was advancing in the service, she was sleeping comfortably and her son was growing up. Sometimes the
husband's place was warmed by one or another lieutenant,
captain or even civil servant. Thus it was in the bed of many a
colonel in St. Petersburg when the husband was away on a
campaign.

Once, however, when her weary lover had fallen asleep,
she heard a creak in the next room. The creak was repeated.
Undoubtedly, the floor was creaking. But she immediately
shook the sleeping guest, pushed him away and threw his
clothes out the door. Then, remembering, she laughed at
herself.

But this also happened in the homes of many other colo-
nels.

XVIII

Peasant men give off a smell of wind, peasant women—of
smoke. Lieutenant Sinyukhayev did not look directly into
anyone's eyes and distinguished people by smell.

He would choose a place for the night by smell, trying to sleep beneath a tree because there rain does not soak in so much.

He walked on and on, never remaining in any one place.

He walked through Finnish villages as if he were a flat stone, a "pancake" being skimmed by a small boy across a river. From time to time a Finnish woman would give him some milk. He would drink it standing up, and continue on. Little kids quieted down and their whitish snot-noses glistened. The countryside closed in around him.

His step changed little. It had loosened up from a stiff walking pace, but his easier, looser, even toylike step was still an officer's military step.

He did not pay any attention to direction. But his course was easy to define. Swerving, making zigzags similar to the lightning on illustrations depicting the universal flood, he went in circles, and these circles slowly narrowed.

A year passed in this way, while the circle was being drawn to a point, and he entered St. Petersburg. Upon entering the city he completed his circle, joining one end to the other. After that, he began to circle the city, and he followed this very same circle for weeks. He walked quickly, in that very same, slightly relaxed military step, for which his arms and legs appeared to be deliberately suspended.

The shopkeepers hated him.

When he happened to pass by *Gostiny Ryad*, they would shout after him:

"Come yesterday."

"Try going backward."

They kept talking about his bringing bad luck; but the old women selling bread, in order to get rid of him, would each give him a loaf.

Little boys, who in every age are remarkably quick to detect weaknesses, ran after him shouting:

"Bandy-legs!"

XIX

In St. Petersburg the guards at Pavel Petrovich's palace cried out:

"The Emperor is sleeping."

The sentries with halberds at the crossroads repeated this cry:

"The Emperor is sleeping."

And in reaction to this cry, as to a windstorm, one after another the shops closed, and pedestrians hid indoors.

That signified nightfall.

On Isaakevskaya Square crowds of peasant men in sacking, driven from the countryside to find work, put out their fires and, covered with rags, lay down right there on the ground.

The sentries with halberds, having cried out: "The Emperor is sleeping," fell asleep themselves. A guard at the Petropavlovsk Fortress walked back and forth, like a clock. In a tavern on the outskirts of the city, the owner girdled in bast sat drinking royal wine with a coachman.

"The end will soon come to Old Daddy Snub Nose," the coachman said, "I was taking important gentlemen . . ."

The palace drawbridge was raised, and Pavel Petrovich looked out the window. He was safe for the while on his island.

But there were whispers and glances in the palace which he understood, and on the streets passers-by with strange expressions on their faces fell on their knees before his horse. So he had ordered, but now people did not fall in the mud as they had always done. They fell *too* eagerly. His horse was tall and he rocked in the saddle. He had judged too quickly: the palace was *not* sufficiently protected. It was necessary to choose a smaller room. Pavel Petrovich could not do this, however, someone would immediately notice the change. "I must hide in the 'snuffbox,' " the Emperor thought, taking some snuff. He did not light the candles. No point in setting someone on his trail. He stood in the dark, dressed only in his underclothes. At the window he took account of his servants. He rearranged things, effaced the name of Benigsen from his mind, and entered Olsufiev's name.

The list displeased him.

"Then my account is not . . ."

"Arakcheyev is stupid," he said softly.

". . . *vague incertitude,* with which that one fawns . . ."

Scarcely a guard was to be seen by the drawbridge.

"It's necessary," Pavel Petrovich said from habit.

He beat his fingers on the snuffbox.

"It's necessary," he reflected, beat some more, and abruptly stopped.

Everything necessary had been carried out long ago, and all proved insufficient.

"It's necessary to imprison Alexander Pavlovich." He was in a hurry and waved his hand.

"It's necessary . . ."

What was necessary?

He lay down and, as he did every night, quickly buried himself under the bedclothes. He fell into a deep sleep.

At seven o'clock in the morning he awakened suddenly with a jolt and remembered something: it was necessary to find a simple and modest man who would be absolutely duty-bound to him alone, and to replace everyone else. And he fell asleep again.

XX

The next morning Pavel Petrovich looked through his orders. Colonel Salso was suddenly promoted to general. This was a colonel who had never begged for titles, nor crawled before people behind the old man's back, and he was neither a braggart nor a dandy. He carried out his duties without complaint or murmur.

Pavel Petrovich requested his service lists. He stopped at the paper stating that the colonel, when a second lieutenant, had been banished to Siberia for shouting "Help" beneath the Emperor's window. He lazily remembered something about that and grinned. It was vaguely connected with some kind of a love story.

How perfectly suited this man would now be, this man who would shout "Help" beneath his window at the requisite moment. He bestowed an estate and one thousand serfs on General Salso.

That evening the name of General Salso burst into prominence. Everyone was talking about him.

Someone had heard how the Emperor, smiling a smile which was long dormant, told Count Palen:

"His division can wait a bit to encumber him. He is required for more important things."

No one besides Benigsen would confess that he knew nothing about the general. Palen winced.

The first gentleman of the chamber, Alexander Lvovich Naryshkin, recalled the general:

"Well, yes, Lieutenant Salso . . . I remember. He was with Sandunov . . ."

"At the maneuvers . . ."

"Remember, a relative of Olsufiev, Fyodor Yakovlevich . . ."

"He is not Olsufiev's relative, Count. Lieutenant Salso comes from France. His father was beheaded by the rabble of Toulon."

XXI

Events happened swiftly. General Salso was called to the Emperor. But on that very day word came that the general was dangerously ill.

The Emperor grunted in vexation, and twisted a button off Palen's coat when he brought the news.

He shouted hoarsely:

"Put him in the hospital, cure him. And if he is not cured, sir . . ."

The Emperor's valet visited the hospital twice daily to check on General Salso's health.

Behind tightly closed doors within the palace, quaking doctors fussed about as if they were sick themselves.

Toward evening at the end of the third day, General Salso passed away.

Pavel Petrovich was no longer angry. He gazed at everyone through a haze, and took to himself, moping.

XXII

The funeral rites of General Salso were long remembered in St. Petersburg and several memoirs have preserved the details.

The regiment marched with furled flags. Thirty royal carriages, crowded ones and empty ones, rolled along behind. That was what the Emperor ordered. Medallions and cordons were carried on pillows.

Behind the heavy black coffin walked his wife, leading a child by the hand.

And she was weeping.

When the procession passed by Pavel Petrovich's palace, he, accompanied by someone else, slowly came out to the drawbridge to watch, and he raised his unsheathed sword.

"My best people die."

Then, after the royal carriages had driven by, he quoted in Latin, following the procession with his eyes:

"Sic transit gloria mundi."

XXIII

And so General Salso was buried, after having lived a full life: a youthful love affair, punishment and banishment, years of service, a family, the accidental mercy of the Emperor and the envy of courtiers.

His name is to be found in the "St. Petersburg Necropolis," and certain historians have even mentioned him in passing.

But the name of the deceased Lieutenant Sinyukhayev is not found in the "St. Petersburg Necropolis."

He vanished without a trace, crumbling into dust, into chaff, as if he had never existed at all.

And Pavel Petrovich died in March of the same year as General Salso—from "apoplexy,"* according to the official report.

Translated by Jane Gary Harris

---

* Emperor Paul was actually strangled in a court conspiracy. However, even in the twentieth century, official Russian historiography maintained that he died of "apoplexy."

EVGENY ZAMYATIN

THE CAVE

Glaciers, mammoths, wastes. Black nocturnal cliffs, vaguely like houses; in the cliffs—caves. And who can tell what creature trumpets at night along the rocky path among the cliffs and, sniffing the path, blows up clouds of white powdery snow: perhaps a gray-trunked mammoth; perhaps the wind; but the wind may be only the icy roar of some enormous mammoth. One thing is clear: it's winter. And you must clench your teeth more tightly to keep them from chattering; and you must split your wood with a stone ax; and every night you must carry your bonfire from cave to cave, deeper and deeper, and wrap more and more shaggy animal hides around you. . . .

Among the cliffs, where in ages past St. Petersburg had stood, a gray-trunked mammoth roamed by night. And wrapped in hides, overcoats, blankets and rags, the cave dwellers retreated from cave to cave. On the Feast of the Intercession of the Holy Virgin, Martin Martinych and Masha boarded up the study; three weeks later they moved out of the dining room and took refuge in the bedroom. That was the last retreat; there they either had to hold fast—or die.

In that Petersburg cave bedroom, things were as they had been in Noah's Ark not long before: clean and unclean creatures thrown together by the exigency of the flood. Martin Martinych's desk, books, stone-age pancakes looking like potter's clay, Scriabin's Opus 74, a flatiron, five potatoes lovingly scrubbed till they shone, nickel-plated bedsprings, an ax, a chiffonier, firewood. And in the center of this whole universe was a god—a short-legged, rusty-red, squat, greedy cave god: the iron stove.

The god was roaring mightily. The great miracle of fire warmed the dark cave. Martin Martinych and Masha—the cave dwellers—reverently, silently, thankfully, stretched their arms toward him. For one hour it was spring in the cave; for one hour hides, claws, tusks were shed and through the frozen brain-crust sprouted green shoots—thoughts.

"Mart, you haven't forgotten that tomorrow . . . ? Yes, I see you *have* forgotten!"

In October, when the leaves have just yellowed and are beginning to wither and droop, there are blue-eyed days; if you tilt your head upward on such a day, so that you no longer see the earth, it is possible to believe that joy and summer still exist. And with Masha too, if you close your eyes now and just listen to her, it is possible to believe that she is still the Masha of old, and that any moment she will laugh, get out of bed and give you a hug—not at all the same Masha whose voice an hour before sounded like a knife scraping on glass, not the same person at all.

"Oh, Mart, Mart! You always forget. . . . You never used to. The twenty-ninth—St. Mary's Day."

The iron god continued to roar. As usual, there was no light: they would not turn it on until ten. The dark shaggy vaults of the cave were swaying. Martin Martinych, squatting on his haunches, drew himself into a knot (tighter, tighter!), and throwing back his head, stared at the October sky so as not to see (oh, not to see!) those faded, drooping lips. But Masha:

"Listen, Mart: if we could light the stove tomorrow at dawn so that all day it will be the way it is now! What about it? How much do we have? Isn't there still about a cord left in the study?"

It had been ages since Masha had been able to drag herself to the Polar study, and she did not know that there it was already . . . Pull the knot tighter, tighter!

"A cord? There's more! I think we have more there. . . ."

At the stroke of ten, suddenly—light! Without finishing his

sentence, Martin Martinych screwed up his eyes and turned away: it was harder in the light than in the darkness. And in the light his face looked crumpled and dull as clay. Many people have clay faces now: like Adam. But Masha—

"You know, Mart, maybe I'll try and get up tomorrow . . . if you light the fire first thing."

"Of course, Masha . . . On a day like that . . . Of course, of course . . . Very first thing."

The cave god was quieting down now, shrinking into himself. Soon he made no sound at all except for a faint crackling. Below at the Obertyshevs' someone had begun to split the gnarled logs of an old barge with a stone ax—and that same stone ax split Martin Martinych in two. One piece of Martin Martinych was smiling a clay smile at Masha and grinding a dried potato skin into the coffee mill for pancakes; and the other piece of Martin Martinych, like a bird which has flown into a room and is trapped there, was senselessly and blindly knocking against the ceiling, the walls and the windowpanes: "Where to get wood—where to get wood—where to get wood?"

Martin Martinych put on his overcoat and fastened a belt around it (one of the cave dwellers' myths is that this keeps you warmer). The pail in the corner by the chiffonier rattled as he picked it up.

"Where are you off to, Mart?"

"Back right away. Downstairs for water."

On the dark stairs, iced over from splashed water, Martin Martinych stood a while, swaying slightly; then he sighed and, clanking the pail like a prisoner's chain, descended to the Obertyshevs': their water was still running. Obertyshev himself opened the door, wearing a rope-sashed coat. He had not shaved for a long time, and his face looked like a vacant lot overgrown with dusty reddish weeds. Through the weeds poked yellow stone teeth, and between the stones flashed a lizard's tail—a smile:

"Ah, Martin Martinych! Here for some water, are you? Please, please, please."

The compartment between the outer and inner doors was so narrow that you could not turn around in it with a pail: it was here that Obertyshev kept his wood. Martin Martinych, the clay man, knocked against the wood, and a deep painful dent appeared in his side. He got an even deeper dent when he knocked against the corner of a commode in the dark corridor. He crossed the dining room: in the dining room was Obertyshev's mate with the three Obertyshev cubs. She hastily hid a soup plate under a napkin: A human had come from another cave, and—God knows!—he might fall on her and seize it.

In the kitchen Obertyshev turned on the faucet and smiled his stone-toothed smile:

"Well, how's the wife? How's the wife? How's the wife?"

"What can I say, Alexei Ivanych? Same as ever. In a bad way. Why, tomorrow's her name day, and I don't even have . . ."

"Who does, Martin Martinych? Who does, who does?"

In the kitchen the trapped bird flew up, beating its wings frantically and darting to the right, to the left—then in sudden despair it dashed its breast against the wall:

"Alexei Ivanych, I wanted to ask . . . Alexei Ivanych, couldn't I borrow just five or six pieces of wood from you?"

Yellow stone teeth poked through the weeds, yellow teeth sprouted from the eyes, Obertyshev became a jungle of teeth which grew longer and longer.

"What an idea, Martin Martinych! What an idea, what an idea! We ourselves are . . . You know very well how things are now, you know very well, you know very well. . . ."

Pull the knot tighter, still tighter! Martin Martinych gave a last twist, lifted the pail and made his way through the kitchen, through the dark corridor, through the dining room. At the threshold of the dining room, Obertyshev pulled out his instant lizard-nimble hand:

"Well, take care. . . . But don't forget to slam the door shut, Martin Martinych, don't forget! Both doors, both, both —hard enough to keep warm!"

On the dark icy landing, Martin Martinych set the pail down, turned around and slammed the first door tight shut. He listened but heard only the dry quaking of his bones and the dotted line formed by his shaky breathing. In the narrow compartment between the two doors he put out his hand and felt around—one piece of wood, and another, and another

. . . No! He quickly shoved himself back onto the landing and closed the door. Now he would only have to slam it a little harder for the lock to click. . . .

But he did not have the heart to do it. He did not have the heart to slam the door on Masha's tomorrow. And on the line formed by his faint dots of breath, the old Martin Martinych was engaged in a death struggle with the new: the old Martin Martinych, the Scriabin one, who knew "Thou shalt not!" and the new one, the cave man, who said "You must!" The cave man, gnashing his teeth, trampled and throttled his adversary, and Martin Martinych, breaking his nails, opened the door and plunged his hand into the woodpile—one piece, four, five pieces he put under his coat, in his belt, into the pail. Then he slammed the door and dashed upstairs with huge animal bounds. Halfway up the stairs, on one of the ice-coated steps, he suddenly froze with terror and pressed himself against the wall: downstairs the door clicked again, and the dusty voice of Obertyshev called out:

"Who's there? Who's there? Who's there?"

"It's me, Alexei Ivanych. I—I forgot the door . . . I wanted . . . I went back—to slam it shut. . . ."

"You? Hm . . . How could you be so careless? You'll have to be more careful, more careful. Nowadays everybody steals, you know very well, you know very well. How could you be so careless?"

The twenty-ninth. From early morning a low cotton-batting sky rent with holes through which an icy wind blew down. But the cave god's belly had been stuffed since early morning, and he hummed benevolently. So let there be holes in the sky, let Obertyshev, that jungle of teeth, count his woodpile—what did it matter: there is only today; "tomorrow" has no meaning in a cave; only after centuries will "tomorrow" and "the day after tomorrow" again have meaning.

Masha got up and, swaying as if in response to secret breezes, did her hair in the old way: back over her ears and parted in the middle. And she was like a last withered leaf fluttering on a naked tree. From the middle drawer of his desk, Martin Martinych pulled out papers, letters, a thermometer, a small blue medicine bottle (which he hastily shoved back so that Masha wouldn't see it)—and finally, from the farthest corner he drew out a little black lacquered box: in the bottom of it there was still some tea, some real—yes, yes, very real—tea! They drank real tea. And Martin Martinych, tilting his head upward, heard a voice very much like the one he used to know.

"Mart, do you remember? My blue room and the piano with the cover on it, and on the piano the ash tray with the little wooden horse, and I was playing, and you came up to me from behind . . ."

Yes, on that evening the universe was created, and the wondrous wise snout of the moon, and the nightingale trill of bells in the hall.

"Do you remember, Mart: the open window, the green sky, and below—from another world—an organ-grinder?"

Organ-grinder, marvelous organ-grinder—where are you now?

"And on the embankment—do you remember? The branches still bare, the water rosy, and past us floated the last blue block of ice, like a coffin. And the idea of a coffin seemed funny to us . . . because of course we would never die. Do you remember?"

Downstairs someone had begun to split wood with a stone ax. Suddenly the sound stopped, and there was some commotion, followed by a shout. Martin Martinych was split in two: one half of him saw the immortal organ-grinder, the immortal wooden horse, the immortal block of ice; while the other half—breathing in a shaky dotted line—counted off the pieces of wood with Obertyshev. And now Obertyshev has finished counting, and, sprouting a jungle of teeth, he throws on his overcoat and ferociously slams the door. And now . . .

"Wait, Masha, I think—I think someone's knocking."

No. No one. No one yet. You can still breathe, still tilt your head upward and listen to her voice, so like her old voice.

Twilight. The twenty-ninth of October had grown old. Worried, peering old woman's eyes—everything shrinks, wrinkles, hunches up under those peering eyes. The ceiling is caving in, everything is flattening out—the armchairs, the desk, Martin Martinych, the beds; and on the bed, completely flattened out like a piece of paper—Masha.

At dusk Selikhov, the house chairman, came. He had once been a strapping two-hundred-fifty pounder, but by now had fallen away to half his size and clattered around in the shell of his jacket like a nut in a rattle. But he still had his old rumbling laugh.

"Well, Martin Martinych, in the first place, in the second place, congratulations to your spouse on her name day. Of course, of course. Obertyshev told me . . ."

Martin Martinych bolted from his chair like a gunshot, rushed to speak—say something, anything. . . .

"Some tea? . . . right away—in just a minute . . . today we're drinking—real tea. Real! I'll just . . ."

"Tea? I'd really prefer champagne, you know. Haven't got any? Well, what do you know! Haw-haw-haw! A couple days ago a friend and I made some brew from Hoffmann drops. It was a howl! We got stewed to the gills. 'I am Zinoviev,' says my friend. 'Down on your knees!' It was a howl! Going home from there I meet a fellow at Marsovo Field with only his vest on, swear to God! 'What's up?' I say. 'Nothing much,' says he. 'Just been stripped clean by robbers, so I'm running home to Vasilyevsky Island!' It was a howl."

Flattened, paper-like Masha laughed in her bed. Tying himself in a tight knot, Martin Martinych laughed louder and louder—to give Selikhov fuel to go on, so he wouldn't stop, so he would talk about something else . . .

But Selikhov was petering out; soon he was silent except for a few gentle snorts. He rattled around in the shell of his jacket; then he got up.

"Well, birthday girl, let's have your little hand. *G.A.F.* What, you don't get it? It's *Greetings And Felicitations,* the way *they* would say it—*G.A.F.* It's a howl!"

He lumbered into the hallway, then into the entry. One last second: now he will either go away or . . .

The floor began to sway and spin under Martin Martinych's feet. With a clay smile on his face, Martin Martinych held onto the doorpost. Selikhov puffed as he stamped his feet into his huge boots.

Mammoth-like in his boots and fur coat, he straightened

up and caught his breath. Then he silently took Martin Martinych by the hand, silently opened the door to the Polar study and silently sat down on the sofa.

The floor of the study was an ice floe; softly the ice floe cracked and broke off from the shore—and it carried Martin Martinych off, spinning him around till he could scarcely hear Selikhov's voice, coming from the far bank of the divan.

"In the first place, in the second place, my dear sir, I must tell you: I'd crush this Obertyshev like a louse, by God . . . But you understand, since he has made a formal declaration and says he'll go to the police tomorrow . . . what a louse! I can only give you a piece of advice: this very day, this very minute, take the wood back to Obertyshev and shove it down his throat to keep him quiet."

The ice block was spinning faster and faster. Tiny, flattened, all but invisible—like a splinter—Martin Martinych replied, but seemed to be talking to himself; and not about the wood but about something else:

"All right. This very day. This very minute."

"Excellent, excellent! He's such a louse, such a louse, I tell you. . . ."

It was still dark in the cave. Clay-faced, cold, blind Martin Martinych clumsily bumped against the medley of things which had been deposited in the cave by the flood. He shuddered: that voice, like Masha's, the way it used to be:

"What were you and Selikhov talking about? Ration books? I was lying here thinking: why not get up our courage and go somewhere where there's sun. . . . What are you clumping around for like that! You must be doing it on purpose. You know very well I can't stand it—I can't, I can't, I can't!"

Like a knife scraping on glass. But what did it matter now? Arms and legs like machines. To raise and lower them you had to have chains and a windlass or ship's hoist, and to turn the windlass not one man but three were needed.

Drawing on the chains with all his strength, Martin Martinych put the tea kettle and pan on the stove and threw in the last piece of Obertyshev's wood.

"Do you hear what I'm saying to you? Why don't you answer? Do you hear me?"

Of course this wasn't Masha, no, it was not her voice. Martin Martinych moved more and more slowly, his feet became bogged down in quicksand; it grew harder and harder to turn the windlass. Suddenly the chain slipped off the pulley; the arm of the hoist dropped down and sent the tea kettle and pan tumbling noisily onto the floor. The cave god hissed like a snake. And from somewhere else, from the far shore, all the way from the bed, came the shrill voice of a stranger:

"You're doing it on purpose! Go away! This minute! I don't need you or anyone else—I want nothing, nothing, nothing! Go away!"

The twenty-ninth of October was dead; dead were the immortal organ-grinder, the block of ice in the sunset-reddened water, and Masha too. And it hardly mattered. For there could be no improbable tomorrow, no Obertyshev, no Selikhov, no Martin Martinych: everything had to die.

Mechanically, remotely, Martin Martinych still went through certain motions. Perhaps he lit the stove again, picked up the pan from the floor and brought the tea kettle to a boil; and perhaps Masha said something to him—he did not hear: there were only the dully aching dents in the clay made by certain words, and by the corners of the chiffonier, the chairs, the desk.

Martin Martinych slowly drew from the desk bundles of letters, a thermometer, sealing wax, the box with the tea in it and more letters. Finally, from somewhere in the very bottom, he drew out the little dark-blue medicine bottle.

Ten o'clock: the lights went on. Electric light—cold, hard, naked, simple, like life and death in the cave. And just as simple beside the flatiron, Opus 74 and the pancakes—the little blue medicine bottle.

The iron god hummed benevolently, devouring the parchment-yellow, bluish and white paper of the letters. The lid of the tea kettle began to rattle, gently calling attention to itself. Masha turned around:

"Is the tea boiling? Mart, darling, give me some, won't you?"

Then she saw. An instant pierced through and through with clear, naked, cruel electric light: hunched in front of the stove Martin Martinych; a rosy glow on the letters, as on the water at sunset; and there, over there—the little blue medicine bottle.

"Mart . . . Do you . . . do you want to so soon . . . ?"

Silence. Indifferently devouring the immortal words—the bitter, tender, yellow, white, blue words—the iron god was purring gently. And Masha, as simply as if she were asking for tea:

"Mart, dearest! Mart—give it to me!"

Martin Martinych smiled from afar:

"But you know, Masha: there's only enough for one."

"Mart, there's nothing left of me now. This is no longer me —I'm going to do it, Mart. . . . Mart, you understand, don't you, Mart!"

Oh, that same voice, her old voice . . . and if you tilt your head upward . . .

"I deceived you, Masha: there's no more wood in the study. I went to Obertyshev's, and between the doors were . . . I stole them—do you understand? And Selikhov came to see me. . . . I've got to bring them back at once, but I burned them all—I burned them all—all of them!"

Unconcernedly the iron god began to doze off. As it flickered out, the walls of the cave still shuddered spasmodically, as did the houses, the cliffs, the mammoths, Masha.

"Mart, if you still love me . . . Mart, remember back! Mart, darling!"

The immortal wooden horse, the organ-grinder, the block of ice. And this voice . . . Martin Martinych slowly rose from his knees. Slowly, laboriously turning the crank, he took the little blue medicine bottle from the table and handed it to Masha.

She threw off the covers and sat up in bed—rosy, swift, immortal as the water once at sunset; then, laughing, she seized the bottle.

"There, you see: I didn't lie here and think about going away somewhere for nothing. Light another lamp—this one here, on the table. So. Now put some more wood in the stove.

"Now . . . Go take a little walk. I think the moon is out— *my* moon, remember? Don't forget to take the key, because you're bound to slam the door, and then there'll be nobody to . . ."

No, there was no moon. Only the cave of the world, silent and immense, and the dark heavy low-hung clouds—its vaulted ceiling. Narrow endless passages between the walls; and dark icy cliffs, like houses; in the cliffs, deep purple hollows: in the hollows, crouched around fires—humans. A light icy draft blows white powder up from under your feet; and over the white powder and icy cliffs, above the caves and crouching humans, with huge measured steps, an enormous mammoth silently moves.

Translated by Richard Ravenal

Nikolai Zhdanov

The Trip Home

Returning home to his study after a long, exhausting conference, Pavel Alekseyevich Varygin set about surveying the
official papers which had accumulated in his absence and had
been put in a manila envelope for him by his secretary,
Nonna Andreyevna. He looked through several forms and
then took up the telegrams which usually came from the
outlying districts and contained various reminders and requests. While reading he made notes with a blue pencil and
set sheet after sheet aside. Finally, only one remained, for
some reason not opened . . . evidently due to the carelessness of Nonna Andreyevna. Varygin himself tore open the
envelope and unfolded the sheet.

"Marya Seménovna died Wednesday, the twenty-fourth,
funeral Saturday," he read. . . .

He left for the country that very night on a slow train with
two transfers on the way: the express left in a day, and he
would have had to wait a whole twenty-four hours.

His wife accompanied Varygin to the door of their apartment, kissed him on the cheek dolefully and said that perhaps she would say nothing to the children: they had not yet
received their marks for this quarter.

"As you will," he replied, and, as he went downstairs into
the yellow light of the street lamps, he thought, "This is
nothing more than a slight annoyance for her."

In the train he spent his time sitting on a bench by a

window looking through the cloudy glass at the grayish band
of earth and the dark silhouettes of trees being carried past.

Varygin had last seen his mother about six years ago. She
had come from the *kolkhoz* "to pay respects," as his wife who
acted a little superciliously toward his rural family had said
afterward.

These six years, it now seemed to him, had gone by completely unnoticed. Once in the fall he had prepared to go to
the country, but his doctors recommended that he look after
his heart, and he went to Kislovodsk.

Sometimes, quite rarely, letters had come from his mother.
They were written at her dictation in some educated person's
handwriting, usually on notebook paper.

"We don't live very well, but we're not complaining," his
mother said. He was grieved, but then it occurred to him that
his mother had never lived especially "well" and the phrase
"we're not complaining" sounded, in essence, quite optimis-
tic.

The train had taken more than twenty-four hours to arrive
at the station of Dvorika. The slow November dawn still had
not chased away the gray shadows of night, which clung to
the low, cold sky and hid under the station roof where potatoes were piled high as a mountain, covered by canvas and, it
seemed, waiting to be shipped off.

He recalled from childhood that right behind the station
there began a small, marshy forest which stretched for about
eight versts and that behind the woods were the villages
called, by the farmers: Lozhkino, Derevlevo, Kashino,
Korkino, Lapshino, Pirogovo, and, finally, *their* village—Tyurino. But there was no forest visible around him now.
Varygin walked across a marshy low place along a fence made
from blackened poles.

On both sides of him rose even mounds of peat. It was
clear that there was farming here. Beyond the low spot there
began a highway which also had not been there earlier.
Varygin waited for a passing truck and went with it up to
Lapshino and then, from there, by foot, to Tyurino.

It turned out that they had already taken his mother to the
cemetery. He found this out near one of the outlying huts

from a middle-aged woman in a dusty soldier's work shirt, carrying well water in wooden buckets.

"And who might you be?" she inquired, looking over Varygin's fine, thick cloth coat.

"Her son," he said.

The woman placed the buckets on the ground and looked Varygin over once more.

"Can it be Konstantin?" she asked. "Why I'm Derevleva, Anastasiya, don't you remember?"

"Our Konstantin died long ago. I'm another brother, Pavel," he explained.

"Well, I myself said that Konstantin had died," the woman joined in, "but my daughter-in-law, you know, had her own version. But what do you care about her! Say, can you find the cemetery? You've likely already forgotten our local places, eh? Klashka!" she cried to a girl who was collecting cabbage leaves that were left on the banks from the harvest. "Run and show him how to get to the cemetery—go straight across the field!"

Following the girl who ran ahead of him, he walked along the field which was hardened but still not covered with snow, stumbling in the uneven places, fighting for breath, and frequently wiping sweat from his face.

They skirted a field that had a fall crop and, walking on a crooked log, crossed a little stream winding into some bushes. Farther on, the shore raised up into a gentle hillock and against the gray sky Varygin saw the old wooden church and the cemetery crosses between the few bare trees. He remembered both the church and the stream, only now they were considerably smaller than they had been earlier. He also remembered the water holes past which they walked. Once they used to wash sheets in these holes. Children said that goblins hid in them.

The cemetery was not fenced and he noticed from afar that someone was standing on the church steps.

"Can I leave you here, mister?" said the girl, slowing down her pace. "There's the midwife who stays at your place. They might tell the teacher that I went to church. Can I leave you?"

"All right, go on," said Varygin.

When he came closer a young woman ran down the

wooden steps of the porch toward him. Her face, reddened
in the icy air, was wet from tears but still radiated health.

"We had already made up our minds that you weren't
coming," she said when he had identified himself. "We were
waiting for the night express. We didn't know how it would
be. Now maybe you will be angry—I myself can't believe it—
but Marya Semënovna insisted that she be buried in the old
way, in Christian fashion. . . ."

Taking off his fur cap and not setting straight the hairs
clinging to his forehead, Varygin went in under the shady
arches where in the semidarkness several slender candles
were burning and three or four figures were standing. The
midwife followed him in and stood by the entrance. He,
however, moved closer and suddenly saw the small, childlike,
dark face of his mother illuminated by the yellow glow of a
candle. He came to a halt and stood, not moving. Before him
he saw only this face.

A priest with sparse gray hair and a lean, bony forehead
was reading a prayer in a sing-song voice, and it seemed as if
he were addressing only his mother who lay immobile with
her bloodless lips pressed together. In the darkness the two-
dimensional faces of the saints drawn on the icon stand
shone forth. There was the odor of incense, and this odor as
well as the words "should'st," "likest," "most exalted"
sounding in the darkness reminded Varygin of his childhood
when he had gone with his mother to this church and even
sang in the choir. All this was so long ago that it was possible
it had never happened. Once the priest passed quite close
and the odor of garlic reached Varygin from his shabby old
surplice.

When the chanting had finished, the women, who had
been hidden in the darkness, closed the coffin, lifted it up,
and carried it away.

Varygin left the church with the others and also helped
carry the coffin through the shaggy grass between the
wooden crosses. He came to his senses only when his mother
had been buried.

Afterward he again crossed the small stream by way of the
crooked log. A light mist, similar to the incense, rose from
the stream, and, as he again walked across the hardened

field, it seemed to him that he had just been in a world that for all practical purposes no longer really existed. . . .

When he returned to the village and went up to the house the midwife first ran up to the porch and, having fished the key from her pocket, unlocked the door. Varygin recalled both this porch and the door with its iron handle, but the gates of the house were different, new, and, as he passed through, he saw a sign on them: "Midwife Station."

Varygin crossed the threshold. To his left a white stove extended to the ceiling, while on the right stood a broad wooden washtub and over it was a clay washstand—probably that very washtub and that very washstand which had been there in his childhood and about which he had completely forgotten afterward and only just now remembered.

The ceiling was much lower than it had been formerly, but the wooden beams slightly sagging in the center were just the same—to that he could swear. There were the old iron hooks from which the cradles used to hang: the first pair, the second, and the third. His father had lived with his brothers, and there were three wives in the home, each of whom had her own cradle. In one of them he, Varygin, had grown up.

"I was mostly in this half," said the midwife, "that's where I take care of my patients. Marya Semënovna was over here. Here is her bed. The bedding is still on it, just like it was."

Varygin looked at the material turned gray with age, and again, not for the first time, the thought that his mother had been in need pierced him painfully.

He took off his hat and coat and wearily sank into a chair. He wanted to lay his head on the table and sink into oblivion. Once all their family had dined at this table. His father had sat under the wooden icon in the corner. Varygin recalled the smell of the cabbage soup and the warm bread with a cabbage leaf stuck to the lower crust. His mother often washed the table with hot water and scraped it with a broken-handled knife. That knot with its dark center had always seemed to him to be similar to a horse's eye. Now the planks of the table had grown yellow and dried up, and the "eye" had become black and cracked.

Notebooks lay on the table in a pile. "Courses for Country Midwives. Notes of Antonova, A.," he read. The letters that sometimes had come from his mother were written in this careful handwriting.

Antonova, A. brought in an armful of wood, kindled the fire, and started the tea kettle. Then she took away the notebooks, got a clean cloth from a suitcase under a shelf, wiped a cup with it, and poured tea for Varygin.

"I'm hurrying off to Lapshino, I have a birth there today," she said. "You will please forgive me."

He didn't want the tea, and he sat there alone, not moving. The life which, when he was a child, seethed in this house, had gone somewhere, and it seemed strange that there remained only these walls and he—Varygin. But he too had nothing to do here and it was necessary to leave. He didn't want to think about leaving. He didn't want to move at all. Where could he lie down? He turned his head to look around.

In a corner on a stand was an old, out of use samovar leaning comically to one side. Its spigot had fallen off and it laughed slyly, looking aslant, as if it wanted to say: "Aha, so you, too, have come unhinged on the road. Lie down next to me, brother!"

Varygin put his hands on the table to get up, and it seemed to him that the table also winked at him with its horse's eye. "So you've finally come back!"

Varygin went over to the bed and lay down.

When he opened his eyes a cold, red band of sunset was shining palely, its reflection in the window. The thought suddenly occurred to him that he had fallen asleep on his mother's bed, where she had died. He got up and moved over to the table. On the wall opposite him was hanging his coat. His hat was on a bench, and behind it in the corner stood the samovar, serious and gloomy, as if offended at something.

Nearby, evidently on the other side of the wall, someone called out in a sharp, nervous voice:

"It's not done this way according to the Party, that's what I'm making a fuss about! If you want to know, nobody can interfere with us village mechanics! What, d'you think this is within the law? A man should know the system infringes on him! . . ."

"They'll take care of that in the District Council," an angry, admonishing voice could be heard in reply. "Get out of here: I tell you a man is resting."

The voices moved away. Evidently the people who were quarreling had gone outside the gates.

In a little while the porch floor squeaked, and a bent-over figure in a short fur coat appeared in the door.

"Are you asleep?" was asked from the semidarkness. A switch flipped, and an electric lamp lit up on the table. Varygin saw a thin old man looking at him with small cheerful eyes.

"Who are you?" asked Varygin.

"Who, me? Moshkarev, Klya. I'm a guard now, but I worked as a blacksmith before. I'm in the guards because of sickness. I keep watch over the blacksmith shop."

He sat down on the chair by the table.

"I brought wood for Antonina Vasilevna. I see that you were sleeping. She probably went to Lapshino, Zoika Sinyukhina is giving birth there again."

"But who cried out?" asked Varygin indicating the wall.

"Pelageya Komkova, the wife of a combine man, a pushy one. They used to be with us in the commune, but now they've been named to the Tractor Corps. She stayed in the *kolkhoz*, but only for the sake of form so that their plot of land wouldn't be taken away—they had over half an acre. Now they've transferred her. That must be the reason why she's done twelve days' work all year. Can a person be like that in a *kolkhoz*? They take their plot and she raises a fuss: 'They've offended the mechanics!' She came here to complain to you. Put her in her place!"

"Didn't they give them a plot?"

"They gave them one. They gave them a fifth of an acre, according to the law, from land outside of the *kolkhoz*, to be taken from separate, vacant land. They decided it in a session of the Village Council."

He paused and then spoke again:

"It must be that you came for your mama's funeral. The final debt. You've respected an old person. You'll be thanked.

It won't be forgotten. They had me ready for the ground, but I didn't make it."

The old man extended one leg and, stretching back, got a partly empty pint bottle from his trousers' pocket.

"Here we are," he continued, growing more lively, "if you're not squeamish about drinking with a working man, we'll drink what God sent. Don't get the impression that I drink much. My niece, Maiya Skornyakova, went to register today with Pëtr Dezhurov, a worker in a cloth factory. They were gay, and I naturally thought of Semënovna. I borrowed a pint and set out. To each his own."

He rubbed his hands as though from cold, looked at the floor, carefully got down two cups, one after another, and poured a little into each. . . .

"Your father and I were great friends. Now, I hear, you're a manager in the Party. That doesn't mean much. We're all people, all the same. Why aren't you drinking?" he asked, stretching out his cup. "Wait a minute, and I'll give you something to eat."

He slid his left hand into his pocket and took out a dark, wart-covered pickle, wiped off the tobacco pieces stuck to it with his palm and broke it in half.

The vodka smarted Varygin's mouth, and he wrinkled his face. He didn't eat his pickle. The blacksmith also had a drink, and he ate his own half of the pickle.

"Well now," he said with satisfaction, screwing up his crafty eyes covered with shaggy shielding eyebrows. "You, it seems, are managers, we are producers, or that's how it seems. Now should we bother with this trifle?"

He unceremoniously shook the still not empty bottle in his hand, and again they both had a drink.

"For some there are funeral feasts, heh, heh, and for others, marriages," said the old man.

Varygin felt a warmth in his chest, and for the first time in three days a feeling of good cheer returned to him.

"And how did my mother live here? Not so bad or how?" he asked.

"Well, she lived like everyone else."

"Really? How did she get her food, for example?"

"Oh, there was nothing to complain of. Our own food

doesn't last longer than till spring, so we go to Lapshino to the combine. There are some who even go to town. The Village Council paid her rent for the house and set up the Midwife's Station here. She got about thirty-five a month. And how much did she need? Sometimes she even had white bread and indulged in store-bought tea. Why, this year they even brought sugar several times, and she also had some. No, you couldn't complain! . . ."

Wheels sounded along the frozen road beyond the gates. Someone was driving past the house on a cart, and the sound of the horse's hoofs and its noisy snorting could be heard.

Then an accordion played somewhere nearby, a gay band walked by the house, and a penetrating girl's voice, breaking into a shout, sang:

> *After the spring harvest*
> *After the district-needs-year*
> *After the bee-keeping courses*
> *I'll part with you, my dear.*

"Our people are enjoying themselves," said the black-smith, "would you like to amuse yourself?" He got up, put the empty bottle in his pocket, and, without saying good-by, disappeared.

Varygin also arose, put on his coat, and went outside. It was already completely dark, but cold stars shone in the places in the sky that were free of clouds. He walked a little way by the gates, shivered from the cold, and looked at his watch. The glowing green hands showed ten minutes to eight. He realized that the express left during the night, and these several hours remaining until his departure seemed unpleasantly long and tiresome to him.

The accordion was playing on the edge of the village and voices, a girlish screech and laughter could be heard. Varygin turned and went toward the house. The soldier's wife, Der-evleva, was waiting for him on the porch. She still had on the working shirt, but a thick woolen shawl was wrapped around her head and shoulders.

"I came to have tea with you," she said sweetly, following him into the hut. "Antonina Vasilevna is worried about you.

She sent me expressly from Lapshino. She couldn't make it herself: Zoika hasn't given birth and is holding her there."

She lit a little stick and set the tea kettle going.

"It's a pity that Semënovna didn't live to see you! How happy that would have made the old woman," Varygin heard her say.

"Was she expecting me?" he asked.

"Well, she didn't say anything this year, but the year before when you promised that you would be coming, she was eagerly awaiting you. She was always saying: 'He'll be coming soon, he'll be coming soon!' But then she quieted down. Now she wasn't offended, not at all. She well understood how hard it is for a busy man to tear himself away. You've probably gone the farthest of all our country people. Afanasy Berezin from Korkino, though, has become a general somewhere in transportation."

Having prepared the tea, she put a cup before him, and sat down at the table.

"We don't have very much to brag about here. We single women in the *kolkhoz* work and work and all for nothing. In a neighboring farm they gave four kilometers to each person, but ours . . ." She waved her hand deprecatingly. "Things aren't getting on so well with us," she said guiltily. Probably she felt uncomfortable before such an important and esteemed person as Varygin that their *kolkhoz* had so few achievements.

"Here's what I wanted to ask you," she continued, undoing her shawl. "Is it right or not what they're doing to us? This year we planted a hundred and eighty-five acres of hemp. But its fiber was too tough. It had blossomed late when the spring crops were getting ripe. We were going to press and stack the hemp, but they ordered us to thresh and ship it all processed. Now what would that do? From us to the collection point is thirty-nine versts, yes, and two ferry crossings, and then you have to wait at the grain elevator! But if you don't take tough hemp away at the right time you won't get 'matyorka,' the fiber from it! But the commissioners ordered: take it away, take it away! Now can't the state, we said, let us wait about seven days? We wouldn't have been in debt. Well, they did it their way. Who knows what's the matter with them! There was nowhere to turn. When they threshed it and took it to the grain elevator the hemp harvest slipped and the unpressed half of it was crushed. Well, the food authorities have probably listed us among the high-quota producers. But we're without food again! Now you judge for yourself, is this right or not?"

"She thinks that everything depends on me," thought Varygin with embarrassment, trying to recall what tough hemp and *"matyorka"* were, and what the connection between them was. But he was just not able to remember.

"It's a political question," he said aloud. "With us the state must always stand above all. Everything depends on the level of mass consciousness."

He was silent, feeling that he hadn't said the right thing.

But Derevleva was listening to him with an expression of satisfaction on her face.

"That's just what I think—it's a political question," she joined in readily, evidently satisfied that the conversation was a truly deep one. "That's so true, what you explained so well. Our masses still do not have consciousness."

In the darkness outside the windows there sounded the whir of a motorcycle.

"It looks like she's returned," said Derevleva. "It seems the farm mechanical engineer has brought her. He comes every Saturday. But he's always busy. Ach, that midwife doesn't understand what's good for her!"

Antonina Vasilevna came in first, and after her appeared a young man with a weather-beaten and cheeky face and a lion-like mane of hair.

"Well, how have you made out here?" she asked animatedly. There remained, apparently, not a trace of her sad mood of the morning.

When she had washed, she sat down at the table, untied a package of bread and butter, evidently purchased in some little shop, and, treating everyone to some, she began to tell what a strong, fine little girl Sinyukhina had given birth to.

It was pleasant to look at her milk-white hands bare to the tight elbows, at her light, womanly movements as she put strands of damp hair behind her reddened ears, at light cheeks now glowing with high color. As she spoke she did not once look at the engineer, but it was obvious that she constantly felt his glance.

"No, she knows what's good for her," decided Varygin, looking at the girl's radiant eyes despite all the cares and difficulties of the day. He thought of his own thickset wife, constantly dissatisfied with something, and of his overfed children: Hena, who at eleven already had a potbelly, and Sveta, who had become like her aunt with her childish face and stout, heavy legs. "This engineer is a happy man," he thought. If long ago life had taken another turn somewhere and he, Varygin, had remained in the country, then, probably, he would now be a completely healthy and strong man. The skin on his face would be tight and smooth like this engineer's. But it was too late to change the past now and, evidently, the future too. And perhaps even if a young woman with such white hands and a supple, beautiful, and strong body now agreed to love him, nothing would have come of it.

"Have you lived in this area long?" he asked.

"Long enough to go away!" she laughed, but a fierce fire gleamed in her eyes. "Over there in the city, away from the rural regions, everything is much more pleasant because of the opportunities at the center of things—you are more cultured and well off there. But they say we are needed here longer."

She looked at the engineer as though seeking his support.

"Yes, there is much work to be done here," said the engineer. "In our region, out of nineteen *kolkhozs* more than half of them are lagging. Small harvests, little profit, the people work unwillingly, eat poorly."

"Why is that?" asked Varygin.

The engineer shrugged his shoulders.

"You should know better than anyone. No one wants to work without pay."

The midwife silently touched the engineer's hands. He got up from the table and began to walk around the room.

Varygin sat, his back leaning against the wall, and chewed the bread. He hadn't eaten since morning. It seemed to him that the engineer was looking at him with hostility.

"Aren't you laying it on a little thick?" he asked in a hoarse voice. "At first I thought that you were an optimist."

The engineer moved to the corner and threw his cigarette into the washtub.

"Optimism," he said when he returned, "is something more intricate than it seems at first glance. Life in the village would be many times better if there were fewer state-supported men of good cheer. One must clench one's teeth and overcome difficulties, not be silent about them. Take, for example, our tractor-mechanics shop. How many hidden possibilities we have there, and no one has any time for this real work! Let's go there tomorrow, and you'll see for yourself."

"I'm leaving today on the express—business!" said Varygin, and he looked at his watch.

The engineer also looked at his watch. The enthusiasm with which he had just been speaking instantly passed away.

"I must be going, Tonya," he said.

She went outside into the hall with him. Varygin could hear them whispering about something on the porch.

"It's probably time for me to go, too," said Varygin when she returned.

"Wait, there is still time. Mitya will tell them at the mechanics shop to send a truck."

Glancing at Derevleva who was quietly washing the dishes in the corner, she awkwardly began to speak about the house: what it would be like now, did he want to stop renting and perhaps sell the house or leave everything as it was?

"Let everything stay the way it was," said Varygin.

There were some things of his mother's left in a chest. He took two old family photographs lying on the bottom of the first drawer. He felt neither the desire nor the strength to sort either through all this or through what the engineer had said and what he had seen here this day.

"Please sort through this yourself," he said and closed the dresser drawer.

The truck arrived much sooner than he had expected. The midwife went with him so that he wouldn't have any difficulty over his ticket.

The road to Lapshino was very bad, but later, when the

truck got on the highway and, its tires softly humming, carried them along the gray ribbon illuminated by the moonlike radiance of the headlights, his usual even disposition gradually began to return to Varygin, and the vexation which remained from the meeting with the engineer faded away.

"Of course," he thought, "our local organizations are still not as regimented as they should be. And sometimes they work unskillfully and crudely and only find excuses to cover it up. But you can't run things everywhere all at the same time. They direct and prompt from the higher levels, but the workers themselves must do the job, the workers themselves!

"Yes, precisely they themselves," he thought again in a minute and was angry that he hadn't said this to the engineer.

They arrived at Dvorika almost an hour before the arrival of the express, and, having gotten his ticket, they sat in the restaurant. The midwife was embarrassed and awkwardly drank the port which he treated her to, continually looking around as though she were afraid of something.

"You should come with me. You could be my secretary," said Varygin in jest. She choked, spilled wine on the tablecloth, and blushed so that he himself felt ill at ease.

On the train, lying down to sleep on the seat in the half-dark compartment where the rest of the passengers were already asleep, he thought with relief that the disturbances and unpleasantnesses of these days were behind him, and he pictured with pleasure how the next day he would enter his warm, well-furnished study and sit in his easy chair at his desk.

Yet the feeling of some sort of guilt did not leave Varygin for a long time. He didn't go to sleep, and through a vague drowsiness his imagination drew for him the wooden crosses against the gray sky, the familiar house, the long plank bench along the wall, the old samovar in the corner, tilted to one side. Behind her well-scraped table sat his mother, her face small and dark as it had been in the church. She leaned toward him and asked, hopefully and expectantly, as Derevleva, the soldier's wife, had asked: "Is it right or not, what has been done to us?"

Translated by Andrew Field

MIKHAIL ZOSHCHENKO

THE ACTOR

This story really happened. It happened in Astrakhan. An amateur actor told me about this.

Here's what he told me.

"Now, here you citizens are asking me whether I have been an actor? Well, I have. Played in a theater. Came into contact with that art. But, really, it's nonsense. There's nothing outstanding in it. . . . Of course, if you give it deeper thought, there's a lot of good in this art. You come out on the stage, let us say, and the spectators look, and among the spectators there are your friends, relatives by marriage, neighbors. You see them winking at you from their seats as if to say: 'Courage, Vasya! Give it both barrels!' And you, on the other hand, make signs to them, meaning: 'Don't worry, citizens, we know a thing or two. You won't catch us napping.'

"But, upon still deeper thought, there is nothing good in that profession. You just get your bile in an uproar. Here, once we were putting on the play *Who Is to Blame?*, with the prerevolutionary setting. It is a very powerful play. In one act, there appear robbers who rob a merchant in plain view of the public. This scene comes out most realistic. The merchant, of course, yells and kicks with his feet. But he is being robbed nevertheless. An eerie play.

"So, we put on this play.

"But just before the curtain went up, one amateur actor, the one who played the merchant, took a couple of drinks.

And the tramp got so flustered in the heat of the production that we saw he was not fit to carry on the role of the merchant. As soon as he came to the front of the stage, he crushed the footlights with his foot, on purpose.

"Ivan Palych, the director of the play, says to me:

" 'We can't let him out on the stage in the second act. He will crush every one of the footlights, the son of a bitch. Perhaps,' he says, 'you will play the part in his place? The audience is stupid; it won't be able to tell the difference.'

"I say:

" 'Citizens, I cannot come out to the footlights. Please don't ask it.' I say: 'I just ate two watermelons. My brain doesn't work so well.'

"But he says:

" 'You've got to save us, friend. At least for one act. Perhaps the other actor will come to his senses after a while. Don't let educational work down.'

"They finally prevailed upon me. I came out to the footlights.

"And, according to the play, I came as I was, in my own jacket and trousers. I only pasted on a little beard. So, I came out. And the audience, though stupid, immediately recognized me.

" 'Aha,' they say, 'Vasya came out! Courage!' they say. 'Give it both barrels!'

"I say:

" 'Courage I've got, Citizens, since the moment is critical. The regular actor,' I say, 'is strongly under the influence and cannot come out to the footlights. He's vomiting.'

"The act started.

"I played the merchant in that act. That is, I shout and try to beat off the robbers with my feet. And I feel as if one of the amateur robbers is trying to pick my pocket for real. I pull my jacket about me, aside from the actors. I beat them off, hitting them straight in their faces, honest!

" 'Don't come near me, you scum,' I say, 'I ask you as a gentleman.'

"But, according to the play, they become more and more aggressive. They get my pocketbook—with 180 rubles—and they try to get my watch.

"I shout with all my might:

" 'Help! Citizens! They're robbing me in earnest!'

"And that produces full effect. The stupid audience is delighted, and they clap their hands. They yell:

" 'Give, Vasya, give! Beat them off, dear fellow! Hit them on the head, the devils!'

"I shout:

" 'It doesn't work, friends!'

"And I continue beating them straight on their snouts.

"I see that one amateur is bleeding profusely, but the others become enraged and more aggressive, the scoundrels.

" 'Friends!' I yell. 'What is this? What should I suffer for?'

"Here the director poked his head from the wings.

" 'Good boy, Vasya,' says he. 'You are playing the part wonderfully. Let's have some more.'

"I see that the shouts don't help because, no matter what I yell, it comes out straight according to the play.

"I got on my knees.

" 'Friends,' I say. 'Director Ivan Palych,' I say, 'I can't go on! Pull down the curtain! They've robbed me of my last savings! They're in earnest!'

"Here, many theatrical experts—seeing that the words don't belong in the play—come out of the wings. The prompter, thanks be to him, climbs out of his booth.

" 'It seems, Citizens,' he says, 'that the merchant's wallet was stolen in earnest.'

"They pulled down the curtain. They brought me water in a ladle. They let me drink.

" 'Friends,' I say, 'Director Ivan Palych,' I say. 'What is this? According to the play, someone has lifted my wallet.'

"Well, they searched the company. But they found no money. However, someone threw the empty wallet into the wings. The money disappeared without a trace, as if it had been burned in a stove.

"You say 'art'? I know your art. I had experience!"

Translated by Jack A. Posin

THE WESTINGHOUSE BRAKE

The thing is, Volodka Bokov was a little bit pie-eyed. Otherwise, of course, he would not have risked such a crime. He was loaded.

If you must know, Volodka Bokov had downed a flagon of Erivan vodka just before the train started, and made up the rest with beer. And as regards food, he ate only one sportsman's wienie. What kind of food is that? So, of course, the fellow got disorganized. Because the combination is very caustic. One's head goes around from it, and various ideas ripen in one's breast, and one feels like showing off before the esteemed public.

So, Volodka got into the train and began to show off a little. He said he was the kind of person to whom everything was permitted, and that even the people's tribunal, in case of any misunderstanding, would uphold his side every time. Because he was—let the public know—of an excellent social origin: his grandfather had been a cowherd, and his mama was the most unsophisticated country-woman. . . .

And so Volodka kept on wagging his tongue. Some sort of a mood hit him—he felt like showing off. And at that point a citizen emerged opposite Volodka in the carriage. This citizen had cotton in his ear and he was neatly dressed, not without luxury. And he said:

"If you keep on telling lies like that a little longer, they'll put you in the clink at the next station."

Volodka said:

"Don't you touch my self-esteem. They can't put me in the clink because of my origin. No matter what I do, I'll get lenient treatment. Because I am a hereditary peasant and proletarian."

Well, that's the kind of mood that hit him! He was drunk, that is.

And the public began to express its displeasure on this score. And the more venomous ones among them began to egg Volodka on. And some fellow in a blue cap, the lowdown soul, said:

"Why, dear fellow! Why don't you smash the window to pieces, and we shall see whether you will be put in the clink or go scot-free. Or," he said, "even better than that: leave the window alone but instead stop the train by turning this handle! . . . This is the brake. . . ."

Volodka said:

"Which handle do you mean? Express yourself more precisely, you parasite. . . ."

The one in the blue cap replied:

"Why, this one. This is the Westinghouse brake. Jerk it from the left to this side. And we'll see what happens next."

The people, and the citizen who had cotton in his ear, tried, of course, to stop the egger-on. They said it was pretty shameful to suggest sober ideas to a pie-eyed man.

But Volodka Bokov got up and so jerked the handle from the left that a cord which had been attached there with a government seal tore loose.

Everybody turned mute on the spot. Silence suddenly reigned among the passengers. The only thing one could hear was the sound of the wheels. And nothing else.

The fellow in the blue cap exclaimed:

"Oh, plague take him, he did stop it! What do you know? . . ."

At that, many jumped from their seats. The blue-cap wearer tried to sneak out to the platform, away from trouble, but the passengers didn't let him. The man with cotton in his ear said:

"This is hoodlumism. In a moment, the whole train will stop. . . . That helps to wear out the rolling stock. Besides, there is the delay."

Volodka Bokov himself got a little scared. He said:

"Stop the one in the blue cap. Let me and him be put in the clink together. He put me up to stopping the train."

But the train, in the meantime, failed to stop at once. The passengers said:

"The train can't stop at once. Even though it is a suburban train, it is entitled to a run after the application of the brake. Eighty yards. And on wet rails even more than that."

But the train, in the meantime, just continued on its way. It went close to a mile, and still there was no perceptible slowing down.

The one with cotton in his ear said:

"It seems the brake is out of order, so to speak."

Volodka said:

"That's what I've been telling you; they won't do a darn thing to me. Put that in your pipe and smoke it!"

And he sat down.

And at the next stop he got out, refreshed himself a little, and arrived home sober as a crystal.

Translated by Jack A. Posin

An Easter Episode

Here, my friends, a holiday is upon us—the Christian Easter.

The believers, like sheep, will drag their sacred cakes to be blessed. Let them drag them! I won't. Enough's enough! Last Easter, friends, somebody stepped with his foot in my cake.

The thing is, I was delayed and was late for the beginning of the ceremonies. I came to the church fence, and found that all the tables had already been occupied. I asked the Christian citizens to make room for me, but they wouldn't. They cussed me out:

"Since you're late, the devil take you," they said, "then put your cake on the ground. Don't crowd and push here: you'll dump our cakes over."

Well, there was nothing else to do. I put my cake on the ground. Whoever was late had to put his cakes on the ground.

And I had hardly had the time to put it down when ringing from all the bells started.

And I saw the priest himself barge along with a brush. He'd dip the brush into a bucket and then splash the water around. Some got it in the snout, some in the cake—he didn't care.

And, behind the priest, father deacon was nobly stepping forward, holding a platter in which he collected voluntary contributions.

"Don't be stingy, Christian people," he said. "Put your coins in the middle of the plate."

They were just passing by me when father deacon became absorbed in his plate. He didn't look where he was going, and bang! His foot went straight into my plate where the cake was.

This took my breath away.

"What do you mean," I said, "you long-maned bozo, stepping into my cake? . . . On Easter night, too . . ."

"Pardon me," he said, "I didn't mean to."

I said:

"I can't make a fur coat out of your apology! I want the full cost of the cake refunded to me! Put up the money, father deacon!"

The procession was interrupted. The priest with the brush stepped into the argument.

"Whose cake," he said, "was stepped on?"

"Mine," I said. "Deacon, the son of a gun, stepped on it."

The priest said:

"I will sprinkle that cake with the brush right away," he said. "And then it will be all right to eat it. After all, it was a clergyman who stepped on it. Your cake will even gain from that. Particularly since I'll sprinkle it twice."

"Oh, no, father!" I said. "Even if you pour the whole bucketful on it, I won't budge! Please refund my money!"

Well, a scandal started.

Some folks took my side, others were against me. The chime master, Vavilych, stuck his head from the steeple and asked:

"Shall I keep on ringing, or stop for a while?"

I said:

"Wait a while with your ringing, Vavilych! Otherwise, under the cover of church-ringing, they'll rob me for sure!"

And the priest was walking around me like a sick person and waving his arms.

And the deacon, the long-maned devil, leaned on the fence, and was cleaning off my cake from his boot with a chip.

Afterward, they gave me a small sum from the collection plate and asked me to go since my shouts were interfering with their business, they said.

Well, I went outside the enclosure and yelled for a while at father deacon. I tried to shame him for a while, and then I went away.

And nowadays I eat the cakes straight, unconsecrated.

The taste is the same, and there's a heap less trouble.

Translated by Jack A. Posin

PELAGEYA

Pelageya was an illiterate woman. She didn't even know how to sign her name.

But Pelageya's husband was a responsible Soviet worker. And though he was a simple person from the country, after five years of living in the city he'd learned everything. And not just how to sign his name, but God knows what he didn't know! And he was very ashamed that his wife was illiterate.

"You, at least, Pelageyushka, ought to learn how to sign your name," he said to Pelageya. "Our name's such an easy one, two syllables—Kuch-kin, but you can't . . . It's embarrassing . . ."

But Pelageya would wave her hand and answer: "It won't do me no good, I figure, Ivan Nikolayevich. I'm slowly getting on. My fingers don't bend special. What'll I study for now and copy out letters? Better let the little Pioneers learn, and I'll live on to old age this way."

Pelageya's husband was a terribly busy man and couldn't spend a lot of time on his wife. He'd shake his head—eh, now, Pelageya, Pelageya. And fall silent.

But one day, all the same, Ivan Nikolayevich brought home a special book.

"Here, Polya," he says, "is the newest self-teaching ABC, compiled according to the latest methods. I'll show you how myself."

But Pelageya smiled quietly, took the ABC, turned it over, and hid it in the bureau—let it lie there, now, maybe it'll come in handy for our descendants.

But then one day Pelageya sat down to some work. Ivan Nikolayevich's coat had to be fixed, the sleeve was worn through. Pelageya sat down at the table. Took a needle. Thrust her hand under the jacket—something's rustling.

"Maybe money?" Pelageya thought.

She looked—it was a letter. Such a clean, tidy envelope, little fine letters, and the paper smelled sort of like perfume or eau de cologne. Pelageya's heart shrank.

"Really," she thinks, "is Ivan Nikolayevich cheating on me all over? Is he really exchanging love letters with respectable ladies and laughing at me, an illiterate old fool?"

Pelageya looked at the envelope, pulled out the letter, unfolded it—she couldn't read it, couldn't make it out on account of her illiteracy.

For the first time in her life Pelageya was sorry she couldn't read.

"Even if," she thinks, "this is somebody else's letter, I must know what's written in it. Maybe my whole life'll be changed on account of this, and I'd better go to the country and work like the peasants."

Pelageya started crying, began remembering that Ivan Nikolayevich had seemed to change recently—like his starting to worry about his little mustache and washing his hands more often. There Pelageya sat, looking at the letter and weeping her heart out. But she couldn't read the letter. And she'd be ashamed to show it to an outsider.

Afterward, Pelageya hid the letter in the bureau, sewed up the jacket and began waiting for Ivan Nikolayevich. And when he came in, Pelageya didn't show she'd seen anything. On the contrary, she chatted away with her husband in a calm and quiet voice and even hinted to him that she wasn't against learning a little and that she was really fed up with being an ignorant, illiterate woman. Ivan Nikolayevich was very glad of this.

"Well, fine," he said. "I'll show you how myself."

"So, show me," said Pelageya.

And she stared straight at Ivan Nikolayevich's even, trimmed, little mustache.

Day after day, two months in a row, Pelageya learned how to read. She patiently formed the words syllable by syllable, copied out the letters carefully, and learned sentences by heart. And every night she took the sacred letter out of the bureau and tried to figure out its mysterious meaning.

However, it was very hard.

Only in the third month did Pelageya conquer learning.

One morning, after Ivan Nikolayevich had left for work, Pelageya got the letter out of the bureau and started reading it.

It was hard for her to make out the fine handwriting, and only the barely perceptible scent of perfume from the paper encouraged her.

The letter was addressed to Ivan Nikolayevich.

Pelageya read:

> Dear Comrade Kuchkin!
>   I'm sending you the promised ABC. I think that in two or three months your wife can completely conquer learning. Promise, dear, to make her do this. Impress her, explain to her how, as a matter of fact, it's repulsive to be an illiterate woman.
>   Right now, for this anniversary, we're liquidating illit-

eracy throughout the Republic in every way, but some-how we keep forgetting our relatives.

Do this without fail, Ivan Nikolayevich.

Best Communist wishes,
Marya Blokhina

Pelageya reread this letter twice and, sorrowfully pursing her lips and feeling some kind of secret hurt, started to cry.

Translated by Helen S. Reeve

THE CHARMS OF CULTURE

I have always been in favor of fundamental convictions.

Even when they started to introduce the New Economic Policy, during the era of Military Communism, I did not object. If it's NEP you want, well, it's O.K. with me. You know best.

Nevertheless, my heart was desperately heavy during the introduction of NEP. As if I had a foreboding of certain radical changes.

And, indeed, during Military Communism everything had been wonderfully free in regard to culture and civilization. In the theater, let us say, one felt free not to take anything off: just sit in what you came in. That was a real attainment.

And the question of culture is a thorny one. Let's take, for example, this same question of taking things off in the theater. Of course, people appear to better advantage without their overcoats—that goes without saying—much nicer and more elegant. But what is all right in bourgeois countries sometimes comes out all cockeyed in our land.

Recently, I bumped into Comrade Loktev and his lady friend, Nyusha Koshelkova, on the street. I had been taking a walk, or maybe going somewhere to wet my whistle, I don't recall now.

They stopped me and began to persuade me:

"Your throat," they said, "Vasily Mitrofanovich, won't run away from you. Your throat is always with you. You'll have a chance to moisten it at any time. Better come with us to the theater tonight. They are playing *The Heater*."

And, to make a long story short, they prevailed on me to go to the theater in order to spend the evening in an atmosphere of culture.

So we came to the theater, of course. Bought tickets, of course. We started up the stairs. Suddenly we're called back and ordered to take off our things.

"Take off your overcoats," we're told.

Loktev and his lady, of course, took off their overcoats in a jiffy. But I, of course, stood in a quandary. I had put on my overcoat right over my night shirt that evening. There was no jacket. And, brothers, I felt that I wouldn't be comfortable if I took it off. "It may lead to a downright scandal," I thought to myself. The thing was . . . the night shirt was not exactly dirty . . . no, the shirt was not especially dirty. . . . But, of course, it was a rough night shirt. A big brass button was sewed on the collar, it so happened. "It's a shame to walk into the foyer with such a large button on," I thought.

I said to the folks:

"I'm really at a loss what to do, Comrades. I'm not dressed properly tonight. I feel uneasy about taking off my overcoat. After all, the people can see the suspenders, and the shirt *is* rough."

Comrade Loktev said:

"Well, let me take a look at it."

I unbuttoned myself and let him see.

"Yes," he said, "indeed the view is . . ."

The lady also took a look and then said:

"I'd better go home," she said. "I can't permit my escorts to walk alongside of me dressed only in their shirts. You might as well have put your underpants on top of your trousers," she said. "It's quite improper," she said, "for you to go to the theater in such a sloppy way."

I said:

"I didn't know I would be going to the theater, you dope. Maybe I rarely wear jackets. Maybe I'm saving them; then what?"

All of us began thinking about what to do. Loktev, the dog, finally said:

"Here's what. I'll give you my vest right here and now, Vasily Mitrofanovich. You put it on and wear it, as if you felt too hot in a jacket."

He unbuttoned his jacket and began to feel and search himself inside.

"Oh!" he said finally. "Gosh darn it! I haven't my vest with me tonight! I'd better," he says, "give you my necktie. It'll be more decent than your present appearance, at that. You tie it around your neck and walk around that way, as if you felt hot all the time."

The lady said:

"I'd better go home, honest. I would somehow feel more at peace at home. As it is, one of my escorts is dressed practically in underpants, and the other has a necktie in place of a jacket. Let Vasily Mitrofanovich ask to be allowed to wear his overcoat."

We asked and we begged and we showed our trade-union cards. But they refused to allow it.

"This isn't 1919," they said, "for you to sit in your overcoats."

"Well," I said, "there's nothing to be done. It seems, Comrades, I'll have to crawl all the way home."

But when I considered that I had already paid my admission, I couldn't go: my legs refused to carry me toward the exit.

Loktev, the dog, said:

"Here's what. You take off your suspenders. Let the lady carry them in place of a bag. And you yourself go as you are, as if you had on an Apache summer shirt and as if you felt hot in it all the time."

The lady said:

"Do what you will, I won't carry the suspenders. I don't go to the theater in order to carry men's things around. Let Vasily Mitrofanovich carry them himself or put them in his pocket."

I took off my overcoat. There I was, standing in my night shirt like a son of a bitch.

And it was pretty darned cold. I shivered and my teeth chattered. And the people all around stared at me.

The lady said:

"Quick, you scoundrel, take off the suspenders. There are people all around. Oh, I'd better go home right away, honest."

But I couldn't take them off in a hurry. I felt cold. My fingers refused to obey me in unbuttoning the suspenders at once.

I did exercises with my hands.

After a while, we got organized and took our seats.

The first act went off all right. The only thing, it was cold. I did gymnastic exercises throughout the entire act.

Suddenly, during the intermission, the people behind us raised a row. They called in the administration. They complained about me.

"Ladies," they said, "are disgusted having to look at night shirts. It shocks them," they said. "Besides," they said, "he wriggles all the time like a son of a bitch."

I said:

"I'm wriggling from the cold. You try sitting here in just a shirt. I, myself, don't feel very happy about it, Comrades. But what am I to do?"

So they dragged me off to the office. They wrote down everything.

Afterward, they let me go.

"But now," they said, "you'll have to pay three rubles fine, according to the court decision."

Such a mess! You just never can tell where your troubles will come from. . . .

Translated by Jack A. Posin

ADVENTURES OF A MONKEY

In a town in the south there was a zoological park. Not a very large zoological park which had one tiger, two crocodiles, three snakes, a zebra, an ostrich and one ape, or, to put it simply—a monkey. And of course all sorts of trifles—birds, fish, frogs and other insignificant nonsense of the animal kingdom.

In the beginning of the war when the fascists were bombing this town, a bomb fell right on the zoological park, and it exploded there with a tremendous deafening racket to the amazement of all the animals.

The three snakes were killed all at once, which, possibly, isn't such a tragic fact; and, unfortunately, the ostrich.

The other animals, however, came to no harm, and, as they say, only had a fright.

Of all the animals, the monkey was the most frightened. Her cage was knocked over by an air wave, and fell from its pedestal. A side wall broke and our monkey fell out of the cage right onto a pathway of the park.

She fell out on the path but did not remain lying motionless as people, who are accustomed to military maneuvers, would. On the contrary. She immediately climbed a tree. From there she jumped on a fence, from the fence to the street, and ran like mad.

Runs and probably thinks, "Eh, if they're throwing bombs here, then I don't like it." And consequently runs with all her might along the city streets.

She ran through the whole town. Ran out on the highway and runs along this highway away from the city. Well, a monkey is not a person. It doesn't understand what's what; doesn't see the sense of remaining in this town.

She ran and ran and got tired. Exhausted; climbed a tree; ate a fly to bolster her strength and also a couple of worms and fell asleep on the branch where she was sitting.

At this time a military transport was going along the road. The chauffeur saw the monkey in the tree. He was amazed. Quietly he stole up on her, put his coat over her and put her in his car. He thought:

"It would be better to give her to some friends of mine, than that she should perish here from hunger, cold and other deprivations."

And so he went on, together with the monkey.

He arrived in the city of Borisov, went about his affairs and left the monkey in the car. He said to her:

"Wait here for me, darling. I'll be right back."

But our monkey didn't wait. She crawled out of the car through a broken window and went strolling along the streets.

And so she goes, like a dear, along the street, strolls, walks about with her tail up in the air. The people, of course, are amazed; they want to catch her. But it's not quite that simple to catch her. She is quick, agile and runs fast on her four little hands. They didn't catch her after all, but only wore her out with senseless running about.

Exhausted, she was tired and, of course, got hungry.

But where can she eat in town? There is nothing edible in the streets. She can't go, with her tail, into a restaurant or a co-op. Furthermore, she has no money, no discount, no food ration-cards. A nightmare.

Nonetheless, she went into a co-op. She sensed that something or other was to be had there. And in it they were supplying vegetables to the populace: carrots, beets and cucumbers.

She popped into this store. She sees a long waiting line. No, she didn't stand in line, and she didn't start pushing people in order to get to the counter. She simply ran along the heads of the customers up to the salesgirl. She jumped up on the counter; didn't ask the price of a kilo of carrots, and, as they say, skedaddled. Ran out of the store, satisfied with her "purchase." Well, a monkey . . . doesn't understand what's what, doesn't see the sense of being without food.

Of course, a turmoil took place in the store; noise, a rumpus. The people began to shout. The salesgirl who was weighing beets nearly fainted from surprise. And really, you can get frightened, if suddenly, next to you, instead of the ordinary, normal customer, something hairy with a tail hops up; and, in addition, doesn't pay.

The people dashed out into the street after the monkey, whereas she runs and chews and eats carrots on the go. She doesn't understand what's what.

Ahead of everyone run the boys, after them the adults, and in back, a policeman, blowing his whistle.

Suddenly, out of nowhere, a dog leaped out and also started after our monkey. At that, it not only yelps and barks, but seriously tries to grab the monkey with its teeth.

Our monkey ran faster. Runs and probably thinks: "Eh, it's too bad I left the zoo. It's easier to breathe in a cage. I will definitely return to the zoo, first chance I get."

And so she runs with all her might, but the dog isn't lagging and just about to grab her.

Then our monkey leaped on some fence and when the dog jumped up to grab the monkey by the leg, she hit it with the carrots with all her strength on the nose. She hit her so painfully, that the dog howled and ran home with a bloody nose. It probably thought: "No, Citizens, I would rather lie peacefully at home than catch a monkey for you and experience such unpleasantness."

In short, the dog ran away and our monkey jumped into a yard.

And in the yard, at that time, a young boy, namely, Alyosha Popov, was chopping wood.

There he is, chopping wood, and suddenly he sees a monkey. He liked monkeys very much, and all his life he dreamed of having some sort of a monkey, and suddenly—there you are!

Alyosha shrugged off his jacket and with this jacket he covered the monkey which cringed in a corner of the stairs.

The boy brought her home; fed her, gave her tea, and the monkey was very pleased. But not quite, because Alyosha's grandmother immediately took a dislike to her. She shouted at the monkey and even wanted to hit her on the paw. All because, when they were drinking tea and the grandmother put her bitten candy on a saucer, the monkey grabbed the grandmother's candy and shoved it in her mouth. Well, a monkey—is not a person. A person, if he should take something, wouldn't do it before grandmother's eyes. But this one, the monkey, did it right in grandmother's presence, and of course, nearly brought her to tears.

Grandmother said:

"Altogether, it is extremely unpleasant when some sort of ape with a tail lives in an apartment. She will frighten me with her inhuman appearance. She will jump on me in the dark. She will eat my candy. No, I categorically refuse to live in the same apartment with a monkey. One of us two will have to be in the zoological park. Should I move to the zoological park? No, better let her live there, and I will continue to live in my apartment."

Alyosha said to his grandmother:

"No, grandmother, you don't have to move to the zoo. I will guarantee that the monkey will not eat anything more of yours. I will bring her up like a person. I will teach her to eat from a spoon and to drink tea from a glass. As far as jumping is concerned, I cannot forbid her to climb on the lamp which hangs from the ceiling. From there, of course, she may jump on your head, but the main thing is, don't be frightened if this happens, because this is, after all, a harmless monkey who in Africa has become used to jumping and leaping."

On the next day Alyosha left for school and asked his grandmother to watch after the monkey. But the grandmother didn't look after her. She thought: "What now; I should look after some monster?" And with these thoughts the grandmother fell asleep in the armchair on purpose.

Then our monkey crawled out through an open transom onto the street, and went along the sunny side. No one knows, maybe she wanted to take a stroll, but maybe she decided to drop in at the store to buy something for herself. Not for money, just like that.

However, at that time an old man was passing by the street, the invalid Gavrilich. He was going to the steam bath and carried in his hand a small basket in which there were soap and underwear.

He saw the monkey and at first didn't even believe his own eyes that this was a monkey. He thought that he was seeing things, since he had had a mug of beer earlier.

There he is, looking at the monkey in wonderment, and she looks at him. Maybe she is thinking: "And what sort of a scarecrow is this, with a basket in his hands?"

At last Gavrilich understood that this was a real monkey and not an imaginary one. And then he thought: "Think I'll catch her. I'll take her to the market tomorrow and will sell her for 100 rubles, and on this money I'll have 10 mugs of beer." And with these thoughts Gavrilich started to catch the monkey, calling, "Kitty, kitty, kitty . . . Come here."

No, he knew that this wasn't a cat, but he didn't understand in which language one had to speak to her. And only later did he figure out that this was the highest creature in the animal kingdom, and then he pulled out of his pocket a piece of sugar, showed it to the monkey and, bowing, said to her:

"Beautiful monkey, would you care to eat a piece of sugar?"

She says: "If you please, I'd like to. . . ." That is, actually she didn't say anything, because she doesn't know how to talk, but she simply stepped up, grabbed this piece of sugar and began to eat it.

Gavrilich took her in his arms and put her in his basket; it was warm and cozy in the basket and our monkey didn't jump out of it. Maybe she thought: "Let this old blockhead carry me in his basket; it's even interesting."

At first Gavrilich thought he would take her home, but then he didn't want to turn back and he went to the steam bath with the monkey. He thought: "It's even better that I go with her to the steam bath. I will wash her there. She will be clean and sweet. I'll tie a bow around her neck and they'll give me more for her at the market."

And so he came to the steam bath with his monkey and started washing with her.

In the steam bath it was very warm—hot—just as in Africa, and our monkey was very pleased with such a warm atmosphere, but not quite. Because Gavrilich soaped her down with soap and the soap got in her mouth. Of course, this isn't tasty, but not to such an extent that one screams, scratches and refuses to wash. Anyway, our monkey started to spit, but the soap got in her eyes and this made the monkey go completely mad. She bit Gavrilich in the finger, tore out of his hands and jumped out of the steam bath like one gone berserk.

She jumped into the room where people undress and there she frightened everyone. No one knew that this was a monkey. They see that something round, white and foamy jumped in, rushing first to the couch, then onto the stove, from the stove onto a crate, from the crate on someone's head and again onto the stove.

Several nervous patrons started shouting and running out of the bath, and our monkey also ran out, going down by the stairs.

And there, at the bottom, was a cashier's booth with a little window. The monkey jumped into this window thinking that it would be more peaceful for her there, and mainly that there wouldn't be so much fussing and shoving. But in the booth sat a fat lady cashier who Ah'd and squealed and ran out of the booth, screaming:

"Help! I think a bomb has hit my booth. Give me some valerian drops!"

Our monkey got fed up with all this shouting. She jumped out of the booth and ran into the street.

And there she is, running along the street, all wet, covered with soap suds and again people are running after her. Ahead of everyone are the boys, behind them the adults, after the adults, a policeman, and in back of the policeman our aged Gavrilich, half undressed, with his boots in his hands.

Suddenly, from out of nowhere, a dog jumps out, the same one which chased her yesterday.

Seeing it, our monkey thought: "Well, now, Citizens, I am a goner."

But this time the dog didn't chase her. The dog only looked at the running monkey, felt a strong pain in its nose, and didn't run, it even turned away. Probably, it thought: "I haven't enough noses in reserve to chase monkeys." But although it turned away it barked angrily: as if to say, run, but keep in mind that I'm here.

At this time our boy, Alyosha Popov, returning from school, didn't find his beloved little monkey at home. He was very sad, and tears even came to his eyes. He thought that now he would never again see his wonderful, adorable little monkey.

And so, out of boredom and sadness he went out on the street. He walks along the street, melancholy, and suddenly sees people running. No, at first he didn't think that they were running after his monkey. He thought they were running because of an air-raid alarm. But then he saw his monkey—all wet and soapy. He ran to her, clutched her in his arms and pressed her to him so that no one would take her. Then all the running people stopped and surrounded the boy.

But then, out of the crowd stepped our aged Gavrilich, and showing everyone his bitten finger, said:

"Citizens, don't let this lad hold my monkey in his arms which I want to sell in the market tomorrow. This is my monkey which bit me on the finger. Look, everyone, at this, my swollen finger; and this is the proof that I speak the truth."

The boy, Alyosha Popov said:

"No, this monkey isn't his, this is my monkey. You see how willingly she came to my arms. And this is also proof that what I say is true."

But here still another person steps out of the crowd—the very same chauffeur who brought the monkey in his car. He says:

"No, it is neither your nor your monkey. It is my monkey, because I brought her here. But I am leaving again for my military detachment and therefore I will give the monkey to the person who lovingly holds her in his arms, and not to the person who wants to mercilessly sell her in the market for the sake of drink. The monkey belongs to the boy."

Then all the people clapped their hands, and Alyosha, glowing with happiness, pressed the monkey to him even tighter and triumphantly brought her home.

Gavrilich with his bitten finger went back to the steam bath to finish washing.

And so, since then the monkey has lived with the boy, Alyosha Popov. She lives with him even now. Recently I went to the city of Borisov and purposely dropped in at Alyosha's to see how she was doing with him. Oh, she lives very well! She doesn't run away at all. She has become very obedient. Wipes her nose with a handkerchief and doesn't take other people's candy, so that the grandmother is very pleased now, isn't angry with her and doesn't want to move her to the zoological park any more.

When I entered Alyosha's room the monkey was sitting at the table. She sat very importantly, like a cashier in the movies, and ate her rice porridge with a teaspoon.

Alyosha said to me:

"I brought her up like a human being, and now all the children and even some adults may look to her as an example."

Translated by Natalie Bienstock